WINGS OF WRATH

And still they watched in silence. So many of them! Black-robed cannibals all of them, drinking in her desperation. She could sense the hunger in them as they watched her struggle. The hate. They were packed tightly about the spell circle now, in a crowd so many layers deep that she could not begin to guess how many Magisters were present. Truly, she would not have thought there were so many in all the world as seemed to be here now—and every single one of them had contributed his power to the spell that was her prison. Now that her senses were fully awake to its power, its glow was so bright that it burned her eyes to look upon it. And it seemed to be strengthened by her own efforts, brightening each time she tried to break free. It was stealing her power, even as she tried to save herself.

BY CELIA FRIEDMAN

The Coldfire Trilogy
Black Sun Rising
When True Night Falls
Crown of Shadows

The Magister Trilogy
Feast of Souls
Wings of Wrath

CELIA FRIEDMAN
WINGS OF WRATH

2
MAGISTER
TRILOGY

www.orbitbooks.net

ORBIT

First published in Great Britain in 2009 by Orbit
This paperback edition published in 2010 by Orbit

Copyright © 2009 by Celia Friedman

Excerpt from *The Hundred Thousand Kingdoms* by N. K. Jemison
Copyright © 2010 by N. K. Jemison

The moral right of the author has been asserted.

A CIP catalogue record for this book
is available from the British Library.

ISBN 978-1-84149-534-7

Typeset in Caslon by Palimpsest Book Production Limited,
Falkirk, Stirlingshire
Printed in the UK by CPI Mackays, Chatham, ME5 8TD

Papers used by Orbit are natural, renewable and recyclable
products sourced from well-managed forests and certified
in accordance with the rules of the Forest Stewardship Council.

Mixed Sources
Product group from well-managed
forests and other controlled sources
www.fsc.org Cert no. SGS-COC-004081
FSC © 1996 Forest Stewardship Council

Orbit
An imprint of
Little, Brown Book Group
100 Victoria Embankment
London EC4Y 0DY

An Hachette UK Company
www.hachette.co.uk

www.orbitbooks.net

DEDICATION

For Betsy Wollheim
Amazing editor
Priceless muse
Beloved friend

ACKNOWLEDGEMENTS

BY FAR, the best part of researching any book is getting to sit down with experts in various fields and hear them talk about the stuff they love. Special thanks for this volume go to John Woodson, whose love of traditional climbing was as infectious as his knowledge was impressive.

Thanks also to my reading team, who really worked their butts off on this one. That's Carl Cipra, Kim Dobson, Paul Hoeffer, Zsusy Sanford, and David Walddon. Couldn't have done it without you guys! Also Fonda Nichols, Steve Rapaport, and Beth Tobin for additional reading support.

Special thanks to Joshua Starr for all his help, especially with the map.

Last but not least, thanks to all the wonderful people at Sylvan for helping to keep me sane while I finished this manuscript . . . Emily Habermeyer and Elise Nicely for being the best bosses ever, and all my students (especially the writing students!) for filling my heart with joy and pride. You guys work so hard that it inspires me to do the same. Keep it up!

The Wrath of the Gods

Kierdwyn

Citadel

Alkali

Skandir

Soladin

Summer Palace

The High Kingdom

Highlands

King's Pass

Corialanus

The Free States

The Sentinels

Sankara

PROLOGUE

THE GODS were coming.

The boy pressed himself down against the hot ground, clinging to the mountain with blackened hands. Broken bits of lava and clumps of ash came loose beneath his fingertips, searing his skin like hot coals, but he hardly noticed. His attention was fixed upon the view overhead, in particular those few places where the thick clouds parted and the sky itself was visible.

They were coming soon. They must be.

They would not refuse the offering.

Beneath his vantage point, in the vast gray bowl of the caldera, a half dozen girls whimpered in pain and terror. They were small things, his age or younger, and bright red blood streamed from cuts on the backs of their legs. The priests had decreed they should be hamstrung before being cast into the caldera, lest they do what the last group of sacrifices had done: flee to the lava pit at its far end to throw themselves in, rather than embrace their destiny. The gods were not pleased when the offerings died too quickly. And when the gods were not pleased the Sleep came, and children died, and crops stood untouched in the fields until they rotted for lack of strong men to harvest them.

The girls were terrified, of course, and the boy winced as one of them screamed, unable to see which one it was, trying not to wonder about it. The Land of the Sun was a small place and he knew the name of everyone in it . . . but once a girl was chosen to be sacrificed she gave up her former name and identity and became only Tawa, a handmaiden of the gods. It was too terrifying to think of them as anything else now, to remember that the girls who had once run with him, jested with him, and played "show me yours and I will show you mine" in the shadow of the great mountain, were set out like lambs for the slaughter, awaiting the gods who would devour them.

Food. The priests never called them that, but that was what they were. Everyone in the Land of the Sun knew it, though no one ever said it aloud. A man could offer up his daughter to be a bride of the gods and feel there was honor in the act, but once he admitted that she was little more than a herd animal being staked out for slaughter, that honor died a cold and miserable death. The flowers woven into the girls' hair ceased to be bridal circlets, no longer crowns of communion but simply a macabre garnish; their cries were no longer the songs of welcome a virgin bride might offer to a majestic and powerful bridegroom, but simply squeals of primitive, overbearing terror.

Little wonder none of the villagers ever stayed behind to see if the sacrifice was accepted, the boy thought. The illusion of sanctity might not survive such close inspection.

Suddenly the clouds overhead seemed to stir. The boy drew his breath in quickly, which made the sulfurous smoke burn his nostrils and set him coughing. He shut his eyes tightly as his chest spasmed, tears streaming down his soot-blackened cheeks as he struggled to keep silent, lest the gods who were surely approaching turn their attention to him before he was ready. And perhaps mistake him for a sacrifice.

Then the fit passed, and the last cough was swallowed, and he opened his eyes again.

And *they* were there.

They clean were—so clean!—cool, clear colors against a blazing sky, ice against fire. Their wings were like the finely veined wings of insects, but broad beyond measure, and so strong that every stroke raised whirlwinds of dust and ash from the ground beneath. Their bodies glistened like the ocean at moonrise, with sparks of blue and purple and colors that the boy did not even know the names of playing across their skin. Their wings were sheets of blue sea ice that cooled the smoky wind with every stroke, and they slid through the filthy sulfurous air like seals through water, poisonous clouds frothing in their wake.

The priests taught that any man who looked upon the gods directly would perish. The boy stared at them despite that warning, naked in his hunger to witness the magnitude of their power, to understand it, to possess it.

One by one the vast creatures dropped out of the clouds, banking low beneath the hot smoke as they glided over the caldera. The girls had stopped screaming now. They still trembled in fear, and one moaned softly in pain as the broad wings beat the smoky air into whirls and eddies all about her, but otherwise they were eerily still, transfixed by the sight of their winged bridegrooms. Even from where the boy crouched he could feel the sheer power of the gods' presence, and it made his blood run cold with fear . . . yet at the same time it stirred his flesh—strangely, uncomfortably—as if he were watching those same girls bathe naked in a hot spring. Unable to move, he watched in silence as the creatures swooped low over the girls, one after the other. The young brides appeared to have forgotten their pain now, and lay back to the last one upon the hot earth, arms reaching out to welcome the creatures as one might welcome a lover. It was a grotesque scene to be sure, but also fascinating, and he could not look away from it.

None of the gods had noticed him yet, or if they had, they did not deem him worthy of their attention. Had any of the boy's people ever seen the gods like this, ever been this close to them without being offered as sacrifice? For the first time since leaving home, he began to think he might really live long enough see his plan through to the end.

And if it worked . . . if it worked . . .

He didn't even dare think about that.

One of the girls was dead now, it seemed, but he could not tell what had killed her. A great god with wings of cobalt and amethyst had swooped down low, as if it intended to strike her, but then pulled up suddenly to join its fellows in the sky, letting out a cry as it did so that filled the caldera. There had been no physical contact; he was sure of it. Yet the girl was strangely still now, motionless in the way that only dead things are motionless, as if all the living strength had been sucked from her limbs. So silent had her death been that the other girls did not even realize she was gone. Or perhaps, in their efforts to offer themselves up to their bridegrooms, they simply did not care.

And then the boy saw what he had been waiting for.

It sat astride the back of one of the gods, a rider more insect-like than human at first glance. Its limbs were sheathed in a blue-black substance not unlike the skin of the great beast itself, making it hard to distinguish where one creature began and the other ended. Lesser wings from the god's upper body were wrapped backward around its rider, creating the illusion of a glistening chrysalis. Even as he watched, the surface of that cocoon slowly parted, its occupant revealed like a locust in season.

The boy's heart skipped a beat. For a single moment the world seemed frozen in time.

So the legends are true.

The creature seated on the back of the god was a man. Not one of the boy's own people, no, but similar enough that he could not mistake it for anything but a human being. The rider's skin was pale, unlike his own, a strange and unwholesome hue that reminded him of clotted milk. His hair was long and matted with dirt and oil, and his close-fitting armor appeared to be slick with oil as well, so that every beam of light that fell upon him caused dark rainbows to dance across its surface. It was a chilling image to be sure, but it was also undeniably a human one. And that was what mattered most.

Girding his courage, the boy drew in a deep breath. *Now,* he thought. *Now is the time.*

He stood.

His legs were shaking, more than they should have been even from his strenuous climb. For a moment he thought he would not manage to stand at all and the landscape swirled dizzily about him; then, by sheer force of will, he made the world stand still and forced his shaking legs to bear his weight. What other choice was there? The gods were watching now, and if he showed any sign of weakness in front of them he might as well just cast himself into the caldera along with the other sacrifices and let them devour him.

When he thought that he had his legs securely under him he drew in as deep a breath as his constricted lungs could manage, shut his eyes for a moment to focus his spirit, and then let out a cry no living creature could miss. Wordless, it *flowed* across the caldera, and into the fuming clouds beyond it.

The gods did not stop their circling, but he knew that they had heard him.

Opening his eyes once more, he looked for the one that had a man astride its back. That one alone had not come low to feed, but was circling high above the others. Had it seen him? If he cried out to it, would it hear his words? The volcano beneath him rumbled and the fragments of pumice beneath his feet seemed to shift slightly in response. Did the gods speak in sounds, like animals and men, or did they use volcanoes as their mouthpieces? So little was known about them!

Then the rider's eyes fixed on him—undeniably human, maddeningly scornful—and he knew that he must seize this moment or lose it forever.

"Take me with you!" he demanded. "I would serve the gods!"

For a moment it did not seem that either the human or his mount had heard him. So he yelled the words again, even louder.

The mountain rumbled again beneath his feet. A whiff of hot sulfurous smoke stung his nostrils.

"I'm strong!" he cried out. "I have survived the cold of the ice and the heat of the testing stones! I've have hunted the sea lion and faced down the snow bear! I am brave enough to face the anger of the earth—"

To come here, he wanted to say. *Brave enough to climb the Mountain of Sacrifice and stand here before you with no weapons, no armor, nothing at all to protect me from the gods' wrath save my own stubborn belief that I can be of value to them.*

The man's eyes were cold, unblinking. Like a lizard's.

Then he turned away.

The boy howled in rage. It was an animal sound that welled

up from the primitive part of his soul without human urging or sanction. One of the girls looked up to see what the source of the noise was, then quickly turned her attention back to the winged bridegrooms. Did she recognize him as a boy she had run with, played with, shared secrets with? Or did she see only a soot-blackened animal howling hoarsely at the sky, as a seal might howl while some predatory beast crushed the life out of it?

Then the talons of one of the gods closed around her and she was jerked off the ground, her neck snapping backward with an audible crack. Apparently the gods did want fresh meat after all.

Not one of them acknowledged the boy's presence.

Not one.

"Take me with you!" he screamed, his voice hoarse with frustration. "I belong with you!"

The gods were rising now, heading back toward the clouds. Several held small girls clasped in their talons, dangling like broken dolls. The sacrifice had been accepted.

The single rider glanced back at the boy, then turned away. His mount circled higher and higher as the glassy wings folded back around him once more.

"TAKE ME WITH YOU!!!"

Then the breath was knocked from the boy's body as something hit him hard from behind. He would have plummeted down into the caldera had not sharp claws grabbed hold of him; with a suddenness that left him reeling, he was jerked off his feet and into the air. Fragmented images from the world below swam in his field of vision, disconnected, unreal. Whirlpools of poisonous smoke. Blue-black wings that beat the air above his head, driving the ground down and away, stroke by stroke. In the distance, beyond the Land of the Sun, he could now see a vast field of white stretching from horizon to horizon. It had no end. It knew no mercy.

I will serve you, he promised the gods. *Better than any other. You will see.*

The gods did not answer.

BEGINNING

And it came to pass that the First Kings wished all men to know of their greatness. So they ordered great towers to be built, each one taller than the last. The towers rose so high that clouds crowned their summits, and the kings declared, "Behold! The gods themselves bear witness to our greatness." Yet still they did not stop building, for each king wished his tower to be the tallest and the grandest of them all.

Each then commanded that the finest silks in all his kingdom should be sewn into banners to hang from his tower, and the outer walls should be covered in gold and silver and adorned with glittering gemstones, and the best musicians should gather along the upper balconies to serenade the air with song, not only from dawn until dusk but through all the hours of the night as well, so that any man who stirred in his sleep might hear their music and know of his king's greatness.

And the fields of the First Kings lay fallow for lack of laborers to tend them; the herds of the First Kings died of hunger in the field for lack of laborers to feed them.

The Creator looked down from the heavens and saw what the First Kings were doing and how their vanity had laid waste to the land.

And He said, "Enough!"

Book of Penitence
Transgressions 7:15–19

CHAPTER 1

I T HAD been cool that afternoon in the pine-clad mountains, and no sorcery was needed to forecast that the coming
night would be a chilly one. In the open plains to the west the
summer heat was relentless and clouds of dust could be seen
rising up from acres of dying crops, staining the sunset russet.
But the mountains were another world entirely. In the cool,
pine-scented shade it was a rare nightfall that did not bring a
cooling breeze in its wake, even in the worst of the summer
season, and this evening was no exception.

Both moons could be seen overhead now, a slender cres-
cent to the west and a nearly perfect orb just above the eastern
horizon; their light filtered down through the thickly layered
branches, mottling the ground with shadows. Peaceful.
Timeless. Ethanus paused for a few minutes to watch the
shadows creep slowly eastward, then turned back to his work,
the collecting of canthus leaves. With night falling it was
getting harder to see, and for a moment he was tempted to
conjure light to aid him in his work. Then the moment passed.
Such things were no longer reflexive for him, as they had once

been. Lighting a lamp took far less effort and no one need die for it.

The plant's sharp, minty scent filled the clearing as he worked. It was strange how much pleasure a simple smell could provide, he thought. Once his life had been full of all the riches and power that morati men could dream of . . . yet nothing then had been quite so satisfying as this simple smell and the sweet peace of a mountain evening.

Finally he had gathered all he could and he rose up, stretched, and then followed the faint glow of lamplight back to his house.

The girl who lay upon a makeshift bed in the far corner of the small house was asleep, as she had been for many days now. He had set her broken bones with care, in the morati manner, not because sorcery couldn't have cured her wounds faster, but because he did not believe in waste. Besides, he'd thought it would be a good lesson for his young student to heal slowly and painfully, like the morati did. Maybe it would teach her something about caution.

Would that it was ever so easy with her, he thought wryly.

As he walked by to add a few leaves of fresh canthus to the teakettle over the fire, he suddenly noted that she had shifted position. Then he saw that one of her the bandages he'd wrapped about her arm had been severed down the middle as neatly as if it had been scored by a knife, to free the limb beneath; the flesh that had once been bruised and broken now looked whole again. So she had been awake while he was gone, for a few minutes at least, and coherent enough to be wielding sorcery. That meant that all her broken bones had probably been repaired, and all other signs of her near-fatal confrontation would likewise have been banished from her flesh. Patience had never been her forte.

He dropped a few canthus leaves into the pot, set it aside, and watched the pattern of steam rise from the hot water as he waited for the herb to steep. Giving her a chance to say something first, if she wanted to. Finally, when the color of the water was a deep golden brown and the smell of it had filled the small cabin like perfume, he poured two cups full, blew on them softly, and walked over to where Kamala lay.

Her eyes were half open but not quite focused; alert, but not yet oriented.

"Here," he said. He gave her a moment to fix her sight on the cup of canthus tea and struggle to a sitting position. As she took the cup from him—her hands trembling slightly as she used them for the first time in days—he reached out and took up a piece of paper that had been lying on the nearby table. "And here," he said, giving it to her, as he pulled up a chair to sit next to her.

She tried to sip from her cup, but her expression made it clear the tea was too hot for her taste. He could see a faint glimmer of power dance upon the surface of the liquid as she bound a bit of soulfire to cool it. How casually she drained a man of life, he thought, to save herself the trouble of a single cooling breath! Yet he knew deep inside that it was anything but casual. The action was deeply significant to her, for it was made possible by her triumph over the limitations of her sex. Killing a morati to cool a cup of tea was a luxury reserved for a precious few.

Thank the gods for that, he thought.

He could see the color come slowly back into her cheeks as the tea warmed her blood; the minty herb would help her clear her head as well. There was a dusting of pale freckles across her brow, he noticed, souvenir of a sunnier clime than his own. For a brief, disconcerting moment he was jealous.

Of what?

She put the cup aside then, her hand still shaking slightly, and turned her attention to the paper in her hand. For a minute she stared at it blankly, as if she had forgotten how to read.

Then her brow furrowed as the writing on the paper came into focus. "What is this?"

"A list of all the unpleasant things I might have done to you while you were asleep. Assuming I did not immediately turn you over to the other Magisters for past crimes. Call it a reminder to you of what the consequences might be the next time you show up half dead on a Magister's doorstep with a death warrant on your head." He sipped briefly from his own cup as he watched her look over the list. To his surprise, she did not answer him with defiance or excuses but just asked quietly, "Are there that many hunting me? Truly?"

"There have been at least a dozen sorcerous queries focused on you since you came here, and some even found their way to this forest. That is not to say that my defenses weren't up to the task, but I would like to know who and what I am defending you against. And why I should do so."

She lowered the cup and shut her eyes. A tremor seemed to pass through her flesh. "They hunt me for killing that Magister? Or something else?"

"Do they know you were the one responsible for that?"

"One Magister knows. I think. He might have told others."

With a sigh he sat back heavily in his chair; the aged wood creaked beneath his weight. "Which one?"

"Does it matter?"

"It might."

"Colivar."

He muttered something under his breath. It might have been a profanity.

"Bad?"

He got up from his chair and walked to the fireplace, pretending that the tea needed stirring. He didn't want her to see his face. "Colivar holds his secrets close," he said at last. "It's not likely he'll tell the others the truth about you unless he stands to gain from it. And he won't hunt you down too quickly, if he thinks that doing it slowly will afford him more entertainment." He looked at her sharply. "But he holds to the Law, the same as all the others. Never forget that. And if he means to keep you alive for a while, it is not for any benign purpose."

She nodded solemnly.

He turned back to her. His expression was stern. "You know you've compromised me by coming here. Didn't you once promise me you would never do that? There are Magisters who would call for my execution as well as yours if they knew that I had given you shelter."

"I know," she whispered. "I'm sorry. I had nowhere else to go."

If she'd argued with him he might have known what to say. But not like this. He was used to a fiery, defiant apprentice, not one with all the spirit leached out of her.

But then again, she wasn't his apprentice anymore. He needed to remember that, even if she kept forgetting it. Once a new Magister was sent out into the world he was his own man— or woman—and no one else of that brotherhood was expected to aid him, shelter him, or even tolerate his company unless he had something to gain from it. And even then there was no guarantee that a so-called ally might not take advantage of a moment's weakness to gain a more permanent advantage. Yes, according to the code they all lived by, she had done the most foolish thing imaginable, arriving on his doorstep the way she had. After breaking the one Law they all were sworn to enforce.

But you are without precedent to start with, my fiery little strumpet. So who is to say there will not be a host of other surprises? I knew that might be the case when I first took you in. So it's my own fault if that gets me in trouble now, yes?

With a sigh he sat down again beside her. Her wild red hair was longer than it had been when she'd left him, he noted. It was almost a feminine length now, falling in bright red wisps almost to her shoulders. No doubt she would cut it again as soon as she realized that.

Ironically, her repeated efforts to deny that she had any concern with her appearance only added to her allure. With her hair grown long, neatly brushed, and plaited in a feminine style, she might have been an attractive woman, but only that. In this state she was something more. Something primal and elemental, he thought. A force of nature.

"It may be that not all of those queries knew what they were focusing on," he said gruffly. He was trying to make his voice as unsympathetic as possible, but old habits were hard to break. "Anyone attempting to investigate your actions, even if he didn't know exactly who was responsible for them, might send a bit of power questing in this direction to seek answers. And I might rightfully respond to such a thing as an invasion of my territory and drive it off. No one will question any of that." He sighed and sipped his tea again. "So I gather you have done something else that others would want to know about? Besides the death of that Magister?"

Her lips tight, she nodded.

"Another breach of the Law?"

"No, Master Ethanus." The words were a whisper.

"What, then? And please remember, I am no longer your Master."

In answer she held out her hand to him, palm up. Sparks of light gathered above it and slowly coalesced into an image of a strange creature with a body like that of a long, dark snake and wings like those of a dragonfly.

Recognition was like a blow to the chest. For a moment Ethanus could not find his voice.

She said, "Prince Andovan called it a Souleater."

He had never seen one before, but he had heard enough of the old tales to recognize it for what it was. And the memory of how those tales ended made his blood freeze in his veins.

"What do you have to do with this . . . thing?"

"I fought it," she told him. "I did as you taught me, and struck for the joints, where its armor was weakest. And it worked." A bit of the old defiance was coming back into her voice. "Wasn't that news worth bringing here? Isn't such a report worth the risk of your harboring a fugitive, at least until she is strong enough to deliver it?"

"You killed this creature?"

"No. I might have, but . . ." She shut her eyes for a moment, trying to think back to what had happened. It all seemed a blur now, especially the last few terrifying moments. "Andovan must have died while I was fighting it. That is the only thing that could explain it."

"Andovan?"

"My consort."

He exhaled in an exasperated hiss. "You learned your consort's *name?*"

To his amazement, her face reddened. "A bit more than that, actually."

"How much more?" he demanded. Fascinated and repelled by the concept. Could you kill a man whose name you knew? Drain him of his vital energy while gazing into his eyes? What would it do to a Magister's soul, to experience such a thing?

"Enough to know that you were right," she said, with rare humility. "We should never learn the names of those we steal life from, lest it weaken our resolve. A weaker spirit than mine might have failed such a test." She met his eyes with a diamond-hard gaze; the flicker of pain in them was so fleeting he almost missed it. "But I'm still alive, yes? So I was strong enough to pass the test. That's all that matters, isn't it?"

Or selfish enough, he thought. *Bloodthirsty enough. Callous enough. For our kind, there is no other measure that matters.*

"You will not be alive for long if you do not keep away from Magisters. And that includes me." His tone was harsh. "You did a foolish thing, counting on my sympathy when you came here. I would expect better understanding from you."

Anger flashed in her eyes. "And I would expect better from *you*. Do you really think that a Magister whom you trained would gamble so heavily on human sentiment? Maybe instead she decided to take a chance that your *curiosity* would be sparked by her confrontation with a creature out of legend . . . enough that you would shelter her until she could share what she had seen. Is that not in keeping with what you taught me? That information is the coin of the realm among Magisters? That a sorcerer will take great risks for the sake of novelty when nothing else will move him? Or did I mistake that lesson also, my Master?"

For a moment he said nothing. It took all his self-control to keep his expression impassive, so that she could not guess what he was thinking. Then he walked to his writing desk, picked up a sheaf of blank papers, a pen and inkwell, and brought them back to her. "Write down all you have seen." He dropped the papers onto her lap and put the writing instruments on the table beside her. "And append a sorcerous image of the Souleater as well, that I might study it in greater detail later." He did not meet her eyes this time; perhaps he was afraid of what his own might reveal. "In the morning, when that is finished, I will take you to the Magisters for justice. As is my duty." He paused. "Do not attempt to leave this house before then, Kamala."

"I will not, Magister Ethanus." Her tone was one of unquestioning obedience. Of course. No other tone would be acceptable where the Law was concerned.

He ached to look at her again, to fix her in his memory one last time. But because it was an ache that came from his heart, he denied it.

"Should they choose to set you free," he said "—unlikely though I think that is—beware of the northlands. Most especially of the sorcerous barrier that holds the Souleaters at bay, which locals call the 'Wrath of the Gods.' I have heard it can play havoc with sorcery, and few Magisters ever go to that region unless their business requires it."

"I understand," she said quietly, nodding.

"A Magister who learned the secrets of the northlands would possess something of value to our brotherhood. Something he might later trade for assistance in . . . sensitive matters."

"I will remember that," she promised.

I really should betray your trust someday, he thought. *Just to remind you that such a thing is possible. Does it make me a bad teacher if I choose not to do so?*

How he ached to have her stay here longer! To drink in her maverick beauty for a bit more time, to bask in her youthful, defiant energy in a way that he had not been able to do while she'd been asleep . . . but it was too dangerous now. If the ones that were hunting her ever got close enough to eavesdrop on her memories, they must not see such weakness in him. He was pushing the limits of the Law as it was; he dared not risk the other Magisters suspecting the depth of his attachment to her.

Not to mention he might then have to admit it to himself.

"I will see you are given fair trial," he said sternly. "That is the most I can do."

And this is the closest I can come to saying good-bye.

"I understand," she whispered. Not saying good-bye either. That was a good thing, he thought. Words could not always be trusted.

Silently he turned back to the door, taking a lantern from its hook as he did so. Behind him there was no rustle of parchment, no sound of an inkwell being opened, no soft scratching of quill on paper. If he had been given such a task he would have spent the whole night working on it, writing until his fingers ached, using the exercise as a chance to review what had happened to him, and perhaps derive some valuable lesson from it. She, on the other hand, would accomplish the assignment with a moment's sorcery—a whisper of stolen life—and then move on to more important things.

Nothing is more important than knowledge, he thought. *Self-knowledge in particular.*

With a heavy sigh he headed out into the night, so that later, if asked, he might honestly say that he had not seen her leave.

CHAPTER 2

H E ARRIVED without fanfare, without servants, without guards. A dozen monks in plain woolen cassocks approached the palace gate together and he was simply one of them, dressed in the same coarse fabric, covered with dust from the same long journey.

The royal guards, on edge ever since Danton's death, gathered themselves into a tight formation at the gate as the small retinue approached. An onlooker might have been amused. It was hard to imagine any weapons such a company might carry that would be cause for concern, but the royal household was edgy without a Magister to guard it, and even though a dozen witches had pledged themselves to aiding in the transition of power—in return for enough gold that they would never have to sell their talents to any man again—it was clear the guards did not consider that good enough.

"Halt!" the captain of the watch called as the party of monks approached the gate.

All but one of them obeyed. That one, a tall man, continued for several steps more, until he stood apart from his companions.

"Halt!" the captain called again, and behind him his men tightened their grips on their lances, wondering what source of trouble might lie hidden beneath those dusty robes.

Then the lead monk raised his hands to the hood that shadowed his features, and slowly pushed it back. "Tell Her Majesty that Salvator Aurelius, son of Danton Aurelius, has returned."

For a moment the captain just stared at him, slack-jawed. It had been almost four years since anyone had seen Danton's second-born, and he had changed much in that time. The gangly youth who had gone off years ago in search of spiritual enlightenment had come into his manhood along the way, and the steady calm that emanated from him now was so uncharacteristic of the young prince the captain remembered that for a moment he was not sure they were the same person.

Then the dark eyes fixed on him, as unnerving in their intensity as Danton's own had been, and he sputtered some words of embarrassment and apology as he knelt before his prince, motioning for his fellow guards to follow suit, while one of them ran off toward the palace to spread the news.

Salvator said nothing, simply motioned for his companions to follow him through the gate. Ten paces before the other monks had been his equals; now, falling into step behind him, they became his attendants.

By the time he reached the palace door the news of his arrival had clearly reached the building and servants who had obviously been surprised by his arrival scurried about in a desperate attempt to look as if they had been expecting him all along. It should not have pleased him, to see them so anxious to receive him properly . . . but it did.

For that sin of pride, he promised himself, he would offer atonement later.

The great oak doors swung open, seemingly of their own accord. The servants who ushered him inside clearly felt that if they bowed down low enough they might be forgiven any other shortcomings. It disturbed him a little how natural it felt to pass them by without acknowledging their existence in any way. It was as if the moment he entered this place his old persona wrapped itself around him, obscuring the man he had worked so hard to become. Was that a good thing? His father would have said it was, but he was not so sure.

He walked far enough that the monks behind him had room to enter. By the time they were all safely inside and the great doors shut behind them, a familiar footstep could be heard approaching. The servants looked away from Salvator as they waited, as if afraid that gazing upon him directly might anger the Royal Heir.

Or perhaps they were afraid of his god, he mused.

Unlike the rest of the palace staff, the castellan who arrived was calm and unruffled. Jan Cresel was some years older than Salvator remembered him, but otherwise much the same. Back in his childhood, Salvator had conspired with the other young princes in various attempts to shake the man's composure. They had never succeeded. The palace could be crumbling down about Cresel, its vast roof about to fall on his head, and he would appear every bit as calm and collected as he was today.

"Prince Salvator." He bowed deeply, formally, at exactly the proper angle for welcoming a future king. "Her Majesty is pleased by your return."

Salvator turned back partway toward his companions, directing Cresel's attention to them. "These good brothers chose to accompany me in order to discourage trouble upon the road. I trust they are welcome here."

"Of course. We are honored to have the good brothers as our guests." His nod toward them was polite but by no means deferential. "The road is long; you must be tired and thirsty." He gestured to a nearby servant, who quickly stepped forward. "See they are assigned suitable accommodations and have food and drink brought for them." He looked at Salvator again. "Is there anything else your companions will require?"

"That is all for now." How easy it was to fall back into his old role. Like an old familiar garment that he had forgotten about but which, donned years later, still fit perfectly. He had not expected that.

"Then, Highness, no doubt you will wish to refresh yourself before making formal presentation. If you will permit me, I will show you to your rooms." Normally the castellan did not take on such duties himself, but apparently this time he thought it was the proper thing to do. Or perhaps he simply wanted Salvator to know that he accepted his place in the new order of things, monk's robes and all. Perhaps not all the servants were equally accepting and he wanted to make a point of it in front of them.

"Not necessary, Master Cresel. I found the journey quite invigorating. Where is my mother?"

The expression on the castellan's face made it clear that he was fully prepared for this turn of events—and any other surprises the young prince might come up with. "Awaiting you, Highness. Of course." He turned slightly, inviting Salvator to follow him. "I will take you to her."

Danton's palace was much as Salvator remembered it . . . and much changed. The halls were the same gray stone, outer walls as thick and windowless as a fortified castle—indeed, the central keep had once served as a fortress, in the days when this region had guarded the vulnerable flank of a newborn kingdom—but there was no longer a sense of gloom about the corners and the dull, aging tapestries that had adorned the walls for as long as Salvator could remember had been either replaced or cleaned. He liked it better this way, he thought, surprised by the brief pang of guilt that followed the thought. As if approving of change was somehow an act of disloyalty.

Any king with a Magister can have his possessions polished and perfect, Danton had once told his son, *or even conjured out of pure gold if he desires. But history, tradition . . . these are things that sorcery cannot counterfeit. These are the true measures of a man's wealth.* The High Queen had gone along with that during Danton's lifetime, of course. But Salvator did not doubt that her first act of mourning had been to assign of veritable army of housekeepers to scrub the place clean and to consign to storage the most faded decorations, or else to have witches restore them to pristine condition. The transformation of his childhood home from gloomy keep to gleaming citadel was both refreshing and—inexplicably—disturbing.

High Queen Gwynofar was waiting for him in the audience chamber. Like the palace itself she was much as he remembered her from his childhood, yet also much changed. The sorrows of the last few months had stolen the blush from her cheeks and though her expression was warm and welcoming at the moment, he could sense the sadness that lay behind it. She was dressed in black, of course. Layers of black, as if each loss required its own separate mourning, with the edges deliberately tattered. The color made her pale skin seem strangely fragile, like that of a porcelain doll. Even in less sorrowful times he had always been amazed by the aspect of delicacy about her, for he had seen her rule by his father's side—weathering Danton's most murderous rages, reining in his worst excesses—and he knew what sort of strong stuff she was made of. Few outside of the family understood her strength. And Danton had played such ignorance to his advantage. Foreign dignitaries, mesmerized by Gwynofar's delicate beauty, would whisper secrets to her that they would never reveal to Danton himself. In their foolishness, they convinced themselves that she would not pass them on to her husband as soon as they were gone. It had always seemed foolish to Salvator, but Danton had assured him that it was a common weakness among men, to let down their guard in the presence of a beautiful woman.

And beautiful she was, there was no denying that. Even in her middle years, shrouded in the black of mourning, she appeared regal and elegant. Those seeing her for the first time would make note of the cascade of golden hair that fell to the small of her back, the clear blue Kierdwyn eyes, and a face that was enhanced rather than despoiled by the first few lines of age now fanning out from the corners of her eyes, drawing attention to their depths. Men would die for such eyes, he thought. Some probably had.

As soon as she saw him, she reached out instinctively toward him: a mother's welcome. "Salvator!" Then she stopped suddenly, remembering what he was; her hands fell down awkwardly by her sides, even though she clearly ached to touch him. "Forgive me. Your vows—"

"The apology is mine to make, Mother." How strange the title sounded on his lips! He had the sudden dizzying sensation of being caught between worlds, unable to manage stable footing in either. "But until my vows are set aside I must hold to them, and yes, that requires I have no physical contact with women." He smiled slightly. "Even my mother."

What did she really think of his faith? The Penitents' view of the Protectors and their mission was far from flattering. Had she taken that into consideration when she'd asked him to return, or had she hoped that such things would cease to matter once he set aside his priestly robes? There was no need to ask the question aloud; he knew what the answer would be. High Queen Gwynofar would have weighed every option before asking her second child to come home. She knew what his religion was about. She understood the risks of such a course. And she had judged it the best of all her options, even so.

So here he was, in this strange place that was no longer home to him, where the very stones under his feet seemed to echo his father's presence. *You served a great dream,* he thought to Danton, *and brought peace to this continent, albeit at the point of a sword. I would have preferred that Rurick inherit such responsibility, but in his absence I will do my best.*

With a smile Gwynofar indicated a nearby table, where a large brass platter of breads and cheeses and another of roasted lamb were flanked by several heavy pewter pitchers and a matching goblet. It was quite an impressive array, given how little warning she'd had of his arrival. Clearly she had been prepared for his return and had even taken into account that he might circumvent the usual protocols in his arrival. Thus had she been with Danton, he remembered, always anticipating his needs. It was yet another quality in her that strangers tended to underestimate.

"I didn't how hungry you would be when you arrived," she told him, "so I prepared a bit of everything."

He was indeed hungry and felt his stomach tighten at the sight of such a banquet. He quelled the sensation with effort, giving thanks to his god for testing him thus. Sacrifice had little value if it came too easily.

His hesitation was clearly not what she had expected. "You are allowed to eat, yes?"

A brief smile flickered across his lips. "It would be a short-lived faith if we were not." He stepped forward to the table, and after a moment's contemplation took up a small piece of bread and a cup of plain water. "However, as a personal offering, I have sworn off all but the simplest fare until my coronation. Doubtless the royal cooks will be relieved."

She drew in a sharp breath as if to protest, but he raised up a hand before she could begin. "You asked me to set aside my vows in order to become king. That I will do, in proper time. Until that hour I am what I am, Mother. You called home a priest. Would you expect me to comport myself as anything less?"

She bit her lip for a moment. "You are as stubborn as your father was, you know that?"

"So my teachers told me. Often." He bit off a piece of the bread and washed it down with a mouthful of water. It quieted the beast in his stomach somewhat.

"However," she said, "You must eat a good meal before your coronation. You cannot afford to look weak before the vassals of Danton's empire."

He opened his mouth to argue the point—but then he saw the resolve in her eyes and he sensed the steel will that lay hidden behind her black silk and gentle manners. It was already a lost battle, he realized. Even Danton had given way to her when he saw that look in her eyes.

Swallowing the last bite of bread (and how his stomach cried out for more!), he turned his attention to a nearby window and the view it offered of the devastated landscape surrounding the palace. "Tell me how my father died. I have heard the public details, of course, but I wish it from your tongue."

It was a horrific tale, one that began with a proud king's mental dissolution and ended in his bloody death at the hands of his own family. Gwynofar played but lightly upon that last part, perhaps not wishing to discuss why the High King's own son had decided he must die. The fault did not lay with Danton; she made that quite clear. A foreign Magister allied to a Souleater had used Danton like a puppet and their family had paid the price for it. Salvator nodded as he listened; that much he had already been told.

But it was when she spoke of the Souleater itself that he listened most closely. It was the first detailed description he had ever heard from someone who had actually seen one of the demons, and it made his blood run cold as a strange elation that was half fear and half awe suffused his veins.

This, this is the Scourge of the Destroyer, that was sent in ages past to humble mankind. My father tried to stand among the gods and he was brought down for it. Now we must await our Creator's judgment as he decides whether one such warning is enough, or whether those ancient horrors must be repeated in their entirety in order for us to learn our lesson.

He did not speak of such things to Gwynofar, of course. She was of a different faith, one based upon human pride, that dreamed of a final battle between Souleater and man, which man presumably might win. It was a primitive faith, simple in its understanding of the world, and in time he would have to address it. But not now. Now was a time for strengthening the bonds of family, not straining them.

We stand at the edge of a precipice, he thought, *one step away from a great and terrible darkness. If we fail to keep our balance, who is to say whether our descendants will ever find the light again?*

"You must decide where you wish your coronation to be held," his mother was saying. "Little else can be done until that choice is made."

With a start he realized that he had missed her last words. *Time for meditation later,* he admonished himself. "Here, of course. What better place to demonstrate the continuing strength of the High Kingdom than Danton's own seat of power?"

She frowned; clearly the choice did not please her. "You know the palace cannot shelter so many. We will wind up with royal encampments in a charred ruin. That is hardly an appropriate setting."

"Perhaps it will inspire them to reflect upon the nature of the world. That life as we know it is but a fleeting indulgence and that same god who created us can just as easily destroy us." He walked over to the table as he spoke and broke off another piece of bread. Reflex. After a moment's thought he put it down again. "Or perhaps it will inspire them to reflect upon the last time this land was cleared, when war ravaged the region, and no prince could afford to offer an enemy cover this close to his gates."

He put down his cup and brushed a few stray crumbs from his robe. "But come now, Mother, show me what changes you have made in this place, and how the ancestor trees have grown in my absence. Meanwhile I shall attempt to answer all the questions you have for me, and we may begin our planning."

———

Sunset lay like a wound along the western horizon, spilling crimson clouds into a bruised purple sky. On the black earth below a hundred lanterns sputtered as workers continued to haul away the charred remnants of a great royal forest, struggling to accomplish it by the deadline they had been given. The ground beneath their feet was bleak and barren as far as the eye could see; only the single castle that looked over it, and the stark mountains to the north, broke the rhythm of the landscape.

Standing alone atop the building's highest tower, wrapping her arms against the sudden chill of the evening breeze, Gwynofar remembered when the forest had burned. Kostas had started the fire—Kostas, that vile creature posing as a Magister who had stepped in to counsel her husband when Ramirus had left them—and then ordered all of Danton's servants to let it burn to its natural end. For three days and nights the sky had spewed forth ash in furious waves, a foul and unnatural storm. At the time Gwynofar had thought the fire no more than an act of spite, meant to strangle her heart with sorrow so that she would be more easily manipulated. Perhaps, she had reasoned later, Kostas had wanted her to hate him so blindly that she would not wonder at the strange supernatural chill that ran up her spine any time he entered a room. But no, even that was not enough to explain it. No matter how much she added up the pieces of the puzzle now it was still not enough. Kostas had served a Souleater. Souleaters fed upon life. What did either of them stand to gain from such utter devastation? Surely her own discomfort, no matter how pleasing it was to him, was not enough to explain what he had done.

There was another piece of the puzzle somewhere. All the instincts in her *lyr* soul told her that it mattered. She had to find it.

"Your Majesty?"

The voice was familiar to her, a memory from a better time. She turned toward its owner with an ache in her heart. *Would that things could go back to the way they were a year ago,* she thought. *Would that the gods had not decided to test us so cruelly.* "Ramirus."

The ancient Magister bowed his head ever so slightly; his flowing white beard stirred in the evening breeze. "I promised you I would come."

She sighed heavily. For a moment words deserted her.

"I take it things did not go well?"

She looked out over the landscape once more. "He means to hold his coronation here, Ramirus. He said that Danton's ruined forest will serve as a reminder to both men and monarchs that life is but a fleeting thing, and that the same gods who created the earth can also destroy it."

"Ah, yes. The creed of the Penitents. A curious tradition." He came to where she stood, near the outer wall, and gazed out upon the landscape beside her. "You made a strange move, choosing that one to succeed Danton."

She did not speak until she was sure she could do so without emotion. "There was no real choice."

"You could have left him in the monastery. He might have spent a lifetime happily chanting his prayers and denying himself a woman's pleasure, and never mourned his lack of temporal power."

"Perhaps," she agreed. "Or instead he might have discovered, after a few years of watching his younger brother rule, that there was more to existence than such a sterile plan . . . and then perhaps he would decide that he had been cheated and he would divide the High Kingdom against itself to claim what should have been his by birthright." She sighed. "My summons was a test. If he had not answered exactly as he had, I would have placed my fourth son on the throne and left Salvator to his strange two-faced god. But Danton's blood is strong in my second-born. Strong enough that when he heard the call to power he set aside his vows of faith to answer it without hesitation. Do you honestly believe such a man would have remained quietly in the background for his entire life? Do you think Valemar would have been strong enough to contain him?"

"Better, perhaps, for a woman to claim the throne."

She looked at him sharply.

"It is not unknown in the north," he pointed out.

"And we are not in the north. Do you not think that a goodly portion of Danton's vassal princes would rebel in an instant if I gave them such excuse? I am foreign-born; they will not forget that. And rumored to be some kind of snow-witch, or changeling, or . . ." She laughed shortly. "I can't even keep track of the rumors these days. Whereas Salvator . . ."

Her voice trailed off into silence. For a moment she shut her eyes.

"You asked him about choosing a Magister," Ramirus said. A question.

She nodded.

"He refused, didn't he?"

"He said his god would not permit such a course. That he would rely upon witches if he had need of power."

"I warned you that might be the case."

"Yes." She bit her lip. "You did."

"And now?"

She shrugged stiffly. "We go on. I make the best of the hand the gods have dealt me. As always."

He nodded tightly. "Then you should leave here, Majesty. As soon as protocol allows."

Her jaw tensed. "I will not abandon him."

"You would not be abandoning him. Merely . . . traveling. Visit your parents. Or your daughters. You told me often enough how much you wished you could see them more frequently. Now is the time."

"He needs me by his side——"

"Your presence here cannot save him from the consequences of his own foolishness." His tone grew stern, as a father's might when admonishing a favorite child. "What will happen the day some prince that Danton pressed into fealty decides he wants no more of Aurelius leadership? Such men have Magisters of their own, you know. And they will be free to act now. There is will be no Law dictating what they may or may not do to your son. Do you understand what that means?" When she didn't answer, he continued, "A single word from an enemy's Magister, and the whole of this palace may come crashing down upon his head. Or the earth may open up to swallow him whole, along with all his household. It is only a matter of time, Majesty. I am sorry, but that's the truth. And I would rather not have you be here to share his fate when it happens."

Her hands clasped the edge of the parapet tightly as she worked to keep her emotions under control . . . or at least to keep Ramirus from seeing them. *There must be a way,* she thought desperately. All the debates she'd had with herself since the night Danton had died raced through her head again. What other path could she have chosen? Danton's High Kingdom was a fragile construct which the wrong move might topple. Now it seemed that the man best suited to inherit it would not survive long enough to do the job.

Then, with sudden insight, she knew what had to be done.

"Make your contract with me," she said. She drew herself up to her full height as she turned to face him, pride lending strength to her words. "I am Queen Mother of House Aurelius. Make your contract with me."

It seemed for a moment that he had lost his voice. "That is . . ." He hesitated, seeking the proper word. "Irregular. To say the least."

"So are Souleaters, and the Magisters that serve them. So is a royal household robbed of three kings in a single night. So is—" She waved toward the black wasteland beyond the castle, her long silk sleeve fluttering in the breeze. "—all of *this*."

"And how do you think Salvator will take it when you tell him you have done this? Defied his will, and invited the wrath of this Destroyer he worships?"

"I won't tell him. It will be our secret."

"It cannot be a secret," he pointed out. "Not if your family is to be protected."

"Then let it be known among Magisters that a contract has been made with House Aurelius. Nothing more. They don't need to know all the details, do they? The mere fact that a contract exists will mean that other Magisters cannot strike at my family. That is your Law, is it not?"

"Aye." He shook his head slowly. "That is the Law. . . ."

"And Salvator would be protected in that case, as my son. Yes?"

"Majesty—" His eyes were hard and cold, but that was not necessarily a bad thing; she knew him well enough to understand that when his emotions were strongest they were most carefully hidden. "What is it you propose to offer in return for this . . . secret alliance? We who serve royalty do not do so for love of servitude, but rather for what we are given in return. The chance to take part in creating and sustaining great nations, to share in our patron's status and posterity. These things cannot be provided by a secret contract. What can you offer that has equal value?"

"To you, Ramirus?" She took a step closer to the Magister; the air between them seemed strangely charged with energy. Was that the magic of her blood coming to the fore again? Ever since the night the Souleater had died she had wondered what its limits were. "I offer that which you desire most. Not wealth, nor status, nor earthly power. I know what it is you really want." Her voice dropped to a whisper, intimate and compelling. "There are secrets in the blood of the Protectors—in those we call the *lyr*—that you've hungered to study for as long as I've known you. Now the Souleaters are returning, and whatever power lies dormant in our bloodlines will soon awaken, as the gods promised us it would. And you can be there, Ramirus, by my side, when it happens. Knowing what the Protectors know, learning the truth behind the ancient legends even as the gods reveal it to us. All that I will share with you and more—fair payment for what I ask in return. Yes?"

She tried to still the beating of her heart as she waited for his answer. *Did you think I didn't know what you were about all those years? Why you had such a keen interest in the tales of my homeland?* But there was far more at stake now than a handful of legends. A contract with Salvator would have bound Raimrus to the service of the High Kingdom. A contract with Gwynofar would bind him not only to her brood but to the business of the Protectors as well. And if the Souleaters were truly returning to the human lands, that was no small thing.

We will need allies, she thought. *All the witches in the world barely managed to contain these creatures the first time. We cannot face them with less power then that.*

"An interesting offer." The night had become dark enough

that it was hard to see Ramirus' expression, but she knew from long experience that it would reveal little to her. "Not one that I would normally entertain—but this is not a normal time, is it?"

Her heart skipped a beat. "You accept?"

"I did not say that. I will consider your offer, both for what I would gain from it, and what I must sacrifice. You know my accustomed habits. I do not set them aside lightly, even for such price as you would offer."

She felt her heart skip a beat. "But Salvator—"

"Is safe until his coronation, and probably for some time afterward. My colleagues will allow him time to choose a Magister Royal. That much is tradition. If you can keep him from making any public announcement of his intentions, he may last quite a while." He looked at her sharply. "You are asking for more than his protection, you know that."

"Yes," she said quietly. "I know."

"And you wish nothing else from me? Nothing of more . . . customary service?"

She looked out over the barren landscape. *Would that we could turn the clock back and start over. Bring back the trees, and Andovan to hunt among them, and my husband and firstborn son to complain about his lack of interest in royal politics. But even you do not have that much power.* "Help the land to recover its strength. Send strong summer rains to nurture the seeds that survived Kostas" fire, so that they grow with all possible speed. Let the field of ash become a field of life, and thus cover over this nightmare that Kostas wrought. For it was no natural devastation and should not be favored by any god."

He nodded. "Very well. If I choose to accept your contract, you shall have fields of grass to comfort you." He bowed his head ever so slightly. "Is that all, Majesty?"

"For now, yes." Later in the night she would make blood sacrifice to the Spears and beg the northern gods to turn Ramirus' mind and heart to her cause. For now, she had done all that one woman could do.

He turned to leave. She knew from experience that he would step into the natural shadows before disappearing or else summon sorcerous shadows to attend him. He did not like the morati to witness his transportation.

"Ramirus."

He paused, but did not turn back.

"Why does your kind make contracts with us at all? You could have anything you wanted with your sorcery, including Danton's throne. Why do you bargain with kings at all, rather than simply become kings yourselves?"

Slowly he turned to look at her. His eyes were black sparks in the darkness.

"Because," he said, "if the world had no structure or limits, we would drown in it."

And then the shadows of the parapets folded about him and she was alone once more.

CHAPTER 3

THE SEERS sat in a circle, hands linked, oblivious to all but the soft rhythm of drums in the background. The spell-song rose from their lips in a shared murmur, a construct of ancient melodies and long-forgotten tongues, mysterious in its harmonies, hypnotic in its power. The great hall surrounding them seemed to dissolve into shadows as they chanted; all the men and women sitting in a circle beyond them did likewise, until the spectators seemed no more than mere phantoms to them. Distant. Inconsequential.

Only the spell mattered now.

Slowly, the air that was contained within the circle of their hands began to stir. At first it rippled softly—like rainwater stirred by a breeze or desert air rising over hot summer sand—then suddenly a gash appeared, as if some unseen blade had rent the air in two. Colors gushed out from the opening, filling the circle with liquid streamers of light: cobalt, ultramarine, violet, viridian. Colors so rich and resonant that they gleamed like gemstones in the dusty air. Soon the center of the circle was a swirling mass of dancing ribbons that throbbed in time to the steady drumbeat. The chanting grew louder then, as the Seers concentrated their power; those spectators familiar with ancient tongues might have been able pick out a few words here and there, remnants of languages from an earlier age, now preserved only in ancient tomes and mystical chants.

> *Hear our summons!*
> *Honor our communion!*
> *Accept our sacrifice!*

The streamers of color were beginning to weave themselves into a picture in the center of the circle. The first shape to become recognizable was some kind of creature. It was long and sinuous like a snake, but it moved in a way that implied more than reptilian intelligence. More streamers knotted themselves about its midsection and then fanned out, taking the shape of broad wings, veined like an insect's. A thousand subtle tones of blue and violet rippled through their substance as the creature hovered in the center of the circle, wings beating steadily.

One of the Guardians watching drew in a sharp breath. The man sitting next to him put a hand on his shoulder, warning him to silence.

Now there was a new shape coalescing in front of the creature: that of a man. He was tall and golden-haired in the manner of the northlands, and well-armed. Even so, he seemed a small and fragile creature compared to the great winged beast looming over him. Then he cried out to the beast as he drew his weapon, a strange, animalistic cry. Every man and woman in the great hall knew the meaning of that sound, and it made cold shivers run up their spines to hear it. The winged creature clearly heard it also, for it turned all its attention upon the lone warrior, just as the legends had said it would do.

The two figures fought.

The strength of the beast was fearsome, but finite. A crossbow bolt to the inside of one shoulder forced it down to earth, where it hissed like an angry lizard.

The skill of the man was great, but untested. The tail of the creature whipped toward him, faster and harder than he had expected, and one could hear ribs shatter as it struck.

And then as the circle of Seers chanted—and the Guardians sitting behind them watched in fascination—the man drove his lance upward through the creature's jaw and into its brain. And then, after the creature's final death spasms, the battle was ended.

For a few minutes longer, the Seers continued their whispering. Long enough for all present to study the fallen creature and take note of important details: the thick armored plates guarding its underbelly; the long, sharp blades fixed to the end of its whiplike tail; the deadly spines running down the length of its neck, back, and tail—save for one small section just above its shoulders where there was only scar tissue. Knotted and twisted whorls of thickened flesh bore witness to where spines had once been. Had they been broken off in battle or removed deliberately? The image gave no clue.

Finally, the chanting ceased.

The image faded.

"May the gods help us," Master Favias muttered.

The Guardian nearest to the doors pushed them open, admitting sunlight into the meetinghouse once more. The late afternoon light picked out a somewhat chaotic collection of carvings that decorated the walls, ceiling, and rafters of the rough-hewn building. Kierdwyn knotwork, Skandir pictoglyphs, battle prayers calligraphed in flowing Tonado script. Forty generations of Guardians had left their marks on this place, all of them carefully preserved each time a portion of the building had to be repaired. According to legend, not a single carving had ever been lost. Wood might rot, mortar might crumble, but the messages left by past Guardians were truly eternal.

The Seers were rising to their feet now, as were all the Guardians surrounding them. Master Favias clasped each Seer by the hand, one after the other, bowing deeply to each, offering the formal thanks of his Protectorate. If their spellsong had been true, if the gods had answered their call for shared sacrifice, then each one of the witches had contributed a portion of his life-essence to their common conjuration. If the spellsong had failed—or the gods were not pleased with their efforts—then one man or woman might bear the cost for all of it. Either way, each and every one of them had been willing to sacrifice a portion of his or her life to serve the Guardians' need, and that must be properly acknowledged.

Some of the Seers took their leave then, clearly exhausted by their efforts; the Guardians bowed in humble respect as they left. A few others chose to remain, waiting to hear what would be learned from their conjuring.

The Master Guardian of Kierdwyn Protectorate looked to Rhys. The latter's expression was grim, and he continued staring at the place where his battle with the Souleater had just been displayed, as if his mind was elsewhere. "You did well," he said.

"I was careless," Rhys responded sharply. Irritably. "I would have died, had a Magister not healed me."

Master Favias walked over to him and laid a hand on his shoulder. "No man has fought one of these creatures for at least a thousand years. Nor even seen one alive, in all that time. Yet you fought one, with nothing better than a handful of myths to guide you, and you brought it down. And then you collected samples for us that will help us prepare for the next battle. *You did well,*" he insisted, "regardless of who may have assisted you."

Rhys bowed his head reluctantly, accepting the praise, but clearly not happy about it.

"Now tell us, where is the cursed creature now? Is the body in a place where we might send our scholars to go and study it?"

Rhys shook his head. "The High Queen tried to have it preserved for us, but was unable to do so. It did not rot as other living creatures do. Within hours of its death its inner organs were already foul from corruption, and its skin was as rotten as that of a week-old corpse. Rotting from within." He shook his head in frustration, remembering it. "I wanted to get a look at the creature's bones, to see if they might be hollow in the manner of birds—that would be a vulnerability worth noting—but by the time I had gotten that far, the creature's skeleton had begun to rot from the inside out, so I could not be sure. Even the few samples I managed to get did not fare well. In the end the cadaver had to be burned to keep its poison from spreading to living creatures. This is all that remains."

There was a table at the far end of the meetinghouse where several small canvas bundles were waiting. The Guardians gathered as Rhys walked over to it and unwrapped the first bundle. Four long, thin bony plates were revealed. Their outer edges were sharp, as finely honed as if some master swordsmith had spent months forging them to perfection; the inner edges were thick and discolored, with fragments of decaying flesh clinging to them that crumbled to dust as Rhys spread the pieces out for inspection.

"These are from the creature's tail. Magister Colivar directed me to salvage them immediately when the creature died. Later, when it became clear that the rest of the creature was rotting too quickly for sample gathering, I wanted to ask why these were unaffected. Whether it was because of some unique property of this particular material, or simply because I had removed them from the body before the putrefaction began. But Colivar had already left and no one else knew the answer." He turned one of the long blades over so that it caught the light; sapphire highlights played along its sharper edge, and a faint musky odor rose from its surface. "This is the part of the beast that our ancestors crafted into knife blades and lance tips to pierce the creatures' hides. Colivar said it was better than steel for this purpose, and that we would probably need diamonds to craft it."

Master Favias nodded darkly. He had been to the armory where the Protectorate's ancient weapons were stored, had noted the strange glassy material out of which many had been made. Tougher than steel indeed, and proof against all manners of rust and decay. Satisfying though it was to know at last what that material was, he was clearly not pleased to be reliant upon the Souleaters themselves for weaponry.

"The Lord Protectors will give us diamonds if we need them," Master Favias said. "What else have you brought?"

Rhys opened another set of wrappings to reveal half a dozen long, curved spines that smelled faintly of rotten meat. "I removed these from the creature's back. They are constructed much like the horns of other creatures, save that the interiors are filled with some kind of spongelike substance. Not much of that remains at this point." He turned one over so that the Guardians could see that the piece was hollow, with strands of some fibrous substance clinging to its inner surface. "Queen Gwynofar suggested that perhaps the Souleater contained within itself some virulent poison, or another vehicle of physical corruption, that was held in check while it was alive. As soon as it died the poison was set free to ravage its flesh, destroying it from the inside out." He put the spine back down. "Needless to say we would need much more observation to confirm such a theory."

He did not say what they all were thinking: *Gods save us from discovering that there are enough Souleaters around to make such a study possible.*

Carefully Rhys unwrapped the third of his bundles. Unlike the others it did not contain a simple piece of Souleater anatomy, but rather a wide, flat box made of wood. This he opened, laying it in the center of the circle so that all might see what it contained.

"This is from the creature's wing."

Even in such a dismembered state, the wing fragment was eerily beautiful. Jewel-toned colors rippled across its surface as Rhys turned it for them all to see, as if the thing were made of liquid gemstones. Slender black struts and the delicate veining between them seemed better suited to an insect's wing than that of a great carnivore; it seemed too delicate to bear such a great weight.

"When I first took this sample," Rhys said, "it required great effort. My knife could barely pierce the wing membrane, fragile though it seemed. And yet, within hours of the Souleater's death . . ."

He picked up the wing fragment, held it in his hand for a moment, then closed his fist around it and squeezed. When he opened his hand again, only dust and tiny shards remained.

"That is all I was able to collect before the creature was past the point of being useful to us," he said quietly. "I should have worked faster."

"What about its mesmeric power?" Master Favias asked, pointedly ignoring the last comment. "Tell us about that."

Rhys bit his lip for a moment as he sought the proper words. "The others who saw it told me afterward that it was ... seductive. They felt drawn to it. Some even felt an urge to offer themselves to it, as a ... as a lover might. Even wished for it to tear out their throat, as though that would be a pleasurable act. They knew that the feeling was wrong, that something unnatural was happening, but even so they could not fight it ... or perhaps, more accurately, they did not *desire* to fight it."

"And yourself?"

"I felt ... a dullness of my senses. A heaviness of thought. And it was as if my limbs belonged to another creature and would not respond to my commands. Every move I made took monumental effort. I used one of the spellsongs to focus myself; without that, I might well have been overcome. But my emotions were never altered. I hated the thing, and I feared it, but I was never drawn to it. I never desired anything but its death, and the death of all its kind."

"So that much is good news," Master Favias approved. "The gods' protection is strong in their chosen warriors."

"Maybe not," one of the other Guardians said. Rhys recognized him as part of the Brusan contingent, a somber man who rarely came this far east. "Rhys is half *lyr*, yes? So he is better protected than most of us. What if the gods were not as generous to the rest of us ... to mere *peasants*."

Rhys' eyes narrowed in anger. He started to move forward, but Master Favias put a hand upon his shoulder once more, this time to steady him.

"Rhys. Please." His tone was respectful but firm. "No insult was given here."

"I am no different than any other man in this company," Rhys muttered.

"In spirit, in strength, in dedication, no, you are not. But in blood? The question's a fair one, my brother. You can ride closer to the Spears than any of us, you know that. You can bear the Wrath beating down upon your soul past the point when other men just cower and flee. If it is your father's special heritage that strengthens you thus, and not just your personal fortitude, then we must be wary of assuming that the rest of us will enjoy the same immunity. Best now to assume that the Souleaters may indeed be strong enough to mesmerize some Guardians, despite this one's failure with you, and figure our tactics accordingly." When Rhys did not respond, he pressed, "That is a good thing, yes?"

Rhys exhaled sharply, but said nothing. His hands at his sides curled into fists for a moment, as he tried to calm his spirit. The fact that Favias was right did not make it any easier. At last he nodded, somewhat stiffly.

"You say that Magister Colivar was present," Favius noted. "I did not see him in the battle."

Rhys nodded. "No. He stood by and watched. So did Ramirus, who had brought me there. Neither lifted a finger to help."

"Perhaps they could not," Favias mused.

"Or will not," a Skandir Guardian offered. One of the few women in the group. "Gods forbid their precious Magister hides should be risked for someone else's welfare."

"Aye," the Brusan muttered. "They are not known for sacrifice, are they?"

Master Favias held up a hand. "Time enough later to complain about Magisters," he said sternly. "Let us hear from our archivists now. Rommel, what have you found that might shed light upon this tale?"

The chief archivist for Kierdwyn, an older man with long gray hair pulled back into a tight queue at the base of his neck, cleared his throat before speaking. "There are records of ancient formulae that were used for treating Souleater hides so that they could be crafted into armor. If the body decays as quickly as Rhys suggests, that would certainly explain why those formulae were considered as important as they were, and why our forebears took such care to preserve them." He stroked the gray stubble on his chin thoughtfully. "Our tradition says that in order to defeat a Souleater, one must wear its armor and wield its weapons. Apparently that is not as simple a process as it sounds."

Master Favias nodded. "We will need samples of all of those formulae. Let us see which ones can be stored without losing their potency. If the creatures do return in force—" he let the words hang in the air for a moment "—our Guardians may have to carry such potions with them to use on the battlefield. The bodies will likely be too far gone to preserve otherwise."

The archivist nodded. "I will send out word to all the archivists and see that trials are begun."

"Good. Good. Now, Rhys . . ." Favias turned back to Rhys. "What of this Magister, this Colivar? You say he gave you information about the Souleaters? Who is he and how much does he know?"

Rhys frowned. "All I can tell you is that he is an enemy of the High Kingdom—or at least he was while Danton was alive— apparently bound in service to one of the southern kingdoms. He is said to be very old, very knowledgeable, and dangerously deceptive. Which, according to Gwynofar, describes most of the Magisters."

"Did you get any sense of where his information was coming from? If there is some ancient text we have not seen yet, we should search it out. Especially if it contains precise information on how to deal with these creatures."

Rhys hesitated. "He spoke very matter-of-factly, as if these were things he'd actually seen, rather than something he'd learned about from written records or artifacts. Though that can't be the case, of course. There were no Magisters until long after the Spears descended."

Favias nodded. "Very well. Then let us collect information on this *Colivar* as well and see what we can come up with. Not only regarding what he claims to have witnessed, but personal details as well. We may eventually have to barter with him for his knowledge, in which case I want to know what sorts of things he values, what peoples and places he favors . . . what sort of *games* he is known to play." He scowled at the last item. The Magisters' penchant for secrecy, and the convoluted tasks they would often require of morati who wanted to learn something from them, were notorious in the northlands. It was the reason that the Protectorates generally relied upon witches for power, trusting to those who were willing to sacrifice a portion of their life-essence for a worthy cause, rather than becoming indebted to prideful dilettantes of sorcery who believed that the entire world existed solely for their amusement.

Not to mention that the Magisters hated the Wrath. Rumor said it wreaked havoc with their sorcery. Most of them preferred not to get within a hundred miles of it, if they could help it. When duty did call them closer they showed up grudgingly, lending their power to the rituals that helped keep the Wrath strong and allowed the locals to approach it . . . but no one doubted when they did that they would rather be somewhere else. Anywhere else.

Maybe they are just afraid of it, Rhys thought, *the way all men are when they come near it. And the rest is just a story they put out so we won't think they are cowards.*

Now that would be something worth verifying, wouldn't it?

"All right now." Favias' tone was strong and confident; if Rhys' news worried him at all, he wasn't letting it show. "We'll need all this to go out to the other Protectorates as quickly as possible. And all the relay houses should be checked to make sure they are manned and ready. When the call to war comes . . ." He drew in a deep breath. ". . . I doubt we will be given much time to respond. So let's make sure everything is in order before that happens."

Forty generations, Rhys thought. It had been forty generations since the first Lord Protectors had established a cadre of warriors whose only purpose was to prepare for the return of the Souleaters. Forty generations of Guardians, each one praying that the world would never need to call upon it. Knowing all the while that such a prayer was futile. The gods themselves had warned that the monsters would return. Now it was happening.

We will be ready, Rhys swore silently.

"Now let us choose who will carry our message," Favias said.

It was the end of the meeting, save for Favias' task of choosing those who would ride to the other Protectorates, carrying word of their discoveries. Rhys knew he was not needed for that. His ties to the Kierdwyn court meant that he would be sent there, as always, to update the Lord Protector. Which meant that he should start on his way as soon as possible. Within days Lord and Lady Kierdwyn would be heading south with all their royal retinue to attend the coronation of their grandchild, Salvator Aurelius. If Rhys didn't handle his business before they left, he might wind up heading south alongside them, and having to speak to both Lord Kierdwyn and his wife on the road.

His stomach tightened at the thought of Lady Evaine.

She would be gracious to me, he thought, *as always.*

That only made it worse.

He slipped out of the meetinghouse quietly, not wishing to disturb the others. Outside the sun was shining, and a brisk summer breeze was whipping the red-and-gold pennants atop the roof with audible force. One well-worn dirt path led down to the stables, another to the Guardians' offering circle. He hesitated for a moment, then chose the latter. He needed to steady his soul before setting out on such dark business.

The path led him into the edge of the forest, away from the smells and the sounds of the meetinghouse. Blue pines crowded closely on all sides of him and the air was filled with their sharp, resinous scent. The path wound between them, inclining slightly as it brought him to the top of a hill. There the pines had been cleared away, leaving a circle of ground bare, with nothing but a Spear in its center.

It was not as large as the ones at the Wrath, and it did not have their baleful resonance, but the pinnacle of twisted rock awakened in Rhys a visceral memory of what the real ones were like . . . and why they existed. For a while he stood still and silent in the clearing, reflecting upon their meaning and upon his mission. Surrounding him were ancestor-trees—or perhaps, more accurately, *protector-trees*—blue pines that had been carved into the likeness of the seven First Protectors. Abeja, Brusus, Han, Tonado, Kierdwyn, Alkali, Skandir. Bark had overgrown their features, making it seem as if the trees had grown into human forms of their own accord. Even being rendered in the same artistic medium could not disguise the fact that the seven were as different from one another as men could possibly be. And why not? They had come from all parts of the known world, brought together by terrible necessity. And when the great war had ended, and the Wrath of the Gods had entrapped the last monsters in a no-man's-land of ice and snow, these seven had stayed behind to guard against the fall of the Wrath, and to found the bloodlines that would someday stand against the Souleaters once more.

The gods had named them *lyr*, and placed special magics in their blood that would awaken when the Souleaters returned. So the legends promised, anyway. By now most of the inhabitants of the northlands had at least a distant blood tie to one Lord Protector or another, which meant that the gift of the gods was in all of them. But the *lyr* were special. They could trace their lineage back to the first Protectors by every branch of their family tree. In them the gift of the gods was concentrated, undiluted; in them, the legends said, lay the hope of mankind.

Rhys was half *lyr* by virtue of the Lord Protector's indiscretion. That had great value among the Guardians. Others would trade places with him in a heartbeat, to have such a heritage.

So why did it make his head hurt? Why did he get angry whenever someone mentioned it?

Because it is not something I earned, he thought bitterly. *Because no matter what battles I face, what dangers I brave, what victories I facilitate, my bastard heritage will always overshadow them.*

"Rhys."

He turned to see who was calling him. It was one of the

Skandir, a woman named Namanti. Like all the Guardian-women from that Protectorate she wore a man's shirt and leggings, the former with its sleeves cut off in deference to the heat of summer. Her well-muscled arms were adorned with wide metal bracelets running up and down their length, and Rhys knew that each one was etched with a design that commemorated some battle she'd won or some trial she'd endured. Her thick yellow hair was plaited with thongs and glass beads, her skin coarse and reddened from exposure to the elements. Skandir Guardians were fierce, he reflected, the women most of all. Sometimes that translated into activities away from the battlefield and sometimes it didn't.

"You missed the ruckus," she told him.

"Over my departure?"

"Nay." She grinned. "You're not quite so important yet, *lyr*." She was using the title to ruffle his feathers and he knew it, so he let it pass without comment. "Favias wanted messengers to carry your news to the other Protectorates; he asked for volunteers. That's when we all realized that there were no Alkali among us."

"None at all?" he asked, startled.

She shook her head. Wisps of blond hair had escaped from their confinement and the forest breeze scattered them across her face. She pushed them back absently, hooking them behind her ears. "Not a single one. Apparently no one has seen any Guardians from there for some time now."

He frowned. "That is . . . odd."

"Aye. Master Favias thought it so. Especially here, so close to Alkali itself. No one has inspected the Spears up there, either—or at least if they did they're not reporting it. Given that we think the Wrath has been breached somewhere, that's no small thing. He wants to send someone in to see what's what. Check the Spears at least, see if the trouble's there." Her deep blue eyes sparkled. "Someone with *powerful blood*."

She knew him well enough to know how the words would make him squirm, and for that reason he refused to take the bait. "Makes sense, if he wants the Spears looked at. Others would be too weak to get close to it without a week-long ritual to pave the way. I hear the Skandir are particularly weak-willed."

She didn't go for his bait either. "Of course, I pointed out you were hardly up to the job, since you don't even speak the language."

He raised an eyebrow. "The Alkali speak a different language?"

"Aye. Leadership does. Sometimes the priests. It's an ancient thing, from before the Dark Times. They don't use it around . . . ah, *outsiders*."

How like the Alkali, he thought. *Anything to set themselves apart.* They were a proud people—some would say arrogant— who never let the other Protectorates forget that they had been masters of the northlands long before the war against the Souleaters brought strangers to their shores. And they were masters of it still, at least in their own minds.

That the Alkali Guardians had dropped out of sight now, just when Souleaters were being sighted again, was ominous indeed. Had they tried to take a stand against the creatures and fallen? It was hard to believe that such a thing could have happened without them sending out a cry for help. But perhaps it had all happened too swiftly for that.

He shook those thoughts from his head. "All right, so who is to be my translator? Some myopic little bookworm, no doubt, that I will have to protect from tree branches as we ride? Assuming he can ride at all."

"You should be so fortunate." She slapped his chest lightly with a folded piece of paper. "Rumor has it you've been assigned an arrogant Skandir who has no great love for the Alkali. Oh, and she's a woman, too. No doubt she'll slow you down each time she needs to take a piss."

He took the paper from her and quickly looked it over. Favias had provided them with a letter of introduction in case their presence in Alkali lands was questioned. That in itself was disturbing; normally Guardians needed no special clearance to go about their duties. "Maybe I'll leave her behind if she takes too long."

"Maybe she's the best shot in the region and you won't get ten strides if you try it."

He refolded the paper and tucked it into his shirt. "Maybe she has drunk too much Skandir ale recently, and thinks her talent is more than it is."

"Ten *kroger* says it is better than yours. Your choice of target and terms."

He shook his head. "I don't carry *kroger*, you know that."

"Then you forfeit, do you?" She smiled pleasantly. "Too easy, Kierdwynner."

He chuckled despite himself. "So who else is coming?"

"No one. Just you and me and the cold, high road. Favias wants us in and out quickly. Up to the Wrath and then across to the east, check out each of the Spears in turn until we find the source of trouble. Preferably before the Alkali even know we are there. Other Guardians have different assignments."

Rhys nodded. He would have liked a witch to ride along with them, even if they never needed to use his power, but Seers were notoriously sensitive to the Wrath, and wouldn't survive that long an exposure. Supposedly it was the price they paid for focusing their witchery on visionary matters; it made them doubly vulnerable to powers that affected the mind. "Dawn, then?"

"If you can get up that early." She pulled out a slender knife with a carved bone handle. "I wouldn't want to strain your noble blood."

He grabbed her wrist and held it tightly. She stared at him for a minute, as if to assess how much real anger was behind the move, then shrugged off his grip. "Easy, Rhys, that's why they picked me as well, you know. Second cousin to someone or something of importance . . . I forget his name. Not as much of the *lyr* blessing as you, but some little bit of it, eh? They figured you'd need that with you, if you had to go close to the Spears."

She looked down at her hand and made a quick cut along the side, shallow and short. Red blood welled up quickly, trickling down the side of her palm. "May the gods of the north guide us and protect us. May they grant us the sight to pick out the enemy, the courage to challenge it in battle, and the strength to send it to the worst bloody hell that the underworld has to offer." She stepped forward and put her hand on the spire of twisted rock, smearing the blood across its surface before withdrawing it.

She offered Rhys the knife.

He cut himself slowly, carefully, along a line that had been cut and healed over many, many times in the past. Unlike her he did not speak out loud, but moved his lips silently as he made his blood offering.

If we are the generation that must do battle with demons, then so be it. Guide us to where our strength is needed. Help us to see that the Second Age of Kings does not end like the first.

His fingers trailed down along the twisted stone pillar, thin lines of red trailing behind them.

And have mercy upon the lyr, he added, *your most precious and ignorant children, who have been promised power without knowing its name, and who may be sent into battle without even knowing what weapons they bear.*

It seemed to him that the ancestor spirits echoed his prayer.

CHAPTER 4

C OLIVAR HAD anticipated that Ramirus' domain would be guarded by sorcerous obstacles, but they were annoying nonetheless. None of them were serious threats, as a Magister measured such things, but they required him to waste time and energy, which was a threat of a more subtle nature.

But that was their purpose, of course. Such obstacles were the Magister's equivalent of a welcome sign, which set out in no uncertain terms what the status of a guest was to be in this place. Each challenge required a visitor to waste just a tad more power in flying over it, or burrowing under it, or burning or fighting or conniving his way through it, to reach the other side. For each such act a visitor must drain more of the life from a consort whose vital energies were finite. Would such exercises force a guest to the edge of transition, so that he might fall helpless later if he tried to use sorcery in Ramirus' presence? Or would he have second thoughts about the business that had brought him here, and perhaps question whether it was important enough to merit such a risk?

It mattered little to Colivar. His current consort was freshly claimed and unlikely to expire this soon for anything short of an all-out sorcerous war. Nevertheless the various entrapments did annoy him, and if he happened to damage a few of them as he flew overhead—setting fire to a forest of enchanted trees, causing a pack of mutated hounds to turn on one another, draining a moat so that all its carnivorous inhabitants were left gasping for breath upon the dry earth—surely Ramirus had expected no less of him. Indeed, even as Colivar flew over the final obstacle, a vast maze of hedges twice as high as a man, he could see rain begin to fall upon the land he had just passed, quenching his fire's fury, distracting the hounds, and filling the moat anew.

He smiled as he flew, for such weather-working was a costly affair that could drain whole days from a consort's life. He had judged Ramirus too proud to sit back and watch as his works were destroyed, and he had not been disappointed.

At the heart of the hedge maze was an imposing manor house built in the northern style, a large and somber building with narrow windows and ivy-covered turrets. It seemed to Colivar that a vague pall of sorcerous irritation hung over it, thick in the humid afternoon air. He reclaimed his human form, brushed a bit of dirt from his black linen shirt, and tried not to let his amusement show as he climbed the great stairs to the entrance. But it would be a mistake to think that the challenge was over merely because he had reached his destination safely. Magisters played a longer game.

The front doors opened at his approach with no human hand to guide them. A whisper of energy, sent to greet him, beckoned for him to follow it. Colivar expended enough athra to confirm its purpose and—when he was satisfied as to Ramirus' intentions—let it lead him deep into the house. Shadowy halls were punctuated by thin beams of dusty sunlight, a setting oddly reminiscent of King Danton's depressing keep. *You served Aurelius for too long, Ramirus.* He thought it loudly, just in case his host was trying to read his thoughts. *It has soured your taste.*

The chamber at his journey's end was a study of sorts, with glass-fronted cabinets containing book, scrolls, and even a few clay tablets. Colivar resisted the impulse to identify the latter with his sorcery. Such tablets could be items of great age, and therefore of great value, or they could simply be another test, a trick, one last temptation for him to waste his power before negotiations began.

Ramirus stood when he entered; it would be hard to say whether his stern expression was meant to communicate respect or distaste. Probably both, Colivar thought. He looked much the same as he had the day King Danton had banished him— long white hair and beard flawlessly groomed, ebony robe falling in graceful folds, expression darkly serene. And why not? Danton was dead now, along with a good part of his family. Ramirus probably considered it divine justice. Even a high king should think twice before insulting a Magister.

"Colivar. What a surprise." Ramirus' tone was dry. "I would offer you refreshment, but I find myself lacking anything . . . appropriate."

The black-haired Magister chuckled. "Poison's all in the moat, eh?"

A cold smile flickered across those ancient lips. Age was an art form to Ramirus, each line and wrinkle applied to his face with the meticulous care of a master painter. It was more than mere aesthetic conceit, Colivar knew. Even by Magister standards Ramirus was said to be old, and for such a man the trappings of physical age were a badge of honor. Even with his eyes hooded by folds of flesh like fine aged vellum, the piercing clarity of his gaze was undiminished. "I would not insult a visitor in such a manner." The velvet words masked a razor's edge. "Not one who comes in peace."

Colivar bowed his head ever so slightly. "You no longer serve the Aurelius, so we have no reason to be enemies."

"Indeed. No more than any two Magisters. Which is not saying much, is it?" He peered at Colivar, studying him closely, as one might do with some strange winged creature that had flown in the window of its own accord, trying to assess whether or not it could be trusted not to make a mess on the rug.

"Please have a seat," he said at last.

Colivar did so, guessing at the chair his host favored and, in a rare show of graciousness, choosing another. "You go without a patron these days, I hear."

"Perhaps. Or perhaps I am simply discreet about my business." Again he smiled, ever so briefly. "It is not a quality I expect you to understand."

The windows were cloaked in heavy curtains, Colivar noted, shutting out the sun. A single amber lamp struggled in vain to illuminate the gloomy chamber. Either Ramirus had absorbed too much of Danton's aesthetic while he worked for the man, or he wished to protect the contents of the room from the damaging effects of sunlight. Which implied that the scrolls and tablets surrounding them were ancient, and probably quite valuable. If so, it was an impressive collection.

"So," Ramirus said, sitting down opposite Colivar in a leather-bound chair that creaked beneath his weight. "What brings you to my domain? Besides a desire for social pleasantries, of course."

He was smooth, Colivar thought. So smooth. You could never get past that smoothness to read what was in his heart, not unless he wanted you to. That was what made the game so interesting with him.

"I was curious as to whether you would be attending Salvator's coronation."

A muscle along the Magister's jaw tensed slightly. "I have not yet decided."

"I hear it's going to be quite the spectacle."

Ramirus shrugged. "I tire of Aurelius spectacles."

The shrug was too casual, the tone too dispassionate. *You are still involved with that family,* Colivar observed. *That is interesting.*

"If that is all you came to learn," Ramirus continued, "you could have sent a letter. The answer would have been the same and the delivery would have cost you considerably less."

"Perhaps I enjoy your company."

"Of course," Ramirus said pleasantly. "And perhaps tomorrow the sun will rise in the west."

Now it was Colivar who smiled. "I could make it so, if it pleased my host."

"Indeed. I would not put it past you to try. Though I imagine even your formidable power has its limits." Ramirus dismissed the thought with a sharp wave of one hand. "You came here to talk to me, Colivar, so speak your mind. I have little taste for pointless pleasantries these days. And be forewarned, if I find your query is not worth my time I may yet charge you for your damages to my estate."

Colivar leaned back in his chair. It was a posture designed to look casual, collegial, but the intensity of his gaze rendered it something quite different, and he knew that Ramirus would recognize it for what it was: the stillness of a predator. "You recall the day the Souleater appeared, yes? Outside Danton's palace?"

Ramirus nodded; one corner of his mouth twitched slightly. "Hard to forget."

Stained glass wings filtering the sun, knife-edged whiptail slicing through air and flesh with equal ease, agonizing beauty wrapping itself around a man's soul . . . Colivar shook off the memory with effort. "As I recall, your arrival at the site with a Guardian by your side was rather . . . serendipitous. Rather incredibly so, to be frank. I find myself . . . curious."

One white eyebrow arched upward. "Do you really expect me to answer that?"

"It never hurts to ask."

"Knowledge has its price, Colivar."

"I did not say I expected it to be free."

Ramirus steepled his fingers thoughtfully. Dust motes stirred in a thin beam of light beside him. At last he said, "The hawk. The one that fought the Souleater outside Danton's palace. What happened to it?"

He shrugged. "I don't know."

He raised an eyebrow. "I find that hard to believe."

"Think what you like. It fell in battle and was gone by the time I went looking for it. I know no more of its destiny than you do."

"And its true identity?"

"A witch, apparently. I have only guesswork on that count, the same as anyone. But it seems the likely answer."

Ramirus nodded. "Then here is the answer to your own question. Fadir came to me and asked for help in manipulating Danton. I realized that the only person capable of that—if anyone was—was his wife, the High Queen Gwynofar. And she . . ." His expression darkened slightly. "Let us say she had good reason not to approach her husband at the time. So I sought out the one person she trusted most, her half-brother Rhys, and transported him to the High King's estate to meet with her, arriving what I hoped was far enough from the palace that Kostas would not sense my presence there. Where the battle you cited was already engaged. So you see, Colivar, no strange coincidence there, simply two roads leading off from a single point that converged a short while later of their own accord. The 'serendipity' of timing simply betrays their common source."

For a long time there was silence as Colivar considered the parameters of their exchange. At last he said, "The hawk was a woman. Whether she was witch or Magister I am unsure— obviously the latter is highly unlikely—but she was an accomplished shape-shifter, as you saw." He hoped that would be enough to satisfy Ramirus. Clearly it was not. The cool blue eyes were merciless. For several long minutes Colivar studied him, trying to gauge just how much he would have to offer the man and just how much the information he got in return would be worth. His opponent waited patiently, the faintest flicker of a smile playing about the corners of his mouth. Win or lose, he clearly enjoyed the game.

Finally Colivar said, "I believe she was the one responsible for Prince Andovan's illness. As well as the death of that idiot Magister in Gansang—Raven, or Flamingo, or whatever his name was." Ramirus' expression remained stonelike, impassive, but Colivar thought he saw a flicker of surprise in his eyes. "And then she was gone, before I could test those suspicions. I have not seen her since."

"The others all think that Raven's killer is dead."

"Yes," Colivar agreed. "I was the only one who knew the truth. Until now."

Ramirus nodded slowly, digesting his offering. As the Magisters measured such things, it was considerable. Finally, his lips set in a tight line, he nodded. "Rhys already knew of Danton's decline, and of the queen's precarious situation. When I asked him for help he told me there was nothing he could do. He said that no words existed that could convince Gwynofar to confront her husband in the manner I desired, and besides, he loved her too much to cause her that kind of pain.

"Those seemed weak excuses to me at the time, but sorcery granted me insight. Apparently Rhys knew what Danton had done to his half-sister. He was afraid that if he went back there again he would lose himself to rage and do something truly terrible to the High King . . . something Gwynofar would suffer for, even more than she was suffering then.

"I was trying to think of some argument that might change his mind when, all of a sudden, he stiffened in his saddle. For a moment his eyes lost their focus and his body shook as if from some sort of seizure. As I was summoning the power to counter it, the fit passed as suddenly as it had come.

"Rhys looked at me as if he had seen a ghost. His eyes, which moments ago had been clear and bright, were now bloodshot and stricken.

"'The monster is here . . . I saw it . . . through her eyes . . .' He stared at me in horror. 'A Souleater.'"

"I did not know at the time that such a creature had returned to the world, you understand, so I imagined that some dark vision had possessed him. But the distinction hardly mattered. He was convinced that the High Queen was in great danger and he begged me take him to her immediately. Which I did. The rest you know."

Colivar drew in a sharp breath. "Witchery?"

Ramirus shook his head. "What I saw that day was not simple witchery. Nor do I believe that Gwynofar consciously chose to send a message to her brother—and he very clearly did not expect to receive one." He folded his fingers one by one as he spoke. "It is said the gods of the north once promised that if the Souleaters ever returned, the Protectors would awaken to some special power. I believe that is what I saw happening. I believe that in her moment of need, Gwynofar Aurelius tapped into some ancient formula whose name we do not even know, and used it to call Rhys to her. Clearly there is some kind of metaphysical connection between them. It may be a connection she shares only with him, or with her family, or even with all of her bloodline. There is no way to tell at this point. Rhys apparently no longer remembers his vision, and Gwynofar was never aware of sending it. Whatever power the gods once hid deep within their blood, it has returned to hiding once more. Not all my sorcery could pry it out afterward."

Colivar's expression was grim. "If it is as you say, it is an ominous sign."

Ramirus nodded. "Yes. It is that."

"If the Souleaters are returning—"

"The northern gods seem to think they are, if ancient legends are to be believed. If not, then some new sort of power has come into the world. Either way things will be . . . interesting."

Colivar's mouth twitched. "That is a bit of an understatement."

Ramirus shrugged. "What are we but spectators? The centuries pass slowly. Mysteries have value. The world changed slowly once, and now it quickens its pace. Only the morati need fear such things."

"Perhaps," Colivar said quietly. "But do not forget what the Souleaters once did to this world. There are parts of that tale which even a Magister should fear."

Ramirus leaned forward; his voice, now a whisper, was strangely fierce. "And do *you* remember those times, Colivar? Not as other men do, who learn of such things from minstrel tales and dusty tomes, but perhaps from knowledge of a more . . . personal nature?"

Colivar drew in a sharp breath. "No Magister existed during the First Age of Kings. You know that as well as I do, Ramirus. The last Souleaters disappeared long before the first of our kind entered the world."

"Indeed. Yet some say you know more than any man alive about the creatures. More than a living man should be able to know. Why is that?"

He shrugged. "Perhaps I am simply old enough to have lived in a time when men remembered more."

"And perhaps I am sharp-witted enough to know that for— what was that charming phrase you once used?—*camel dung*."

"So what, then?" Colivar's eyes narrowed. "Am I not really a Magister, but something that existed prior to the Great War? Is that what you are implying?" Dramatically he spread his arms wide, as if in invitation. "Test me, then. Taste the sorcery that binds me to my consort. Know for yourself the truth of what I am."

Mad though the offer was, for a brief moment Colivar thought Ramirus might just take him up on it. Certainly there was a fire that sparked in the white-haired Magister's eyes at the suggestion. If Colivar was truly opening himself up for inspection, might there not be some way to take advantage of that, without getting sucked into a consort's bond and devoured in the process? It was a tempting prospect, and Colivar felt a rare thrill as he braced himself for possible assault. It was rare that two Magisters of their age and power tested themselves against each other directly, and anything rare was an experience to be savored . . . even if it was not without its dangers.

But then the moment passed. "I know what you are from the taste of your sorcery," Ramirus assured him. "Or did you think all those obstacles outside were just for my amusement? Your power is as cold as a demon's prick."

Colivar chuckled. "Now you flatter me."

"Hardly." Ramirus leaned back in his chair once more. "The day is coming when we may well need to cooperate with one another. *All* of us, Colivar. Else the world may fall to these creatures once more."

"Then the world is doomed," he responded. "For I cannot imagine Magisters making the kind of sacrifice that would be required to save it."

"Perhaps sacrifice would not be necessary this time. Perhaps if we knew our history better, a better way might be found."

Chuckling softly, Colivar stood. "You do not yet have the coinage to buy all my secrets, Ramirus. Though I am flattered by your interest." He nodded respectfully as he stood. "Now if you will excuse me, I have a variety of preparations to make before Salvator claims his crown. So much to do." He smiled. "You understand, of course."

Ramirus stood to see him out, and took it upon himself to walk him back to the front door of the manor. An uncharacteristically respectful gesture. The exchange of information sometimes brought that out in him.

"You really should come to Salvator's coronation," Colivar said along the way. "It may well prove the largest gathering of our kind since the night of Andovan's suicide." *You do remember that, don't you? The night Danton humiliated you in front of all of us?* "Already there are wagers being placed among the Magisters as to which enemy will strike him down the moment the crown is placed upon his head. And to think, it would only take a handful of words to keep it from happening—nothing more than the name of a Magister to sponsor him—but that is the Aurelius pride in action. Or perhaps it is Penitent pride to blame. Such a distasteful religion." He shook his head. "Foolish morati, all of them. My money is on Corialanus, by the way. And death for Salvator within twenty-four hours of the moment that he first puts the crown upon his head." He bowed his head slightly. "Please accept the information as a courtesy."

"You are most gracious." Ramirus' expression was impassive—unreadable—but his tone was dry. "And I shall consider your advice for what it is worth." He waved his hand toward the door and it began to open. "In the meantime, try not to destroy too much of my property on the way out, will you? I should hate to have to send you a bill for it."

Indeed. And how much does one pay for a three-headed moat monster these days? "I shall do my best," Colivar promised. "Assuming of course that your property does not get in my way again."

"It will not stop you from leaving," Ramirus promised. And a spark of cold humor glimmered in his eyes. "In fact, Colivar, I feel confident in promising you that no sorcery of mine will *ever* keep you from leaving."

Nevertheless, it was not until he saw his visitor fly over the enchanted forest, demon-hounds howling at him from below, that he returned to the lamplit comfort of his library to continue with his research.

CHAPTER 5

A MONTH AGO, the Queen of Sankara might have been pleased by the success of her gathering.

The heads of all twenty-six Free States were in her grand atrium now, accompanied by such spouses, advisers, and, in some cases, courtesans as had traveled with them. Servants in flowing silks moved among the guests, silent and graceful, offering silver platters heaped with the costliest delicacies of the region: fresh peacock hearts, marinated lark tongues, date pastries topped with shavings of gold leaf. Music played softly in the background—a sensual melody from the southern deserts—and a delicate incense warmed the air, carefully chosen to complement the perfumes in vogue.

If anyone had questioned in the past whether a Grand Council meeting should be held in Sankara, they did not question it now. Other princes might provide a meeting room where the leaders of the Free States could hash out policy issues, but who else could host such a fete as this afterward?

"What a delightful gathering," the Duke of Surilla gushed to her. He had found a young man among the attendants that suited his fancy and had spent the last hour eating his fill of whatever delicacies the boy was serving, to keep him from wandering away. Other hosts might have simply provided the duke with a promise that the servant would join him in his bed later and prided themselves on a job well done. Silly fools! Pleasure was not simply about hunger fulfilled, but a multi-course feast in which seduction was merely the first remove. And so the good duke must stumble about the task of asking her if later that evening the boy would be, ah, *free,* to attend to his desires. And Siderea told him that her attendants were free to do as they pleased, and so the boy might meet with him after hours if it pleased him to do so. Now the duke must wonder and worry each time his blood grew heated, and continue to eat from that one particular tray until his stomach could hold no more, and offer up flattery and flirtation and perhaps even some expensive gift to earn the night's ending that he desired. Which was all as it should be. Siderea's servants were well versed in such games and took a genuine pleasure in manipulating her guests. And why not? The boy was free to keep whatever gifts he might earn, while the duke drank deeply of the illusion of *conquest.* Far more fulfilling for him than if she had merely told him the truth—which was that her servants would of course accommodate his sexual needs. What kind of a hostess would she be otherwise?

Yes, by all her normal measures, it was a most successful party.

But while her guests laughed and flirted, and she moved from one to another with wine in her hand and a smile on her face that made each guest feel absolutely certain that he was the one person the Queen of Sankara really cared about, her heart was cold. The joy on her face was no better than a mask, and even the pride she felt at the success of her party was a pale shadow of what it should have been. Empty pleasures. The one thing she wanted most was beyond her reach, and no man here could provide it. Which made all other pastimes seem cold and futile.

Could her guests see the weakness in her? Could they sense the doom that hung about her like a shroud? Or was she hiding it artfully enough?

Don't think about that, she ordered herself. *Focus on the business at hand.*

The council meeting had been peaceful enough, but ultimately unproductive. As she had expected it to be. She was not one of those Free Lands monarchs whose head was in the clouds, nursing dreams of political unity and cooperative enterprises. She was a realist. The Free States had banded together to face down the threat of the High Kingdom and to keep Danton Aurelius from claiming the valuable trade ports of the Inner Sea one by one. Individually the twenty-six tiny nations might have fallen to him, but together they had proven strong enough to fend off his military attentions. No one dared leave the alliance because to do so was an invitation to certain conquest.

But now Danton Aurelius was dead. That threat was gone. In his absence the so-called Free States were likely to devolve into what they had been before his reign: a bunch of squabbling, disorganized municipalities, more interested in warring with each other than in serving any common interest. Oh, there were a few exceptions. The ruling houses married their children to one another to establish alliances by blood and sometimes that actually worked for a while. Sometimes a whole generation might pass without overt aggression between two particular states, although the shadow war of corruption and assassination continued on unabated. And of course Sankara itself was prosperous enough—and strong enough—that it had never needed to fight with its neighbors over land or gold. But on the whole, the lords of the Free States were a fractious lot, more interested in who owned what particular stone along their common shoreline than in any dreams of mutual prosperity.

Danton had been the Other. Fearing him, they had united. Who would fill that role for them now? Salvator Aurelius wanted peace, she'd heard. A Penitent monk who hated war, inheriting a warmonger's throne! That was of no use to anyone.

"My compliments, Lady Queen. A most impressive gathering."

Lost in reverie, Siderea had not seen or heard anyone approach her. She masked her surprise with a delicate laugh of pleasure. Never mind who was talking to her; they would read into that sound whatever message they most wished to hear. "You are too kind," she purred, turning to face the source of the words.

The speaker was a stranger to her, a man of indeterminate age, thin and hard, with black hair that fell in a sharp-edged bowl cut above lean, angular features. His jawline was without any hint of shadow, which made it likely that no more than a handful of hours had passed since his last shave. On a day when both lords and servants had been bustling about since dawn without a moment to spare, that seemed . . . odd. His long robes hinted at wealth in their fabric, but not in their styling, and they offered no clue as to his origins. Garnet silk: the color of pomegranates and blood. His words had a foreign flavor to them, but it was not an accent she recognized. That was odd as well; the great port city of Sankara was favored by merchants and travelers from all the great cities of the world, and Siderea had heard their accents and dialects often enough to recognize them. This one was hauntingly familiar to her, but she could not place it.

The Witch-Queen made a point of knowing the faces and names of all those who attended her gatherings, and even the servants who traveled with her guests. No man should ever be in her house whom she could not identify. The fact that she did not know this one was . . . disconcerting.

He smiled, and there was a hint of dry satisfaction about the edges of his mouth, as if he sensed her consternation and took pleasure in it. "Your reputation does not do you justice."

"You are not one of my guests," she said coldly.

"Not one of your invited guests," he agreed, "but one that I think you would welcome nonetheless."

He reached out and took her hand in his own—her left hand—and raised it to his lips. Something about the gesture sent a warning chill down her spine. She was about to pull her hand back from him, and perhaps call for the guards to evict him, when he folded his other hand over hers and said softly, "Permit me to admire your taste in jewelry."

She opened her mouth to respond as his arrogance deserved . . . but then she saw what he wore on his own hand, and the words died on her lips. For a moment the whole world seemed to blur about her; the only point that was steady and clear was the deep blue cabochon ring on her left hand, the one the sorcerer had given her . . . and this man's matching ring, now positioned right beside it. Deep blue, almost violet, with other colors that swirled and shimmered in its depths.

"Perhaps there is some place where we might speak privately," he suggested.

She looked back at her guests, blinking as the world came back into focus. They all seemed to be happily occupied for the moment. Her servants would see to any needs they had. If she did not tell someone she was leaving, no one was likely to notice her exit. For a brief moment she contemplated calling a guard to her side, just in case, but a cold and stubborn determination filled her. If these men were what they claimed to be, then their business with her was something not even a trusted servant should hear. And if it was not, and this was some kind of trap . . . how much was there left to lose? A few years of life? Maybe only a few months? The time for hedging her bets was long past.

"Follow me," she said, and her heart was suddenly pounding so loudly in her chest she could no longer hear the music.

Through the palace she led him, past sitting rooms outfitted in velvet and gilt, with diamond-paned windows that looked out over the moonlit harbor. One maidservant rushing about her business turned a corner and almost ran into them; lowering her head to the floor in obeisance, she offered up whimpering apologies until they were out of sight. Siderea hardly saw her. She was remembering the night a sorcerer had visited her on her balcony, his face hidden by shadows, promising her a means of surviving the loss of her soulfire in return for . . . what? He had not specified. But she did not doubt that there would be a price, or that it would be a large one.

Finally they came to a small study away from the traffic of the evening. Siderea closed the heavy doors behind them, then drew herself up as she turned to face him. He had caught her off guard in the atrium, but she would not allow that to happen again. A bit of unorthodox behavior might be tolerated, given the circumstances, but even that had a limit. She was still a queen.

The first visitor had played similar games with her, she recalled.

Though she had not been able to see his face clearly at the time, nor heard his voice above a whisper, she realized now that his accent had been much the same as this man's. Were they the same person? She decided to take a chance on it.

"This is the second time you have entered my home without proper introduction," she pronounced. The flicker of surprise in his eyes was all the confirmation she needed. "Perhaps it is time to remedy that."

A curt nod acknowledged her insight, but also warned her that the game was far from over. "You may call me Amalik."

"Not your true name, I gather."

The thin lips twitched. "It is the one I use in this region. The only one you will hear others use, in referring to me."

"Fair enough." She allowed herself to smile slightly. "I assume you know mine."

"Aye, Lady Queen. Your name, your title, your history—as much as any man knows of the latter, of course—and your . . . *situation*."

Could he hear how loudly her heart was pounding? It took all her composure for her to keep her expression neutral. *This is a stranger who may have nothing of value to offer*, she reminded herself. *Nothing but dreams of manipulating royalty with promises and shadows. Until he proves he is more than that, give him nothing.* "You must have ears among the Magisters, to know of such things."

"Not all men require the permission of the Magisters to take a piss. Majesty."

The vulgarity might have offended her if the overall senti- ment did not sit so well with her current mood. "You have witches serving you, then?"

"No, my Queen. Not witches."

"Who else has the power to ferret out secrets that have never been spoken aloud? Much less offer a solution to them?" She folded her arms across her chest. "Perhaps you do not understand quite as much about me as you claim."

His dark eyes narrowed. "There are more powers in the world than Magisters and witches," he told her. "Others keep to the shadows and are rarely seen by men. Or women."

"And you claim to have access to such a power."

"I do."

"And are offering to use it on my behalf."

"No, my Queen." Again the flicker of a smile. Not a warm thing, that expression, but cold and reptilian around the edges. "We—I and my allies—are offering you control of it. Yourself."

Keeping her expression carefully composed, she turned away from him for a moment. There were a few leather tomes on the sideboard nearby; she opened the cover of one and stared at the illuminated pages without seeing them as she tried to digest his seemingly incredible offer. It didn't help that a sudden wave of physical weakness came over her at that moment. It took all the strength she had to set her limbs so solidly that he did not see her falter. The moment of weakness passed as quickly as it had come, but the warning of it was clear: she had very little time left.

"You seem very certain this . . . power . . . will serve my need."

She could hear him walking up behind her. Close, too close. She could feel the coldness of his presence near to her back, and for some reason it made her skin crawl. "It will allow you to extend your life," he said quietly, "beyond the normal span of the morati. It will replace the vitality that a lifetime of witchery has drained so that you can live as the Magisters do, unfettered by common mortality. That is what you seek, is it not?"

She did not answer him immediately. She focused her

attention on the delicate page before her, running her fingers over the smooth surface of the gold leaf while she tried to order her thoughts. How she wished she had enough witchery left for one last spell! A single spark of soulfire could reveal this man's true intentions, sort out truth from falsehood. But she dared not risk it. She had too little life left to her already; she could not afford to sacrifice another hour, even for that.

And he knows all that, she realized. *If he understands my situation, as he claims, then he knows he is free to lie to me. That I have only my human senses to rely upon.*

But what if he was not lying? What if there really was some new power in the world, neither sorcery nor witchery, that could sustain her? It was a heady thought. Also an unlikely one. But she had run out of other options and could not afford to let the possibility go untested.

She turned around to face him again. Because he had probably intended his physical proximity to unnerve her she did not back away, but instead drew about her such regal aspect that it was he who instinctively took a step backward. It was important not to look weak now, important for him to view her as a powerful queen, not a desperate beggar. "Such gifts are not without a price," she said sternly. "Speak on that."

His eyes narrowed. "Those whom I represent are not merchants, come to haggle over a handful of coins. They are men of power, seeking a woman of equal power as an ally."

"Men?" The edge to her voice was undisguised. "They are all men?"

He bowed his head in assent. "Aye."

"That is the way of Magisters, is it not?"

"Except that we tender you an invitation to join our ranks, while they—may I be blunt, my Queen?—left you to die."

The words were like a slap across her face. Yes, the Magisters had left her to die. Used her when it pleased them, to bind their pitiful backstabbing brotherhood together, and then thrown her on the trash heap when they were tired of her. Like the rind of a fruit that had been sucked dry of juice. Who cared if the flies ate what was left?

Did the Magisters even suspect how much she hated them now, she wondered. Not damned likely. They were narcissistic bastards, all of them, blind to anything that did not revolve around their own desires, their obsessions, their petty rivalries.

The thought of possessing some power that they had no knowledge of was a heady one. The thought of surviving long enough to actually turn the tables on them, to make them pay for their callous abandonment of her, was almost too sweet to contemplate.

But words were cheap. Any fool might offer them. And if her years as queen had taught her nothing else, it was that a woman in power attracted fools like honey attracted flies.

"What proof do you offer that any of this is true?" she challenged. "Or do you think that I will swear my allegiance to a complete stranger for a handful of pretty words that any good actor might invent? How do I know that you even have allies?"

The cold, reptilian eyes flickered with amusement. What if he could read her thoughts? It would not be beyond the reach of a witch to do so, she realized suddenly, and certainly not beyond a Magister.

"When the time comes for you to claim this power, Majesty, all will be made clear to you. And you may choose then whether to go forward or not with full knowledge of all your options. Is that satisfactory?"

"*When the time comes?*" Her heart skipped a beat. "You claim to know my situation, then speak casually of waiting." She glanced toward the door. "Perhaps I have wasted my time after all."

The man's eyes narrowed. How alien they seemed in that instant, how lightless! Not like human eyes at all. "There are things that must be set in motion before you can join us. Certain natural processes must be completed first. We have done all we can to hurry them along, but—"

"How long?" she demanded.

"A lesser month at least. No longer than a great month at most."

She exhaled in a soft hiss. "Then why come to me now? Why speak of these things to me tonight, when—" *when I may not be alive a month from now* "—when you cannot deliver what you promise, or even prove that such a power exists?"

"I came tonight to see if you were interested in such an offer. If not, we will seek elsewhere."

"For another woman?"

"Yes."

"A woman of power?"

"A queen in spirit, if not in title. No one else can accept such a gift."

"And was I your first?" she asked. "Or have you approached other queens before me and been rejected?"

A muscle along the line of his jaw twitched. "There have been no other queens," he said. His expression was impassive, but she could sense the hostile energy coiled just behind it. He was not accustomed to bargaining with women, or with masking his emotions; the strain of it showed. "There are others who can take your place, if need be."

Take her place in what? *In claiming an unnamed power that must have a woman to master it.* The whole idea was mad. Every rational fiber of her being was crying out for her come to her senses and throw this miscreant out on his head—and perhaps have him meet with a convenient accident on the way home, thus silencing a man who seemed to know far too much about her private business. Surely a wild tale like this deserved no better treatment.

But what if there is some truth to all this? she thought. If even one word out of twenty was true, that still hinted at secrets worth learning. Risks worth taking. Didn't it?

She had to know the truth.

Drawing in a deep breath, she steeled herself for what well might be her last act on earth. *May the gods help you if you are lying to me, Amalik. If so I will have you torn limb from limb for making me waste the last hours of my life indulging your delusion.*

Focus. Focus.

Reaching deep inside herself to where the final sputtering embers of her soulfire lay hidden, she struggled to claim one precious drop of power to bind to her purpose. Her dying soul did not part with its substance easily; it would have been easier to thrust her hand between her ribs and rip her heart out of her body than it was to claim that tiny portion of power.

But she had not risen to her throne by being weak-willed, nor had fear ever kept her from doing what she needed to. Her body trembled as she focused upon that dying flame, her flesh growing cold as it sensed the closeness of Death, but she remained focused on her objective. And in the end she claimed it—one precious drop of her soul's strength, divorced from the whole, that she might shape to her will.

Carefully, so carefully, she crafted a truth-telling spell, knowing that she must make it perfect, absolutely perfect, for in this enterprise there would be no second chance.

(And how much of her life had this effort already cost her?

Was Death laughing at her as he watched, amused by her desperation?)

"All that you have told me of this power," she whispered hoarsely, "all the promises you have made and the reasons you say you are making them . . . you swear before the gods, all these thing are true?"

"Aye, my Queen." There was an edge to his voice that had not been there before. "By the gods I swear it."

She released the power to do its work and shut her eyes, feeling her spell fill the room between them: testing the stranger, tasting his substance. *Hunger. Lust. Impatience.* Powerful emotions roiled within him, primitive in their intensity, strangely inhuman in their tenor. *Hatred. Dominance. Desperation.* His outer aspect might appear civilized, but the depths of his soul were just the opposite. Dealing with him would be dangerous beyond words. But what of the prize he had promised? Did it exist? Might she really lay claim to it, if it did?

Then she tasted the truth of his words and a shiver ran up her spine.

He does not lie.

Slowly she opened her eyes. She did not need to say anything to him; he could read in her expression what she had learned.

You expected me to do this, didn't you? That was part of your plan from the beginning. The reason you could speak to me in riddles like you did. You knew that I had the power to see through your games, if I were willing to make the sacrifice to do it.

And you wanted to see if I were willing, she realized suddenly. *This was a test, wasn't it? Of strength. Of commitment. Perhaps of desperation.*

Only one decision was possible now. Only one promised a chance of life.

"What do you ask of me in return?" she said quietly.

Amalik smiled coldly. How calm his outer demeanor was! As if he and she were bargaining over some trinket of jewelry that had no real value. But she had seen inside him and knew the truth: whatever these men wanted her for, their hunger for it was every bit as driving as her hunger for life itself. "A token. A test. To seal our bargain."

"Such as?"

"You are planning to attend the coronation festivities for the new High King, I believe? Position yourself in the palace. Earn his favor. It should not be difficult for someone of your talents. Our plans may require some influence in his court. You will provide it."

But that is only a secondary goal, she thought. *The hunger that burns within you is for something much simpler, a goal far less civilized than courtly politics.* "And what is it you want him influenced to do?"

"For now?" He chuckled softly. "To be true to his faith. To be confident in Sankara's friendship so that he does not look too closely in this direction. And to distrust the many Magisters who will be vying for his favor. I assume the latter will be no problem for you?"

Now it was her turn to smile. "No. None at all."

"Later there will be more concrete assignments, I am sure. But for now that will suffice. Let us say simply set the ground-work for him to trust your counsel, so that in the future your words will have power." He raised up one black eyebrow. "So do we have a bargain, my Queen?"

There was a voice that whispered deep within her soul, warning her to be careful. Reminding her that the welfare of Sankara was not necessarily well served by such a plan. The Free Lands needed a war, or at least the threat of war, to keep them unified. A peaceful, happy High King was not necessarily a good thing for them.

But if there was even a remote possibility that this man could deliver what he promised—even a shadow of a chance—could she afford to turn him away?

He asks no more of me than what I would do anyway. Assess the weaknesses of this new king, play him like an instrument, wrap him about my finger. If not for political influence, then for the sheer sport of it. How often do the gods give me a monk to play with? And by the time this stranger and his allies return to ask for more—by then I shall know more of what their game is all about. Who knows? Perhaps we shall bargain anew when that happens.

"Aye," she said quietly. "We have a deal."

The voice in her soul was silent.

CHAPTER 6

THE MIRROR in front of Salvator was not one of his father's sorcerous accessories but a simple sheet of polished metal set in a tall wooden frame. As such it was a less than perfect reflector that made his lean form look even thinner and his angular features somewhat awry. That did not bother him, of course, though it did seem to bother his mother.

What bothered him was the stole about his neck. The long strip of embroidered cloth hung down the front of his robe on both sides, its foundation fabric encrusted with so many layers of embroidery and so many gemstones that one could no longer see the original cloth. Which was not what bothered him, of course. Well, it was not what bothered him *most*.

With a sigh he lifted it off over his head and held it out to Gwynofar. "I am sorry, Mother. I cannot."

"It is part of the coronation regalia," she said quietly.

"I understand that."

"It represents your family's history," Gwynofar said firmly. "Your heritage."

"Again, I am sorry. But I cannot wear it."

She exhaled sharply in frustration. "All the Aurelius kings have worn this stole at their coronations, since the first one that claimed a crown. Each has added his own signs to it. His accomplishments. These—" she indicated a section of the intricately embroidered piece near one end of the stole "—these are all your father's triumphs. The victories that brought the High Kingdom into existence. Without them you would have nothing to rule over."

"I understand all that, Mother." His tone was infinitely patient. "But we will have to find some other means of honoring Father's work."

"I had all the sacred symbols removed," she said, still not taking it from him. "You know that, yes? There is nothing here that speaks of any god but yours. Only human history—centuries of it—reaching back to the First Age of Kings—"

"And that time was many things to many people, Mother— we could argue over it for years and reach no agreement—-but one thing cannot be argued. Whatever the First Kings did, ultimately demons were sent to punish them so that mankind was driven back into the darkness for centuries. Some would argue we are only just now recovering from that blow. Yes?" When she did not answer he asked, "Do you wish me to begin my reign by tying myself to that disastrous age?"

"Your father did," she said coldly, "and he was a great king."

For the first time since his arrival at the palace, a shadow of anger passed over his face. "My father's last days were lived in the shadow of a demon. Let us never forget that. Nor the fact that demons have now been seen in other places as well. This world is on the brink of utter devastation and I for one do not intend to forget it."

He drew in a deep breath then, and shut his eyes for a

moment as he muttered a prayer under his breath to settle his spirit. Then he held out the stole to her. "Forget past glories. We will make new ones. Commission a stole to be crafted that celebrates my father's triumphs, and those of the kings that came before him. But not back past the Dark Times. That is all I ask."

She hesitated, then nodded tightly and accepted the stole from him. "You will at least wear silk, yes? Something appropriate to your rank? Not that . . ." She indicated his monk's robe. ". . . *burlap*."

A flicker of a smile softened his expression. "It's wool, Mother, but, yes. Never fear. I shall wear the most expensive silks you can procure, and a feather in my hat besides, if you so desire it. Festoon the ground with priceless gems and I will walk on them in golden shoes while dancing girls strew rose petals upon the ground for me to crush underfoot. All this I will do if you deem it appropriate." His expression darkened; he put his hand upon the stole. "But not this. I cannot celebrate the age of sin, not without inviting the Destroyer to punish us again. Is that how a new king should begin his reign?"

She bit her lip for a moment. Then, with a sigh, she began to fold the stole, her pale fingers smoothing the delicate embroidery with every turn. "You are as stubborn as your father was, you know that?"

"Aye." He nodded. "And you would not have asked me to take up his crown if I were anything less. Would you?"

———

"We have space enough in the palace for your vassals," Jan Cresel told him, "providing they do not bring large retinues with them. Some may prefer to remain in the field for that reason. It should not be seen as an insult. Nor should your invitation be framed in any way that will cast aspersions upon those whose might choose such a course, or make them feel pressured to do otherwise. Some princes do not travel ten miles from home without a veritable army to accompany them; they will want the space to spread out and put on a show worthy of their retinue."

"To build their towers," Salvator said quietly.

"The invitations will be rendered with suitable diplomacy," Gwynofar promised. "As always."

"You have other names on the list," Salvator pointed out.

Cresel nodded. "Allies of Danton, who will be looking for a clear sign that you mean to continue in his footsteps, at least where they are concerned. Offering them rooms in the palace will be seen as a sign of favor that will help keep them focused upon you rather than upon the blandishments of your enemies. But do bear in mind that any of those who accept your invitation will be doing so in the hopes of catching a private moment with you sometime during the festivities. Some will simply want reassurance from you, others. . . ." He hesitated.

"Others will wish to see if the new High King will be easier to manipulate than his father." He smiled slightly. "You see, Master Cresel? I do understand the game."

"You can expect every noble house with a marriageable daughter to arrange for an introduction sometime during their visit. Needless to say you should remain as neutral as possible in all such meetings. Should you so much as twitch an eyelash in some girl's direction, the gossipmongers will see it transformed into a marriage proposal within an hour. Which can sometimes be as much trouble as the real thing." He smiled dryly and offered Salvator a leather portfolio. "I have assembled reports for you on the candidates worthy of your attention . . . and a few warnings regarding those that are not."

"And what do you advise?" Salvator asked. "Regarding marital prospects."

Cresel hesitated. Clearly he was not accustomed to being asked for this sort of advice. "I would advise waiting," he said finally. "Neither allies nor enemies know what to make of you just yet. For so long as a man believes that his kinswoman might win your favor, he must act to keep that option open. The moment you make a choice in such matters—or even appear to be swayed in the direction of a particular choice—he is free of that obligation. So for now, let them dream their dreams while you take stock of your options. And try not to be too . . ." He paused uncomfortably, seeking the proper word. ". . . *affected* by their charms."

Salvator looked sharply at him. "Do you know what my father did, Master Cresel, when I told him I meant to enter the monastery? He brought in a whore to teach me about love. Well, actually, he brought me a bevy of whores. Some earthy and crude, some elegant and sophisticated, the whole gamut of feminine charms. He said that I should experience Woman in all her guises before choosing to forego such pleasures forever." He shrugged. "Obviously his hope was that after a night or two of unfettered debauchery I would no longer have the heart to go through with my plans. Alas, he did not understand enough of the Penitent faith to realize that he had in fact given my sacrifice greater value, and thus had only fuelled my determination." The chair creaked as he leaned back in it. "The point of the tale is, Master Cresel, the fact that I rejected the cruder pleasures of this world for four years does not mean I do not understand their power. Quite the contrary. I assure you I will mistake neither passion nor political alliance for love. I know that decisions made in the heat of the night rarely survive the morning's inspection. So please, do not fear that my innocence will lead me down some dark and terrible path. I am better armored than most to face that particular enemy."

He reached out for the guest list that Cresel had compiled and nodded as he approved its contents. He had spent the last few days studying all the lineages and households of significance, and was pleased to see that most of these looked familiar.

Then he came to one name that surprised him. Raising an eyebrow, he looked up at Cresel. "Siderea Aminestas?"

"Aye, Sire. The one they call the Witch-Queen."

"I know what they call her. Why is she on the list?"

"Because she is the most powerful monarch in the Free States and bringing her into your sphere of influence would not only guarantee access to the southern shipping lanes, but it would make Corialanus think twice about testing you. Lest it find itself having to defend two borders at once."

"You are assuming she is interested in such a relationship. As I recall, she was a thorn in father's side. He blamed her for uniting the Free States against him."

"Her people have communicated her interest. Not directly, of course. But they have been pulling strings behind the scenes to get her this invitation. Which means your options are presumably open."

Gwynofar raised an eyebrow. "I think I can guess what 'options' she has in mind."

Salvator chuckled. "And if so, where is the risk in it? She is too old to bear children, so even seduction has its limits. She cannot become my queen, and I am sure she would not wish to be my concubine. But if she imagines that she can manipulate me with her charms, then she will focus on that game for as long as it has promise and not do other, more destructive things. Why dash her hopes prematurely?"

"This is not one of your father's whores," Gwynofar said quietly.

"And I am no longer the innocent young boy that those whores serviced, Mother." He handed the list back to Cresel. "You have done well. I approve these names. And I will study the notes you have given me on all the well-born maidens who will be vying for my favor; thank you for that research." He pushed his chair back and rose to his feet. "Mother, would you be so good as to work with Master Cresel on the invitations?"

She nodded. "Of course."

Cresel seemed about to speak again but bit his lip instead. It was an uncharacteristic hesitation. Finally he offered, "Will you be wanting some . . . ah, special accommodation . . . for after the coronation, Sire?"

Salvator blinked. "Of what sort?"

"You have indicated you will not set aside your vows until the ceremony. Which means that immediately afterward you might be . . . let us say, subject to distraction. Not the best state for a new king to be in, when first impressions matter so very much. Perhaps we should arrange for . . . let us say, a private interlude?"

Salvator scowled. "I have practiced self-discipline for four years, Master Cresel. Do you think me so poor in my learning that such things are necessary? What would my father have said to that?"

Gwynofar offered quietly, "Your father would have said that any man who imagined he could set aside four years of celibacy and keep a clear head directly afterward was a creature blinded by his own pride."

Salvator stared at her for a moment. Then he chuckled softly. "My father did not understand my faith well enough to wield such an argument, Mother. Though I do appreciate your concern. However, I can assure you that I am up to the challenge. If there is indeed some demon of lust inside me that imagines it will be unleashed the moment a crown touches my head, then it is bound to be sorely disappointed." After a moment's thought he added, "As for this Aminestas—do see that she needs to bribe someone to earn her invitation, will you? I would hate to make things too easy for her."

"I shall that she is properly challenged," the castellan promised.

As Salvator left the room he could sense all the questions left unspoken, the arguments unvoiced. And they were not entirely without merit. How sure was he, really, that he could watch while every eligible young woman in the High Kingdom was paraded before him, plying her best seductive tricks, and still remain cool-headed?

It is a spiritual trial, he told himself stubbornly. *I will be stronger for having faced it.*

But he devoted an extra hour to prayer that night. Just in case.

CHAPTER 7

IF SHE flew high enough, Kamala could see the Wrath.

It had no physical substance, but the same mystical Sight that had enabled her to see Ethanus' sorcery in her childhood was apparently sensitive to it. Even so it was not visible in its own right, more in how it affected the things around it. A subtle dark shimmering in the air that hung low around the horizon, turning the mountaintops to mist. A sense that things were out of focus, when her powerful hawk eyes should have had no problem seeing everything clearly.

If she stared at it long enough it seemed she could begin to feel its baleful power as well. A cold chill crept up her spine, confusing the rhythm of her wing stroke; her heart filled with a sudden desire to be heading somewhere else, anywhere else. It was hard to continue flying north once the effect had taken hold. If she stared at the Wrath long enough it became hard to fly anywhere.

But the Guardian named Rhys was heading north, directly toward it, and so she followed.

She had picked up the man's trail outside some kind of

meetinghouse in the Kierdwyn Protectorate, where dozens of his kind were gathered. Finding him had been no easy task, since all she'd had to go by was a fleeting moment's memory from outside Danton's palace, snatched just after the Souleater had struck her down from the sky. There had been no more than a few seconds for her to absorb the battle scenario in all its surreal splendor: A single warrior bravely standing his ground against a creature out of legend. A white-bearded Magister who seemed content to watch the battle, not lifting a finger to help. And Magister Colivar, standing off to one side as if stunned, his hands clenched into fists at his side. Lying on the ground, her breath knocked out of her by her sudden transition, she'd watched just long enough to see the warrior thrust his spear into the great creature, to feel the earth shake with its death convulsions, and then she had fled the scene. Any longer and the Magisters would surely have found her there . . . and their wrath was something she feared even more than Souleaters.

Now the Souleater's killer was heading north, with a woman by his side. Kamala had learned enough about the Guardians from snatches of conversations overheard outside the meeting-house—a hawk's hearing could be as good as its eyesight with sorcery to enhance it—to understand why this one had been able to bring the creature down. If anyone really knew what the Souleaters were about it would be these specialized warriors, who trained and studied and meditated each day in the stead-fast belief that their ultimate destiny was to do battle with the creatures. And of them all, only this one had proven his capacity.

Kamala had followed these two Guardians for days now, soaring high overhead until her borrowed wings ached. Each night she descended to some secret place that was out of their sight and reclaimed her human flesh, forcing herself to focus upon being human again until the ecstasy of flight faded from her memory and she could sleep, albeit fitfully. Then the sun would rise all too soon and the warriors would saddle up again, and the journey would begin anew. . . .

If any man knew what the Souleaters were about, this one called Rhys nas Kierdwyn surely did.

If he had been alone she might have approached him directly, but he was not. And for reasons Kamala did not fully understand, the presence of a woman by his side made her uneasy. It probably wouldn't have if the woman had been decked out in a stylish riding gown, trailing silk skirts sidesaddle over the flanks of her mount. Such a woman Kamala would simply disdain and dismiss, a mere traveling accessory to the one who really mattered. But no, this woman was clearly a comrade-at-arms in every sense of the word. And that bothered her.

Why?

You are jealous, she thought.

What a bizarre thought! Jealous of a morati?

Jealous of how he accepts her.

The woman was dressed in a man's garb, but not in any manner that kept her true sex hidden. She had not flirted with the men outside the meetinghouse as a normal woman might have done, but Kamala was willing to bet that the other Guardians were not unaware of the difference between them, or its sexual potential. Yet they all kept a respectful distance, of their own accord. Sometimes one or the other would make a joking comment about her effect on them all, but even then they were laughing with her, not at her.

True acceptance.

It burned her to see it. Why? Because they accepted this warrior woman for what she truly was, not for some role that she must play in order to win men's favor? Because she did not have to pretend to be something less than a woman to win a respected place among them?

If the Magisters had half so much tolerance, Kamala thought bitterly, things might be very different for her now. And at night, in her fitful dreaming, she imagined what that might have been like for her. To be part of their brotherhood without the need to deny her sex. Simply accepted.

She kept her distance.

———

Rhys and Namanti reached the top of Branwyn Ridge just before sunset. It had been a hard day of riding and the horses were clearly less than enthused about being prodded up the steep incline at the end of so many grueling hours. Namanti's mount in particular, a bulky Skandir-bred gelding with thickly tufted ankles, whinnied repeated protests as she urged it up the slope. The two packhorses, laden with supplies for the journey, suffered in stoic silence behind them, but found the going no easier.

There was supposed to be a pass some miles farther north, but neither suggested they ride that far before nightfall. They were coming close to the Wrath of the Gods now, and the next few miles might well bring them within its sway. No man in his right mind would spend a minute more in that baleful region than he had to. Not to mention that animals could often sense the Wrath before men did; sometimes horses would panic when they caught their first whiff of it, and bolt for freedom in a desperate attempt to get away from some unseen, unnamed enemy. In a place like this, where even a sane horse found the footing precarious, such behavior could result in injury or even death.

As the gods had intended, Rhys reflected darkly.

On the other hand, a man could pit the force of human self-control against the ancient curse, and perhaps stand his ground for a while. Some did better than others. A few men, like Rhys, could get to within sight of the Spears before the pressure became unbearable. When men had to go closer than that it generally took a good bout of drinking to get them started, and twice as much drinking when they came back home to forget what they had seen. Sometimes for public rituals a handful of Magisters would be brought in to mute the curse's power so that the local reigning *lyr* could offer prayers of thanksgiving in the very shadow of the Spears without being driven mad. But even that was a temporary fix at best. And the fact that the Magisters hated the Wrath and would rather be anywhere else on the face of the earth than within reach of its power was not lost on anyone.

Rhys remembered one day not so long ago when he had come close enough to a Spear to touch it without such assistance. That he could remember the incident without cringing was a testament to how weak the Wrath had become.

If its power is fading, then it cannot protect us any longer.

Daylight was fading now, and the mountainous landscape ahead of them was an eerie sight, misty shadows creeping toward the east like ghostly fingers. Here and there the low-angled light would pick out the upper edge of a granite cliff, or the summit of some wind-carved monument, setting the tip alight with bright orange fire. It was an ephemeral beauty that vanished moments later, as quickly as it had come, as dusk conquered the peaks and the shadows of the coming night grew deep and black.

"You wanted to come up here tonight. Why?" Namanti rode

as close to Rhys as she dared, given the restlessness of her mount. The husky creature had been trained for battle, and could stand its ground in the face of a full cavalry charge if necessary, but the Wrath emitted a different kind of fear. Clearly the horse was not happy at all about this journey. "Remind me."

Peering into the distance, Rhys looked for motion. Any motion. They were close enough to the Wrath now that animals would be loath to make their home here, which meant that the only creatures moving among these shadows should be those who had some pressing reason to do so.

Or men.

But he could see nothing. The shadows were already too deep, the valleys too dark. They had come too late.

"I've had an odd feeling all day," he murmured. "Of being watched, somehow. I was hoping . . ." His voice trailed off, fading into silent frustration. At last he shrugged. "It's too late to see anything from here."

Her expression was solemn. "You know that's a common reaction to the Wrath, yes? Sensing enemies where there are none?"

He stared out over the mountains. "I know."

"This feels different than that?"

He nodded.

"All right, then. That's good enough for me." She wheeled her horse around and nodded toward the south. "I saw a place a short bit back that will serve for a good camp. Out of sight from most directions, with a good vantage point for a sentry. I assume we're keeping watch from now on?"

He nodded, but still did not move.

"Rhys?"

"I had a dream last night, that something was waiting for us in Alkali." He shook his head. "Something that won't cross the border." He pointed to a set of three stark granite spires rising up from deep within the Alkali Protectorate. The tips of the Three Sisters glowed orange against the darkening sky. "Somewhere near those."

"You sure?"

Lips set tightly, he shook his head. "I'd hoped if we came up here I could see something to confirm it. Not sure what. But it's too dark to see anything at this point."

She said it quietly. "Bad dreams are also a symptom of the Wrath."

This time he nodded stiffly. "I know." He turned his horse southward to follow her; his expression was grim. "Believe me, I know."

He'd been this far north before, several times. He knew what the magic of the gods could do to a man's mind, even a man who was half-*lyr*. He knew that rational thought became progressively more difficult as one approached the Spears, and paranoia took root all too easily. He knew that when you got close enough every rock seemed to hide an enemy, and every breeze seemed to carry baleful sorcery in its wake.

But that doesn't mean nothing's out there, he told himself stubbornly. And he took the first watch himself that night, knowing that he would not be able to sleep.

———

The Guardians were traveling a strange route that sometimes proceeded logically, following the low points in the topography but at other times snaked its way directly over the tops of ridges or mountains, as if the two travelers were seeking the most difficult possible path. At one point the going was so difficult that Kamala could tell that the horses were straining to make the climb, while she could see that a few miles ahead of them there was a dip in the ridgeback that would have allowed for easy crossing. From what she could hear of their conversation they seemed to know the pass was out there, but they still chose to take the harder route. Perhaps they had gotten as close to the Wrath as their horses could tolerate. Even from the height of her skyborne vantage point Kamala could see how edgy the animals were becoming and it was not hard to figure out why. Most of the native wildlife had fled this region long ago, and those few animals that had remained behind were scrawny, nervous things, barely half the size that they should be. If left to their own devices, Kamala had little doubt that the horses would turn tail and head south as fast as their hooves could take them. More than once the two travelers had to work hard to urge their mounts forward, yanking on the long reins that led the pack animals to get them to cooperate.

The lack of local wildlife had complicated Kamala's journey considerably. In the form of a hawk she generally had little trouble bringing down enough food to sustain herself, and while the human Kamala might have gone hungry rather than sink her teeth into a raw, bleeding field mouse, something about being in bird form seemed to negate her normal disgust. With a hawk's wings to carry her through the air and sorcery to enhance her senses and her speed, hunting did not usually take any more time than unpacking supplies in human form would have. But now, in this benighted region, things were no longer so easy. Her sorcery was showing signs of becoming affected, and since she relied upon it for hunting, that was not a good thing. One night she decided to try a more direct approach and simply conjured food for herself. The spell took more than an hour to focus properly and eventually produced a loaf of bread teeming with worms and a half a round of cheese that smelled so vile she couldn't bring herself to taste it. Better to go hungry.

Little wonder that the Magisters hated this place, she thought. She hoped that soon the Guardians she was following would reach a place more amenable to sorcery; otherwise Kamala might have to abandon her current course long enough to go back and fetch supplies.

Or you could always talk to the Guardians, she reminded herself. *They carry enough food for three.*

But she wasn't ready for that yet.

She did attempt to weave a spell over the two travelers that would ease their nerves a bit. They had taken to looking over their shoulders on a regular basis, and sometimes their eyes strayed upward, as if seeking enemies in the cloud-filled sky. From what she could pick up when she eavesdropped on them, it seemed that the proximity of the Wrath was making them both unnaturally edgy. That would have been a simple matter to correct back home, but in this region it took her more than an hour to polish the spell that would calm their fears. It was necessary, though. She didn't want to take a chance that one of them would notice the hawk that was following them day after day, or guess at its nature. Not yet. She wasn't ready.

You are not being watched, her sorcery whispered to them. *You are not being followed.*

For now, it seemed to be enough.

———

"I was surprised you didn't want to go to the coronation," Namanti said as she separated their saddlebags from the rest of the equine gear.

Rhys looked up from the fire he had just started and blinked. "What on earth made you think of that?"

"Queen Gwynofar is your half-sister, yes?"

He used a stick to prod the woodpile so that air could flow freely through it. Tiny flames flickered beneath the pile of bark and branches. "It's not Gwynofar who's being crowned," he pointed out. "And I'm certainly not needed for the ceremony."

"No, but it's her son. A rather important day for her." She dropped the bags down by the fire. "Horses are all taken care of," she told him. "Ragnar hates this place, but he's still eating." Rhys nodded. Namanti's mount was an ill-tempered creature who was clearly not pleased about their current journey. No surprise, really. He was a bulky animal, bred for hard work and trampling down enemies in battle, not meant to be dancing along cliff edges like a mountain goat. Rhys had been hoping Namanti would choose a more agile mount when they got closer to the Wrath, but for now she seemed determined to stick with this one. So he had to put off hoping that the unpleasant creature would lose its footing at the edge of a cliff. At least while she was riding it.

Namanti sat down cross-legged on the ground beside him and began to unpack their evening meal: salted meat, hard cheese, a small portion of dried fruit, and two hard, dry cakes from Skandir that she said would help keep them strong. The latter were clearly an acquired taste, but the fortitude of Skandir warriors was renowned throughout the Protectorates, and they always seemed to carry the miserable things with them, so Rhys ate one whenever she offered it. With a good swig of ale to wash it down, of course. Or two.

"My first duty was here," he said, using his hunting knife to cut off a hunk of cheese. "Bringing the Souleater samples back to Master Favias, reporting to the Guardians what I'd seen. And now they need us to attend to the Spears. That's much more important than attending a ceremony I have no part in." Long tongues of flame were beginning to lick at the sides of the woodpile. He leaned back on his heels, watching them with satisfaction. "Gwynofar is *lyra*, she will understand."

Namanti nodded as she dropped down beside him, unplugging a waxed leather skin full of ale for herself. "So tell me why the Lady Protector tolerates your presence at her court. I admit I've always wondered."

He raised an eyebrow. "You're very inquisitive tonight."

She shrugged. "It's a boring ride. Indulge me."

He sighed and for a minute just stared into the growing flames. They had traveled far enough north by now, and ridden high enough into the mountains, that the summer nights were growing chill; the warmth of the fire would be welcome when the sun finally went down. "I don't know, Namanti. That's the gods' honest truth. I should be the last person she wants in her home, by any civilized measure—"

"You earned her respect somehow? Or maybe charmed her with your good looks?"

Rhys snorted and took another deep swig from his own skin. "Given that I was all of ten years old when she first saw me, I somehow doubt that."

"Even in Skandir, where it's expected that a ruler will have his share of concubines, the children of such unions aren't welcome in their father's house. Laws of inheritance and all that. If bastards weren't officially disowned, then the whole system could fall to pieces. At least that's what I've been told."

"Then it's fortunate I'm not from Skandir, isn't it?" He took a bite of the hard, dry cake and quickly washed it down. It was better if he didn't actually stop to taste it. "All I know is that I was still a child when a servant from the royal court showed up at our home, asking after me. My mother had always hinted that someone 'of rank' was responsible for my birth, so I assumed it a query from that mysterious personage. How proud I was, to have my father sending servants to ask after me, as though I were something more than the product of a night's drunken debauchery!" He grimaced as he dislodged the last bits of Skandir cake from his teeth and swallowed them. "But he just looked me over rather distastefully, like one might do with an overripe melon in the market, searching for bruised spots, or maybe some sign of worms." He paused. "It wasn't until some time later that I found out the servant had been *hers*. Evaine Kierdwyn had just found out about the product of her husband's indiscretion and wanted to learn for herself whether his seed grew true in peasant soil or not." He drank deeply of the ale, letting it spread in warm waves out to his fingers and toes. "Had the Lord Protector not been *lyr* himself it would probably have not mattered to her at all . . . but he was, you see, so it was all tied up in Protectorate tradition. A child with the 'gift of the gods' isn't something you just forget about. Even if you really do wish it had never been born."

"Do you think that's how she feels?"

He hesitated before answering. "No. I don't. It's how she *should* feel—it's how *I* would feel in her place—but she's never shown any sign of it. She's been nothing but gracious to me any time I visit. As if I were . . . something other than what I am." Why did that make him feel so bitter? He took a long swallow of the ale, letting the skin hide his expression from her view. "Mostly I try to stay out of her way. Though Favias does rather seem to enjoy sending me to court with his messages. I think the situation amuses him."

"Would you have been welcome at the coronation had you gone?"

He stared into the distance for a moment. "Salvator will become High King with or without me there to watch. It's just as well I had other business. And what would my place be there, anyway, amid all the crowned heads and their retinues? A guest of Gwynofar, taking up space in a palace that should be reserved for the High King's most valued vassals? Or perhaps banished to the far reaches of the field, as my social station merits, too far away to be any more part of the proceedings than a house servant would be, or a local peasant hawking his wares." He capped the skin, put it down on the ground beside him, and sighed. "My duty is here. Gwynofar will understand. Anyway . . ." He smiled faintly. "The last thing Salvator needs right now is an illegitimate half-uncle wandering around the palace."

How reasonable it sounded when he explained it that way, he thought. Almost enough to ease the ache in his heart.

"I'm sorry," she said. Just that, and then silence.

It took him a minute to realize she had put her hand on his shoulder. A companionable gesture, rather than intimate. The kind of gesture a man might make. He shrugged it off.

"I'm going to take a piss," he said.

She said nothing as he left the camp, making his way through the pine trees to where a small stream flowed softly over the rocks. There he stood for a minute, eyes half shut, drinking in the sounds and the smells of the pine forest. Trying not to think about the event taking place hundreds of miles to the south of him and what might have happened had he attended it.

Never mind, he told himself. *Soon you will be near enough to*

the Wrath that you will long to be back among the civilized dis-
comforts of Lady Evaine's court.

———

Kamala woke up suddenly.

At first she thought it was an animal foraging nearby that had disturbed her sleep. She had cast a simple spell to keep the local wildlife from tripping over her during the night—what little wildlife there was in these cursed latitudes—but that didn't mean some scrawny creature might not be making enough racket outside the spell's border to wake her up. For a moment she lay very still, trying to tell if that were indeed the case. But whatever creature had awakened her was silent now. A smart move on its part, she thought. Especially with game as rare as it was these days. Yesterday's field mouse had not been all that satisfying.

No sound this time. Nothing that merely human senses might catch wind of. Still, without a doubt, something was out there.

She lay frozen for a moment, not even breathing, straining all her senses to the utmost. But she heard nothing moving. No, less than that: she heard nothing at all. No breeze rustling through the trees, no insects scrabbling in the dirt, not even water flowing over the rocks in the stream just downhill from her. Nothing.

A chill of pure dread ran down her spine. Carefully, secretly, she gathered her athra to her, trying to look as if she were still half asleep so that whatever had silenced the natural sounds of the mountain landscape would think she was still unaware of its presence.

And then a stick broke.

She sat up suddenly, just in time to see the black-robed figure in the moonlight disappear again. The color of his clothing drank in the light, leaving no doubt as to his profession. A Magister. For a brief second their eyes met—just long enough for her to see that his were filled with hate—and then the night folded in around him and she could no longer see him at all. But he was still there. Oh, yes, she knew that for a fact. Her human senses could not locate him any longer, but now that she was fully awake her sorcerous sense could detect his handiwork. Spells had been wrapped about her campsite while she slept, she saw that now, layers upon layers of them, like the sticky web of a tent spider. The magical strands glowed fitfully, as if they'd been woven from some sickly power; no doubt that was the effect of the Wrath being so close by. If so, then the curse of the gods might have just saved her life, for she read clearly in the webwork surrounding her the baleful intent of its maker and knew that if the construct had been perfect, she would have slept until it was too late to save herself.

She tried to transport herself away, focusing upon an apparent weak spot in the web for her directional focus. But her athra seemed slippery somehow and she could not control it. Was that the effect of the Wrath as well? Or was the spell surrounding her acting to constrain her sorcery?

Shadows were beginning to stir on all sides of her now, and she knew with a sudden sinking feeling that there was more than one Magister present—many more. Apparently news of her crime had gotten out. How they had tracked her to this place she did not know, but one thing was certain: if she did not break free of their spell she was doomed.

She tried to put on wings again, adopting that feathered form which had served her so well in the past few days. But the change was agony; hot needles pierced her joints as her bones cracked audibly, and the soft tissue of her body felt like it was on fire. Gritting her teeth against the pain, she struggled to force her flesh into the shape she desired. Never before had she come so close to losing control of her body . . . or her courage.

They will not take me down without cost, she swore.

They were coming into focus now, stepping forth from the shadows as they surrounded her, standing just outside the spell circle. So many Magisters! She did not have time to look for familiar faces; instead she leaped into the air as soon as her wings were stable, throwing herself at the high point of the barrier with all her strength, aiming for what seemed like a weak point in its structure. For a moment the sorcerous webwork entrapped her, and she struggled desperately to free herself. *Must get out!* The Magisters watched in silence. *Must break through!* Her claws scrabbled desperately at it, but to no avail. Finally it released her and she fell back to earth. Like a bird in a cage she began to panic, flying toward the barrier first in one place, then another, throwing the full weight of her body against the spell circle, ripping at it with her talons and her sorcery. Feathers flew from her shoulders. Blood dripped from her claws. But the encircling spell remained undamaged; she could find no place weak enough in its construction to allow her to break through, either by physical or metaphysical effort.

And still they watched in silence. So many of them! Black-robed cannibals all of them, drinking in her desperation. She could sense the hunger in them as they watched her struggle. The hate. They were packed tightly about the spell circle now, in a crowd so many layers deep that she could not begin to guess how many Magisters were present. Truly, she would not have thought there were so many in all the world as seemed to be here now—and every single one of them had contributed his power to the spell that was her prison. Now that her senses were fully awake to its power, its glow was so bright that it burned her eyes to look upon it. And it seemed to be strengthened by her own efforts, brightening each time she tried to break free. It was stealing her power, even as she tried to save herself.

Must get out! Must!

Trembling with fear and exhaustion, she reclaimed her human flesh so that she might better control her sorcery. The skin of her arms appeared bruised and lifeless, and blood dripped from her fingertips. What was happening to her? The uncertainty of it was more unnerving than any direct assault would have been. Violence she knew how to deal with. Violence she knew how to answer. This . . . this she did not.

The Magisters watched her, unmoving. They were chanting softly now, it seemed to her, but the language was one that she did not understand. Nevertheless she knew instinctively that they were voicing words of power, such as a witch might use to focus his athra before a major undertaking. But a Magister had no need of such tools. What in the name of all the hells was going on?

Then she saw that the webwork about her was thickening, shifting, closing. Where there had been small open spaces before to offer her hope, slender strands of power now splayed like darning threads, drawing them inexorably shut. Desperately she gathered her athra to her and struck out at the baleful construct, directing all the force that was in her soul at the one point that seemed weakest but she could barely raise a whisper of power now, and the spell circle remained unharmed.

"What do you want?" she gasped. "Tell me!"

They continued their chanting. So many Magisters, joining

their life energies together in one great effort . . . how could any one human being hope to stand against them?

The last holes in the web were drawing shut. Strands of light began to assemble themselves into letters and words, all in a language she did not understand. It was hard to see anything beyond them. The webwork itself was dimming, but the letters remained clear. She tried in desperation to call up enough power to interpret them but the power would not come to her. Even worse, the glowing letters seemed to draw strength from her efforts, as though her own athra was feeding them. The spell that surrounded her was sucking all the power out of her soul. . . .

"It was an accident!" she screamed. Or tried to. The tissues of her throat were dry and cracked and she could barely force out any sound, much less recognizable words. "I didn't mean to kill him!" What little volume she could muster seemed to be absorbed by the glowing letters as well; they pulsed with light as they drifted toward her. The spell wall behind them was growing dark now and she could see nothing beyond it, only those unknown symbols that floated in the air before her, waiting for another offering of her life energy. Whatever power she raised to fight this thing it would absorb; whatever spells she cast to save herself it would devour.

And then suddenly the last of the light was gone, the glowing letters sputtered out, and there was darkness. Panicked, she struck out toward the barrier, but her hands moved only a few inches before they hit solid stone. Reaching out in other directions, she found the same thing: rock on all sides of her, above and below as well, roughly carved and clearly not natural in its formation.

She was entombed.

Bleeding hands scraped against the unseen wall to no avail. She could feel something chiseled crudely into the rough surface. Letters. Surrounding her. Spells—powerful spells—that would slowly but surely steal all the life force that was in her and transform it into—

What? What did they want? What was happening to her?

Wordlessly, she screamed. Opened her mouth and let the terror pour out until the stone walls shook from the force of the sound and surely the animals beyond it would hear its echo and flee and—

She was lying on a bed of leaves with no stone tomb enclosing her.

No words of power.

No Magisters.

For a moment she just lay there, stunned, trying to absorb what had just happened. Her heart was pounding so hard that it seemed about to burst from her chest. Her whole body was drenched in a cold sweat. Her hands, her hands . . . she brought them up before her face and saw that they were undamaged. No blood. No blood.

The sudden relief was more than she could handle; she rolled over on her side and retched. Long, shuddering spasms shook her as her body vomited up all the terror of the past hour. It seemed to go on forever.

It was a dream, she thought when at last the fit was over. Lying on her side on the rocky ground, feeling as if she ought to kiss the soiled earth beneath her cheek, so glad was she to be back in the real world again.

Then: *No. It was more than a dream.*

She had never been prone to nightmares. Even in the darkest days of her childhood, which were filled with more pain than any young girl should have to endure, her sleep had been free from torments. Her brother used to awaken crying in the middle of the night, whimpering of monsters and darkness, but she never had. *Her* monsters had walked the earth during the day and paid with grimy coin for the right to abuse her; sleep had been her one true refuge.

The Wrath was known to give men nightmares, she knew that. Indeed, she had expected to have bad dreams once she entered this area; it was a risk she'd accepted in order to follow the two Guardians. But this . . . this had been something more than a simple nightmare. She knew that for certain, without quite understanding how she knew. This was a vision that mattered. But what part was significant and what part was simply the product of her own fear? She had no idea how to begin to sort it all out. And yet it mattered. She knew that instinctively, in the same way she knew that the sun would rise every morning. *It mattered*.

The Guardian would know what it meant, she thought. If only she dared ask him.

Shivering in the chill dawn light, she wiped her face clean on a handful of grass and began to make her way down to the stream to wash herself.

CHAPTER 8

THE LAST time Colivar had seen Danton's palace, the land surrounding it had been a study in devastation. Blackened earth and the charred skeletons of trees had stretched as far as the eye could see, and the smell of stale smoke and burned flesh had hung heavy in the humid summer air.

Now that same landscape was a brilliant and colorful thing, with a lush carpet of fresh grass underfoot—so new it had not yet had a chance to scatter its first seed—and a veritable metropolis of colorful tents and pavilions staked out upon every available inch of solid ground. A channel had been established to bring in fresh-flowing water from a nearby river, with several pools providing focal points for the encampments surrounding them. And perhaps even more important, large refuse pits had been provided at the far end of the estate, with servants waiting to shovel a layer of dirt over each new offering, to keep the air smelling sweet throughout the festivities. All in all, Colivar mused, it was quite an impressive transformation.

If it had been the intent of the Aurelius family to erase all memory of the land's former devastation, they had done so admirably.

Each delegation had its own assigned space, and the larger groups had established veritable cities of canvas, complete with feast halls, formal audience chambers, and, in some cases, temples to one god or another. Uniformed guards patrolled the canvas walls that demarcated the boundaries of their domains, and in some cases elevated walkways had been erected inside the walls, so that those men might have a clearer perspective. It was mostly for show, of course. Any delegation of rank would have a Magister Royal in attendance, and if some lesser encampments did not have a Magister on its regular payroll it would have surely scrambled to hire one for this gathering. Which meant that there would be no real trouble, Colivar thought dryly. Magisters valued their peace.

At the far end of the field was a single pavilion set apart from all the others. Its fabric was black—that rich and impossible shade of black which only sorcery could produce—and if one approached closely enough, one could feel a cool breeze stirring about its walls, regardless of the angle of the sun or the heat of the day. Few morati came near enough to find that out, of course. They understood the message embodied in its color, preferring to steer clear of anything which so obviously—and aggressively—belonged to the Magisters.

Entering the pavilion's cool confines, Colivar offered up a bit of his own sorcerous power to help maintain its comfortable temperature. Visitor's courtesy. As his eyes adjusted to the shadowy interior he could make out furnishings that were rich and luxurious, if somewhat mismatched. Each Magister had apparently donated key pieces in his style of choice to the whole, with little thought for the overall effect. Or perhaps they simply did not care to adjust their offerings to suit the taste of others. It was hard to say. Social events with this many Magisters in attendance came along only a few times each century, so they had never had the time to work out exactly how such things should be organized. Or the interest.

Colivar gazed at the collection for a few moments, then bound enough power to tweak the colors here and there; when his sorcery settled, all the pieces were rendered in a rich but tasteful combination of burgundy, scarlet, and gold. Much better. He added a few embroidered floor pillows of his own to the collection and then headed over to the sideboard, where bottles of wine and platters full of delicacies were waiting. A chill wafted upward from the plates and bowls whose contents required cold storage, soothing after the day's heat.

There were three other Magisters inside the pavilion: Lazaroth, Tirstan, and another one from Gansang whose name Colivar could not call to mind. He nodded a greeting to them all as he poured himself some wine. "So," he said. "Any news worth hearing these days?"

"Lemnos has fled Kierdwyn," Tirstan said. "If you regard that as news."

Colivar sipped his wine. It was a complex vintage, with subtle and pleasing undertones; whoever had conjured it had excellent taste. "Not a great surprise. No Magister serves in a Protectorate for very long."

"He says the Wrath is getting worse these days," Lazaroth offered dryly. "Apparently it was more than he could handle."

Colivar raised an eyebrow. "Do you believe that to be true? That the Wrath is changing?" When Lazaroth didn't answer immediately he added dryly, "I am guessing from your self-satisfied tone that you are the one who claimed Lemnos' post, but if I am mistaken in that assumption, please do let me know."

Tirstan chuckled softly. "You are not mistaken."

The other Gansang Magister lifted up his cup in a toast. "Permit me to introduce Magister Royal Lazaroth, newly sworn to the service of Stevan and Evaine Kierdwyn, of the Kierdwyn Protectorate. May he have a bit more staying power than his predecessor." He drank deeply from his cup.

Tamil, Colivar recalled suddenly. The Magister's name was Tamil. "Certainly an interesting post," he mused, "given all that is happening these days. No doubt it will put you front and center at Salvator's festivities, Lazaroth."

Lazaroth snorted. "Hardly. You forget his damnable religion. Lord and Lady Kierdwyn have asked me to steer clear of him as much as possible . . . thus I am passing the time in such *delightful* company as this." There was a dry edge to his tone that came up just short of being overtly insulting. Lazaroth was not in a good mood.

"Yes," Tamil said, "and what is all that about, anyway? I must admit I don't pay much attention to morati religions. What exactly is the problem with this one?"

"The Penitents believe there is one god," Colivar said, "who acts as both Creator and Destroyer to keep the world in balance. Mankind offended him during the First Age of Kings, so he created the demons we call the Souleaters to teach him a lesson in humility. Civilization collapsed as a result, the First Kingdoms fell to ruin . . . you know the rest. Presumably that was enough to satisfy this god, for he eventually allowed the demons to be driven off. And so here we are today. Man's duty on earth now is to acknowledge the sins of his forefathers and do penance for them. While trying not to offend again."

Tamil raised an eyebrow. "Well that seems rather . . . depressing. But what is the issue with Magisters?"

"We are tools of the Destroyer," Colivar said quietly. "The embodiment of Pride."

Lazaroth chuckled darkly. "Our sorcery is unclean. It corrupts the human soul. Etcetera, etcetera." He took a deep drink from his cup. "Of course, to be fair, the Penitents are not so very far from the truth in that, are they?"

They are not far from the truth in any of their beliefs, Colivar thought darkly. Shadows of memory stirred in the deepest recesses of his brain, fleeting images of things and people that were better left forgotten. "It will be interesting to see what happens to their faith when it is confirmed that the Souleaters are returning. Will they believe that their Creator has rejected them? Or that he is testing them once more? The latter could prove . . . unpleasant."

"Fanatics are strengthened by adversity," Tamil pointed out.

"Aye," Tirstan agreed, "and meanwhile Salvator seems to be doing well enough with only witches to assist him. A king can afford the cost of such service."

"And what do you all think of the rumor that he has made a secret contract with one of us?" Lazaroth asked them all.

Colivar's eyes narrowed. "I doubted it myself, before I arrived. But now . . ." An expansive gesture took in the whole of the land surrounding them. "Let us say this place is a lot greener than it should be."

"Witches can make the grass grow," Tirstan pointed out.

"Aye, but it's unlikely that a Penitent monk would order a man to shorten his lifespan for such a prideful purpose." He scuffed at the thick grass by his feet; the blades were so closely packed that it was impossible to get a clear look at the ruined earth beneath it. "This is a Magister's work, without question. The only question is, whose? And what has been asked in return?"

Lazaroth chuckled. "So now we all have a mystery to occupy our minds when the morati festivities grow dull. Well done, Colivar. I shall invite you to all my parties."

"At any rate you have lost your wager." Tirstan grinned. "If Salvator has agreed to a contract with one of us, then no sorcery can touch him."

"That is assuming everyone plays by the rules," Tamil pointed out.

"True enough." Lazaroth's dark eyes were fixed on Colivar. "Though the price for breaking the Law is considerable, is it not?"

Colivar's expression was unreadable. "As it should be," he said quietly. He put his cup down on the table and with a short wave of his hand bound enough sorcery to clean it for the next user.

"Now, if you gentlemen will excuse me, I have a few errands to run for my own patron . . ."

He started toward the door of the tent, but Lazaroth's voice stopped him.

"She is here, you know."

Colivar looked back at him. "Who?"

"The one you all doted on, while she had something you wanted. And now have abandoned to face death alone." He smiled; it was a dark expression. "How she must hate you for that! As I might myself, if I had a woman's heart."

Colivar's lips tightened. He said nothing.

"Of course, the morati have no more value to us than maggots. Aye? But this one was allowed to believe she was something more. How cruel, to learn the truth at last! From queen to maggot, all in a handful of days."

Tirstan snapped irritably, "That's enough, Lazaroth."

"At least I did not use her as some others did." Lazaroth's eyes glittered coldly. "So doubtless her resentment will not focus on me. That's some kind of comfort, isn't it?"

For a moment there was silence. Colivar considered all the responses he might make, and found none of them up to his standards. Finally he left the pavilion without answering, leaving the Magisters that remained behind to discuss the question to death in his absence.

Such words should not bother him. They should not bother any Magister. Such men left their human instincts behind with their first transition, and with it all compassion. Surely he, Colivar, knew that better than anyone.

We have done her no wrong, he told himself. *Her days were numbered from the start, and not even we can change that.*

But Lazaroth's words echoed in his brain for many hours, and not until sleep came at last, deep in the night, was he able to let them go.

———

"Your Majesty?"

Siderea smiled as she turned to greet the young woman who was addressing her. It took some effort. Although she was standing in the middle of the grand pavilion at the campsite provided for the Free States, surrounded by a bevy of rich young men who would be all too happy to shower her with compliments and attention, her mind had been elsewhere.

Three times now she had passed by Magisters in one place or another, all of them men she would once have called her lovers. Each had been fastidiously polite, and one had even asked after her health. Her health! Did the idiots think that she didn't know the truth about her own condition? Or did they believe that engaging her in petty social repartee as if nothing were wrong would somehow make the situation better for her?

They could save her if they wanted to. She believed that with all her heart. Oh, they made grand speeches about how no woman could join their sorcerous society; she'd heard enough of those arguments to write a book on the subject. Feminine nature was too weak, or too unstable, or else just too *unmasculine* to master "true power." But that didn't mean they couldn't do anything else for her. They had preserved her youth well past its normal limits already, hadn't they? Surely they had some other trick up their black sleeves that could buy her a bit more time.

The truth was, they had chosen to let her die. And not one of them had the decency to admit to it. Or even to offer her a moment of honest sympathy. Gods, how she hated them all!

But the moment's business called for a convincing smile, and so she fixed one dutifully on her face as she offered her hand to the young woman who had approached her. She was a pretty young thing, who curtseyed very nicely, touching her hand briefly with her own, as if not quite sure how much formality was called for. A charmingly sincere moment.

"Forgive me for bothering you," she said. Her cheeks flushed slightly (a delightful pink!) but her gaze was steady and strong. "I was hoping you might be able to spare a moment for a question or two? I do not mean to impose . . ." She looked about at the men surrounding them, several of whom winked suggestively or raised their glasses as her gaze fell over them.

Siderea caught her meaning immediately. *Women's business.* The thought brought a genuine smile to her face, for the first time in many hours. "Of course, my dear. Here, come with me. You gentlemen will all excuse us, won't you?" She beamed at the peacocks surrounding them, while steering the young woman toward a quieter corner of the tent. "In the meantime, you are . . . ?"

"Petrana Bellisi, Your Majesty. Of House Bellisi."

Bellisi. Of course. That was one of the names that had been raised as a possible marital prospect for Salvator. Duke Bellisi ruled one of the smaller Free States, but he was well connected by treaty and marriage to just about all the others, which meant that his eldest daughter possessed an impressive political dowry. If Salvator wanted to conquer the Free States by alliance rather than by warfare, marital ties to House Bellisi would be a good first step.

Intrigued now, Siderea took stock of the young woman's assets while they walked. She was a lovely young thing, with the sort of creamy white skin that men loved to write songs about, and a natural rose hue to her cheeks and lips that other women might pay a fortune to imitate. Her figure looked pleasing enough, but it was currently laced into a sober gown of dark brown wool that did her no service. Far too conservative for this sort of setting, and the color did nothing for her complexion. No doubt a man had picked it out for her, Siderea thought. No woman with eyes in her head would ever have picked out such an unflattering shade for herself.

It's a monk's color, Siderea realized. Shaking her head in amazement, at how little men understood about . . . well, about anything.

Grateful to have something to focus on other than her own brooding thoughts, she directed the girl to a pair of unoccupied chairs. "So what can I do for you, my dear?"

The girl sat down carefully, smoothing the folds of her gown as she did so. Then she smoothed them again, delaying the moment of revelation. Clearly she did not know how to begin. "I find myself in need of advice," she said at last. "And I am told you are the best one to ask."

Siderea smiled her most charming smile, trying to put the girl at her ease. "How could I resist such flattery? Tell me what it is you seek."

"My father means to introduce me to King Salvator after his coronation. He says that I should do my best to make a positive impression, even though I will not have very long to do so."

"Indeed." Siderea nodded in agreement. "Every young woman that imagines herself a High Queen will be doing exactly the same. All week, no doubt. I imagine Salvator will be quite overwhelmed."

"But you see, that is my question." Her slender hands twisted in her lap. "I do not know . . . that is, what sort of. . . ." She looked pleadingly up at Siderea. How dark and wide her eyes were, and how lustrous! Brush a bit of kohl about the edges, and courtiers would scribe poems to praise them.

Siderea reached out gently and took the girl's hand in her own. "I understand," she said quietly. "And you did right in coming to me. After all, I too have a vested interest in seeing a daughter of the Free States win Salvator's hand."

"They say that no one knows men better than you. That once you have set your eyes upon a man, he cannot possibly resist you."

"And you wish me to teach you that art?" she asked. "In a handful of hours?"

Petrana blushed. "I would never ask so much of you. Of course."

Perhaps not, but the concept was intriguing. Siderea could not engage in marital politics on her own behalf, being well past the age of fertility, but directing a pawn in that game could be delightful sport. Of course, Petrana would have to become a proper pawn for that to work out properly. But that would not be so very hard to manage, would it?

"I am not averse to teaching you my art," she said, brushing a stray lock of hair from the girl's cheek. "But it will require more privacy than we can manage in this place. Perhaps you will visit me sometime after we return home? So that we can devote some proper time to it?"

"I—I would be honored, your Majesty. Thank you."

"In the meantime, how to make sure Salvator has the proper impression of you this week . . ." She steepled her fingers thoughtfully. "He is a man, you know. He may have been a monk in the past and he may soon be a king, but he is still a man. Too many forget that."

"He has lived as a sworn celibate for four years," Petrana said. "My father says that is what matters most."

Siderea chuckled. "Yes, it matters, though few will understand how to take advantage of it." She leaned forward intently. "Shall I tell you what mistakes your rivals will make? They all assume that is Salvator is defined by his celibacy. That after four years without a woman, he will so vulnerable to games of desire that he will forget about everything else. Some of them will wear their most suggestive gowns, far more daring than their normal attire, hoping that he will be so blinded by the sudden upwelling of lust that all other things will cease to matter. In this they forget that he is an Aurelius, raised by a powerful monarch, and suckled on politics at his mother's breast. He will want a wife worthy of sharing his throne with him, and whatever lust he feels will be in that context. A woman who is too blatant with her temptation, who goes too far in catering to his lust, may appeal to him as a concubine, but he will never place the crown of the High Kingdom on her head.

"Others will make the opposite error, and assume that because of his background Salvator has an innate distaste for all pleasures of the flesh. That is due to simple ignorance of his faith. The Penitents have no issue with natural desire. Their monks offer up self-denial as a personal sacrifice, to balance out the sinful excess of nonbelievers. Once Salvator sets aside his robes, he will be stepping into another role. And the last thing he wants as High King is to be treated like a monk in the bedchamber. Yet some women will dress up in their most conservative gowns, covering over all the features that a man would have interest in seeing in an attempt to play to that side of his nature. Trust me, their names will be forgotten before the sun sets." Picking at a fold of Petrana's skirt, she said. "I take it your father chose this for you?"

Petrana nodded.

Siderea sighed. "Never let a man pick out your clothes, my dear. Unless that is part of your seduction. They think they know how to manage it, but really, they haven't a clue."

"So what do you suggest, then?"

"Put on something attractive that compliments your coloring. The sort of gown you might wear to receive well-born suitors at home. Modest but appealing. Let him see that you have interest in him as a man, but that you are also a tasteful, intelligent woman who can engage his mind. Follow his lead in conversation, but do not be too shy to have an opinion if it is called for. And if he changes tack in mid-conversation, then that is a good thing. You are being tested.

"I do believe that four years in the monastery have left their mark on him, but not in the way that your father expects. Salvator may have been trained in his youth to excel in political manipulation, but he left that world for a simpler one, in which casual lies have no purpose. I expect that he is on his guard now, well aware of the complex plots being woven about him, knowing that he must rise above them all if his crown is to be respected. It is a task he is clearly capable of—else another child of Danton would have claimed the throne—but you can be sure that it exhausts his spirit. So give him something genuine. Wear clothing you are comfortable with so that you can be yourself in front of him. Speak from the heart when you address him, and if diplomacy demands that you must downplay some particular subject matter, then turn his attention to something else. He knows the game and will follow your lead. But do not lie to him. Nor compliment anything about him or his kingdom that you do not truly admire. Vapid flattery is abhorrent to such a man, and those women who practice it today will be forgotten tomorrow." She leaned back in her chair. "While you, on the other hand, will offer him a brief respite from the whirlwind of courtly artifice, and he will remember you favorably for it."

Petrana smiled slightly. "That does rather go against what I have been advised."

Siderea shrugged. "By old men and dried-up maidservants. Whom do you trust in such matters?"

The girl bowed her head respectfully. "Your expertise is renowned."

"Expertise?" Siderea chuckled softly. "I do my research. That is all. No man is such a puzzle that a proper study of his background will not reveal some crucial weakness. But you must read the signs properly, else all your effort is wasted."

Leaning forward, she touched a finely manicured finger to Petrana's cheek, stroking the petal-soft skin. A pleasing blush rose up beneath her fingertip. "I will give you more lessons later," she promised. She was close enough now that the perfumed warmth of her breath filled the space between them. She could see the girl's nostrils flare as she absorbed it. "You will come and visit me and I will teach you all that I know. That is what you desire, yes?"

"Yes. Please."

"Then that is what you shall have." Siderea leaned back again, letting her hand fall to her side. "Now, if you will excuse me, I do have some other matters to attend to." In truth she had no real reason to leave, but it was always important to close such a meeting on the proper note. To leave her companion wanting more.

"Of course, Your Majesty." Petrana stood up quickly, and curtseyed respectfully. "I am grateful for the time you have given me. And all your advice."

At least the girl seemed more confident now. That was a good sign. A High Queen must be confident.

She definitely had promise.

It was not until Siderea left the encampment some hours later, heading back to her chamber in the palace, that she realized just what it was she had said.

You will come visit me and I will teach you.

A few days ago she'd had no future. Now she was planning for one. Did that mean there really was hope for her? Or was she just so desperate that she would embrace a stranger's lies in order to pretend that there was?

Either way, there was no denying that she felt a bit better now. And when she passed a Magister on her way to the

palace she gave him no more than a brief nod of acknowledgment. Anticipating how delightful the moment would be
when he and his kind finally realized they were not the only
game in town.

CHAPTER 9

"THIS ISN'T right."

Rhys scowled at the map in his hands then studied the land just ahead of them. The map clearly showed a narrow pass in front of them. The land didn't.

With a muttered curse he went back to his horse and dug out the leather-bound volume of maps that Master Favias had given them. In it were copies of every survey the Guardians had ever made of this region, including detailed drawings with notes scrawled all over them. The archivists were meticulous about keeping their work up to date, and made sure that every map was updated or replaced as soon as new information was discovered. One never knew when a particular quirk of geography might prove important, if not in guarding the Protectorates while the Souleaters were in exile, then certainly in the war that would ensue once they returned. The question of how to best move men and supplies from one point to another might well prove pivotal in that final conflict, and the Guardians intended to be prepared for it.

But.

According to all the maps that Favias had given them, there should be a pass right in front of them now, a low saddle between two high, sharp ridges. The reality was not nearly so accommodating. There was indeed one ridge to the left of them that more or less matched the drawings, and then another to the right of roughly the same proportion that ended in tall, jagged peaks. But the latter was a broken thing, with a deep gouge in its western flank, and beside it, filling in the pass, was a veritable wall of stone. A few scraggly vines and year-old saplings were struggling to take root in the scree along the lower slope, while the upper portion rose naked and forbidding, sharp stone fragments silhouetted against the early morning sky. Far too steep to climb comfortably and bad ground for horses even if it had been level. Not good. Not good at all.

"Earthquake, most likely." Namanti stood beside him, studying the map in his hands. "Common enough in these parts. Looks like it split a good piece off that one." She pointed to the broken peak, and with a wave of her hand traced the path of falling rubble. If she was right, nearly half the formation had collapsed.

Lips tight, Rhys nodded.

She looked down at the map again. "Do we have anything more recent than this?"

He looked through the book, checking the date in the corner of every drawing. The most recent map of this area was from a few years back; there had been no notes appended since. He could understand why Master Favias had been concerned about that. Every summer Guardians were sent out to check on all the Spears and to make note of any changes in the terrain surrounding them. Even if nothing were out of place it was customary for the survey teams to add a dated confirmation to the records, just to verify that the trip had indeed been made. The archivists made sure that all those signatures were reproduced, along with the original drawings, each time a map was copied. With Guardians traveling to different Protectorates on a regular basis, and each of them bringing news of recent inspections with them, it was rare that any change took place which all the archivists didn't know about. Doubly rare that a book like this would be lacking such important information as the closure of an important pass.

But it looked like no Guardian had traveled this route for a long time. Or if one had, he'd made no record of the fact.

It was hard to say which concept was more disturbing.

"It's cut off the western approach," he muttered. "Even if we try to circle around to the other side, there's no guarantee the route will be passable when we get there."

"What other option is there?"

Damn the Alkali, he thought, as he searched through the material Favias had given him. *Even their mountains are uncooperative.* At last he found a map of the region directly to the east of them, where a route that snaked along a long, narrow valley, parallel to their current route had been marked; it headed directly towards Alkali's westernmost Spear. "Here. This is the main Alkali approach route. What their own Guardians would be using, if they were doing their job. We should be able to cross over to it without too much trouble."

For a moment she said nothing. He could guess what she was thinking. The Skandir and the Alkali were not fond of one another, which was hardly a surprise given that they'd been rivals before the Spears fell. Now that the will of the gods demanded they cooperate with one another the Alkali and the Skandir were not openly hostile, but it was no secret that they were unhappy about the arrangement. Namanti had accepted this assignment in good faith, willing to act as interpreter if such was needed, but Rhys had no doubt that she was secretly nursing a hope that they wouldn't cross paths with any of the locals. As was Rhys, truth be told. Traveling the Alkali route increased their chances of doing just that.

But this far north they will all be Guardians, Rhys thought. *No one else has any reason to come up here. And Guardians we can deal with.*

"All right," she said at last. "Alkali route it is."

He glanced up at the sky, taking the measure of the sun. A single hawk circled high overhead, searching for prey along the barren landscape; otherwise the sky was empty. *Would that we had your vantage point,* he thought to the bird, *to see what lies ahead of us.* "We can still make good distance before nightfall," he assessed. The summer days were long in this region, which made traveling easier, though it was sometimes hard to stay asleep long enough to feel rested. It was said that there were places beyond the Wrath where the sun never set at all, but ruled the sky through all the day and night for months on end, followed by an unnatural darkness that smothered the icy land in blackness for just as long. No plants could thrive in such a place, nor any of the animals that depended upon plants for food. It was one of the reasons why the first Protectors had driven the Souleaters to the far north and imprisoned them there; bereft of sunlight on their wings for months at a time, lacking any living creatures to feed upon, they were sure to perish.

Except it hadn't really been a sure thing, had it? Because no sooner had the Spears fallen than the gods announced that mortal men must stand guard over them, and should hone their weapons against the day when the dreaded creatures would return. So what did the gods know about Souleaters that the Guardians did not? Not even Seers had been able to shed light upon that mystery, though generations of them had expended their life-essence trying to do so.

So much knowledge was lost in the early days, Rhys mused. *Would that we had kept the kind of records back then that we do now!*

Speaking of which . . . he drew out one of the writing tablets they'd brought with them, spread its wooden covers open to reveal the smooth wax surfaces within, and began to sketch details of the landscape before them. His bone stylus moved quickly, impressing images into one of the wax surfaces, along with explanatory notes. Archivists would translate it later into proper cartography with the proper labels. For now he just wrote down everything he saw that might be significant, and trusted to the experts to sort out what mattered from what didn't. Given how long it had apparently been since a Guardian had come to this place, he didn't want to risk leaving anything out.

With a final glance up at the sky—and a parting nod to the lonely predator circling high overhead—he mounted up once more, and he and Namanti turned their attention to finding a way across to the eastern valley.

———

It wasn't natural.

That was all Kamala could think, as she circled high above the wall of rubble that blocked the Guardians' path.

It wasn't natural.

Did they know that?

She saw them pull out their maps and their tablets as they tried to work out the best route to follow. If they'd been farther south she could have revealed herself to them and offered to help, but after her failure in conjuring edible food she was hesitant about working any sorcery this close to the Wrath. Besides, what explanation could she give for having followed them? No witch would be wasting her life energy for two people she didn't even know in the middle of nowhere. Did she want these two guessing at the truth and perhaps bringing back word of it to their respective peoples when this was over? *We met a female Magister up north. Don't know who she was or why she was there.* Word would get back to Colivar and his ilk soon enough, and then she would be hunted in earnest.

From overhead she could see that what had looked like a simple rock-slide from their vantage point was in fact something else entirely and she was pretty sure that no simple earthquake had caused it. Even without sorcery to call upon, her Sight could pick out the glimmer of power along the ragged edges of the shattered mountain. Something—some*one*—had set this all in motion. But why in this particular place? Judging from the maps that the two Guardians had consulted, there was only one answer possible. Whoever had blocked this pass hadn't just wanted to slow down any travelers coming from the west; he'd wanted to channel them to another road entirely, one that ran through the heart of Alkali territory.

Maybe if she hadn't used her sorcery on the Guardians earlier they would have realized that. But her own power had blunted the edge of their suspicion, and now that they were closer to the Wrath she didn't dare take the risk of trying to unweave that spell. Helplessly she was forced to watch as they turned their horses toward the only viable path, making exactly the choice that *someone* had intended them to. They couldn't hear the echoes of power that whispered from the mountainside as they passed by. They couldn't see the glimmering force that played along the edges of the shattered peak. While she—who could hear the whispers, who could see the signs—had no way to warn them of danger to come, unless she wanted to stand in their path in her human skin, waving her human hands and shouting out the news as they passed by her.

And who was to say they would take her advice even if she did that?

She followed them for a while, brooding as she rode the mountain thermals, wrapped in her own dark thoughts. Then, with sudden determination, she began to beat her wings against the wind, picking up speed. If she could do nothing else she could at least reconnoiter the land ahead of them. If she was right and they were heading into a trap, she should find that out. This close to the Wrath it was unlikely that anyone would be taking precautions against being spied on from overhead; the odds were good that if something was out there, she would be able to find it.

Back when she had studied with Ethanus she had learned to read maps, but those had been finely fashioned documents that she could study at her leisure, with sorcery to help focus her sight or clarify arcane markings if required. It was quite another thing to snatch a glimpse of a map from hundreds of feet in the air and then try to match it to a living landscape with no sorcery for assistance. Not to mention that whoever had shattered a mountain in order to herd visitors to the east might well have worked other changes in the landscape as well, and those would not have been recorded. But the long glen that Rhys and the woman were heading toward seemed a large enough feature on the map that even an ill-trained hawk should be able to spot it from overhead. Or so she hoped.

Keeping the Three Sisters in sight to guide her, Kamala headed eastward, scanning the ground below her for any sign of what Rhys had called "the Alkali route."

She was not disappointed.

From the air, it looked as though some vast blade had sliced open the earth; probably the locals had legends about ancient gods doing just that. The bottom of the narrow valley was flat and rocky, with the remnants of what must have been a sizeable stream running down the center of a gravel bed; it was but a trickle now, with puddles and pools on both sides of it, remnants of a wetter season. She saw no evidence of human passage along the bottom, but that meant very little; anyone smart enough to be using this place for a trap would be savvy enough not to leave behind any obvious sign of his presence.

Heart racing in anticipation, she rode a warm breeze up and over the eastern wall of the glen and began to examine the land beyond it. She thought she saw a narrow path worn into the brush, but there was no way to tell if it had been made by men or by beasts. The latter was unlikely, though. Most of the larger animals had abandoned this region long ago, and those that remained were too small in number to be leaving such a clear sign of their presence. Human, then.

She did not follow the trail directly, but wove back and forth across it in what she hoped was the normal manner of a hawk searching for prey. The last thing she wanted was for her quarry to wonder why a raptor was following his path.

And then she saw them. Their helmets caught her eye first, gleaming in the low-angled sunlight. Soldiers. There were at least half a dozen of them on her side of the valley, and now that she knew what she was looking for, she could catch the glint of several others on the far side as well. All of them carefully positioned so as to be invisible to travelers in the glen below them.

Bad.

The portion of the valley that they had chosen to keep watch over was steep and narrow; no horse would be able climb out of it easily. Farther ahead, around a slight bend, there was a blockade of sorts, and then beyond that, a path leading down from the summit of the western side that the guards might use to descend safely. And she remembered a place she had just passed by, about half a mile back, where the slope of one wall had been moderate enough that armed men might clamber down it safely, perhaps with ropes to guide them.

Very bad.

She had seen enough. Circling high over the heads of the waiting soldiers, she turned back toward the south. There was no longer any question of what she must do. If she wanted those two Guardians alive to serve her own needs, then she would have to turn them away from this trap. And there was only one way to do that with the power of the Wrath fouling her sorcery.

She flew back to the place where she'd originally entered the glen, calculating that before the day was out the Guardians would pass by that spot. She found herself a thicket of dense brush where her transformation back into human form could be hidden from sight and buried herself in the heart of it, just in case there were scouts wandering about. Her wings ached from the long flight, but the freedom they gave her would be sorely missed. From this place she could sense the baleful power of the Wrath coursing down the long glen, foaming like white water as it rushed southward. The kind of sorcery required to take on animal form was complex and risky under the best of circumstances and unthinkable in such a setting. Whatever challenges she faced from now on, she'd be facing them in human flesh.

Drawing in a deep breath, she tried to still the pounding of her heart. Reclaiming her human form would be risky here, but it should still be manageable. All living flesh had an innate preference for its natural form and would return to that form if sorcery did not actively prevent it from doing so. All she had to do was unweave the spell that had given her feathers and wings in the first place, and the rest should come naturally.

Quiet. Quiet. Reach inside for the power at the core of the soul. Stolen power, sweet power. Grasp it, claim it, use it to unweave the spell that has bound the flesh to a foreign form. Feel bone and sinew responding. Reshaping. Cast aside the sorcery that has made it into something other than human, make it free it to become what it once was—

And power burst forth from the center of her body, engulfing her in molten sorcery, unfettered by any human spell. Too much, too fast! Her body could not contain it. The flesh of her arms and legs began to liquefy, blood and sinew losing any semblance of cohesive form; fluid oozed forth from a twisted skeleton as convulsions of transformation wracked her frame. Feathers appeared upon her fingertips and then were gone as they switched helplessly back and forth from one form to another, unable to fix on a single identity. Kamala felt herself screaming, but her ears had melted and could not absorb the sound. Her skeleton cracked audibly as it expanded, contracted, expanded again. Her rib cage shrank to avian proportions around her human heart, strangling its beat, then expanded in a burst of pain.

You cannot survive without a viable body for longer than a few seconds, Ethanus had once warned her. *Never forget that.*

Gasping for breath whenever her lungs were coherent enough to allow for it, Kamala struggled to impose a human template upon the formless agony that was her flesh. Vital organs took shape at her command and then collapsed into themselves seconds later as raw transformative energy surged through them. Her heart managed half a dozen beats, then dissolved. Her lungs drew in two breaths, and then collapsed. Her limbs were clothed in skin one moment, and skinless in the next; red and blue veins snaked their way around her body, throbbing erratically as her heart struggled to reconstruct itself and then burst, spilling her life's blood out upon the ground.

Men who have their heads cut off have been known to blink for second or two afterward, Ethanus had taught her. *That is all the time you can count on having, once your body can no longer sustain you.*

The pain was fading now, but that was not a good sign. All the sensory input she had was beginning to fail her; her flesh was expiring. But the spirit within her, that had gotten her through First Transition and beyond, refused to die. Struggling to control the power, she forced her heart to take shape once more, and then poured all her force of will into it in one last desperate bid to reclaim conscious control of her flesh. With each surge of blood a portion of her indomitable will flowed outward into her body, and with it all the force of her human identity. *This is what the flesh must become!* she screamed silently at her body. *This is its natural state!*

And slowly, painfully, the tide of chaos receded. Inch by inch her body restored itself to what it was supposed to be; organ by organ it resumed its functioning. Finally, after what seemed like an eternity, she lay upon a bed of bloodstained grass, simply human. Simply breathing. Grateful to be alive.

After another eternity, she found the strength to open her eyes and look around her. Only that much strength, and then they fell shut once more. But she had seen what mattered.

It was dark. The sun had set long ago.

She needed no sorcery to know that the Guardians had passed her by.

She had failed to save them.

———

The sun was beginning to go down by the time Rhys and Namanti reached the valley floor, and the high ridge to the west of them cast shadows across the dried riverbed. For a moment they both pulled up their horses, considering the options.

It had been a long day. Rhys was used to riding long distances, but after the push to reach this point by sunset, even he was exhausted. Namanti's mount was starting to get edgy—edgier than usual, that is—and even a brief stint without a rider had not done much to sooth his nerves. All of them needed a rest.

Together the Guardians stared at the road ahead and considered what they had seen that day, why they had come.

"We could make another few miles before nightfall," Namanti offered.

Grimly, Rhys nodded. Human exhaustion was a compelling argument, but the duty of a Guardian was even more compelling. Something was wrong in this part of the world, and the sooner they figured out what it was, the better. He sighed as he kicked his horse into motion once more, hearing him snort in indignation at the order. *Soon,* he promised him. *The day is almost done. Have patience.*

They rode in silence through the lengthening shadows. The rhythmic creaking of leather and the jangling of tack took the place of conversation as the horses splashed their way through a succession of puddles, scattering frogs with each step. For reasons no one understood, amphibians seemed to be immune to the Wrath. Yet one more ancient mystery that the Guardians had failed to unravel.

As they rode on, the valley began to narrow. Its walls rose up higher and higher on either side of them, until the last rays of direct sunlight were blocked; the puddles ahead of them turned to sleek black glass that fractured into a thousand glittering droplets as their horses splashed noisily through them.

Time to call it a day, Rhys thought. It might take them a while to find a stretch of ground that was dry enough to camp. Better to do that before the last of the light was gone.

His eyes were focused on the ground ahead when they came around a bend and suddenly found their way blocked. They had to pull their mounts up short to keep from barreling into the obstruction; the pack horses following behind them neighed in confusion as they paused to take stock of the situation.

There was a tree lying across the streambed, effectively blocking any forward movement. It was a thick conical pine with long, close-set branches that appeared to have tumbled down the eastern wall of the valley. Rhys took note of the loose mound of dirt and rocks that must have come pouring down the valley wall when it fell. *Must have been a victim of the spring rains,* he thought. Such things were not unusual in this region, but they could be damned inconvenient.

It was too thick an obstacle for them to lead the horses through it, and too high for them to jump over it safely. They'd have to move the cursed thing out of the way. Muttering invectives, Rhys prepared to dismount and motioned for Namanti to follow suit. He hoped they could get this taken care of before full darkness fell.

But even as began to swing his leg over his saddle, he paused.

Something was wrong. He couldn't put his finger on what it was, just that it was . . . wrong.

He looked over to Namanti. She hadn't dismounted either, and from the look on her face she had the same sense of misgiving. It was a strange sensation, as though the mental capacity he needed to analyze the situation was there inside him, but he could not access it. He'd never felt anything quite like it before.

Then Namanti hissed softly. He followed her gaze to the roots of the fallen tree. It took him a minute to realize what she had seen, but when he did, his blood turned to ice in his veins.

They hadn't torn loose from the ground.

They'd been *cut*.

Before he could draw in another breath a crossbow bolt struck him in the shoulder, hard enough that it almost knocked him from his saddle. Namanti's Skandir mount squealed as it was struck by a second bolt, and he could see her struggling one-handed to keep him under control as she reached behind her for the small shield that hung from her pack. Hot pain lanced through his arm as he pulled his own horse quickly around, causing the next bolt to miss him by inches. Two more struck the leather packs strapped to his saddle. The shots were coming from directly above, which was bad, very bad. There was no way for them to go forward with the tree in their way, and no shelter in sight save the tree itself, which arrows could easily pierce. The only chance they had was to flee back the way they had come, but any ambush worth its salt would have made preparations to cover such a retreat.

They were trapped.

One of the pack horses squealed and went down; Rhys got his own mount out of the way just in time to avoid being carried down with it. Ignoring the molten pain in his arm, he pulled out the letter that Favias had given them and held it high. "We are Guardians!" he cried, angling it so that those high above them could see its seal. Every human being that lived in the Protectorates should respect such a sign. Even the bandits of the region gave Guardians a wide berth, either respecting their mission or simply because they feared retribution by a cadre of warriors said to be favored by the gods themselves.

But these men respected nothing.

With a sudden cry of defiance Namanti wheeled her horse around to face the valley wall and urged the beast into a run. At first Rhys thought she was going to try to get it to jump over the tree near its top, where the branches were smallest, in the hope it could carry them far enough to avoid being impaled when they landed. But then he saw that she was not heading for the tree but for the valley wall itself. There was one place where the slope was not as extreme as elsewhere and she was heading straight for it. He watched in fascinated horror as the massive beast leaped for the wall, momentum carrying him up the steep slope as his great hooves dug into the rocky earth, fighting for purchase. What the horse lacked in agility he made up for in raw power, forcing his way up the impossible slope step by step. Bolts struck him in the neck and shoulder as he climbed, and blood poured down his coat. Still he kept going, fighting for every inch, an angled ascent that would soon bring him over the top of the tree so that he could come down safely on the other side.

She's going to make it, Rhys thought in awe. Readying himself to follow suit if she did.

But then the powerful hooves missed their grip; clods of earth went flying in all directions as the horse scrabbled desperately for purchase. Namanti shifted her weight, trying to help the horse regain his balance, but his momentum was gone now, and gravity's grip was closing fast.

Gravity won.

The fall was not long, but it was brutal. Namanti was thrown from her saddle as the great horse struggled to right himself and was caught by one of his flailing hooves. Rhys heard the snap of bone as she landed hard amid the tree's sharp branches. A moment later the horse came down on top of her and Rhys heard a sickening thud as nearly a ton of horseflesh slammed into the ground . . . and into her. Where one of her arms was visible he could see that it was broken in two places. Her head was twisted over to one side, her neck at an angle that implied the worst.

With a cry of anguish, Rhys pulled his horse around and began a mad gallop southward. Never mind the ambush that might be waiting for him there; he would ride right through it if he had to. A terrible black mourning filled his heart, an utter determination to escape this trap and see that those who had brought Namanti down paid for it with their lives. If he had to brave a field of arrows to do that, then he would. There was really no other option, was there?

Then his horse carried him around a bend, and he saw what was waiting for him and he pulled up, desperately, feeling his horse skid on the wet gravel underfoot as he tried to stop himself in time.

In front of him was a line of men, all in identical helmets

and breastplates, and in front of *them* was a line of stakes, each one as thick as his arm and fashioned in a deadly point. Each stake was fixed in the ground in such a manner that it was angled toward him; any horse bearing down upon such an array would surely impale itself . . . and its rider.

I am going to die here, he thought in despair. He pulled out his sword from its saddle harness, but it was an empty gesture. He couldn't get close enough to any of his attackers to use it without killing himself in the process. Then, for a moment, the entire world seemed to slow down around him. The strange mental fog that had possessed him at the tree was suddenly gone; each thought in his head became crystal clear and focused.

It was said that one of the gifts of the *lyr* was that of a common consciousness. That a *lyr* who died in the service of the gods might bequeath memories of his death to his kin, for the sake of the greater battle. If so, then let that be his last act. He focused his attention on his attackers, drinking in every detail of their appearance—their race, their uniforms, their weaponry—inscribing it all as deeply into his memory as he could. Who was to say if the legends were true, or if his father's blood alone was enough to give him access to the *lyr*'s special powers? Time seemed to hold still as he studied his enemy, so maybe that was a good sign. Perhaps his death would not be in vain.

Then he heard a voice order, "Dismount!" and time resumed its normal pace.

He slid from his saddle, his left leg almost collapsing under him as it hit the ground. Apparently he'd taken an arrow in his thigh during his meditation; only now did he feel the burning sensation of it. With effort he managed to stand upright, gritting his teeth against the pain. They would see no weakness in him, he swore. He would not give them the pleasure of seeing weakness in him.

Several men stepped between the close-set stakes and walked toward him. His grip tightened on his sword, but he did not raise it up. They could easily have taken him down with a barrage of arrows with no risk to themselves; the fact that they were approaching him on foot instead might mean they did not intend to kill him after all.

Then something struck him on the back of the head, sending the world spinning. He tried to turn to face his attacker, but his wounded leg wouldn't support the twisting motion; a second blow landed as he fell to his knees in the stream bed. *Remember this,* he thought to the *lyr,* as his vision began to fail him. *Avenge me!*

The roar of blood filled his ears as a third blow fell, then there was only darkness.

CHAPTER 10

THE GREAT tent gleamed in the sunlight, brilliant white beneath a clear blue sky. From the central poles flew golden banners emblazoned with the two-headed hawk of House Aurelius, snapping in the wind as if to make sure that they were noticed. The side poles were topped with finials in the shape of a hawk taking flight; in the bright morning sunshine the polished golden feathers were almost too bright to gaze upon.

Of similar brightness was the company gathered inside. Male and female, young and old, there were too many in attendance to count, and all were dressed in their finest silks. Princes and nobles stood with their households, family and attendants, all clad in their heraldic colors, so that it was possible to judge the size of every retinue in a single glance. Their colors—and their wealth—dazzled the eye.

The only ones missing from the crowd—and they were notice-able by their absence—were the priests. The pantheistic faiths of the region were not happy about Salvator's elevation. Not happy at all. Who could predict whether this monk-turned-king might take it upon himself to cleanse the High Kingdom of its many temples? Danton Aurelius had been a ruthless man, sometimes even a brutal one, but at least he had steered clear of any interference with religion. *I have enough enemies already without pissing on the gods,* Danton used to say. Not so his son. Salvator's god was known to be a jealous, vindictive deity who acknowledged no rival to his power. The last time mankind had angered him he had brought the First Age of Kings to its knees—or so the Penitents claimed—and nearly wiped out the human race in doing so. The only thing that kept him from throwing his weight around now was the limited size of his following; a faith born of guilt and self-denial was limited in its appeal to the masses. But with a Penitent monk about to claim man's greatest empire, that picture could easily change. No, the priests of other religions were not happy about Salvator's elevation at all, and those who were attending the coronation stayed far to the back of the crowd and tried not to draw attention to themselves.

At one end of the tent was a grand dais, with two sets of silk-cushioned chairs flanking a single throne. Those who had been to one of Danton's formal courts would recognize that the throne was his, and would know that the personal emblems of all the ruling families of the High Kingdom had been worked into its intricate carvings. It was a large and heavy piece, as Danton had been large and heavy, and it stood upon a small secondary dais of its own, high enough above the throngs of guests that one could see it even from the back row.

It was time.

A line of trumpeters that stood the length of the great tent split the air with a sharp fanfare; immediately all chatter was silenced. A herald whose tabard was emblazoned with the double-headed hawk stepped up to the dais and struck his staff upon it three times, producing a booming sound that filled the sunlit space. He waited until all eyes were upon him, and then announced, in a voice that carried clear to the back of the hall, "Her Royal Highness, Shestia Aurelius Casca." Normally there would have been a long string of titles to follow that one, but today those other titles did not matter. Those who sat upon the royal dais were Salvator's blood kin, family of the deceased High King, and that was the only position that mattered.

Gwynofar's youngest daughter entered the hall from the far end on the arm of her husband and walked the length of its central aisle by his side. She had inherited her mother's delicate build but she held herself with a pride and a presence that would have made her father proud. The couple was halfway down the aisle when the next of the family was announced— Tesire Aurelius Signaste—who progressed down the aisle in her turn. As each of Gwynofar's daughters reached the royal dais their husbands released their hands, allowing them to ascend to their seats alone. Thus had the line of Aurelius done for centuries, when leadership passed from one generation to the next.

Watching her fourth son Valemar announced next, Gwynofar tried not to think about all the deaths that had made this cere- mony necessary. Tried not to remember the recent funerals for Danton, Rurick, and Andovan, and the three days of official mourning that followed. Hundreds of people had filed past the polished caskets, paying their respects. The bodies that had been repaired and preserved by witchery so that all three men looked as if they were sleeping peacefully and had not in fact died violently at the hands of their own family and guards. Salvator in his priestly attire had offered up prayers that were singularly moving, attesting to a kind of emotive power she had never known he was capable of. How Gwynofar had wept those nights, as all the sorrow of the past month overwhelmed her! How she had wished she might awaken to discover that the deaths of her husband and sons were no more than a bad dream and the Souleater's flight a mere fantasy!

But today all that mourning was to be set aside. That was part of Aurelius tradition, and difficult as it was, Gwynofar recognized the wisdom of it. Commoners might have the luxury of living in the past, but monarchs had to look ahead, to anticipate trouble and be prepared for it. Greater kingdoms than Danton's had fallen to ruin when their rulers forgot that simple rule. Or were perceived to have forgotten it.

Next to be announced were Gwynofar's own parents, the Lord and Lady Kierdwyn. Tall and elegant and effortlessly graceful, the couple smiled as they walked arm-in-arm down the aisle, finally taking their place to one side of the Aurelius brood. How different they seemed from Danton's hawk-faced get! Sometimes Gwynofar suspected that Danton had taken her for bride not only for the sake of political expediency, but to mellow the harsh features of his line.

And then it was her turn.

"Her Royal Majesty, High Queen Gwynofar Kierdwyn Aurelius."

Slowly she walked down the long aisle, her long formal gown and ceremonial mantle trailing behind her, a uniformed honor guard flanking her on each side. Heads were lowered respectfully as she passed by, but she looked neither to the right nor to the left, nor did she even glance downward as she gathered up her skirts to ascend to the dais. A servant stepped forward and lifted the mantle of state from her shoulders, stepping back into the shadows with it as she seated herself upon the throne.

The chair had been built to accommodate Danton's formidable frame, not such a slender build as her own, but she had enough nobility of spirit to fill its seat. Likewise Danton's crown seemed to sit comfortably upon her head, although in fact she'd had to add an inner band of quilting to make it fit. For this ceremony she could not wear her own.

And for that one moment she was, without question, the single most powerful person on the continent. High Queen in her own right, heir to the greatest empire in recent centuries. Tradition might require that one of Danton's male descendants claim his father's throne, but until that transfer took place, it was hers. A heady elixir, if a temporary one.

There was silence for a moment, tense and anticipatory, and then a stirring of movement at the back of the tent. No trumpets sounded this time, as thirteen monks in long brown robes walked up the center aisle, two lines of six with a single tall figure at the head of the formation. Brown wool brushed the ground around coarse hemp sandals, deep hoods casting faces into shadow, rendering the monks anonymous. As they approached the dais the twelve stopped walking, their leader taking a few steps more to set himself apart from them, much as they had done outside Danton's palace when Salvator had first arrived.

Heart pounding, Gwynofar stood. She had always found the rituals of state strangely intoxicating, and this one was no exception.

Gazing into the depths of the shadowed face, she pitched her voice to be heard by all those who watched. "Who comes before me to claim the throne of the High King?"

Slowly the figure reached up and pushed the hood back from his face. Many of those assembled had never seen Danton's second child in the flesh, and a rustling sound filled the tent as people craned their necks trying to get a clear view of him. "I am Salvator Aurelius," he said, "eldest living son of Danton Aurelius, and rightful heir to his kingdom."

The secondary dais lent Gwynofar enough height that she could meet him eye to eye. There was no warmth in her mien, nor any sign of affection, only a cold and formal dignity.

"You are the son of a king," she pronounced, "but you wear the uniform of another calling. No man can serve two destinies at once." Sternly she folded her arms across her chest. "The time has come to choose your path, Salvator Aurelius."

In answer, he reached up to the neck of his robe and began to unfasten it. Two servants hurried forward, one on each side of him, and as he opened the front of the voluminous garment they lifted it off his shoulders, allowing him to slide free of it, while a third removed his hood.

Beneath the brown woolen robe Salvator wore a long white gown, stark in its simplicity. Set against the peacock complexity of the court surrounding him, its plain white surface seemed to blaze with a pure and perfect light, drawing all eyes to him. He wore no jewelry save for a simple leather belt, also white, with the Aurelius hawk worked in gold upon the buckle.

Turning away from Gwynofar—and toward his audience— Salvator took his discarded robes from the servants, folded them reverently, and held them out to the monks.

"Bear word to your brothers that the priest they once knew as Father Constance has left their fold, and is no more. The vows of a monk that he once offered in your company are exchanged this day for the vows of a prince, and for his oath of service to his subjects."

The two monks nearest him bowed their heads respectfully as they received the discarded robe. Then the small company of brothers turned as one and left in the same manner they had come: silently.

Salvator turned back to face his mother. Despite her attempts to maintain a stoic expression, Gwynofar could not wholly mask the glow of pride in her eyes.

Reaching up to her head, she lifted Danton's crown in both hands, slipping out the band of quilting as she did so. "Accept the crown of Danton Aurelius, and with it the burden of leadership."

"I do so accept it," Salvator said. And because she was standing a level above him, she was able to place the crown upon his brow without having to strain.

She reached about her neck to remove the newly-embroidered stole that she wore—it was long enough to brush against her ankles—and placed it around his neck instead. The gold-encrusted embroideries were all the more dramatic for being set against the brilliant white of his gown. "Accept the stole of Danton Aurelius, and with it the lessons of history."

"I do so accept it," Salvator said.

She motioned to the servants who had removed the mantle from her; they draped it over Salvator's shoulders now and fastened it with golden cords across his chest. "Accept the mantle of Danton Aurelius, and with it the charge of law."

"I do so accept it," he responded.

Lastly, she held out her hand for Danton's sword of state and a servant gave it to her. Its jeweled sheath glittered as she held it out to Salvator. "Accept the sword of Danton Aurelius, and with it the authority of war, which carries with it the hope of peace."

"I do so accept it," he said, and he took the sword into his own hands.

How like a king he looked in that moment! She wished that Danton could see him thus. He would have been proud.

Finally she stepped away from the throne itself. "Accept the throne of Danton Aurelius," she said solemnly, "and with it, sovereignty over the High Kingdom, and all its lands, people, and projects."

He stepped up to the dais, turned, and sat down in the great carved chair. "I do so claim my father's kingdom," he said.

Only one more thing was needed now.

"The heirs of Aurelius will judge your claim," she told him.

One by one, his brother and sisters came and knelt before him, acknowledging his sovereignty over their father's kingdom. One by one they publicly relinquished any claim they might have had to Danton's throne, and offered him their support and loyalty. For most of them it was merely a formality, but she did watch Valemar closely, alert for any sign that he thought his monkish elder brother should have left the field of politics to him. But there was nothing. Last but not least the Lord and Lady Kierdwyn came forward, and though they did not kneel, and owed him no subservience, offered formal recognition of their grandchild in his new role.

It was done.

Fanfares blared from both sides of the great tent. The herald announced the new High King in his finest voice. Salvator took it all in as if he had spent the last four years preparing for this moment, and in that moment he looked so much like his father that Gwynofar had to fight to hold back tears from her eyes. *Not yet,* she told herself. *Soon you can seek out some more private place. Time enough then to weep.*

And then came the final announcement. Those vassals who wished to offer their obeisance might do so now; those allies who wished to receive formal acknowledgment of their treaties might also come forward. It was a public call for acknowledgment of the new monarch and it might have been a risky maneuver under other circumstances. But Gwynofar had arranged in advance for a goodly number of nobles to respond properly, so there was little danger of embarrassment. By the time a dozen princes had stepped forward to acknowledge Salvator's new rank, it would be too public an insult for anyone else to refuse to do so. Whoever might have his doubts about whether a religious hermit could rule Danton's kingdom effectively would hold his peace for now.

Nonetheless she watched alertly for a few key faces, and not until the prince of Corialanus had come forward and offered his respectful congratulations did she dare to take a deep breath.

He is going to be all right, she thought, feeling a knot in her chest loosen for the first time in weeks. *Everything is going to be all right. . . .*

The sky overhead was black with only a single moon inhabiting a field of stars. All over the field surrounding the palace lanterns were being shuttered, bonfires banked, torches extinguished.

The long day was finally ending.

Salvator's face ached from the unaccustomed stress of controlling his expression for hours at a time. His mind ached from trying to remember all the names and faces he had met since his elevation. His body ached from ending four years of celibacy without so much as a parting nod, and then diving right back into the pool of temptation as if he had never left it. Dozens of noble ladies had been presented to him by well-meaning brothers, fathers, and regents in the hope he would find them appealing when the time came to contemplate his marriage options. Half of them had dressed like courtesans, in the hope he would find their jewel-bedecked assets tempting, and the other half were covered up from neck to ankle in the hope that they would be viewed as morally respectful choices. Not one of them had a clue what he was really about.

There had been one who stood out, though. A pretty little thing from one of the Free States—what was her name, Petrana?—who had seemed genuine enough. In the midst of the political maelstrom, with factions on all sides of him fighting to manipulate him, such a presence was refreshing. Of course it might well be a studied subterfuge, as so much in the world of royal politics was but still, she was an intriguing prospect. And a tie to the Free States could be advantageous for him, provided their informal confederation did not fracture in Danton's absence. His father had never had access to those ports, or their attendant markets, though he had coveted them. Perhaps marital diplomacy could accomplish what war had failed to do.

But there was no reason to rush any of that. The more mystery there was about what sort of woman he might choose for his queen, the more his allies would be attentive and his enemies would be kept off guard. Patience in this case was the most effective strategy.

Soon enough he would retire and be released from this exhausting day. It was a respite long overdue for an ex-monk who had spent the last four years rising and setting with the sun. In the morning, of course, it would all begin anew. All sorts of festivities would be hosted by one delegation or another, as befitted a crowd that had traveled so long and so far to get here. And Salvator could not afford to relax—genuinely relax—for a single minute of it. The future of his empire depended upon the impression he made in these few days, on men who were watching like vultures for any sign of weakness or inconstancy. A heavy burden to bear.

But there was still one piece of business left for this evening, unless he mistook that game. And so he had left the halls of his palace, where guests still wandered in twos and threes, laughter resonating between the ancient stone walls, to seek a more private place, atop the highest tower in the palace complex. Long ago armed sentries had kept their watch here, with the land spread out bare and vulnerable on all sides, so that no enemy could find shelter from their scrutiny. Then the threat of war had moved to distant places and a forest had been allowed to take root. Now the land was bare of trees once more, burned to the ground by a servant of corruption. When the last torch was extinguished and the last guest departed, there would remain only that stark reality.

The land itself prepares for war, he thought darkly.

The soft whisper of silk on silk alerted him to another presence on the rooftop. He turned to face its owner.

The Witch-Queen of Sankara appeared surprised. Of course "Forgive me, Your Majesty. I did not know you were up here." Her voice was soft and musical in cadence, artfully pleasing to the ear. "I did not mean to disturb you."

"You do not disturb me," he answered. *How could you do that, when I came here to draw you out?*

She was dressed in layers of silk tissue the colors of sunset, with a pattern of delicate gold flowers embroidered across the outermost gown. The soft fabric hinted at the shape of her body with pleasing subtlety, teasing the eye with the curve of a breast or a thigh briefly as the night breeze pressed against it, then falling free once more and concealing all. It was hard to resist doing what masculine instinct would prefer and fix his eyes where they would stand to catch the finest view when the next breeze stirred. Instead he met her eyes. They were wide and black in the moonlight, twin pools of black crystal. A few drops of belladonna could provide such an effect, if nature fell short.

"There is enough view here for two to enjoy," he said, and he made room for her to stand beside him.

She had been introduced to him earlier in the day, of course. One introduction among the dozens that mattered most. Even then she could not help but stand out from the crowd. Her deep copper skin was muted now by the moonlight, but in the bright light of day it had gleamed with exotic splendor as she moved through the crowds with an innate sensuality that defied all attempts at male understanding. The flesh stirred to see her walk without the brain understanding why. Such a woman required no décolletage to draw men's eyes to her, nor any of the other sartorial affectations that passed for flirtation among her less talented sisters. Indeed, Salvator thought that once or twice he had seen a flicker of disdain in her eyes for women who had clearly invested their hopes in such mechanisms. It was a strangely cold look, with a fleeting hint of something darker behind it, peeking out from behind the civilized mask. An intriguing insight.

She had not made any attempt to talk to him at length during the day, or to capture his attention by any other means. Hardly a surprise. In the midst of the day's festivities she had been surrounded by vulgar distractions, like a fine jewel in a gaudy setting; now her only competition was the moonlight.

"You are most gracious," she allowed, bowing her head ever so slightly. Something tinkled softly beneath her skirts as she joined him at the parapet; a hidden bit of jewelry making its presence known? His instinct was to seek it out, but he kept his eyes focused carefully upon her face. No reason to hand her such an easy victory.

She looked out over the landscape and sighed. "Such a beautiful view. I wish I could have come up here earlier. It must have been magnificent at sunset."

"We have both had our duties to perform today," he said. "Perhaps in the future there will be more time for such simple pleasures."

One delicate, plucked eyebrow arched inquisitively higher. "You do seem to be taking all this rather in stride, considering how much your world has changed in a fortnight." She laughed softly. "I think I would still be numbed by shock, myself."

"Ah, but a king does not have the freedom to be numbed by shock. Or a queen, I should think."

"True enough." The dark eyes sparkled. "Perhaps that is the ultimate test of royalty. To be surprised by nothing." A subtext purred beneath the words: *You are doing quite well so far, my king.*

The unvoiced compliment pleased him more than it should have. Was there witchery behind it? Or simply the natural power of feminine flattery, contrasted against four years of isolation? *She would not be willing to sacrifice her life's essence for such a simple spell,* he guessed. And: *It would be a point of pride for her, to accomplish her seductions without witchery.*

"There have been many tests of late," he said quietly. Not trusting himself to say more.

She smiled and looked out over the landscape, gracefully offering a change of subject. "I admit I did not expect the land to be so well recovered, so soon. Quite an impressive sight."

"We were fortunate," he said, following her gaze outward.

Only a few torches were lit now, leaving only the moonlight to illuminate the vast stretches of land. Sparks of light kissed the high points of tents and banners as moonbeams fixed upon them, shivering slightly as a few stray clouds passed overhead. "There was rain nearly every day, a rare thing in summer. Plants can grow quickly if Nature is accommodating."

"Ah, see now, if you had not told me that, I would not have assigned Nature the credit. I would have said to you that your witches were skilled, and that their offerings spoke well for your throne."

A shadow passed over Salvator's face. "I would not order any witch to expend his life-essence for so trivial a thing. Nor would I accept such a gift, if it were offered."

"You are an unusual man, then. Most kings welcome power however it is offered."

"Most kings are not Penitents," he said quietly.

She turned back to look at him. For the first time, he sensed hesitation in her. Was it a genuine emotion or simply another serving of polished artifice? She moistened her full lips with her tongue as she considered, then said, "I hope it would not be . . . out of line . . . to ask a question of you? Regarding your faith?"

"Not at all." He smiled faintly. "Many have done so this day. Many more will in days to come." He did not add that few of the questions had been respectful, though they had all been voiced respectfully. His faith was an alien thing to most of his guests, and the presence of monks wandering among the gaily-clad peacocks of his court, watching silently as vain young nobles proudly fluffed their tails before their fellows, was a sober reminder of that. Not that it had stopped the peacocks from staging their displays over and over again. Or kept them from asking about Salvator's years in the monastery, with the same distaste as one might ask a prisoner from a dungeon how many maggots were in his daily bread. "Please speak freely."

She smiled at him. "You are most gracious, Your Majesty." A slender hand moved forward as if to touch him lightly upon the arm, but then paused, and fell gracefully down by her side once more. It was far from the first time today that a woman had hesitated before touching him, but unlike the other incidents, this one seemed to be born of respect for his faith, rather than fear of it. A refreshing change, even if the move was as likely to be carefully staged as all the others.

"Please," he said. "Call me Salvator."

She inclined her head ever so slightly, acknowledging the offer. "Only if you will call me Siderea in turn."

He nodded. "So be it." With a sigh, he leaned back against the parapet. The gesture appeared casual, but it had as much to do with physical exhaustion as any social statement. "So what do you wish to know about my faith, Siderea? Since it seems for once we will not be interrupted."

She leaned against the parapet beside him; the soft silk of her gown lay fluid along the curves of her figure. "It cannot have escaped your notice that we are the only two monarchs on this continent that eschew any formal contract with Magisters. Certainly it is common wisdom that no man can claim a throne without them." She circled one finger slowly about a stray tendril of her hair as she spoke. "There are those who have questioned my judgment for my own choice, though it is no secret that I maintain social ties with various Magisters so that they tolerate my eccentricity. Yet you do not seem the type to flatter and fete the Magisters in order to remain in their favor. You simply . . . reject them. I must admit that I am curious about why you would choose such a high-risk course." She smiled. "You understand . . . I thought I was quite alone in my prejudices, until you came along."

Salvator nodded. *Aye, we are kin in that much, whatever other differences there may be between us.* "The Magisters represent power without price. As such they are a corrupting influence that disturbs the natural order of things. The Penitents believe they were sent to mankind as a temptation after the last of the Souleaters were gone, to see if we had learned the proper lessons from that invasion. Apparently not, for the world was then subjected to another century of darkness." Salvator's expression grew solemn as he remembered the details of that darkness. Far too disturbing to be shared in such a casual exchange. "It is said that during the latter half of the Dark Times the Magisters destroyed all of man's greatest works, and killed all the leaders who would have led him back into the light. But for sorcery, the Second Age of Kings would have begun much earlier than it did."

"And do you believe that is what truly happened?"

He shrugged. "History tells us that our ancestors lived in darkness for generations after the Great War, long after the last of the Souleaters were gone. Have you ever heard a better explanation for it?"

"No," Her voice was soft, her tone thoughtful. "No, I have not."

"I believe there is not a night that goes by that they do not hunger to be restored to the kind of unfettered power they once enjoyed. If not to wield it openly, then by virtue of their influence over mortal kings. And if we become corrupt enough to allow them that influence . . ." He drew in a deep breath and held it for a moment, trying to settle his spirit; if he became so strident that he drove her away, that served no one's purpose. "Perhaps that is why the Souleaters have returned now. Perhaps it is a warning. At any rate, I for one will not serve the Magisters' agenda."

"That is a very brave stance," she said quietly.

He shrugged stiffly. "It takes no great courage to risk one's life in service to one's god. I would be more afraid of a life lived without faith, that had as little direction as the life of an insect." He shook his head. "But forgive me, your words inspire darker reflections than I think you anticipated—"

"It is your passion," she said softly. This time she did put a hand upon his arm: a light touch, like the wing of a butterfly. "You need never apologize for passion. Not to me."

He forced himself not to look in her eyes. There were too many secrets there, swimming in the shadows; a man could get lost in them. "So what about you?" he asked "Why do you take such a risk?"

She laughed gently; the jewelry hidden under her skirts tinkled softly as she shifted her position. "Oh, I am afraid I have not nearly so compelling a tale to offer. Nor so exalted a cause. I simply find them insufferably arrogant. When I first came to my throne they tried to tell me how to run my country, and it did not sit well with me. Now they offer the same words to me as 'friendly counsel,' but I am not beholden to them as other princes are, so I do not have to listen. Or obey."

A faint smile spread across Salvator's face. "Now you see, *that* is true courage." He bowed his head ever so slightly. "I salute your spirit, my lady."

On sudden impulse, he reached out and took her hand in his. Raising it to his lips he kissed it, his eyes never leaving hers. A subtle perfume rose from her fingers, warm and pleasing. Her skin was like silk.

She did not move closer to build upon the moment. That intrigued him. A common seductress would surely have done so, taking his gesture at face value, pressing the moment's advantage. This one was playing a much more complex game.

Or perhaps it is not the game I thought it was.

Somewhere in the distance a bell sounded, tolling the hour. Midnight. The sound seemed to disperse the moment's magic. He held her hand a moment longer, and then reluctantly released it. Her fingertips stroked his palm as they withdrew, leaving streamers of fire in their wake.

"So much to do in the morning," she said softly. Regretfully.

He chuckled. "Now you see, that is where a retired monk has the advantage over a lady of the court. My day's work has always begun at dawn. To sleep even an hour longer than that would be . . . unimaginable decadence."

"Well, then." She reached up to his face, her index finger tracing the line of his cheekbone, feather-light. Despite his best intentions, it made his loins tighten in response. "Shall I wish you decadence, then? Or would that offend against your faith?"

Using a silent prayer to settle his spirit, he managed to keep his voice steady. "Only if I may wish you the same," he said, hoping the words sounded more natural than they felt. Suddenly he was out of his element, and no longer sure of . . . anything.

But she did not press the moment's advantage. Or perhaps she did not notice it? He offered her his arm and she took it, and together they walked to the narrow door that led back downstairs, into the tower. Her walk was poetry in motion. How many months had she practiced it—how many years—before it became that fluid, effortless glide? It was impossible not to watch. Impossible not to feel his blood stirred by watching.

She paused at the door, as if considering something. Her finger stroked the weathered oak thoughtfully.

"Corialanus will be trouble," she said at last. "You have won them over by your manner, at least for today, but they will surely test you in the future. It would be good for you to have a friend in the south, who might learn of trouble when it was still in the planning stages and give you fair warning of it."

He nodded solemnly. "Such a friend would have my eternal gratitude. And such favors as I might render in return."

She did not say more, but glanced back at him with a silent, secret smile, then slipped through the door and was gone. Her perfume took a few minutes longer to dissipate, and he did not move again until the midnight breeze had carried the last of it away, cooling his flesh as it did so. As much as his flesh could be cooled.

You have passed your first test of temptation, he told himself. *Take strength from that knowledge. Build upon it.*

But it was a long, long while before he could stop thinking about her.

QUICKENING

The passion of the beast is in man's heart; let no man give it sovereignty

Lest his soul turn aside from all things human, and the music of the angels be forgotten.

Book of Penitence
Meditations 24:1,2

CHAPTER 11

NYUKU REMEMBERS:

Cold. Knife-edged white sheets of pain: wind-driven, flesh-scoring. They lanced through the boy's soft flesh and sliced to the center of him until his heart felt like a jagged icy mass, threatening to shatter with each and every heartbeat.

He could see the broken body of one of the sacrifices dangling from the talons of the god flying right ahead of him. She had struggled briefly when the god had first grabbed hold of her, but terror and cold had finally robbed her of life; now she dangled like a shattered doll from her captor's claws, her hair dusted with frost, her eyes glazed and lifeless.

That would be his fate soon enough if they did not bring him to some kind of shelter, the boy thought, shivering violently. But at least he still felt cold. He was savvy enough to understand how important that was. It was when you stopped feeling cold that you knew you were about to die. Supposedly the gods had designed Man thus so that he would have a warning sign when he overstepped his bounds, and a chance to retreat to safety before the frigid wrath of the gods snuffed out his life.

The problem was that in this situation, there was no retreat possible.

The priests taught that the world had been created out of ice and snow; both land and sky were originally frozen solid. But the gods had discovered that such a place could not sustain life, and every attempt they made to populate it failed miserably. Finally a god named Kuta had stolen a piece of the Sun and buried it deep within the earth, so that the land directly above the Sun Stone thawed and water ran freely there. Then Man was created, along with all the plants and animals that required sunlight and flowing water, and they were given that place as a home. And so the world was created.

The boy had always been skeptical of such tales. But now, looking down upon his world from the vantage point of the gods themselves, seeing with his own eyes how the Land of the Sun gave way to endless fields of glittering whiteness in every direction, he could believe that the entire world had indeed been dead once, and that if mankind's precious fragment of the Sun ever expired, it would become dead once again.

It should have been a humbling thought, but it wasn't. There were gods who tended to the sacred fires of the Sun and men who served those gods. It was whispered that those men carried sparks of the Sun with them so that they might brave forbidden places where the heavenly light never shone, and that they even rode on the backs of the gods as if they were true companions to them, rather than humble servants. The boy had never been sure those tales were true until today, but now that he had seen it for himself at the caldera he could think of nothing else.

Some men rose above the normal status of men to share in the freedom and the power of gods.

He was determined to be one of them.

A sudden gust of frigid wind burned his eyes and he shut them for a moment, struggling to blink away the pain. When he opened them again the world below him had changed. A thin line of jagged gray protrusions now jutted up from the whiteness, like the half-buried bones of some long dead animal. But then his captor dropped down toward them—so suddenly that he thought for one heart-stopping moment that he had been released and was falling—and he realized the "bones" were in fact a line of jagged hills, robbed of scale by the featurelessness of the white plain surrounding them. Clearly that was their destination.

He saw another god swoop low, carrying a man upon its back. Or at least he thought it was a man. A set of small wings from the god's shoulders had folded back over the figure, encasing it in a glossy, blue-black cocoon. At first glance it did not look like a man at all, but rather like a part of the god's own body. Only when he kept staring at it could he make out enough features to figure out the truth.

The boy shivered.

Below him now he thought he could make out the faint throbbing glow of a sacred pool nestled between two of the hills. Warmth. That meant warmth. Then a black vein of open water came into view, not unlike the narrow channels that surrounded his homeland, when the ice began to crack in the spring. *A piece of the Sun has been buried here as well,* he thought in awe. Who would have imagined that there was another such place in the world? Certainly the priests had never hinted at it. Did they know about it? Or was he the first of his people to learn of this secret place?

He watched in amazement, the cold forgotten, as the ice and snow beneath him gave way to naked earth, and then to sparse patches of vegetation surrounding a steaming lake. He could see no herd beasts, but surely they were there. And wild beasts, hungry to feed upon those herds.

And men?

In a rush of blue-and-violet wings, one of the great creatures landed by the edge of the lake. Others followed. Each kept apart from its fellows, roaring belligerently if another god came too close, baring razor-sharp teeth in warning. The boy had heard killer seals roar like that when rivals crossed their paths in the mating season; it was a sound of mindless rage, primal and terrifying. He shivered with fear at the thought of being set down in the midst of such a scene, even as he hungered for the warmth of a Sun Stone beneath his feet again.

But his captor had other plans. Though his god banked down low toward the lake at first, he pulled up suddenly before reaching it, and veered sharply to one side. The movement was so sudden and unexpected that it drove the breath from the boy's body. Even as he struggled to take in a lungful of frozen air, the sky about him suddenly went dark; in his weakened and distracted state it took him a minute to realize that his captor had flown into a gap in the hillside, broad enough in its entrance to accommodate the great wings. They passed into the depths of a vast cavern, its floor covered with patches of mud and loose gravel. Then the great talons opened at last and the boy fell roughly to the floor. Sharp pumice bits scored his shoulder and arm as he landed on them. For a moment he lay there, breathless, feeling the dull heat of his blood seeping out through dozens of lacerations. Dimly he was aware of his god bellowing as it left the cavern, no doubt some sort of challenge to the gods below. How like beasts they sounded! He would have expected gods to have a language that was more harmonious, more . . . civilized.

Then he realized suddenly that the ground beneath him was warm. Likewise the air was no longer painful to his lungs, but robbed of its wintry chill by what seemed a fragile, tentative heat. He drew in a deep breath, feeling precious warmth seep into his flesh. His fingers and toes throbbed in pain as they buried themselves reflexively in the warm pumice grit beneath him, almost as if they were creatures independent of his will, seeking the Sun Stone buried far below. For a moment he was aware of nothing save a purely animal hunger for warmth. In that moment he would have buried himself in the gravel from head to toe if it had been deep enough, and been happy to bleed for it. He lowered his face to the ground, eyes closed, oblivious to anything but the life-giving heat beneath his cheek.

"What is this?"

It was a male voice that broke his reverie, in an accent so thick the boy could hardly understand the words. "Are they sacrificing boys now?"

"Does it matter?" a second voice challenged him. "Food is food."

"Food stays out there," the first man said gruffly. "This one has been brought in here. Why?"

The boy blinked and looked up, trying to focus his wind-burned eyes on the men that suddenly surrounded him. There were maybe a half a dozen of them in all, and as he watched, still more stepped forward from the shadows of the great cavern. They were not like the men of his own people in appearance, nor even like each other, but a mismatched group of individuals, as foreign to one another as different species of animals. One was tall and thin and pale of skin, with yellow hair falling in long, tangled locks about his anemic features. Another was almost black of face, with eyes that stood out like white stars in a midnight sky, and a thick layer of black fleece in the place of hair. Another had eyes without lids, only slits in his face through which black pupils shone. The boy blinked as he twisted around to see them all, trying to absorb their strangeness. Yet though they were all different in size, shape, and coloring, they had one thing in common that chilled the boy to his very core. Their eyes. Different shapes and different colors and sizes, some of them human in form and some more lizardlike, but all of them without exception were haunted, hollow things. As if their owners had gazed upon something so terrible that their very spirits had been sucked out of them, and what was left was not quite human. The eyes of living men did not look like that, the boy thought, shivering. Were these men ghosts? Was this the place of eternal warmth where the spirits of the dead were said to reside? If so, was he being allowed to see it as a living man, or had he died in the cold skies during his journey here, so that his spirit truly belonged in this realm?

"He cried out to be brought to us," a third man announced. He was a lanky creature with sharp, protruding joints and equally sharp movements. His tight-fitting garments glistened with an oily sheen that shimmered blue and violet, neither fabric nor sealskin nor any other substance the boy could identify. The others were dressed in different sorts of garments—some sleek and long and cut from a single piece, others fashioned out of smaller fragments, cobbled together in seemingly random array—but as his eyes adjusted to the shadows of the cave, the boy could see that all their clothes were made of the same curious substance. It looked like it was the same color as the skin of the gods, as if the great creatures" wings had been wrapped around these men and then fixed in place. Or perhaps these were not truly men at all, he thought, but some supernatural amalgam of human and god, and the blue-black coverings were not clothing at all, but a kind of composite skin. Perhaps these were half-breeds, who might in time transform themselves fully into gods. Or maybe they were the cripples of their kind, the failures, who acted as servants to those who were fully transformed, and in return were permitted to share the heat of their caverns, but could never grow their own wings. His mind buzzed with possibilities, too terrible and too wonderful to contain.

Is this what you want to become? an inner voice whispered. *Truly?*

He thought of his village, struggling against the twin demons of cold and darkness, always so close to losing the battle. Of young girls mutilated so they could serve as sacrifices. Of the great Sleep that would come over the village sometimes, a weakness so terrible that crops would rot unharvested on their stalks and herd beasts would waste away while the villagers lay in a mindless stupor, too weak to care about anything. And then when the great Night came his people would die in droves for lack of food stores, and death would rule the land.

Heart pounding, the boy forced himself to his feet. Whatever these creatures were, it was unthinkable that he should display weakness before them. "I have come to serve the gods," he told them. And then, his heart beating thunderously, he added, "Like you do."

For a moment there was silence. Then one of them—a stocky man with long red hair, who wore a breastplate made up of coarse patches of god-skin—threw back his head and roared with laughter. "You wish to *join* us?" He slapped his thigh. "To join *us?*"

The flush of shame that came to the boy's cheeks was a hot thing. "Yes."

"Ambitious," the dark-skinned man assessed. His eyes gleamed like fresh snow against the eerie blackness of his face. "And spirited."

A stocky and bald man spat on the floor in disgust. "Iceborn brat. He knows nothing of the world save the legends we gave to his priests . . . and you know what those are worth. A sheep come to stand among the wolves, bleating to be one of them."

"We were once sheep ourselves," another said quietly. This one was a tall man, olive-skinned, with long black hair as sleek and as glossy as wet sealskin. "Or do you forget?"

"We are more than that now," the bald man growled.

"Are we?" The words were softly voiced, but the boy sensed the challenge behind them. "Are we really?"

In a distant part of the boy's mind—the one square inch not frozen solid by ice or fear—he suddenly realized that the men had spaced themselves evenly about him, and that each was very protective of the space surrounding him. Whenever one of them moved too close to another, his neighbor would warn him off with a low growl, and the intruder backed quickly away. What would happen if he didn't? Would they roar at each other like the gods were doing down by the lake? Fight each other as beasts would fight, until one was subdued or even destroyed?

"What is your name, boy?" It was the black man asking.

He drew himself up as proudly as he could. The heat from the ground had finally reached his bones, so at least he was no longer shivering. They must be very close to where the Sun fragment was buried, for this cave to be so warm. "Nyuku," he said. "I am called Nyuku."

"So the food has a name." The bald man snorted. "Now are you satisfied?"

"We need new blood," said a man whose hair and skin were

as pale as moonlight. Nyuku could see blue veins in his cheeks, pulsing as he spoke. "You know that."

"Weak as a sheep, this boy is." The speaker had red hair, bright red, like the skies at sunset. "Fit for the cooking pit, nothing else."

"We have a clutch approaching its first season." The speaker this time was a thickset bearded man with broad features not unlike those of Nyuku's people. His voice was quiet and even in the manner of one who is secure in his own authority and need not prove it by volume or coarseness. "And no one to offer to the victor. Why? Because the girls given to us are weak, and for every living child one of them bears for us, five more are lost in the womb. And the ones that survive are too timid to please the ikati. So we have lost half a dozen candidates already. Do you wish to lose more?" He looked at the boy as one might look at a hunk of seal meat. "This one is strong, and almost old enough for his seed to have value. Maybe he will strengthen our stock."

"The iceborn are food," the redhead muttered. "Nothing more."

The bearded man's face darkened suddenly in anger; he took a step forward into the circle, and such was the sheer force of his presence that the boy instinctively moved backward to give him room. "Is this *your* colony?" he demanded of the redhead. His voice was not loud, but it filled the chamber with unexpected force. "No! It is *mine.* So if you mean to challenge me for primacy . . ." he turned slowly so that each man must meet his eyes in turn; Nyuku could feel the energy crackle between them like lightning as one by one they met his gaze, then turned away. ". . . Do it now. Otherwise, *hold your tongue.*"

For a moment it seemed the entire world was frozen. Waiting.

The boy held his breath. Somewhere—thousands of miles away it seemed—one of the gods roared its defiance. But none of the other gods answered it, and after a moment or two it became clear that the men in the cave were not going to answer this man, either.

The redhead was the last to look away. "If that is your will," he muttered. There was cold hatred in his voice, like that of a dog on a choke leash, forced to heel.

"It is."

The redhead drew in a deep hissing breath and the muscles in his legs twitched, as if making ready for combat. For a moment all was silent, within the cavern and without, as the two men took each other's measure. Then the moment passed. The redhead released his breath and nodded stiffly. The bearded man looked about the circle, clearly ready to confront anyone else who had issues with his leadership. But whatever the power was that had almost caused these men to turn on one another, it seemed to have passed.

Nyuku drew in a shaking breath as the leader of the god-riders turned to him. He sensed what was required and lowered his eyes as a dog might, acknowledging its master, but inside his chest his heart pounded wildly in defiance. *Someday I will be the one who commands these men,* he promised himself. *And they will all lower their eyes to me . . . including you.*

"We were all tested once," the leader told him. "We chose to come here, then chose to remain here, to become something other than *human*. It pleased the gods that we did that, and they felt that we had proven our right to stand among them. But the sons that we breed for them now have never been tested. They are born to this fate, they do not choose it, and the gods do not accept them."

Suddenly he came to Nyuku and grabbed him by the hair, pulling his head back until their eyes met; the man's gaze was a dark and terrible thing, more like that of a beast than a human being. Everything inside Nyuku screamed to pull away, to wriggle out of the man's grasp even if he had to leave half his scalp behind to do it, to prove to him that he would not be so easily humbled but he held himself still, heart pounding wildly, sensing the nature of the test that was taking place. The other men had given way to this one. If he did as well, he would not be allowed to join their number. That much was plain.

For a long time the bearded man stared into his eyes. Finally he released him, pushing him back with a force that sent him skidding across the knife-edged gravel.

"This boy's been tested in coming here. That's a choice, isn't it? Maybe the ikati will respect it." A dark, twisted smile flickered across his face. "Or maybe they will decide he's food after all, and devour him whole."

Between gritted teeth Nyuku said "I am not *food*."

The bearded man waved his hand dismissively. "That is for the gods to decide. And best they do it when they are not hungry, yes?" He glanced meaningfully toward the cavern's entrance, drawing Nyuku's gaze in that direction.

He means the girls, Nyuku thought. *The sacrifices.* A wave of sickness rose up inside him but he swallowed it back, hard, unwilling to let these men see any sign of weakness in him. Did he care so much for the girls of his village that he would mourn their deaths? Or was he willing—and able—to let go of his former life, and embrace this one with a full heart?

It was a test. Everything here was a test.

"Let them decide," Nyuku said steadily.

He could feel energy crackling between the men, sparks of

unvoiced frustration and defiance. One wrong move and they would turn on their leader. One foolish word on Nyuku's part and they would tear him to pieces.

Then: "So be it," the bearded man proclaimed at last, and his tone left no room for protest. "The gods will decide."

A hot flush of triumph coursed through Nyuku's veins. He gritted his teeth with the effort of controlling his expression. Once he had dreamed of joining the servants of the gods. Now he hungered to rule them.

He must never let the current leader see that in him, he knew. Not until he knew how to make the dream real.

Thus it begins, he thought with satisfaction.

CHAPTER 12

TUKKO HATED the Wrath. He hated being near enough to feel its baleful presence. He hated having guard duty close enough to it that any time he tried to relax, nightmares would cling to his mind like beetles to dung. You'd feel a bug crawling inside your helmet, or catch sight of a snake out the corner of your eye, or even think you heard your commander whispering bad things about you as you came on duty, and you'd bear it as long as you could without moving, just in case it wasn't real, but then eventually you'd become convinced it *was* real, and you'd pull off your helmet, or jump back as the snake lunged for you, or ask your fellow guards what was being said about you . . . all for nothing. The Wrath conjured enemies where there were none, and it made them seem believable. Even big strong warriors like Tukko were not immune.

Yesterday had been different. For the first time since taking up this cursed post, they'd actually gotten to *do* something. Mind you, Tukko didn't really understand why they had attacked the two Guardians, but orders were orders. *Stop any foreigners who are traveling along this route*, Anukyat had said. Truth be told, it felt good to fight something that could bleed and die as opposed to the usual illusionary phantoms. It made him feel like his job was worth doing, which he hadn't felt in a long time.

Now those two strangers were back in the Citadel, their dead horses were in the process of becoming the evening meal, and life was getting back to "normal." For Tukko that meant a long ride to various checkpoints, delivering what had to be delivered and collecting reports of anything his superiors should know. Not a glamorous job by any measure, but Anukyat said it was important, so it must be done. Something about things being "finely tuned" and progressing "like clockwork." Whatever that meant.

He heard a moan in the bushes.

His hand went reflexively to the short sword he wore at his belt as he pulled up his horse. There weren't a lot of animals around here and there shouldn't be any people other than his own company. Everyone from the fight yesterday had returned home unharmed—not a big surprise when you figure how neatly the trap had been sprung—so if someone was wounded, it wasn't one of his people.

Holding his horse steady, he strained his ears and thought he heard the sound again.

It sounded like a woman.

Slowly he urged his horse forward, one step at a time. The sound seemed to be coming from up ahead, behind a thicket of brush. The land surrounding it was mostly open, with few obstacles to conceal enemies. He looked carefully around, just to make sure. You couldn't be too careful in this region.

Finally he reached a position where he could see what was making the noise.

It was a woman.

She wore nothing but the scraps of what might have been a shirt, which did not do much to hide a rather shapely body from his view. Her limbs were dirty and there was blood streaked on her forehead, as if something had struck her there. She had her arms wrapped about her knees and she lay on her side moaning softly, not even aware of his presence. Every now and then a tremor of fear ran through her, the way it might with an animal that was trapped and had nowhere to run.

For a minute or two he just watched her, looking up periodically at the surrounding landscape to be sure that there were no surprises coming. Guard duty had prepared him for many things, but not this. Finally he dismounted, and when she still seemed to be unaware of his presence, cleared his throat.

Startled, she looked up. Her green eyes filled with fear and she began to scramble away from him, muttering things that sounded like pleas for him not to hurt her.

He could not see anyone else nearby, and there was no sign of anything that might explain why she was here. But as she moved he caught a flash of dried blood on her thighs, which combined with the fear in her eyes to draw a pretty clear picture for him, of one thing at least. Whoever had left her here had used her pretty harshly before departing.

"It's all right," he said quietly. He wasn't used to calming terrified women, and didn't quite know what tone of voice to use for it. "I won't hurt you."

Shaking visibly, she regarded him as a field mouse might a hungry hawk. But at least she stopped crawling away. "Where am I?" she whispered.

He gave her the common name for the northern Alkali mountains. Those who dealt with the Wrath on a daily basis usually called it much worse things. "Where are you from?"

"Rayt," she whispered hoarsely. "I was traveling with a trade caravan . . . that is . . . there were bandits . . ."

"Not from here, though." No caravan in its right mind would travel this close to the Wrath.

She shook her head. "No, they . . . farther south . . . they brought me here afterward." Then her nervous hands came in contact with the short ends of her red hair and hers eyes widened. "They cut off my hair! Oh, my gods, they cut off my hair . . ." She began to weep.

He tried to focus on the bigger picture, rather than those portions of a rather shapely body which were revealed as she shifted her position. The Lord Protector would not be pleased to hear that there were bandits using these mountains for cover. This woman might have information that would be of value to him. If so, then bringing her back and delivering her personally to his superiors was the order of the day. But there was only one way to do that—well, two, if you counted the option where she rode the horse and he walked back—but it was a long journey and he didn't like to be out in the mountains after nightfall.

"Listen," he said, pulling out the cloak that he kept with him for night jobs. The mountain evenings could be chilly. "I'm going to take you somewhere safe, you understand? But you will have to ride with me to get there." The green eyes grew wide and fearful. He tried to look directly at them, and not at the taut, full breast that had slipped free of its cover. "I won't hurt you, I promise." There was a growing tightness in his groin now, which was making it hard to think clearly.

She bit her lip for a moment, and then, very hesitantly, nodded.

She let him help her up, wincing in pain as she moved.

He handed her the cloak and turned away while she wrapped herself up in it. Then he mounted his horse, shifted forward in the saddle as far as he could, and gave her a hand up behind him. She had some trouble mounting—*probably used to riding sidesaddle,* he thought—but then finally managed to get onto the horse behind him, legs astride. The sudden heat of her thighs against his own was disconcerting, and the fact that this new position pressed his groin up hard against the forward curve of the saddle didn't help matters. Her hands wrapped about his waist from behind, her breasts a warm pressure against his back. Thank the gods she couldn't see what effect she was having on him. Given what he guessed her kidnappers had done to her before discarding her in the middle of nowhere, that would scare her off for sure.

They'll have use for her information at the Citadel, he thought as he focused his thoughts on that, rather than on the soft heat of the woman behind him. *I'll be rewarded for finding her.*

He did not even hear the whisper of his sword being drawn from its sheath until it was too late.

———

Water engulfed Rhys, cold and choking, dragging him back from darkness. He tried to draw in a deep breath but another wave broke over him and he breathed it in. Coughing, he struggled to turn himself over so that gravity would help him empty his lungs, but his hands were fixed behind his back and he couldn't manage the maneuver. All he could do was gasp for breath helplessly, like a beached fish, turning his head to the side when he finally began to cough the fluid up.

No more water, then. Only pain, and a pinpoint of light before him. The back of his head felt like someone was pounding on it with a hammer. His left shoulder and right leg were on fire, and each time he tried to move them, fresh pain lanced through them.

"You awake now?"

Someone kicked him roughly in the side, which made his body jerk away, sending new spears of pain shooting down his wounded leg. But his vision was starting to come back to him now, and he could see the three men standing above him. One was holding an upside-down bucket, no doubt the source of his recent drenching. He seemed to be enjoying Rhys' discomfort.

Then one of them saw his eyes focus and ordered, "Get him up."

The other two grabbed him by his arms and lifted him roughly to his feet. The pain from his wounded shoulder nearly made him pass out again. One of the men reached out with a length of cloth and wiped it once across his face, quickly. Possibly he had meant to remove the spittle that Rhys had coughed up, but in its wake the cloth left streaks of grime that did not smell good. Hard to say which was worse.

"He'll see him now," the third man said, and he nodded for the other two to drag Rhys along. Along the way he cast the bucket aside, and Rhys could hear it land noisily on some stone surface. There was the sound of water dripping in the distance, but he could not tell where it came from.

He tried to walk, but his right leg had stiffened from its wound and he found it hard to move. They neither slowed nor stopped for him, but merely dragged him along at the same inexorable pace, whether his feet were under him or not. It hurt far less if they were under him, so he struggled to keep up.

Where am I? he thought desperately. His surroundings offered no clue. The narrow, windowless stone corridor they were dragging him through might have been in the lower levels of a keep anywhere in the known world, and there was no telling what manner of building stood over it. But they could not have taken him very far in his current condition, he told himself. And Magisters did not like to go close to the Wrath, so it was unlikely that anyone had provided sorcerous transportation to move him. Which suggested that he was still in the Alkali Protectorate, and probably not very far from the place where he'd been taken down.

I am a Guardian, he thought, as his wounded arm was jerked half out of its socket by an impatient escort. *No man has any reason to harm a Guardian.*

But he no longer had Favian's letter of passage on him, and after what had happened in the glen, he wasn't all that sure they would respect it if he did.

They dragged him into a large room that was so brightly lit by comparison to where he had been that he blinked his eyes in pain as they adjusted. His two escorts forced him to his knees, and one of them grabbed him by the hair and forced his head to bow down before releasing him. He was in no condition to argue with them. There was a single figure at the far end of the room; as Rhys raised up his head once more it walked slowly toward him. As he struggled to get his eyes to focus properly he could hear booted footsteps and the jingle of spurs.

"Identify yourself," a harsh voice commanded.

The nebulous dark shape in front of Rhys finally resolved into the figure of a man: short, broad-shouldered, physically powerful. There was no mistaking the Alkali cast to his features. Glancing about the room, Rhys saw that all the other men present—and there were only men—were of the same type. Black-haired, ruddy-skinned, with broad features and narrow, almond-shaped eyes, the Alkali had not changed in appearance since the day the Wrath had fallen. Or so it was said. Certainly they disdained to take mates from among the other peoples of the north, claiming that "foreign blood" was inferior to their own.

"My name is Rhys." His voice was raw and rasping; it was hard to make the words form properly. "Rhys sera Kierdwyn." Normally he would not lie about his heritage—normally there was no need to—but he was suddenly wary of admitting to his royal ties. *Sera Kierdwyn* meant only "servant of Kierdwyn," and was a name that any man who served the royal famly might claim. "I am a Guardian of the Wrath," he said. Even in this battered state, there was pride in his voice as he spoke the title.

"Indeed. A Guardian. How fortunate for us." The man's tone was dry. "I take it you believe the Alkali Protectorate does not have Guardians of its own. Otherwise our loving brothers to the west would have no reason to enter our territory. Yes?" He waited for a response, and when Rhys offered none his voice grew hard and cold. "Why are you here, Guardian of the Wrath? Tell me honestly, for I can read the truth in a man, and lies will cost you dearly."

He drew in a deep breath, trying to steady his nerves. *You are innocent of any wrongdoing,* he reminded himself. "The Guardians of Kierdwyn feared that the Wrath has been weakened. They saw that their brothers in Alkali had gone silent. They sent us here to seek out the reasons for those things."

"Indeed. How benevolent of them. How . . . paternal." The black eyes narrowed; it seemed to Rhys they burned with hate. "And so they sent a Skandir into the heart of our territory, with no word of warning to precede her. For our own good, of course. Is that the story?"

A sudden lump in Rhys' throat made it hard for him to speak. "Namanti . . . is she . . ." He could not finish the question.

"The Skandir bitch? Dead, and lucky to be so. Her interrogation would not be half as pleasant as yours, I assure you."

He shut his eyes for a moment. *Don't let him see how much that affects you. Don't let him have that power over you.* "We carried a letter," he said hoarsely. "With the seal of Kierdwyn's Master of the Guard. In accordance with custom—"

"Where?" His interrogator spread his hands wide. "I see no letter." He looked to the men who had brought Rhys into the room, now flanking him. "Do either of you recall this person having a sealed letter?"

"I do not," one said.

The other shook his head. "Nor I."

Rhys hung his head. He didn't want his captor to see the fury in his eyes.

"You see, Rhys nas Kierdwyn? I warned you not to lie to me."

He wanted to scream out his indignation, he wanted to curse this man before all the northern gods—how dare he treat a Guardian of the Wrath like a common criminal! He wanted to—

And then it sank in what had been said.

Shaken, he looked up. His interrogator was holding a leather-bound book open in one hand and was leafing slowly through the pages. Favias' maps. "You signed and dated your notes, you know. Such a well-trained Guardian. I am sure your Master would be quite proud of you." He snapped the book shut. "So you are the son of a Lord Protector, but not one officially acknowledged as such. Very interesting."

There was nothing he could say that would make the situation better, so he said nothing.

"That would make you half *lyr*, would it not? Possessed of the gift of the gods. Whatever that is supposed to mean."

Rhys drew in a deep breath, fighting to stay calm. "If you know that I am *lyr*, then you know why I was sent here. If one of the Spears has been damaged, you will need someone to repair it—"

His interrogator slammed the book of maps down on the floor, silencing him.

"You really do not understand, do you?" He lowered himself in a crouch until his eyes were level with Rhys' own. "*There are no gods,*" he whispered fiercely. "All the things you were ever taught about them were *lies*. All the missions you have undertaken in their name were hollow tasks. Meaningless. The Wrath is the work of men, nothing more, and if you understood the source of its power you would vomit up every lesson you'd been forced to swallow. An entire lifetime of lies." He stood again; his expression was dark. "The gods—if there are gods—are surely laughing at our gullibility."

He's mad, Rhys thought. He glanced at the other men, who seemed unshaken by the tirade. *They're all mad.* Most likely the Wrath was responsible for that. The Guardians knew how to resist the power of that ancient curse, but few men outside their ranks would be able to do so. Spend enough time within range of its baleful magic and you might begin to believe all sorts of crazy things—including dark fantasies like the one this man had just described.

"Please," he said. Struggling to keep his voice calm, to remove even the faintest hint of confrontation from his tone. "Let me speak to your Master of the Guard. Give him my books, let him read my notes, let me explain to him why I was sent here. He knows our customs and our purpose. He will know how to judge me."

The interrogator stepped back. His black eyes narrowed. "Do you know who I am, Rhys nas Kierdwyn? Do you have any idea where you are?"

Rhys hesitated, then shook his head.

"I am Anukyat," he pronounced. "Master of the Guard for the Alkali Protectorate. So now you know."

Rhys opened his mouth, but no words would come. The room seemed to spin about him.

"Take him back," Anukyat ordered the men standing behind him. "Lock him up. We may have use for him yet, or at least for his *lyr* blood . . . now that the gods no longer have any use for him."

The two Alkali Guardians lifted Rhys by the arms again, and dragged him away.

———

"Hold, there!"

The guard approaching the Citadel gate was not mounted, but walking beside his horse. The animal was limping badly and clearly was in no condition to support a rider. A makeshift bandage around the guard's head was covered with blood, obscuring much of his face and covering one eye; where his skin was visible it looked as if it had been ground into the dirt. He, too, was limping.

"More fighting today?" The sentry asked. The guard shook his head, then winced and put a hand up to his face, as if trying to hold back the pain. "What, then? Took a fall?"

The guard grunted and nodded. "Cursed scree," he muttered hoarsely. Then he bent over coughing, disappearing behind the bulk of the horse. When he stood up again, the sentry could see a trickle of blood coming from his mouth.

"Best see the chiurgeon right away," the sentry said, and waved him on in.

With a curt nod, the injured guard and his horse limped into the courtyard. After a moment of looking around, he located the stables and led the animal in that direction. A young boy in a well-worn tunic ran out to greet him as he unlatched his supply pack from the saddle and slung it over his shoulder. The same for his weapons. The boy waited patiently until he was done, then wordlessly took hold of the horse's reins and began to lead the animal gently away, clucking reassurances to it as they went.

They would find the rock wedged into its shoe soon enough, Kamala thought. Hopefully it would look like an accident.

Positioning the heavy pack so that it would shield her face from view, she studied the courtyard for a moment and then, having gotten her bearings, headed toward the shadows behind the barracks.

Rhys' cell was dark and damp and barely three paces across in either direction. Not that he was likely to be pacing any time soon. A heavy iron cuff on his ankle secured him to a chain that was fixed to the back wall of his prison, with just enough room to allow him to lie down on a moldy straw mattress or to occasionally piss in the metal pot they had provided. Even so, the turnkey who pushed his food and water through the slot in the door, just far enough for him to reach it, did so with obvious unease. Evidently he thought that Rhys was dangerous.

It could have been worse. They'd chained his arms behind his back when the chiurgeon came to examine him, which had made the man's inspection of his shoulder exquisitely painful. Two burly guards had pinned him down for the examination itself, as if they were afraid that even in his weakened state he might overwhelm them. But at least the poisons in the shoulder wound had been drawn out and a poultice applied, and the same had been done to the deep puncture in his thigh. They might hate him here and they might fear his strength, but for whatever reason, they clearly wanted to keep him alive.

At least for now.

Exhausted by the day's events, he lay back upon the dank mattress and wished he could fall asleep. He knew that he would need all his strength for whatever came next, so he shut his eyes and did his best to relax, despite the throbbing of his wounds. And maybe he even did sleep, on and off. Maybe, in the dim twilight of his cell—lit only by a few weak beams of lamplight that squeezed through the barred window in the door—he passed in and out of sleep without realizing it. Certainly nightmares could hardly be worse than his current prospects.

What in the name of the gods had happened here?

For a thousand years now, the Guardians had served the Protectorates. A thousand years of training to fight an unseen enemy, of searching high and low for every scrap of ancient lore that might help prepare them for battle, a thousand years of willingness to brave the most fearsome curse known to mankind if the gods required it of them. Ten centuries of utter dedication by men and women who answered to no greater politics, served no foreign purpose, acknowledged no distraction. Their neutrality was sacrosanct, their honor was legendary, and, as a result, there was no place in the Protectorates where they were not welcome.

Until now.

There are no gods, the Master of the Guard had told him. *You serve a lie.*

What could make such a man abandon his faith and turn him against his own kind?

Show me the cause, Rhys prayed to his gods. *Teach me how to address it, that the Guardians may remain strong, and we can serve you as you intended.*

With a sign he shut his eyes, exchanging one pain-filled darkness for another.

And while you are at it, please get me out of here.

The new prisoner made Kato nervous.

He shouldn't have. He'd been a turnkey for ten years now, first in the keep of a southern lordling with a penchant for imprisoning his political enemies, now here in the Citadel. The job was much the same. Keep the doors locked. Make sure the prisoners were fed enough food to keep them alive, if not to keep them comfortable. Call for help if anything unexpected happened.

But.

You weren't supposed to put Guardians in prison. He knew that.

You also weren't supposed to question a Master of the Guard. Not in public, not in private, not even in the darkest recesses of your own head. Ever.

So when those two rules came into conflict, what were you supposed to do?

Don't think about it, he told himself, as he made his rounds, peering into the grated slot in each door, checking to be sure each prisoner was present and alive. The latter mattered more with some than with others. *Just do your job*. In truth the place was nearly empty, despite its impressive capacity. Prisoners didn't last long this close to the Wrath—a mind already weakened by confinement and fear couldn't stand up to that malevolent power for very long—so anyone of real value to Master Anukyat was generally sent south for safer keeping. Maybe that would happen to this Guardian, eventually. Maybe he'd be gone soon, and Kato would not have to worry about him anymore.

With a sigh he settled down onto the rough-hewn bench he had placed opposite the Guardian's cell and poured himself a cup of warm ale from a ewer on the table beside him. Anukyat's Citadel was located at the farthest reaches of the Wrath's power, which meant that a sane and healthy man could get through a day well enough, but Kato didn't envy the soldiers who had guard duty farther north. Sometimes he thought he heard them screaming in their sleep. Or maybe that was himself he heard screaming, in the grips of his own Wrath-born nightmares. Either way, this was a cursed region for sure. If you asked him (not that anyone ever did), the ancient Alkali warriors who had abandoned the Citadel in the first place had had the right idea.

On the other hand, working in the shadow of the world's most fearsome curse meant you were paid generously, which did a lot to compensate for the nightmares. Or so Kato told himself.

Sighing heavily, he took a long, deep drink of his ale. He was so lost in his own reflections that he almost didn't notice the footfall on the stairs.

Almost.

He put his cup down and looked up at his visitor, half expecting to see some messenger from Master Anukyat, or perhaps the man himself. No doubt he would want to look in on his newest charge, Kato thought. Make sure he was alive and all that.

But it wasn't Anukyat, or his messenger. In fact, it wasn't a man at all.

She was tall and barefoot and dressed in nothing but a man's linen shirt, open down the front. Her legs were impossibly long and the hem of the shirt, falling to her upper thighs, seemed barely enough to cover her. Where the neck gaped wide on one side the inner curve of a breast was visible, its ruddy tip teasing the eye through the thin white fabric. And her hair! It was a bright red, the color of fire, and wild in its style, as though she had only just rolled out of someone's bed.

He tried not to stare at her, but failed miserably. He did manage to shut his mouth after a moment, but that only left him speechless.

"You are Kato?" the apparition asked him.

Dumbly, he nodded.

She smiled and began to walk toward him. The sight of her breasts swaying beneath the thin fabric made all the blood rush to his groin, leaving his brain high and dry.

"Someone upstairs said your job was tense and you would appreciate a little . . . relief. Is that true?"

"Who—who said that?" he stammered.

She took a step closer to him, and put one hand against his chest. He could smell her closeness as her index finger traced a line down his doublet, down to the ties of his codpiece. She pulled at the end of one tie until it released, then slid her hand inside the garment. "Now that's a secret. Let's just say you don't owe me anything for this—it's all been taken care of." She stroked the swollen length of him, up and down, an agonizing rhythm. "Someone must like you a lot," she whispered, closing her hand about his balls. The pleasure of it was too much to bear; he closed his eyes and moaned as he reached out for her—

The hand inside his codpiece suddenly grabbed his flesh and twisted it. Gasping, he tried to push her away from him, but then she brought up her knee into him, hard. Pain exploded in his groin, and from there spread in waves to every inch of his flesh. It was suddenly hard to breathe. Impossible to control his body. He doubled over with a cry—

—and the ewer came down upon the back of his head. Once. Twice. Blinded by pain, he could not protect himself. The third blow finally deprived him of consciousness, which seemed a mercy; he lay still, crumpled in a heap at her feet, his hands still clasped about his wounded pride.

She looked down at him for a moment, prodded him with her bare foot once to make sure he was really unconscious, and then set the ewer aside. A quick glance about the chamber revealed where his keys were hanging, on a large brass ring by the fireplace. She went to fetch them, peering into each prison cell as she passed. When she came to Rhys' her eyes lingered just long enough to meet his own, then turned away.

Rhys had witnessed enough of Kato's seduction through the small window in his cell's door to catch the gist of what had happened, if not all the fine details. Holding his breath, he waited to see what she would do next. Clearly she meant to free someone here, and if that someone was not him, then he was ready to bargain with her.

But it was to his cell that she returned, and after throwing the bolt open, she entered the gloomy space.

"Rhys nas Kierdwyn, I assume?"

He tried to stand in a dignified manner, despite his shackles. "I am. And you are—"

"For now, a friend." She came over to where he stood and knelt down by his feet. One after one she tried the keys on her ring in the locks of his shackles. "We can make proper introductions later."

After three tries she found the one that fit the lock; the iron ring on one ankle fell open. The same key worked on its mate and he was free at last.

"Now bring him in here." She nodded toward the sleeping turnkey.

Rhys' leg wound throbbed as he hurried to collect the body, but he was pleased to see that the leg still supported him. The wound in his shoulder was not doing as well, and when he tried to lift the turnkey up he discovered that his arm wasn't strong enough for such action yet; he had to settle for dragging the heavy body back into the cell where she was waiting for him.

She knelt by the side of the body and, in a methodical and efficient manner, stripped it of all its clothing. The body beneath was dirty and rank, with an ugly bruise already rising on its groin. The woman ripped the hem of the man's shirt, tearing several long strips of fabric from it. When she began to tie the man up with them, Rhys crouched down by her side and helped. Soon they had the naked man trussed up like a pig for feast, with a gag in his mouth that would muffle any cries he tried to make. When that was done, the woman shackled him in Rhys' place, then threw the threadbare blanket that Rhys had been given over him. In the darkness of the cell, one would have to look closely to see that anything was amiss.

"Wait here," she said, and she left the cell. He waited. A moment later she came back with a bundle of clothing in her arms, and handed him the top half of it. A uniform, with several armored pieces wrapped in fabric.

"Don't talk," she warned, as he opened his mouth to ask her questions. "Just dress."

Silently, he did so.

She had brought him a guard's uniform, identical to those that his attackers had worn. She had one for herself as well. If she hadn't warned him to silence he might have made some comment about how unlikely it was that she could pass for a man, but when she slipped on the leather cuirass and buckled it tightly at the side, he was glad he hadn't. The stiff leather compressed her breasts and added bulk to her waist, and her broad shoulders added an additional note of verisimilitude. Up close the illusion would never hold, but from a distance, or in shadow perhaps it would work.

"Here." She had something in her hand. A stick of charcoal? "Stand still." She spat on her finger and rubbed it along the black stick, then applied the color to his eyebrows.

"Is that necessary?" he asked.

"Have you seen any blonds in this place?" She cocked her head as she regarded her work, and he noted that her own eyebrows had been darkened as well. On the woman the change seemed less unnatural; he had not even noticed it before.

Spitting in her palm, she added a bit of charcoal and then mixed it between her hands. The result she patted along his jawline; the shadow of a beard? You're taller than the locals as well, you know. Try not to make that too obvious."

He watched as she put her own half helm on, tucking her hair up into it so that its fiery red color was hidden. He did the same with his own. Though he could not imagine they would actually pass for locals, the attempt at subterfuge was comforting.

The blanket stirred a bit. A soft moan sounded from under it.

"I hope you're strong enough for traveling," she said. "We have a lot of distance to cover tonight if I'm to get you far enough south to send you home.."

His breath caught in his throat. "Home?"

"Yes. Kierdwyn, right? I'm guessing that a day's travel can get us far enough that I can send you directly. All we will have to do is evade pursuit until then . . . and I have some tricks that will render our trail all but invisible to morati eyes."

"Witchery?" he asked.

Her eyes sparkled in the shadows. "You might say that."

A witch could send him home, all right, though she'd have to give up years of her life to do it. Transporting living creatures was one of the most strenuous magics in a witch's repertoire, he'd been told. Which was why Guardians relied upon mundane vehicles of travel whenever possible.

But even if she were willing to make that sacrifice—even if she could get him home—that left so many questions un-answered . . .

"I need to go back north—" he began.

"I don't think so." She rolled up the turnkey's clothes and her own discarded shirt into a tight bundle and tucked it under her arm. "The road to the north is swarming with soldiers. Unless you want a repeat performance of what happened to you last time. . . ." Her voice trailed off suggestively. "At any rate, my job is to get you out of here and bring you home, and that is exactly what I'm doing. So unless you want to walk all the way to Kierdwyn, we have to get far enough from the Wrath that I can transport you safely. That's at least a day's ride due south, by my calculations. I hope you're up to it."

He wanted to argue with her, and for a moment almost did. Didn't she understand what was at stake here? The Wrath was unstable, a damaged Spear might be the cause, and now it looked like the Guardians of Alkali—or at least their leader—were insane enough to attack any foreigners passing through their land. If Rhys left this region now, it might become so well fortified later that no Guardian could get through at all. Surely that mattered more than his own personal safety!

But he saw the warning in her eyes, and said nothing. *We will argue about it later,* he promised himself, *when we are somewhere safe.*

"Very well," he said. Whoever she was, she was risking her life to save his own; that was worthy of respect as well as gratitude. "Lead on."

They locked the cell door behind them, and she added the ring of keys to her bundle. "If all goes well, we will have until the end of your jailer's shift before this is discovered. If it doesn't ... well, less than that." She picked up the lamp from the turnkey's table. "Follow me."

He did so.

Up one turn of the staircase she reached into what looked like a decorative alcove, felt about a bit, and finally opened a door. He would not have guessed it was there if she had not shown it to him. Beyond it was a narrow passage, with large, irregular blocks of rough-hewn stone for walls; the look and feel of the place was different from any part of the building he had seen so far. Almost like a different place entirely.

"Servant's passage," she whispered. "Part of the original structure, or so they tell me."

"They?"

She looked back at him; her lips twitched briefly into

something that was almost a smile. "Servants and whores will talk to their own kind," she said. "Especially if the listener has sympathy for their trials. I, of course, am the embodiment of feminine compassion."

"Is that how you got the uniforms?"

Now she did smile, albeit briefly. "No, that was simple thievery. Not much of a challenge, I'm afraid. This place is rather isolated; I'm sure no one ever thought a common thief would wander through, so they took few measures against one." The smile faded. "I couldn't get to the armory, though. Not enough time. We'll have to make do with what we've got."

She led him through the narrow passageway, following what appeared to be a set of directions she'd memorized; frequently she had to stop and concentrate to remember the next bit of it. Who had given her such detailed information? A servant angry at his masters who saw a chance to work mischief? A slave seduced by her charms who dreamed of winning her favor? A soldier down on his luck aching for the kind of relief that only a woman's caress could offer? He had seen her work her wiles on the turnkey and wouldn't put anything past her.

And then they reached the place she was looking for. She felt about the wall until she found the latch that had been described to her, then shuttered her lantern. No telling what was on the other side.

Slowly, carefully, she eased the door open. No sound came from the room beyond. No light shone from any nearby source, though a faint ambient glow was coming from somewhere. She nodded to Rhys and then slipped through the opening, adjusting her lantern so that a tiny beam of light might be released. Only that, and no more.

He followed.

It was hard to make out what manner of room they had entered, for the lantern only illuminated one detail at a time. As she turned it from one side to another, Rhys saw a large trestle table, walls full of hanging pots, and at the end of the room, a fireplace as tall as a man with a cast iron rack inside it. A kitchen? She swung the light up, illuminating a handful of dead birds hanging from the ceiling, along with slabs of salted meat. "Get a few of those," she whispered, as she laid the turnkey's shirt on the table. He was just tall enough to pull them down. There were shelves full of supplies at the other side of the room, and they raided those as well. It was clear the woman had been here before and had already decided what she would take; the operation was smooth and silent, and when they were done, the stolen stores were wrapped into a tight bundle and tied securely with a strip of the turnkey's shirt.

"You have two choices now," she whispered. "We can sneak out of here by the back way, and I think we can get out safely enough without anyone noticing us, assuming the information I was given is accurate. . . ."

"But?"

She looked at him. "It will not get us horses."

He bit his lip, considering. Under the best of circumstances he would not like to travel this region on foot. And these weren't the best of circumstances. Within hours, if not sooner, the rogue Master Anukyat would realize that he had escaped, and would surely mobilize every Guardian in the vicinity to hunt him down. The only hope they had was to get far enough away before that happened. On horseback, that might be possible. On foot . . . he shook his head, his expression grim. "And if we want horses?" he asked. "What is required?"

"Subterfuge," she said. "And the luck of the gods."

He nodded grimly. "Then we let the gods decide."

Taking up the bundle of supplies, he followed her to the far end of the room. There was a heavy door there, with a small window set into it; a trickle of light came in through the iron grate, making it easier to see. She peered out through the grate and then pushed open the heavy iron bolt on the door, trying to make as little noise as possible. As the door swung open one of the cast iron hinges groaned; the two of them froze, holding their breath while they waited to see if anyone would come to investigate. But no one did, and after a few more seconds of waiting the woman nodded, and pushed the heavy door all the way open.

Fresh air flowed across his face, cool and sweet. Never mind that if you smelled it closely you could make out the distant odors of horse manure and decaying garbage. To Rhys it smelled of freedom. For a moment he just drank it in, taking stock of the scene that surrounded him. Night had fallen during his imprisonment, and in the sky overhead he could see a single full moon, shining clear and white. It was close to midnight, then. They would have enough natural light to travel by for hours yet. That was good.

He wondered if she had taken the moon's schedule into account in making her plans. He would not put it past her.

Once the door was safely shut behind them she led him to a shadowy path tucked behind a series of shelters and stalls, out of sight of the open courtyard. From one building he heard a brief bout of masculine laughter, drunken in tenor; the sounds of gambling. Barracks, most likely. Passing so close to Anukyat's soldiers made his heart skip a beat, but no one noticed them. As she had noted, people here did not seem to worry about invasion from within.

Thus far the gods seemed to be favoring them.

Finally she paused, and waited for him to come up beside her. "Stable," she whispered. Not that she needed to point it out. The smell of the building just ahead was thick and heavy, a mixture of hay and manure and well-oiled leather; no rider could have mistaken it. There was an open space they had to cross to get to it, and she paused warily, looking in all directions to see if there was anyone that might witness their passage. Finally she nodded to signal him that all was well, and they bolted toward the rear of the stable where the shadows would protect them once more. As he did so he turned his head back to steal a glance at the building he had so narrowly escaped from.

And he stopped.

And stared.

Behind them—directly behind the Citadel itself—a vast stone spire soared, so high that mists gathered about the summit, giving it a fairy aspect. Its surface was striated in the manner of wind-carved monuments, but dramatically so, magnificently so, with long, deep furrows running vertically toward the summit, punctuated by even deeper holes that gaped like caverns in its surface. Through one he even thought he saw moonlight shining, as if it passed all the way through. The Citadel grew outward from the monument's base, and in the midnight darkness it was impossible to see where the natural structure ended and the man-made one began.

Then his rescuer struck him between the shoulder blades, hard enough to jar his damaged shoulder, and reminded him of what he was supposed to be doing.

He followed her into the darkness of the stable without another look back.

There was just enough moonlight coming into the stable that she did not need to unhood the lantern at first; they were able to see into the stalls as they passed by, measuring the occupants against their need. A few horses snorted quietly as they passed by, but most of them seemed to be asleep. Judging from the construction of the building, the stable had been small to start with, and then was expanded several times. The first section they passed through had stalls that were open to view, with nothing but a half wall to separate human visitors from the equine inhabitants, but a later addition had more enclosed stalls, with waist-high gates set between sections of planking as tall as Rhys himself. That promised cover, should they need it, and they chose a pair of animals whose stalls were of that type, and not in the direct line of sight from the entrance.

Moving to the end of the row, where the tack was hung, Rhys quickly gathered the supplies they would need to saddle their mounts. The woman let him make all the choices in that operation, taking items from him as he handed them down without comment, and carrying them quickly and silently to the stalls they had chosen. There were other supplies stored there as well, to outfit those guards who needed to travel long distances in pursuit of their duties, and he gathered up every-thing he thought they might need in the wilderness, if indeed they decided to travel all the way to the Spears. Extra blankets. Extra feed. Vessels for water. Canvas for shelter. It was obviously more than the two of them needed for the journey she had mandated—a simple day's ride to the south to escape the Wrath's influence—but she said nothing when he brought it back to the stalls. Maybe that was a good sign. Maybe she already knew that he would try to talk her into the longer journey, and was considering whether she might not agree.

In the vast open spaces of the Protectorates horses were an integral part of life; it was nigh impossible for someone to reach adulthood without knowing how to care for the creatures. Yet it was clear from the first few minutes that his companion knew nothing of saddling horses, not even the most elementary steps. She tried to help, following his lead, but it took less effort to just wave her back and do all the work himself, than to try to explain the fine points of equine gear under such circumstances. So where was she from, then? How did she get out here, in the middle of nowhere, without the basic skills that mountain travel required? Spreading an extra blanket under each saddle, wrapping some extra hardware in soft cloths before packing them inside the saddlebags so they would make less noise, he could barely contain his questions. How was it she had showed up just in time to rescue him? He didn't dare start asking her until they were safely out of here. Gods alone knew if she would answer him, even then.

"Shhhh!" Her whispered warning made his heart skip a beat. Straining his senses to the utmost, he realized suddenly they were no longer alone. In an instant her lantern was hooded again; the only light they had now was the faint bit of moonlight coming from the far end of the stable, and the distant flicker of another lantern approaching. Rhys could hear footsteps coming toward them, and what sounded like a man singing softly under his breath as walked slowly from stall to stall, checking on their occupants.

The woman rushed to get their supplies out of sight behind the solid portion of the wall, reaching as far as she could without taking a step so that the rustling of the straw underfoot did not betray her. He was impressed by how quietly she managed it. The instincts of a thief, no doubt. As for himself . . . he had gone too far in saddling the horse to be able to strip the tack off in time. All he could do now was remove the bridle and bit from its head and quickly throw a blanket over the rest of the animal, in the hope that whoever was passing by would not look too closely at the creature. He tried to get the horse to shift its position so its rear end was behind the solid portion of the wall and it moved a few steps in that direction—but then he heard the singing coming way too close for comfort, and he gave up the effort and pressed himself against the wall beside his rescuer, their hearts pounding in unison as they waited.

This would be a good time for delivering that luck, he informed his gods.

The singing came closer; a beam of light fell upon the adjoining stall, picking out the features of the horse inside it. Beside him Rhys could feel the woman trembling, but whether it was from fear or excitement he could not tell. He could sense the energy that was wound up tight inside her, ready to be released in an instant if required, and her knife was already in her hand, waiting for his signal. She clearly would not hesitate to attack, if that was required, and perhaps even to kill.

Then the light passed into their stall. It flashed along the head and mane of the horse, then moved toward the forward edge of the blanket Rhys had thrown over it. The animal whinnied softly as it turned away from the light, and then the voice and the lantern moved past them.

They waited a long while in the darkness, until they heard the man complete his rounds and leave the stable. And still they waited. There was no room for error.

Finally the woman peered around the corner, and nodded. "All right," she whispered. "He's gone now." But she did not put away her knife, and while Rhys resumed dressing the horse she remained at the gate, as alert as a mountain lion watching for signs of prey.

Finally both horses were ready to go. He led them from their stalls, handed her the reins of the shorter one, and vaulted up onto his own. "We try to ride out as though we belong here, is that the idea? Trust in the fact that they don't normally have any reason to inspect outgoing guards too closely?"

She nodded. "If the gate is open we should have no problem. If it is not, then as I said . . . subterfuge and luck."

She place her foot in the stirrup and tried to mount. Her balance was wrong on the first try and she cursed softly as she landed back on the ground. Her second try was more successful . . . but far from graceful.

He reached over and caught her rein, and waited until she met his gaze. "You do know how to ride, don't you?"

She flushed angrily. "Of course."

"How well?"

"Well enough," she snapped. But the split-second of hesitation before she answered told another story.

He muttered the names of several northern deities under his breath. *Do you have any idea what kind of horsemanship is required to ride in these mountains by moonlight?* There was no need to ask the question. Clearly she had no idea.

The god of mischief must be laughing himself to death right about now.

"The sentry will most likely be on the left side," she said. "I look more like a native than you do right now, so I will take that side."

He said it simply. "No."

"You are too tall to pass for a native," she pointed out. "Best to let me draw his notice."

"Height will not matter so much in the darkness if all else is right. Whereas a guard who does not ride like a guard will be recognized as a fraud by any light."

Anger flashed in her eyes again. She wanted to argue with him; he could taste it. But she didn't.

"Here," she said at last. She reached out to hand him something. "You will need this."

It was a messenger's tube made of beaten copper, the sort that documents might be placed in to protect them from the rigors of travel. He nodded, as the final piece of her plan fell into place.

As suicidally insane plans went, it was not a bad one.

Together they moved toward the stable doors. She rode well enough to keep pace with him, to his right and a few feet behind, a position that would make it hard for the sentry to see her as they approached his station. He hoped she would be able to keep up when things got more challenging.

Rhys urged his horse into a canter as they left the building, and she followed suit. It was a risky speed under the circumstances, that gave them less than a minute before reaching the gate. But the alternative was a trot, and that was the gait most likely to betray an unskilled rider. Besides, they had to move fast enough to convey a sense of urgency, if this was to work.

He focused his attention on their point of exit, and the uniformed man watching over it. The gate was closed, as he had expected it would be this late at night. Their current pace would take them right into it if it wasn't opened in time. But that, too, was part of the plan.

Courage and luck, right?

The sound of hoofbeats approaching drew the sentry's attention. When the man's eyes met his own, Rhys held up the tube for him to see. Knowing that such men relied upon their instincts, he tried to exude a sense of urgency and authority: he and his partner were legitimate messengers, handling some business so urgent that there was no time to wait for the sun to rise before setting out, or even to pause while the gate was opened. Anyone in service to the same master would surely respect their need for haste and facilitate their exit. . . .

For one brief second time seemed to stand still as the sentry considered. Was it dark enough to mask all those details of their appearance that might warn him that something was wrong? Apparently so, for he turned his attention to the gate, and with a short cry ordered forth servants from the shadows to open it.

Just in time.

The woman at his side reached up to adjust her helmet as they passed through, using her right hand to shield her face from the servant on that side of them, but the man was too busy getting out of the way of the thundering horses to be paying attention to fine points of her appearance. And the gods were indeed on their side, or so it seemed. The gate itself cast such a shadow in the moonlight that they were all but invisible as they passed through it.

No one called for them to stop. No one raised an alarm. The massive doors swung shut slowly behind them, and Rhys could hear its iron bolts falling back into place, securing Anukyat's Citadel once more.

They didn't dare slow down while they were still within view, but followed a well-worn path that probably served the regular patrols, leading southward. The path was much used, which served their need well; it would be nigh impossible come morning for anyone to pick out which hoofprints were theirs, or to know for certain whether a set of prints that broke off from the main path belonged to them or not. If they could put a few miles behind them before Rhys' absence was discovered and get out of sight of the Citadel's watchtowers, they might have a chance to get away safely.

Southward.

There was a monument to the right of them, similar to the one Rhys had seen at the Citadel, and another some miles to the west. The Three Sisters. Tradition said that the famous trio of landmarks was located too far south to be subject to the Wrath, but the words of his witch companion seemed to imply otherwise. If so, then the Wrath was expanding its area of influence. Weakened at the source, perhaps, less focused in its power, but bleeding out into the surrounding landscape. That was not a good piece of news.

Something is wrong in Alkali, he thought stubbornly. *And I am not leaving here until I find out what it is.*

Suddenly his companion reined in her horse, and he followed suit. They had come to a crossroads of sorts, where several freshly trod horse paths intersected the one they had been following. If they changed direction now, it was unlikely any pursers would be able to detect it. Later they could leave the second path behind and set out across truly virgin landscape, with no one the wiser.

This was where he must part company with his companion, then.

He looked up at her, and to his surprise found her smiling. It was a subtle, secretive expression, replete with hidden meaning. For a moment he did not quite know how to respond. It seemed like he had been traveling by her side for weeks, rather than just a handful of hours. Facing death together made for a strange sense of intimacy.

"You risked your life to free me, back there," he said quietly. "And I don't even know your name."

She seemed startled, somehow, almost as if his words had surprised her. But why should they? Surely she could not have entered the Citadel's gates, much less contrived such complicated plans to get him out safely, without realizing the danger involved? Or had she just forgotten that her promise of proper introductions was still unfulfilled? "Kamala," she said. No family name, no place name, no honorific. He could not even place the region the name was from. It was as much a mystery as she was.

"Thank you, Kamala." He wanted more than anything to question her further—where had she come from, how did she learn of his plight, why had she risked her life to free him?— but somehow the moment didn't seem right for it. And besides, they were not out of danger yet. "I will repay you for all that you have done for me today. I swear it."

She did not answer him, but turned her horse around and started to ride once more. Instead of heading southward, as he had anticipated, she turned off down a side path that headed roughly east. Then stopped, and waited for him.

Now it was his turn to be startled. "Change of plan?"

"Not at all." Her eyes sparkled like emeralds in the moonlight. "We're heading north, aren't we? Back up to the Spear, yes? Isn't that what you wanted?" She indicated the well-scuffed earth beneath her feet. "We can follow this path for a while to confuse pursuit, then leave it later on to strike out in that direction."

"I thought . . . I thought you said you had to go south."

"So I did—while your jailer was listening. Did you not notice that he had stopped struggling, when I spoke of our plans?

He didn't want me to realize he had regained consciousness. Tomorrow morning, or whenever he is discovered, he will have valuable information to barter with to save him from his master's wrath. So then the guards will know where to look for us. Good news all around, don't you think?" The emerald eyes glittered. "That is, assuming we don't spend the whole night here discussing it."

She smiled, then turned her attention back to the east and started riding. After a moment he touched his heels to his horse's flanks and started after her.

Courage and luck.

———

You risked your life to free me.

The words were strange, uncomfortable things. Kamala did not know how to absorb them.

Had she really done that for him? Risked that same eternal life that she had once bartered her soul to possess, that might now be cut short by a single sword stroke in a place where the best sorcery was befouled, and could even turn against its maker?

She had not even thought of her actions in those terms before. Had not analyzed her own motives, or the risk involved. All she had known was a flood tide of fury that the Guardian she had intended to use for her own purposes had been stolen away from her. Guilt, perhaps, that her own failure had allowed his capture. Frustration, that she had found a means to gather priceless knowledge, only to have it snatched from her grasp. Arrogance, that she refused to acknowledge there was any man she could not outthink, or—failing that—seduce.

She had been foolish. She had taken chances. The risk had been high.

Ah, but the prize is surely worth it, she told herself. *Knowledge that even the Magisters do not have. Knowledge that can be bartered for greater things.*

Far to the north, the Wrath was waiting.

CHAPTER 13

MIDNIGHT.

Siderea Aminestas awakened suddenly from a sound sleep. Her heart was pounding as if something had frightened her awake, but the shadowy bedchamber was peaceful and silent and the only other presence she could sense was that of her maid, encamped beyond the threshold of the room.

So what was the cause? She focused her attention inward, trying to catch some hint or memory of what had disturbed her, but all she could remember were bits and pieces of dreaming, none of them helpful.

Rising from bed, she wrapped a robe of fine gold silk around her, more out of habit than of need; the night was pleasantly warm with a balmy breeze blowing in from over the port, rich with the smells of summer. But she felt a need to wrap something around herself. To give her hands something to do while she tried to calm herself.

But her heart would not stop pounding. Did her body know something that her intellect did not? Was there enough innate witchery left in her soul that it had sensed something amiss, something that should make her afraid—or perhaps excited—that her mortal senses could not detect?

In another day, another lifetime, she would have called for guards to attend her. But that did not suit her current circumstances. She'd twice played host to a visitor who liked to circumvent normal protocol, and in case this had something to do with him, she wanted as few witnesses around as possible.

Almost a month now. She went to bed each night wondering when he would come back to her. If he would come. If she would still be alive when he came. . . .

Quietly she walked out into the corridor. A servant stirred sleepily, ready to serve her. "Shh," she whispered, "there is no need." The girl sighed and returned to whatever dream she'd been enjoying; judging from the smile on her face it was a pleasant one. At the entrance to the royal wing a pair of guards waited; they snapped to attention as they heard Siderea's soft footfalls coming their way. "All is well," she told them. They would not worry about her safety unless she gave some sign that they had to. Royal tradition might demand a retinue of guards to protect her, but who really expected a witch of her obvious power to be in danger in her own demesne? The one time she had been threatened, years ago, she had dispatched the troublemaker before her guards could take their first step. Word of that had spread quickly. No one had threatened her since.

Of course, no one knew that the power that had once protected her was now gone.

She would not give them cause to suspect it.

Down the hall she walked, softly, the ends of her silk gown fluttering behind her like wings. She did not think about where she was headed, but simply walked; her feet seemed to know where they should go. At last she came to the place where a marble archway offered passage to a balcony overlooking the harbor. Of course. It was where Amalik had met with her the first time, when he had given her a ring and a promise. Now she understood.

Her heart still pounding, she took a moment to compose herself before stepping out onto the balcony.

He was there. Dressed in a tunic of midnight blue, with high leather boots of the same color. The color made his coarse skin look pale as moonlight.

"It is time," he said.

She didn't realize she had been holding her breath until she suddenly exhaled it. "Then . . . what? What is needed?"

"Tomorrow you will come with me into the mountains." He gestured toward the northwest, where the steep flanks of the Sentinel Mountains crowded Sankara against the sea. "Alone."

"Alone?"

He bowed. "The secret is for your eyes alone, my Queen."

"We go by witchery, I assume?"

"Not for this matter, I am afraid. You will understand why when we arrive. . . ."

"So we ride? Like ordinary mortals? Is that your intent?"

He nodded.

She looked out toward the mountains. They rose abruptly from the fertile plain, with no gentle foothills as a prelude. They were steep, too steep for farming, and without a clear pass for miles; the tallest peaks had snow upon them even at the height of summer.

One could become lost in such a range, and no one would ever know it.

One could hide secrets there, and no one would ever see them.

"I cannot ride there alone," she said.

His eyes narrowed; there was a flicker of anger in their depths. "Are you setting conditions now?"

"I am telling you the simple truth. If you do not think that my guards will follow me when I leave here, and watch over me secretly if I try to order them back—or that my people will not take note of me riding alone through the city without servants in attendance—then you do not understand the ways of royalty. We are never *alone*."

"I can shield you from their eyes so that none will see you. Until we reach the mountains."

"And will I be coming back here, after this . . . revelation?"

"If you choose to."

"Then I cannot simply disappear. It would raise too many questions." She silenced his protest with a wave of her hand. "You say you wished your business kept secret. Well, if so, that is not the way to manage it. Remember, all it takes is one Magister to catch the scent of mystery, and all your secrets will be revealed." The word *Magister* curdled on her tongue as she spoke it. "Unless you and your allies are proof against sorcery, it is best not to draw their interest in the first place."

He scowled. "So what do you suggest?"

She considered. "A special outing, to collect herbs of power from secret places in the mountains, that I can trust no one else to handle. If my people believe it is witch's business they will not ask too many questions. I will come up with some reason for your attendance. You may lead that group as close to the mountains as you think appropriate, and we will worry about leaving them behind after that."

He clearly was not happy about her suggestion. No doubt it would bring her people closer to his secret destination than he wanted, but that could not be helped. Would he stand up to her, she wondered, give her orders, demand that his original conditions be obeyed? It was clear that he wanted to, and she knew from their previous dealings that he did not feel bound by the usual rules of protocol. There was a black fire inside this man, and she was willing to bet that being given orders by a woman, queen or no, was stoking it to greater and greater heights. What did he hunger for more right now—the masculine catharsis of dominance reasserted, or the more civilized satisfaction of effective cooperation? The answer would tell her much about how to manipulate him in the future.

(*In the future*. What a powerful, wonderful phrase that was! There had been a time not long ago when she had not had any future.)

"It will be as you describe," Amalik said stiffly. "My Queen."

So, she thought, *the hidden fire is contained once more.*

For now.

———————

She traveled with eight guards to protect her, as well as a handful of servants to see to her personal needs. Of course her servants believed that she had the power to handle any trouble that might arise, and even cook her own food, if necessary, with a wave of the hand if required. But because she was a witch rather than a Magister, it was their job to see that she did not have to. And so the whole party of them must come along, carrying such tents and rugs and silken cushions as a queen must have in the wilderness.

Amalik was displeased by all that, and he made no secret of it. He clearly hungered to travel faster, and less encumbered, and he took every opportunity to let her know it. And while she would not have brought along servants simply to irritate him, it could not be denied that the more agitated he became, the less careful he was about hiding his true self from her. By the second day of travel she had ascertained that he was not used to dealing with nobility, or with women, or perhaps even with people in general. Indeed, he seemed happiest when he was riding out ahead of them all, perhaps pretending that he was riding alone, with Siderea following obediently and silently behind him. A good thing for both of them, she mused, that he had never had the opportunity to test that fantasy. It would not have lasted long.

At night he would disappear, presumably to make his own camp somewhere in the wilderness. Always he positioned himself ahead of them: fearful, perhaps, that one of her guards might scout the way ahead and see something he should not. Promptly at dawn he would return, looking as if he had neither slept well nor managed even a cursory cleaning, pacing his horse back and forth in a bad temper while her retinue packed up their things.

But then came the morning of the fourth day when he brought back two other men with him. They shared his lean and hungry look, but there the similarity ended. One was ebony-skinned, with knotted tangles of black hair that cascaded down to his shoulders and a coarse cuirass of some blue-black leather that looked as if he had not taken it off for several years. The other was a short man, yellow-skinned and black-eyed, with bony, skeletal features that seemed better suited to a day-old corpse than a living man. He, too, was dressed in grimy leather armor of a sort, of the same color and texture as his companion's. Siderea shuddered as they approached the camp, and her guards hurried into position ahead of her, challenging them. Her other servants stopped what they were doing and stared, not knowing how to respond to such an unexpected presence.

Are these my new allies? Siderea wondered. Her hackles rose at the thought. *What have I gotten myself into?*

Amalik faced her; his expression was impassive, but she knew him well enough by now to guess just how much he was enjoying the moment. "You may leave your guards behind now," he said. "These men will see to your needs the rest of the way," he said.

She drew in a deep breath, while her servants turned to her in disbelief. *You have no choice,* she told herself. *For better or worse, this game must be played out to its end.*

She turned to her guards. "I will be going on alone. These men will protect me."

"But Majesty—" their leader protested.

She waved him to silence. "Do you doubt my capacity to handle trouble? Or perhaps it is my judgment you question."

His face paled. "No, Majesty. Of course not."

"Well, then. You have your orders." She looked out over the small company. "You will all wait for me here until I return. You will not, under any circumstances, follow me. Is that clear?"

They all bowed their heads in assent. Which was good; if she did not meet their eyes, they would not see the uncertainty in her own.

She looked at Amalik and mouthed: *how long?*

He hesitated, then held up fingers: four at first, then five.

"A week," she ordered. "Wait for me a week, without leaving this place."

Her horse was saddled and waiting. A servant ran up to offer her a lift with his hands, but she mounted without it. The desert-style pants that she wore under her skirts slid over the polished leather with a whisper as she settled herself astride in the manner of a man. One of the few southern customs she still maintained.

She, too, was restless.

"Do not follow me," she commanded one last time, as she kneed the horse into motion.

The faces of Amalik's allies were expressionless, but she could sense the same black fire burning behind their eyes. *Lovely companions I have now,* she thought grimly. There was a musky-sweet odor that hung about the newcomers, less than pleasant at close quarters. Apparently the source of their power did not value either bathing or perfume.

Amalik did not lie, she reminded herself. *The power I need is out there, hidden in the Sentinels. If these are the only men that can bring me to it, so be it.*

"Lead on," she told Amalik, and when he and his companions began to ride north, she followed.

———

Mountains loomed on all sides, loosely covered in rocky soil and thin, dry grass. The horses stumbled on the steep slopes several times, and if she had ridden sidesaddle she probably would have fallen off sometime in the first hour. As it was, her thighs ached from pressing tightly against the sides of her mount, trying to keep her seat properly. When Amalik finally signaled for them to stop, she could barely dismount on her own.

But she'd be cursed if she'd let one of these filthy men touch her.

Amalik waited until her legs were steady beneath her, then said, "We walk from here."

Picking her way with care, she followed him up a rocky slope. The black man stayed behind to lead the horses off somewhere;

the other fell in behind her. Suddenly she heard a shrieking in the distance; not a human sound, nor that of any beast she knew. Her legs, already sore, grew weak beneath her. "What is that?"

"All is as it should be," Amalik assured her, without turning around.

He led her over one ridge, then toward another that was yet higher. It was a path no horse could have managed. The strange cry rang out again while they were climbing. This time the sound was louder, and clearer, and seemed to her to taste of rage. A blind, bestial fury that echoed from the very heavens. Amalik did not break his stride for a moment, or otherwise acknowledge the sound. Siderea tried to do the same, but her heart was racing.

It's what we're heading toward, she thought. *It's why this "secret" of theirs needs to kept be so far from human habitation. So no one else will hear its cries.* For the first time since Amalik had visited her, she was truly afraid. But it was important that these men not see the fear in her. To allow them to do so would give them too much of an advantage over her.

And then they came over the top of the last ridge, and stood along its crest, silent and solemn . . . and she saw.

Directly ahead of her was a narrow ravine that stretched beyond the limits of her vision to both the right and left of her. Whatever river had carved it ages ago had long since disappeared. The walls were steep, nearly vertical, and barely a few yards across from one another at the widest point. From the depths of the ravine rose a terrible smell of rotting waste and decayed flesh and other unwholesome things, as well as a low keening sound that played upon her nerves like fingernails on slate. What in the name of all the hells was down there?

She wanted more than anything to turn and run, but that would be an unacceptable show of weakness. Gods alone knew what Amalik had brought her here for, but if the situation turned bad she would need all her wits about her. She took a few steps away from the men, so that they would have to close the distance before being able to touch her. A minimal precaution. Then a rustling from deep in the canyon drew her attention, and she edged a few steps farther, leaning as far forward as she could safely manage to see what was down there.

Whatever it was, it was large and dark-skinned and covered with dirt. It let out a terrible cry, and the sound pierced through her to the bone: hatred and fury and pain and hunger and misery, all bound up in one nerve-jangling shriek. Against her better judgment, Siderea edged closer to the lip of the chasm, trying to get near enough to see the creature clearly without risking a fall. The men remained behind at the ridge; perhaps they realized that if they moved so much as an inch in her direction she would withdraw. The creature was moving in and out of shadows as it paced up and down the length of the ravine, making strange noises as it did so. She could see where steep rockfalls had blocked its way at both ends. Here and there along its path were piles of broken bones, and in one place the rotting remains of what looked like a horse. That certainly explained the smell. Strangely, no flies were visible. Behind the reek of foulness there was a strange, musky-sweet odor that took her a moment to identify. It was the same scent she had picked up on the guards she realized. Stranger and stranger.

She shifted her position, trying to see even more. The creature seemed to be large, but it was keeping close to the wall directly beneath her, and she could not get a clear view of it. She did catch sight of a long black tail trailing behind it that twitched with every step; perhaps it was some sort of monstrous lizard? She had heard of such in other lands, but not so close to home. What relationship did any of this have to the question of sorcerous power? Reptiles couldn't be witches.

And then the creature's feverish pacing brought it into a shaft of sunlight, and she could see it clearly at last.

"Oh, my gods." She whispered the words instinctively as she stumbled backward, so suddenly that she almost fell. Part of her mind recognized what the creature must be, from myths she'd heard and ancient murals she'd seen; the other part insisted that such a thing was simply not possible and she must have gone mad if she thought it was.

She looked back at Amalik. His expression might have been carved in stone for all the emotion it betrayed. He nodded.

A Souleater.

It was long and sinuous with blue-black scales crusted with mud and debris that ran down its length. Vast wings that might have fanned out from its back in a more open space were pressed tightly against its sides, trapped by the unyielding canyon walls. As she watched, the creature struggled in vain to beat its wings, keening in obvious frustration as it did so. Clearly it was trying to take flight; clearly, in this narrow canyon, it would not be able to do so.

She looked back at Amalik again; there were so many questions crowding her mind she could hardly pick one to ask. Finally she managed, "This . . . this is the power you spoke of? This creature?"

"They harvest the energy of life," he said. "More than they need." He looked down into the ravine. "She can replace what you have lost."

Siderea stammered, "S–she?"

"She is a female of her kind. Only a female of *our* kind can draw upon her strength." The black eyes turned to her again. "You now understand why you were chosen."

The creature in the chasm moved suddenly. With a speed that seemed impossible, it headed straight for the rockfall at one end of the ravine. Siderea saw sharp talons flash against the rocky slope as raptorlike claws dug in deeply for traction. Pebbles and dust were scattered in all directions as the creature began to climb, and Siderea stepped back instinctively, wanting to be far away from the place where it would emerge—

And then something vast and dark swooped down from overhead. With a gasp Siderea stepped back as its shadow fell over her and almost lost her footing on the rocky earth.

Another Souleater.

With a cry of warning the new arrival plummeted down directly toward the female. It was twice her size at least, and its clean, sleek body glinted in the sunlight. The female drew herself up and seemed ready to fight, but she was smaller than the other, and somehow Siderea sensed she was not in condition for combat. At the last minute she drew back, hissing in rage as her attacker forced her to release her grip on the rock pile. Siderea watched in horrified fascination as she fell back to the floor of the canyon, bellowing in pain as one of the fragile-seeming wings was crushed beneath her. The length of the canyon echoed with her cries as her attacker withdrew, apparently satisfied.

It did not want her free to fly, Siderea realized. It had forced her back into the canyon, where the walls were so close that she could not spread out her wings. The rockfalls that had entrapped her had probably not been accidental, but part of a deliberately crafted prison.

What in the name of all the gods was going on here?

She turned up her eyes to follow the larger Souleater back to its perch, high overhead, and to her shock saw a handful of others as well, equally large, perched on various high points about the canyon. Legendary creatures; the stuff of nightmares. They were watching the female in the ravine intently, ready to move the minute she made another break for freedom. Men were standing beside them, craning their necks like hungry vultures as they watched the show. Siderea saw her yellow-skinned guide standing right beside one of the creatures and now that they were next to each other, she could see how his garments resembled the hide of the creature, albeit dulled by a patina of hard use. Creatures out of ancient nightmare, allied to men who wore their skins. . . .

It was all too much to absorb. She put her hand to her fore-head and felt a wave of dizziness come over her. For once it was not the product of her weakened condition, but sheer emotional overload. Her hands were shaking, and she did not know how to still them. All she could think of was the image of the Souleater from King's Pass that Colivar had conjured in her palace . . . a dark, demonic creature rising up over a field of gutted bodies, drawing its strength from human suffering. Is that what these men had allied themselves with? How was such a thing even possible? The last time Souleaters had ruled the earth, human beings were their chosen prey. To see the two species standing side by side like this implied things that her mind was not ready to accept.

Then the female began to stir once more, struggling to free her left wing from where it had been pinned beneath her. Only she didn't have enough room to manage the maneuver. She cried out again, a long keening note that was filled with pain and fear. A wounded animal might cry out so, begging for help. Then two black jeweled eyes turned to Siderea and fixed on her; their power washed over her in a wave and for a moment it seemed she could feel the creature's pain as though it were her own.

"They need sunlight on their wings," Amalik said. He had come closer to her than she had intended to allow, but she couldn't take her eyes off the creature. "She grows weaker every day without it."

"Then why do you keep her down there?" Siderea demanded. Her throat felt as raw as if she had been screaming herself. Was it possible she felt sympathy for the creature? *They eat human souls*, she reminded herself. *They nearly destroyed the entire world, once.*

"She does not understand that if she flies too high, or heads in the wrong direction, men may see her. And we have no way to tell her that. So she cannot be allowed fly."

She finally turned to him, blinking slowly as she struggled to focus on what he was saying. "You think . . . you think that *I* can get her to understand that?"

"If she accepts you."

"And what if she doesn't?" she demanded. "What then?"

She could see him hesitate; perhaps wondering if he should lie to her? "Then you will be consumed," he said at last. Calmly, quietly, as though this whole enterprise was utterly sane. "As were those who tried before you."

A cold shiver ran down her spine. "You said I was the *first*."

"I said you were the first *queen*," he corrected her. "There have been other women." He looked down at the wounded Souleater again. "Not for this one, of course. She has only just matured. They cannot relate to humans as anything other than food until their third instar. That was why we had to wait before we could bring you here."

"And she can do that now? Relate to humans?"

"Let us hope so, my Queen." He turned back to her. "Otherwise this will be a short-lived relationship."

"Where are the others?" she demanded. "The other Souleaters. What happened to them?"

For a moment he was silent. Siderea could hear the wounded female panting below them, trying to regain her strength before struggling to her feet again.

"If she were allowed to fly free," he said at last, "our presence would be discovered. And we are not ready for that yet."

Sickness roiled in the pit of her stomach. From which of many horrors? That of the suffering beasts, the women fed to them like slabs of meat, or her own likely fate? It was impossible to untangle her emotions, to focus on any one sane thread. "You've driven this one mad," she whispered hoarsely. "So what do you expect? If I were her, in this condition, I would tear the first human being that came near me to bloody bits. That's what happened the other times, isn't it? You turned these . . . these *things* into crazed beasts, and they vented their rage on the first human being that got within reach." She could hear the anger rising in her voice; it was a stronger emotion than fear, so she embraced it gratefully. "And then you killed the creatures for falling short of your expectations. And you started all over again. How many more will you kill?" she demanded. "Of them? Of your own kind?"

"It is more than that to us—" he began angrily. Then he took a deep breath, clearly trying to control himself; his voice grew steadier, but there was still a fire smoldering in his eyes. "We gave them the partners we thought they wanted. The only

kind we had ever seen them accept. Young girls, impression-
able, that could grow to adulthood alongside them. It should
have worked."

"So you fed a mouse to a tiger and were surprised when it
got torn to bits. That doesn't give me great confidence in your
judgment." Was the creature listening? she wondered suddenly.
Could it hear the echo of fear in her voice? The cries in the
chasm had ceased; the labored breathing had subsided. Siderea
had the impression that it was waiting for something. How
much did it understand of what was going on?

If I had even a year's worth of soulfire left in me, she thought,
*I would go running from this place as fast as my feet could carry
me. And never look back.*

*Of course, if I had any soulfire left in me, I would not be here in
the first place.*

"So this time we brought in a tiger for our tiger," Amalik
said. "A witch with a lifetime's experience of power; a queen
with a lifetime's experience of command. A good match by all
measures, since the creature you see before you will be a queen
among her own kind. So the only question now is whether you
have the courage to grasp this opportunity, and make it your
own, or whether you would prefer the lingering death of a senile
witch, with your kingdom crumbling around you."

She hissed softly. The creature in the chasm raised its head,
aroused by the sound.

"What do you have to lose?" Amalik pressed.

"Do not pretend you would let me go home to die in peace.
Not after I have seen this . . . thing."

There was silence.

Finally he said to her, "No. I am sorry. There is no going
home."

"Do not lie to me ever again," she said sharply, and she turned away from him.

The female Souleater had come to the part of the ravine that was closest to Siderea. Her eyes were large and multifaceted and fixed upon Siderea with unnerving intensity; their color was a black so deep that it reminded her of the Magisters.

Bile rose to her throat, sour and bitter, at the thought of them. *Don't let yourself be distracted,* she ordered herself. *What little hope you have of surviving this mad enterprise surely depends upon thinking clearly.* "What is it you expect me to do?"

She could hear his sharp indrawn breath at the question. "Go to her. And if you believe that your gods care about such things, then pray."

No god I know of would approve of this madness.

Slowly she walked toward the highest point of the rockfall, a few yards beneath the edge of the ravine. Black jeweled eyes watched her from down below. She didn't dare look at them directly for fear she would lose the last of her courage. For a moment she hesitated, and it seemed to her all the world was still. And quiet. So quiet. Not even the insects were stirring.

There is nothing left to lose, she reminded herself.

With trembling hands she lowered herself to a seated position on the ravine's edge, and prepared to drop down into its depths. Then the great creature hissed. Her breath caught in her throat. Souleaters were said to mesmerize their prey before they devoured their souls. How close did she have to be for that to happen?

Nothing to lose, she repeated to herself. A mantra of false courage . . . but it was all she had.

Slowly she lowered herself downward into the ravine. She hung on to the cliff's edge as long as she could—would that the moment could last forever!—and then, finally, she abandoned herself to fate and dropped down the rest of the way. The rocks were sharp and loosely packed, and as she hit the mound they shifted beneath her feet and she fell. The thin silk of her summer gown was little protection. Pain shot up her left arm as the sharp rocks tore through both fabric and flesh; she could feel warm blood trickling down her arm as she struggled to right herself.

The Souleater did not make a sound, but she could sense it watching. Waiting.

She took a minute to catch her breath and wrapped the long silk sleeve tightly about her arm to stop the bleeding. The creature still hadn't made a move toward her. Was that a good sign, or was it simply waiting until she came down to it, away from the rockfall where the other Souleaters might attack it? Clearly it was afraid of them.

That is something we have in common, she thought.

Trembling, she worked her way down the rocky slope as best she could, wincing every time her damaged arm was jolted. But the pain was a good thing: a finite, rational sensation that helped her focus on something other than fear. The stale air within the ravine became more and more overpowering as she descended, a rancid perfume of rotting meat and stale animal droppings. For a moment she thought she would vomit—as if that would make things better!—but she managed to get enough control of her body to limit herself to a few dry heaves.

If the creature had attacked her during that bout of sickness, there was nothing she could have done to stop it. But when Siderea finally looked up, she found the Souleater was still not moving. It was hissing softly with each exhaled breath, and its muscles were tensed like a wolf about to strike, but for now it was just watching her with those eerie, unnatural black eyes.

Waiting.

Now that she was on its level she could see how large the creature really was, and how poorly it had fared in its captivity. The filth of the ravine was spattered all across its hide, and its delicate paned wings streaked with mud and waste and dried blood; this recent injury had clearly not been its first. Flakes of dried skin were peeling from its hide in several places along its flanks and high about its neck. Did it shed its skin like a reptile? Was it in the midst of that transformation, perhaps? Or was the blue-black hide a more permanent skin that had suffered more permanent injury? Fury filled Siderea's heart as she looked upward, to catch sight of the human and inhuman vultures perched high overhead. She could only see two of the Souleaters from her current position, silhouetted against the brightness of the open sky, but it was clear that those two were sleek and clean, their blue-black scales glistening in the sunlight. That was the final indignity. Rage welled up inside her, on behalf of the miserable creature before her. She hated the Souleaters who had forced such indignities upon one of their own kind. She hated the men who had conspired with them. She hated the Magisters, who were like them in so many ways. Vultures, the whole lot of them, human and otherwise, who cared only for their own masculine hungers, and not a whit for the suffering they caused. The hatred welled up inside her, magma-hot, and she shook for trying to contain it. *Let it go,* an inner voice whispered. *It hurts too much to hold it inside. Just let it out.*

She screamed. It was a terrible, primitive sound that should never have issued from a human throat. The walls of the ravine shook as echoes coursed up and down its length . . . and then shook again as the female Souleater let out a cry of its own. For one terrible instant the two of them were as one, screaming out their defiance to the same enemies, bound together in a communion of hatred . . . and then Siderea staggered and fell, as the power of her fury left her. She felt empty inside, but that was a good thing; something within her had been cleansed, and her soul felt right again.

Now the Souleater was moving toward her. The creature stepped slowly, clearly wary; perhaps it thought Siderea might call down the bigger ones to punish it if it came too close. Siderea could smell its presence as it approached, and she thought she could pick out the musky-sweet odor of the Souleater itself from underneath the rankness of the canyon. It seemed that for a moment she could sense the life inside the creature as well, the soulfire at its core. Hot, so very hot. She hungered to warm herself at that fire, to let its heat fill her, restoring her vitality. Among humans, only children had souls that bright; she had never sensed anything like it in an animal before.

The creature's head moved slowly forward, until it was close enough that Siderea could feel its hot breath on her face. Trembling, she stood her ground. Its teeth were sharp and angled backward like a snake's; its faceted eyes reflected Siderea's sweat-streaked face in a thousand mirror-shards. Unexpectedly, she felt a strange sense of communion with the creature. Both of them surrounded by vultures. Both of them hating, and fearing, and despairing. Sisters, across the bounds of species.

With effort, she raised herself up from the rocky slope. Her arm throbbed with pain and she could feel blood trickling down to her fingertips, but she pushed herself upright and managed to get to her feet once more. Then, drawing in a deep breath for courage, Siderea took a few hesitant steps toward the

Souleater. The jewel-like eyes followed her as she moved, but the creature made no move to stop her. Not even when she came close enough to touch the thing.

For a moment Siderea hesitated; then she put her hand upon the creature's thick neck. Beneath her fingertips she could feel the pulse of its heartbeat, alien in its rhythm but familiar in its substance. This fearsome creature was no supernatural construct, no demon, but an animal wrought of flesh and bone, capable of suffering and bleeding—and hating—as powerfully as any human. She could feel the hate through her fingertips now, a warm, vital energy that vibrated along its skin. How powerful the emotion must be, for her to be able to feel it in her weakened state! Normally she would have had to use witchery to sense such things.

You can imprison us, she thought to the vultures waiting overhead, *but you cannot possess us. You can torture our flesh, but you cannot control us. And if we die in this place because of your arrogance*—she stared into the Souleater's eyes, and understanding came to her—*then you will lose the one thing that matters most to you.*

There was strength in that knowledge.

She turned back to the rockfall, no longer fearing to have the deadly creature behind her back. She knew it would not hurt her. The mound of rubble looked steeper than it had from above. No helping that. With a muttered prayer to the god of desperate causes, she began to climb back up. Slowly—painfully—trying to use only one hand to steady herself whenever possible, she made halting progress up the treacherous slope. One time she did indeed fall, and landed hard on her wounded arm; as pain shot up through her shoulder she heard the Souleater cry out behind her. *I'll be all right,* she promised her silently, and then: *We'll be all right.*

As she neared the top of the mound she could see that Amalik had come to the edge of the ravine to meet her. But the mere sight of him, after all that he had done to the female Souleater, was intolerable. "Get out of here!" she whispered hoarsely, as she reached the top of the mound and stood. Her own voice sounded harsh to her, and barely human. "And take all these others with you!"

He opened his mouth as if to speak. To do what? Give her orders? Demand answers? Rage, hot rage, welled up inside her at the mere thought. "*You will all leave here,*" she commanded, in a tone that would brook no disobedience. "*NOW!*"

Whatever Amalik had expected from her, this was clearly not it. Uncertain, he looked up to his companions for guidance. She growled low in her throat. He'd wanted a tiger, right? Very well. Now he had one. Gods help them all if they treated her like anything less.

Finally, hesitantly, Amalik backed away a few steps from the ravine's edge. Her soft hiss made it clear that it was not far enough. An hour ago he might have argued with her, or perhaps even dared to give her orders. Now . . . now their relationship had changed. He wanted something from her—something that she still had the power to deny him—and now that Siderea understood that, he had no cards left to play. He was no longer master in his own court, but petitioner in hers.

Which was as it should be.

He signaled something to the men and monsters beyond her line of sight. Siderea felt her heart skip a beat; were the others going to leave now, as she had commanded, or would they come down to the ravine and try to force their will upon her? If the latter, then she would go down fighting. Behind her she felt the Souleater brace herself, ready to fight alongside her. It was an odd sensation, to know that without words. The mesmeric power of the other Souleaters would be unable to affect her now that the female had accepted her; she knew that instinctively as well. So let them come.

One of the Souleaters swooped down low over the ravine, close enough to her that its wingstroke raised dusty whirlwinds from the earth and the breeze from his passage stirred her hair. In another time and place she might have cringed from such an approach, terrified of the massive creature. But not here, not now. No weapon in his arsenal could be more terrifying than her descent into the ravine had been and she had passed that test. These vultures would not have the satisfaction of seeing her afraid ever again.

One by one the other Souleaters followed the same path, passing over her head with a cry, and then headed out over the mountains. She thought she saw something clinging to the back of one of the creatures that might have been a man, crouched down low over its shoulder, but from where she was standing she did not have a clear enough view to be sure. No matter. What was important now was that they were leaving here, men and Souleaters both, because *she* had ordered it.

Below her, in the ravine, the female was now moving toward the rockfall, trying to pull her damaged wing free as it did so. Siderea winced, her own arm throbbing in sympathy. She might have risked descending again to help the creature climb if she thought it would do any good. But there was nothing she could do in such a tight space that would be of any use, and she would probably wind up crushed for her efforts. "It's all right," she said quietly. Did the Souleater understand her words? If not, would she at least understand her tone? "They're gone now. Everything will be all right."

How surreal this whole scene was! How casually she spoke to one of the greatest predators on the planet that (if legends were true) fed upon the souls of human beings. She did not look so fearsome now. Siderea could feel waves of fear rising up from her as she regarded the rocky slope that was her only path to freedom. "You have to climb out yourself," she said. As if the creature could understand human language. "I can't help you. I'm sorry."

The female began to climb. Slowly, unsteadily, digging each taloned foot deep into the mound of scree before daring to move the other, bracing her long tail against the solid ground beneath her for as long as she could. Siderea felt every jarring step as if she were the one making the climb. The damaged wing trailed behind the creature, freed now, but useless. She could see it twitching as the creature tried to use it for balance, and she winced each time it did. There was no need to tell this Souleater that she mustn't fly, Siderea thought grimly. It would be a long time before that wing could support her again . . . if ever.

Finally, exhausted by her efforts, the great beast reached the top of the mound. There she shuddered visibly, eyeing the distance yet to go. From here it was several yards straight up the wall of the ravine. The vertical surface offered few footholds sufficient to support a human, none of them large enough to support such a creature. Her head jerked about as she studied the walls surrounding her, but there was no better place that might be reached on foot. The long tail coiled and uncoiled like an agitated snake as she searched for some solid patch that she might brace herself against, as she had on the ground below. But up here there was only loose rock that shifted with every movement.

There was no easy way up.

Finally the Souleater settled herself opposite a section which seemed more navigable than most, and tension rippled along her flanks as she prepared herself for motion. Then, with a force that sent a shower of rocks flying in all directions, she leaped upward, struggling to use her wings to add every possible inch of height. It was a desperate move, and Siderea sensed that it might indeed have worked if imprisonment hadn't weakened the creature so badly. As it was, the Souleater didn't make it to the top. Her talons grabbed for the edge of the ravine and struck dirt just beneath it. If the ground had been more solid, perhaps that might have been good enough for her to work her way up. But as Siderea watched in horror, the earth started to crumble from underneath the great claws, sending a warning cascade of dirt and rocks plummeting down into the ravine. For a moment she thought the Souleater would go down with it, and she backed instinctively out of the way, lest she crush Siderea when she fell. Then, in a seeming act of desperation, the creature whipped her long tail over the edge of the ravine, shifted her weight, and attempted to lodge one of her feet against a narrow stone ledge off to her left side. Siderea held her breath as she watched. She could hear a crack as the tail impacted something, then it pulled taut, providing a counterbalance. The earth stopped crumbling then, as the Souleater's weight shifted to its new foothold; the sharp talons of her other foot had a precious second in which to dig deeply into the ravine wall for purchase . . . and then, with a final effort, the creature was over the top and out of sight.

Siderea fell to her knees on the rock pile, exhausted. She felt as if she had been the one struggling to climb the wall, and was only slowly coming to realize that her own ascent had yet to begin. But then the long, sinuous tail snaked back down into the ravine, heading toward her. She did not draw away from it. Pythonlike, it found her by touch and began to wrap itself around her, smooth coils kneading her flesh as it shifted its grip, tightening itself about her torso. Even when she saw the sharp blades at the end of the tail and felt them pass right by her face, she felt no fear. Perhaps she trusted the creature now. Or perhaps she was simply too exhausted to feel fear. One thing was certain: whatever primitive strength had sustained her while the other Souleaters were challenging her, it was gone now.

And then the muscular tail pulled Siderea off her feet, dragging her upward. She was scraped against the wall of the chasm, jolting her damaged arm; she winced in pain but did not cry out. Then she was pulled up and over the edge and dragged onto a patch of sunlit earth beyond. The snake coils finally relaxed, releasing her. She did not have the strength to crawl out of their embrace, but simply lay where she had been deposited, resting against the dirt-encrusted hide, gasping for breath. She could feel the creature's pulse against her cheek, and it seemed she could hear her powerful heartbeat in the distance, slowing now that the terrible exertion was over. But that must have just been an illusion. In actual fact her senses were fading now, and she could barely hear a thing. She knew why. The last sparks of her soulfire were sputtering out and a strange chill was seeping outward from her heart. The sunlight was growing dim as her vision began to fail her. This mad day's trials had finally exhausted the last of her life-essence.

I saved you, she thought to the creature, despairing. *Will you not do the same for me?*

A final shudder of pain coursed through her body as she shut her eyes. Her limbs seemed to be distant things, no longer her own, but impersonal objects, controlled by another. She flexed the fingers on her good hand, trying to banish the strange feeling, but it persisted. She tried to flex her injured wing but the sharp edges of the fractured struts cut into the flesh surrounding them, making the slightest move agony. The wing had to be laid out properly, she knew that. It would heal if it were laid out properly, and not otherwise. Gritting her teeth, she struggled to stretch out the part of it which had not been wholly shattered, and finally, keening softly in pain, she managed to get perhaps half of it spread out upon the earth. No more was possible.

Sunlight. Warm, welcoming, intoxicating sunlight. Sunlight such as this creature has never known it. Born in shadow, raised in shadow, imprisoned in shadow. Waves of light beat down upon her wings now, warming her blood, soothing her pain, quelling her fear. Her heart strengthens within her chest as sun-warmed blood fills it, driving the healing power outward to every fiber of her flesh. Even her damaged wing trembles as the warm blood flows through it, throbbing with fresh vitality. But sunlight cannot reach the parts that need the healing most, nor fix into their proper place fragments of bone that are all askew. Keening in frustration, she tries again to move the damaged wing, which starts it bleeding again. Precious healing fluid trickling down upon the ground, where the magic is worthless—

Siderea opened her eyes. For a small eternity she just lay there, unmoving, her cheek resting against the creature's tail, feeling the warmth of the sunlight course through her flesh. The *creature's* flesh. Was this some strange dream that preceded death? If not . . . then what? She tried to rise up and, to her amazement, was able to do so. Her wounded arm still ached, but the pain was no longer blinding; she swayed for a moment on her feet, then they were steady beneath her. Far steadier than they should have been, given her condition. The sunlit world seemed bright again. Her senses were functioning.

She was healing.

She took one step, and then two, and at last, when she was sure that she was steady enough to walk, began to work her way around the Souleater's body. She could see where one set of wings had been splayed out across the earth; shimmering highlights ran up and down their length each time the creature drew in a breath. They were not like the wings of the other Souleaters, but longer and fuller, with veils of shimmering membrane trailing down from their lower edges. Fairy wings, she thought, as she watched them shimmer cobalt and violet in the sunlight. Strangely, madly beautiful.

The creature turned her head to follow her, black eyes watching as she made her way around to the other side. There . . . there was the damage. One of the main struts, a slender bone that swept out from the creature's shoulder to the outermost tip of its wing had been fractured in at least a dozen places. Razor-edged shards of bone had cut into the tender membrane, leaving parts of it in tatters; the whole of that wing was crusted with blood. The Souleater had paid a heavy price for its escape.

Siderea crouched down before the broken limb and slowly, carefully, began to work the pieces back into position. Dark red blood slicked her hands, making it hard for her feel what she was doing; she wiped them off on what was left of her riding gown and continued. The Souleater keened softly as she worked, clearly in pain, but it made no move to stop her. It understood that she was trying to help.

Finally all the bits of bone were lined up in roughly the

proper configuration, and the torn membrane smoothed down into position as best as it could be. As she stepped back and looked at her handiwork, Siderea realized that her own arm had stopped bleeding. Apparently she had healed herself, without even realizing it.

Her power had returned.

Hesitantly—oh, so hesitantly!—she summoned the supernatural vision that she would need to look within herself. That she was able to do so at all told her volumes about her condition; a mere hour ago such a thing would have been impossible. Heart pounding, she turned her witch's vision inside herself, seeking the fire that burned at the center of every human soul. The source of all life, all witchery.

And she gasped as it came into focus. No longer merely a dying flame which any metaphysical breeze might extinguish, but true soulfire, steady and strong. There was no mistaking the change, or its significance; dying witches did not possess such energy.

For a long time she just stared at the Souleater. A distant part of her brain remembered that it was one of the most feared creatures on the face of the earth whose cousins had once brought human civilization to its knees. She should rightly fear it. Any sane person would.

She had passed beyond sanity long ago.

Hands trembling—from exaltation now rather than fear—she tore a length of fabric from the hem of her gown and began to clean the damaged wing. She could sense the creature flinching in pain as she rubbed off the crusted blood and filth, but it made no protest. It needed sunlight on its skin to heal. As each new inch of membrane was exposed she could feel the sun's heat seeping into it, warming the creature's blood . . . and her own.

I will be whole again, she thought, awed by the revelation.

Finally, she had done all she could. She stood back and watched the Souleater in silence for a moment or two, watching the rise and fall of her chest as she rested, sunlight playing across the wounded wing in ripples of azure and violet. What a strangely beautiful creature she was, Siderea thought. The ancient legends spoke only of terror and death, and hinted at strange mesmeric powers, but said nothing about beauty. Little wonder that men had been mesmerized by these creatures when they first appeared in the sky. Little wonder that it had been so hard for them to muster any real defense against them.

Slowly, carefully, she lay down beside the Souleater, resting her head against its shoulder. She could feel the thrumming of its heart against her cheek, a strong and steady beat now, slowing gradually as the great creature slipped into sleep. Closing her eyes, she tried to let go of all the tension of the past few days—and all the pain of the last few hours—and just lose herself in its musky-sweet perfume. Gradually, her own heartbeat slowed to match the pulse of the creature; the rhythm of her breathing stilled to match the Souleater's own.

And the sunlight warmed her wings as they slid into sleep.

CHAPTER 14

KAMALA COULD hear the screaming in her sleep.

Or at least she had two days ago, when she had last slept. The best she'd been able to do since then was to lie on the ground with her eyes closed, waiting for dawn to come. Rhys seemed to think that it was important they do at least that much, even though she was pretty sure that he wasn't sleeping either. The body must rest, he told her, even if the mind could not.

Gods alone knew what the horses were going through.

Rhys said they should not have started hearing the screams yet. The fact that they were doing so was apparently another sign that something was seriously wrong in this region, and the cause of it was surely only a few day's travel ahead of them. He said that one used to be able to approach the Wrath quite closely before the death-screams became audible. And the pain-screams. And the hunger-screams. The Guardians used potions to counteract the effect but all his potions had been left behind at Anukyat's citadel. Along with his maps.

Shivering, Kamala turned over in her leafy bed, wishing

she could have a single hour's peace in which to sleep. But that could not be managed by any means the Guardians knew of, and of course sorcery was out of the question this close to the Wrath. A spell for silence was as likely to melt her eardrums as it was to do anything useful.

Daring to open one eye, Kamala saw that the sun was rising at last. With a weary sigh she sat up and saw that Rhys was already up and about, checking on the horses that were tethered near the stream. Long leather leads would allow them to drink freely and graze on the thick summer grass nearby at will—assuming they calmed down enough to do so. Did the horses hear human screams also, Kamala wondered, or were their nerves being stretched to the breaking point by some equine equivalent? Perhaps the sound of other horses being tortured to death? As the animals paced restlessly at the farthest reaches of their thin leather leads, it was patently clear that all their instincts were crying out for them to break free and run from this place as if all the demons of all the hells were after them. Thus far only Rhys' quiet mastery had kept them from doing so. How much longer would that last?

"That won't hold them," she said. "Not if they really want to go."

Rhys looked over at her. He had stopped shaving days ago, and his jaw was speckled with stubble. Didn't trust his own hand with a knife anymore, he'd said. "It's not meant to." He came back to the campsite and knelt down by the brush beds they had assembled the night before. "If they panic so badly that it drives them to break the leads, then it's time for them to go. Prey animals can only remain here so long before their minds snap. Predators last a bit longer." He handed her the pack with the food in it. "Ugly thing to see, an insane horse. Best they should escape the place before that happens."

"I take it we're not riding today." She tried to hand the pack back to him without opening it, but he wouldn't take it. "I have no appetite in this place," she protested.

"All the more reason to eat something." He stared at her until she gave up with a sigh, and fished a hunk of cheese and a strip of salted meat out of the bag. He was right, damn it. "And yes, I think this is as far as the horses should go. I had some potions with me to calm their nerves down a bit—we use them often when we patrol this far north—but they're gone now." His expression hardened. He didn't often speak of what had happened to him in the Citadel, but it was clear that Anukyat's betrayal of the Guardians' cause was something he could neither understand nor forgive.

He squatted down by her side and dug out a few strips of dried meat for his own breakfast. Nothing fancy today, nor anything that required preparation. His mind was elsewhere.

How like Andovan he looked right now, with the low-angled light of early morning setting his golden hair afire! When she had first noticed the resemblance she had thought it a quirk of her own sentiment, replacing the face of this warrior with that of her former consort and lover. But then one night Rhys had told her about his family history, so now she understood the truth. The same inheritance had molded them both; the same *lyr* blood ran in both their veins. Magical blood, he had told her. The stuff from which heroes were conjured.

Strange, how his voice became bitter when he said that. As if such an inheritance were a curse to him, rather than a gift. He was full of mysteries and bitterness, unlike the doomed prince who had been his nephew. That one had been half *lyr* as well, but it'd had no real meaning to him. His fate was meant to play out in the halls of kings, not in the lairs of monsters.

"So how close are we to this Spear thing?" she asked.

He hesitated. "Judging from the strength of the Wrath here, I would normally say less than a few hours' journey, but who knows? The curse used to be much more isolated; one could actually come within sight of a Spear before feeling its full power. Now?" He shrugged. "We will be there before nightfall, that much I'm sure of. Or at least as close as we are able to get to it."

"I thought the Guardians repaired these things. Surely you can't do that from a distance?"

"There are the potions I told you of, and also special rituals, designed for that purpose. Sometimes the Magisters help with those, though you can tell how much they hate it. However, as I no longer have any of those things with me, we shall have to make do with simple courage." He looked at her. "You don't have to come all the way, you know. You can wait here until I return. There's no shame in it."

She could feel her expression harden. "I'm not a coward."

"You're also not a Guardian. You have no duty driving you."

But I have my own reasons for being here, she thought. *And they are as valid as yours.*

"I will go as far as I can," she told him. And clearly he had learned enough of her nature by now not to argue with her further.

They left their camp as it was, pausing only briefly to smother the fire so that the surrounding forest would be safe. Rhys wrapped some of the food in a linen cloth and tucked it into his pocket, and both of them took their water skins, but otherwise they left the supplies behind. The message was clear, and chilling: if they did not come back within a day or two, they would not be coming back at all.

Rhys had fashioned lances on their second day of freedom, stripping two long, straight boughs of leaves and then sharpening the tips. Hardened by fire, they now made excellent walking sticks, and they helped Kamala keep her balance as they worked their way up the rocky hillside. They climbed without speaking, but not in silence. The voices were always there. Screaming in pain. Warning them to flee. Bearing witness to a suffering more terrible than anything they had known in their lives. Or so it seemed to Kamala.

Directly ahead.

———

What exactly are these Spears? she had asked him during the first long day of riding. *Why does so much depend upon them?*

We don't really know, he had told her. *Tradition says that the gods cast them down from the heavens in the final days of the Great War, to affix a curse to the land. In the places where they struck the ground it was split open, and the blood of the Earth Mother spewed upward. When it cooled, it formed a shell about the Spear itself, protecting it. We keep the shells in good repair to protect what is inside them, so that the Wrath will remain strong and true, but I do not know of any man that has seen what is actually inside one, or heard any tale that hints at what they really are.*

———

Terror.

Dark, cold waves of it. Rushing over her with a roar, filling her lungs, choking off her breath.

Go away! The voices screamed at her. *Run! There is still time!*

Magisters stirred in the shadows surrounding her, their fingers tracing signs in the air, weaving spells to entrap her. She refused to look at them. They were not real. The Wrath had summoned them once in a nightmare and now it had done so again in her waking moments, but they were still nothing more than an illusion that drew its strength from her deepest fears.

You don't understand! the voices screamed. *You can't understand!* Magic clawed at the inside of her head like a wild animal in a trap. *Flee while you can! To stay here is death!*

"Kamala!"

It took her a moment to sort out the one human voice from the cacophony. Rhys. She struggled to look at him—to focus upon him—and finally managed it. His own face was ghostly white, all color drained from it by the force of the supernatural assault. Did his *lyr* blood make him immune to the voices, did it quiet them enough that he could still think clearly? Or was he more sensitive to them than she was, more able to make out exact words and warnings, but somehow granted the spiritual fortitude to stand against them? His expression was dark and terrible, and for a moment she sensed how hard it was for him to focus on her when the source of the disturbance was right before them.

Then he took her hand and squeezed it. She shut her eyes and for a moment—a single moment—managed to focus her mind upon that contact, to draw strength from it.

Ahead of them was a vast plateau, flat and desolate. There were no trees within sight, only an endless tundra with a thin cover of scraggly grass punctuated by tangles of dry brush. In the center of it was a single butte, a flat-topped granite island rising up from a black and desolate sea. One whole side of it had been broken apart, leaving a huge concave gap in its side. Winter's ice, perhaps, shattering the ancient stone.

Atop it was the Spear.

It stood twice as tall as a man, or perhaps even taller, a

monument of mottled stone that seemed alien to everything around it. Its surface was a malformed, tortured shape, as if a cone of rock had somehow been stretched and twisted out of all natural proportion. It had probably been located in the center of the butte at one point, but centuries of erosion had worn the structure away at its base, and now that one whole side of the butte had broken away, it no longer had the support required to sustain itself. The lower portion of one side had broken open, revealing a hollow interior. Some of the rocks that had fallen were suspiciously regular in form, Kamala noted. Bricks? Whatever lay beyond them, inside the spire, was hidden in darkness. Maybe that was because the sun was on the wrong side for visibility. Or maybe it would have been dark inside the thing regardless.

"Broken," Rhys whispered hoarsely. Strangely, the terrible screaming that had been with them for hours now did not drown out human sound; Kamala could hear the clear note of disbelief that was in his voice. Whatever sort of damage the Guardians usually repaired, it was clearly nothing on this scale. "No wonder the Wrath was disrupted."

"You can repair it, yes?" When he said nothing she pressed, "Isn't that what Guardians do?"

He did not answer her, only stared at the thing for a moment longer, and then, with a grim look upon his face, began to make his way forward, toward the shattered spire. She wanted to follow him—she tried to follow him—but she could not make her body obey her. Every time she tried to force one of her legs to move, to take a step forward, the power of the Wrath would wash over her in a wave, and it took all her courage not to turn around and flee from the place in mindless terror. If she stood still, if she made no effort to approach, it was tolerable, albeit by a slim margin. Her whole body shook from the force of it, but at least she did not run away.

She watched in fascination as Rhys slowly approached the butte. He sounded like he was muttering prayers under his breath; asking his gods for protection, perhaps? Weren't they supposedly the ones that had created this thing in the first place? The ghostly voices flowed over him, screaming their warning, but they could not turn him away, or even slow his steps. Was his *lyr* blood shielding him from the worst of their assault, or was his sense of duty simply stronger than his fear?

She watched as he reached the butte at last and climbed to the top of it, then approached the Spear itself. Though the damage was on the side of the spire, he approached it from the front; perhaps that was the path of least magical resistance, she thought. She could see him trembling as he finally knelt down by the opening to see what was inside, though whether that was because of fear, or simply the physical strain of the last few days catching up with him, Kamala could not begin to guess.

And then he drew back suddenly, as if shocked. He wrapped his arms tightly about himself; his body began to shake violently. It was as if some power had taken hold of him and he could not break free.

Long minutes passed. Fear whipped around Kamala like a whirlwind. Still Rhys remained as he was, arms clutched over his midriff as if there were some unbearable pain centered there. He was no longer moving, but frozen in place. It was an eerie, inhuman stillness. As if he were carved from the same stone as the monument before him.

Time passed. The sun shifted its position. The voices screamed in Kamala's brain with such force that it brought tears to her eyes.

Still Rhys did not move.

Something was wrong, Kamala realized. Something all his training had not prepared him for.

She was going to have to go to him.

She tried to take a step forward, but it was like trying to walk in a hurricane. Black emotions came rushing across the open tundra, howling as they enveloped her. Shutting her eyes, she used the skills that Ethanus had drilled into her to try to focus her mind inward, to regain control of her flesh. *Go back!* the voices screamed at her. *Death is here! Turn and run!* But Rhys was not running away, and so she would not either.

Shutting her eyes for a moment, she summoned the memory of his hand holding hers. The warmth that had flowed through his touch. His protectiveness. The source of that warmth was up ahead, and it needed her. The knowledge she sought was up ahead, and he was guarding it. The voices could scream their warnings all they liked; the magic of this place could fill her head with illusions and pain; none of that would keep her from going to him.

Move! she commanded herself. Forcing her limbs to obey. Slowly, torturously, one leg moved forward. Then the other. Raw emotions battered at her soul as she moved, wave after wave of sorcerous assault. *Hunger. Pain. Fear.* She struggled to stay focused on her body and on the few feet of black earth just ahead of her. At least the ground was solid here; thank the gods for small favors. After days of riding across mountains and through rivers, that was a veritable luxury.

Time ceased to exist. So did the voices. Ethanus had taught her how to focus inside herself in preparation for the day when her First Transition would require such skills; now she applied them here. Illusions of pain ripped through her flesh, but she knew them for what they were and ignored them. Shadowy figures draped in black robes reached out with their sorcery to bind her, but she refused to acknowledge their existence. Somewhere a creature was starving to death, and its hunger reverberated within her flesh as if it were her own; she focused upon moving her feet, one after the other, and keeping her balance as she did so. If the Wrath overcame her now and she fell, she was not all that sure she would be able to rise up again.

Then, finally, she reached the butte and began to climb. Her hands were covered with blood by the time she reached the top; she could not remember the exact cause.

She looked at Rhys and was shaken to her very core. What had she expected to see? Terror in his eyes, or perhaps the black vacancy of supernatural possession. What else could overwhelm such a man so that all his faculties deserted him?

Tears.

She saw tears.

She reached out slowly and touched one. He started violently, as if awakened from a trance by her touch, and he reached up and grabbed her hand. His grip was so tight it was painful.

"Look!" he rasped. "Tell me what you see!"

She leaned forward to peer into the dark space inside the Spear. At first she could see nothing at all, save that the interior space seemed to be regular in shape—cylindrical with a domed top—and had some kind of runic figures scrawled all over it. The script was familiar somehow, but she could not remember where she had seen it before.

Then her eyes adjusted to the dim light, and she saw.

There was a mummy inside. Maybe a living body once, when it had first been sealed into this space, but subjected by now to centuries of cold, dry mountain air. Its skin, stretched tightly over an armature of sharp-edged bones, was the color of tree bark, and its posture and expression made it clear just how the owner had died.

Kamala turned away from the spire and leaned over the edge of the butte just in time to vomit.

Its mouth had been frozen by death in mid-scream, its final expression; its spindly, shrunken arms were thrust outward as if to batter at the inside of its prison. Its fingers . . . its fingers were shattered at the tips, Kamala saw. Scraped raw and bloody as their owner had tried desperately to claw his or her way out. But there was no door in this prison, nor window. No escape. Whoever this was, he had been left to die slowly of thirst and starvation, suffocating in this space as his mind became delusional for want of food, of air . . . of hope.

And memories came welling up from the inner recesses of her soul as her nightmare engulfed her once more.

—*Bleeding hands scrape against the wall to no avail. She feels something chiseled crudely into the rough surface. Letters. Surrounding her. Spells—powerful spells—that will slowly but surely steal all the life force that is in her and transform it—*

—*Wordlessly she screams, opening her mouth and letting the terror pour out until the stone walls shake from the force of the sound. And the animals outside this magical tomb will hear its echo and flee, for the sound will be so terrible that not even a demon would dare to approach—*

Her sleeping mind had recognized the Wrath for what it was and tried to warn her.

Now she, too, was trembling.

"He was right." Rhys' voice was hollow. "Anukyat. He knew."

No god had created this spire. No god had condemned this

person to death or deliberately crafted a horror chamber to turn his last hours into agony. This was done by human hands.

"They killed all the witches," Kamala said. Wincing at the taste of the words in her mouth. "That must be why there were none of them left after the war with the Souleaters. Every one of your Spears contains a human sacrifice."

Only witches could have served for such a sacrifice, she thought. No one else could expend all the vital energy of a human lifetime in a brief span of days; no mere human being could have provided such terribly efficient fuel for the curse that bound them.

She gazed out across the tundra; her Sight could barely pick out the shimmer of the Wrath stretching across the land from east to west, a grim and compelling power. "It is the energy of death," she whispered. "Human fear, human starvation, the madness that comes of being buried alive, all concentrated by these spells written here, a lifetime's worth of soulfire released in a brief span of hours, then woven into a barrier—"

"Who made the spells?" he demanded. "Who did this to him?"

She shook her head and whispered, "I don't know."

"Willing? Was it willing? The legends say the witches sacrificed themselves. . . ."

She shuddered. Was it possible that any man or woman would agree to such a fate? "I don't know, Rhys." How many Spears were there, in all? Dozens on this continent at least, and supposedly more wherever dry land was available around the world. The whole of the polar region had been circumscribed, a line of Spears to guard the human lands forever. A seemingly impenetrable barrier, whose mortar was death.

How many witches had died for this? Who had killed them?

"We can't fix this," Rhys said. His voice was a hollow thing. "The spells are broken. Look . . ." He grabbed up a handful of shattered brick and let it run out between his fingers. Whatever figures had once been drawn upon it were beyond restoration now. "No man would know how to redraw them." She saw him open his mouth to say more, then shut it again. *No man would be willing to,* his expression said. *We are Guardians, not murderers.*

Closing her eyes for a moment, fighting to shut out the terrible power of the place, Kamala tried to think clearly. "We need to copy the figures," she said at last. Ethanus would know how to decipher them, or at least how to begin researching them. "Bring them back with us, for others to look at." Maybe something could be done to restore the Wrath to strength without repeating the atrocities that were used to establish it in the first place.

If so, the Magisters would surely value such knowledge.

Rhys shuddered. For a moment he was so still that she feared she had lost him again; then, with a nod of determination, he pushed his left sleeve all the way up his arm, baring his flesh. Taking out his knife, he unsheathed it one handed and then pressed the point against his forearm . . . and began to cut.

"Rhys!" She reached out for him but he pulled away from her.

"Did you bring pen and ink to this place?" he demanded. "Wax tablets, perhaps? Because I know that I didn't." He stabbed the knife into his shirt sleeve, tearing through the fabric. "Maybe we can weave a tapestry instead, with this. Embroider a record. What do you think? Or maybe . . . maybe you can work some witch's spell here, so we remember everything? Oh, but wait. No spells here. So that won't work."

His eyes met hers, and she saw they were filled with madness;

his blond hair, made wild by the wind, clung to his tear-stained face. For a moment he just stared at her, and then, when she made no further move to stop him, he returned to his work. Copying the runes from the inside of the magical tomb, carving them into his flesh. "Not so deeply," she whispered once. "If you bleed too much you will not make it home." But he didn't seem to hear her. The self-mutilation was an act of penance, the flow of blood a purification. Now and then he winced as the knife cut into his arm, and it seemed to her that he drew a savage satisfaction from the sensation. Pain was communion with those who had come before him, who had suffered and died so that he and his people might live.

Finally he had copied all that he could. She helped him roll down his shirt again, wrapping the sleeve snugly about his arm to staunch the flow of blood. He made no move to help or hinder her, but accepted her ministrations in stoic silence. When she reached across him to gather up a handful of the shattered brick he did not move, but stared off into the distance. In shock. She put the sample in her food pouch and then, gently, took his face in her hands.

"Rhys. Rhys." She shook him gently until his eyes fixed on her. "We have to go now. We have to go home. Can you walk?"

He hesitated, then nodded.

She helped him get to his feet. Helped him climb down from the butte. Mercifully, his state of shock seemed to be sparing him the worst of the Wrath's power, and concentrating on his welfare seemed to be helping her. Or perhaps it was because they were leaving this place. The power of the barrier was focused on driving living creatures away, so that none would be able to cross: fleeing it now, Kamala and Rhys had its metaphysical current at their back.

Hours passed. Night fell. Exhausted and drained, Rhys stumbled through the darkness. Exhausted and drained, Kamala tried to guide him.

Eventually the screams faded into silence, and with them the power of the Wrath. Not knowing where they were—nor caring—the two of them lowered themselves to the rocky ground, arm in arm, and slept at last.

Mercifully, they did not dream.

CHAPTER 15

 OMETHING WAS wrong.
S   Approaching Siderea's hilltop palace, Colivar could not pin down the source of his disquiet. Nothing seemed out of place, at least to his casual inspection. Brilliant white columns gleamed in the sunlight as they did on every other summer day; the salt-laden breeze blew in from the sea in its accustomed manner; even the distant murmur of human activity in the port far below was its usual timbre and volume. No, everything looked and sounded perfectly normal.

So what made him so sure that it wasn't? It was something he sensed viscerally, as an animal does, without having a name for it. A fleeting unease that he could glimpse out of the corner of his eye, but not look on directly. It was a kind of thing he had never felt before, and since there were few things in the world that he had not experienced—sorcerous or otherwise— it bothered him.

Perhaps it was simply the lack of welcome that seemed so odd. He was accustomed to having a servant run up to him the moment he arrived so the absence of one was noteworthy.

Evidently Siderea no longer expected surprise visits from sorcerers—or perhaps no longer welcomed them. He could hardly blame her for the latter. The Magisters had not exactly treated her well of late. Lazaroth's comment about maggots came to mind.

And then, at last, a servant appeared. The man wasn't exactly jubilant to see him, but at least he was properly respectful. "Magister Colivar." He bowed deeply in respect. "You are here to see Her Majesty?"

"If she is receiving," he said, berating himself a moment later for expressing himself in such a manner. A Magister should never appear obsequious.

"Of course, my lord. Please follow me."

Colivar was led into the palace and taken to a receiving chamber, where he was left to wait. That was also a new custom; normally Siderea put all her other business aside when a Magister came calling. Nothing about the room itself looked any different than the last time he'd seen it, but even so his hackles rose as he entered. Whatever disturbance he had sensed outside the palace was clearly active in here as well.

Then Siderea entered. She looked lovely as always, of course, but a trained eye could pick out the change in her demeanor, from her usual languid elegance to something colder. Not a great surprise. The fact that she had made him wait had warned him what to expect.

"Colivar." She raised one eyebrow as she looked him over, as if not quite sure what manner of creature he was. Then she held out her hand to him, inviting the appropriate homage. "It has been some time."

He walked over to her, took her hand in his, and lifted it briefly to his lips in greeting. He could smell a strange perfume rising from her fingertips, some kind of warm, sweet scent with undertones of musk. It seemed oddly familiar to him. One more part of the puzzle.

"And to what do I owe this great honor?" she asked, slipping her fingers free of his grasp.

He made sure his disquiet did not affect his tone, asking with accustomed lightness, "Can a humble sorcerer no longer visit?"

A fleeting smile came and went, though her gaze remained cold. "Come now, Colivar. You were never humble."

"Even a sorcerer can be humbled by beauty, lady."

"Beauty fades in time. And not even the Magisters can save it, in the end. At least that's what some of them have told me. Is it true?"

Inwardly he sighed. "I wish that it were otherwise," he said, with rare sincerity.

The dark eyes narrowed. "Do you really?"

"Of course. How could you doubt it?"

She folded her arms across her chest. "So, would you teach me true sorcery, if you could? Would you make me like yourself, so that I might survive the ages?" The black fire in her eyes burned fiercely, hungrily. "*If you could.*"

He drew in a deep breath before answering. "It is not within my power, Siderea. You know that."

"Because no woman can wield true sorcery. Isn't that right? We are . . . what? Too weak to master it? Too flighty?" She shook her head. "Do you know the answer to that, Colivar? Can you tell me why I must die? Can any Magister?"

For a moment he was silent. There was no right answer to such a question, and he did not know which wrong one to choose. "I don't know," he said finally. "No one knows." Hopefully she would accept that at face value. "I am sorry, Siderea."

Even if Transition were possible for women, it would not be possible for you. You are simply not inhuman enough to survive what that change requires.

With a heavy sigh she shut her eyes. For a long moment she was silent. He could sense some great internal struggle going on, and he respected her enough not use sorcery on her to eavesdrop on the details. Finally, she whispered in a trembling voice, "Why did none of you tell me? Why did you leave me alone to discover the truth?"

He shook his head. "I don't know, Siderea."

"I expected better of you. After so many years. . . ." She turned away from him, biting her lip. "I expected better of all of you," she whispered.

"You know better than anyone else how few morati we become involved with. The rhythm of mortal life is alien to us. As are its accustomed sentiments." He sighed. "Accuse the Magisters of many things, lady. Gods know, we probably deserve them all. But never believe that we would not drive death from your door if that were possible."

How convincing his words sounded! And it was the proper thing to say to her, even if it were not really true. Colivar suspected that most of the Magisters would not lift a finger to help her if they thought the price of it was having a woman invade their exclusive brotherhood. Siderea was like a king's concubine in that regard; good enough to share a man's bed, not good enough to share his throne. Thank the gods that would never be tested.

What about me? he wondered. *Would I give her the gift of eternity if I could?*

He didn't know the answer.

Gently he took her by the shoulders, turning her back to

him. The strange, sweet perfume that she wore filled his nostrils, stirring his blood unexpectedly. He put a hand to her cheek and felt the life pulsing fiercely within her. *This one will not go quietly to death,* he thought.

"I cannot preserve your life past its natural span," he said gently. "But I will help you as I always have, in other things. Those favors which my kind has provided for you, you will have so long as you walk this earth. I promise you that."

"And when I need you?" she whispered. "What then? I have no way to call for help."

Her words were a sudden reminder of something he had forgotten. Something they all had forgotten. It took all his self-control not to let the shock of that realization show on his face.

She had tokens from all her sorcerous lovers. Personal items which could be used to call to them . . . or to focus less benign spells upon them, if she so desired. What would become of that collection when she died? Which of the Magisters would get to it first? In the secret and subtle wars that sorcerors waged against one another to fend off the ennui of immortality, such a collection was beyond price.

She did not have Colivar's token any longer. He remembered that now. She had used it to call him to her when the messenger from Corialanus had brought news of the Souleater, and he had never replaced it. So he was safe. The same could not be said for the others.

"I will keep in touch," he promised softly. His mind raced as he tried to figure out where she would have stored such a thing and what sort of magical defenses might surround it. "If you need me I will know it, and I will come to you."

The black eyes filled with gratitude. For a moment she hesitated, then she embraced him. Tangling her fingers in his long hair as she wrapped her arms around him, burying her face in his neck. Clutching him with all the desperate strength of a drowning woman. And when he put his arms about her in turn, she wept. All the fear and uncertainty seemed to come pouring out of her in deep, gut-wrenching sobs. He was tempted to use his sorcery to blunt the edge of her emotions, but then he thought, *No. Do not toy with her as you would with a common morati. She deserves better than that.* And so he held her until the flood tide finally receded of its own accord. Until she broke the embrace of her own volition, and stepped back from him.

"I am so sorry, Colivar . . ." Wrapping her arms about her, hands tucked out of sight, she breathed the words. "This is not your burden."

He conjured a handkerchief and used it to wipe the tears from her face. "You have nothing to apologize for. Save perhaps befriending men who are not worthy of you."

She lowered her eyes and nodded. He could see her trembling now, as she struggled to regain her composure. But it was clearly a losing battle. Finally she looked up at him, her wide eyes pained, and said, "Colivar, this is all too much to deal with. Your coming today . . . I was not prepared. Would you . . . would you understand if I said I needed to be alone for a while? To process all this? I am so sorry. . . ."

"No need to apologize," he answered quickly. He kissed her gently on the forehead one last time, feeling her shudder beneath the contact. So much pain. So much fear. He genuinely wished he could do something to help her.

"I will be back," he promised her. Whispering other things as well, to soften the edge of his departure.

But his focus was no longer upon her sorrow, and when he finally got far enough from the palace to be sure that she was not watching him, he crafted a tendril of power to go search for her tokens. He gave it an hour to do its work. It turned up nothing. Oddly, that pleased him.

The fact that she is merely a witch does not mean she is foolish, he thought.

He wondered how many others of his kind would have to learn that lesson the hard way.

You should have ripped his throat out with your teeth.

The Souleater's indignation was so powerful that for a moment it was as if Siderea could indeed taste Colivar's blood on her lips. Sweet, sweet blood! How she hated him, and all his kind! It had taken all her art not to let that hatred show while Colivar was here. Not to let him guess the truth.

Our territory! Inviolate! The Souleater's thoughts were a storm within her. Not voiced in human language at their source, those thoughts, but translated somewhere within her own brain so that she might understand them. The process was becoming more and more natural to both of them as time went on, but no more gentle.

It is all good, she thought back to the creature. *Trust me.*

A hot wave of anger enveloped her. She no longer feared such onslaughts, but let the bestial emotion surge freely through her, drowning out her human instincts. It was the stuff of life that transferred power from the Souleater's flesh to her own, and she welcomed it as she would welcome the embrace of a lover.

Trust me, she whispered to her winged consort when the worst of the hate-storm finally subsided. The power in her own soul was so strong now that she could feel its heat tingling in her fingertips. What sorcery could the Magisters possibly wield that was the equal of the Souleater's vitality? Poor, doomed souls, wrapped in their black shrouds, imagining themselves invincible! Someday she would beckon to them and they would come to her, tearing each other to pieces in the hope of being allowed to touch her. Sweet, sweet vengeance!

Trust me, she whispered again to her consort. Soothing thoughts. Loving confidence.

He trespassed! He offended!

And he will pay for it, she promised.

She opened her hand and gazed with satisfaction upon the long black hairs that lay across her palm, tangled between her fingers.

"All in good time," she whispered.

CHAPTER 16

AS THE butterfly's wings fanned slowly up and down they began to change color. First the orange spots along the outer edges grew larger and darkened, then they transformed into deep violet patches. Next, two white streaks radiating out from each side of its body merged into one and then curled back upon themselves, forming intricate knotwork designs along the base. Following which the tiny white spots on the creature's body began to move about as well, gathering into rosettes reminiscent of a leopard's coat, a strange configuration for an insect.

The butterfly sipped from its flower once more, seemingly oblivious to its amazing transformation. Then it beat its wings quickly and was borne aloft on the breeze to be swept away from them.

"So your witchery will work here?" Rhys asked.

"So it seems." Kamala would have liked to test her sorcery against some larger template before entrusting a human life to it again, but no real witch would waste athra like that. Until she was ready to let her true status be known she would have to limit herself to the sorts of tests that a real witch might enact.

She looked back at Rhys. The fact that they had gotten out of Alkali territory safely—and were now beyond the range of the Wrath's corrupting influence—had done little to improve his spirits. There was an emptiness in his eyes that made her shiver, as if a part of his soul was now gone. Her gentlest touch received no response at all, or if it was noticed, was simply shrugged off. She had watched him lie awake in the moonlight for many nights now, and wished that she could do something to sooth his spirits. But she had not been willing to take a chance on how the Wrath might warp her spells. Now that sorcery was possible again, she didn't know where to begin. What did you do to help a man who had lost his gods?

They had made love once. If it could be called that. When they had traveled far enough south that the screams of the Wrath could no longer be heard, and had stolen enough sleep to restore their strength, he had awakened in the depths of the night and reached out for her, and she, stirred by the same wordless need, had responded. Life calling out to life, in the shadow of destruction. It was quick and desperate and when it was done he lay in her arms shivering, and she understood why. No words were offered, nor any asked for. Some things defied the bounds of language.

In the morning they had saddled up their horses and started on their way once more. They never spoke of that night. He never touched her again. Now and then she thought she saw something flickering in the depths of those empty eyes, a tiny spark of human emotion that was struggling to break through to the surface. But because she didn't know how to fan it properly—or if should be fanned at all—she let it be.

He had not slept since then, and was clearly exhausted, but perhaps he deemed that better than nightmares.

Gazing at the land ahead of them now—windswept plains cloaked in tall grass, with patches of dense brush, a different universe entirely than the land that surrounded the Spear—he told her, "You don't have to do this for me."

"It's safe here," she assured him. "My spells will work properly now."

"Safe for me. Not for you." The tiny spark flickered in his eyes for a moment, a brief defiance. "We do not ask our witches to give up their life-essence for us unless there is no other choice."

"You didn't ask for it," she pointed out.

"Transporting someone costs you dearly, does it not?"

"It costs much soulfire." In fact, the transportation of living creatures was one of the most costly tasks in the sorcerous lexicon. Removing a sentient being from one place and materializing him in another with all his living systems intact—not to mention his memories—was the ultimate test of any sorcerer. Or any witch, for that matter. The cost in athra was immense. The slightest mistake could be fatal. "But that is my concern, not yours."

She had already taken the necessary precautions. As soon as it had seemed that her powers were stable once more she had gone off by herself to burn out her current consort. Though she'd had no idea how much athra she had wasted in her struggle to shape-shift near the glen—or even how long the struggle had taken—she had felt she could not afford the risk of losing consciousness at some inopportune moment.

It was the first time she had ever done such a thing, but she knew the theory of it well enough. Waste the athra in pointless exercises, drain one's consort of the last of his life-essence, and force the next Transition to take place, claiming a fresh source of life. It took surprisingly little time to do; apparently her consort was nearly exhausted. A mere whisper of sorcery was all that was needed to drain him of what little energy was left. It was a humbling discovery. Truly, if she had not forced the issue now, when it was relatively safe to do so, she might well have lost her power in the midst of some more precarious procedure such as transportation. What happened to a sorcerer who lost control of his power when his physical body was *nowhere?* She shuddered to think of how close she had come to finding out.

It is not enough to grab hold of immortality, Ethanus had taught her. *One must be careful not to lose one's grip.*

There had been a whisper of some other power in the area that she had sensed as soon as her own was restored. A spell of searching. Wary of any sorcery on a good day, downright paranoid at the current moment, she had turned it aside with care. *Nothing here of any interest,* she had told it. *Whatever you seek, look elsewhere.*

"I am fully capable of riding home on horseback," Rhys insisted. And indeed he seemed ready to try. But in his current state she doubted he would get very far. Stubborn male pride. It made men do foolish things just to prove that they didn't need help. And the weaker they were, the more the game mattered to them. The eternal paradox of the male psyche.

"Try it," she said with equal stubbornness, "and I will pick you up off your horse to send you home, and that will cost me more soulfire in the end. Is that what you want?"

He gritted his teeth and shook his head and looked like he was going to argue with her further but then, with a sigh, he surrendered. Arguing with her required energy and right now he had very little to spare. "What do you need from me?"

"Where do you want to go?"

"Home." He whispered it. "To make my report. That is my duty, is it not? A Guardian is a creature of duty."

She had to ask. "How much will you tell them?"

"I don't know." His gaze was dark and empty. "Do I serve them best by telling them truth? Revealing that their heritage is a sham? That their ancestors" grand self-sacrifice was in fact a hideous atrocity? How will they do battle with the Souleaters then, knowing that? What will they draw upon for strength?" He sighed heavily. "I won't know until the words come out of my mouth, I think."

"I'm sorry." She whispered the words. "I wish I could help you."

"You have done more than I would ever have asked for. You know that."

She was not used to people being grateful to her; it stirred uncomfortable emotions. "I will need something to link you to the place you want to go, as I've never been there. Some sort of physical relic to help anchor that end of the spell."

"Anukyat's men took all my supplies. Including my focus for the meetinghouse. Does that mean you can't send me there?"

"Probably not. I'm sorry."

Cursing softly under his breath, he began to pat down his clothing, as if trying to remember what he still had on him. As one hand brushed across his chest he felt something lying beneath the bloodstained fabric. Fumbling inside the neck of his shirt, he pulled out a leather cord he wore as a necklace with a small stone threaded on it. He held it in his hand for a moment, his eyes shut; clearly it had memories attached. Then he took it off and handed it to her. "Will this do?"

The pendant was a small river rock with a natural hole

through the middle. Anukyat's men had clearly not deemed it significant enough to steal from him. "What is its significance?"

"Gwyn gave it to me, years ago. For luck." He laughed bitterly. "You see how well it worked."

"Where did that happen?"

"In Kierdwyn. The Lord Protector's keep."

"It might take us there, then." She turned it over in her hand, considering. The thing had no natural power, but many people ascribed good luck to such formations. "Or it might take us to wherever she is now."

"Either will do," he said quietly.

"We will have to leave the horses behind." As a sorcerer she could transport them easily enough, in fact, but no true witch would waste that much vital energy.

For once he did not argue with her, but simply nodded. "There is good forage here, and with luck they will find their way home in time. Or perhaps they will choose to stay here, without human masters."

He limped over to where the horses were waiting and carefully removed their last few bits of tack. She could see him wince once as he had to reach higher than his wounded arm wanted to go, but he would not ask her for help. Male pride.

"Rhys, let me tend to your wounds now."

He shook his head. "There will be healers when we get home. You have wasted too much life on me already."

"That is my choice to make, Rhys." When he did not respond she added, "Please."

He hesitated, then sighed and nodded.

Slowly, carefully, she untied the neck of his bloodstained shirt and pushed it back over his wounded shoulder so that she could see where the Alkali arrow had pierced him. The joint was stiff and it clearly pained him to move it, but the hole was clean and it was healing fairly well. Silently, secretly, she bound a bit of sorcery to speed up the process and ease the pain, but no more was necessary. Then she gestured for him to take a seat on a nearby tree stump and waited while he rolled up one leg of his breeches, so that she could look at the gash in his leg. As she had suspected, that wound was not doing well. Hard riding had kept it from closing properly and the surrounding flesh was red and swollen; a thick yellowish fluid had oozed out from one corner of the gash, and dried blood had crusted along its edges. She could see him biting his lip when she inspected it, trying not to admit how much it pained him to have it touched. Not good. Not good at all.

She drained the malevolence from the ugly wound, drawing out the poisons that were festering deep inside it. Then she used sorcery to weave the edges of the torn flesh back together, starting from the deepest point and working outward, toward the surface of his body. And she communicated to his body that all was well, so that the blood inflaming that region would disperse and the swelling subside.

Physical healing was easy enough. What she did not know how to do was attend to the wound in his soul.

When the scars of battle had been dealt with, she directed her attention to his self-inflicted wounds. Thus far he hadn't let her touch them, or even look at them, and she was afraid for a moment that this would still be the case. But apparently he no longer had the strength—or perhaps the heart—to resist her efforts. Numbly, he pushed the bloodstained sleeves up his arms so that she could take a look at his handiwork.

His arms were a gruesome sight. Reddened flesh was cross-hatched with shallow cuts and covered with streaks of dried blood.

Gently she brushed her fingers down the length of his arms, one at a time, using sorcery to cleanse the wounds, wondering at the meaning of the mysterious shapes he had copied. Strange angular figures covered every inch of his left arm in jagged, uneven rows. He had tried to etch a few figures into his right arm as well, when he'd run out of space, but the latter attempt had been far less successful.

For a long, silent moment she studied the strange shapes, binding enough sorcery to be sure they were burned into her memory forever. Then she took his left arm in her hands. It was stiff and painful and she handled it gently, summoning soulfire to her as she stroked the wounded skin once more with her fingertips.

"Leave the scars there," he ordered her. "Just like they would have healed on their own, without witchery."

She didn't point out to him that such self-mutilation was no longer necessary. She could easily summon a tablet for him to write on, to copy the precious signs, so that they could safely be erased from his flesh. But that wasn't what this was about, for him. There were other wounds inside Rhys, soul-deep wounds, that required pain for healing. To be scarred by his journey was somehow part of that formula. She didn't understand why—she wasn't sure he did either—but for now, she simply urged the cuts to scar over until they were no longer a series of swollen and infected gashes, but neatly fashioned ridges of reddened scar tissue: a surreal calligraphy.

And because his gaze was elsewhere for a moment, she was able to alter some of the symbols without his noticing. Every third or fourth sign was changed by a stroke or two, or transposed with another figure. Whoever attempted to read this text, even if he knew what language it came from, would have a serious challenge ahead of him. Then she wove a spell about the scars to guarantee that that no one would be able to detect her tampering, nor summon a vision of the original writing without her consent. Rhys would not notice the change, of that she was certain. Now she had made sure that no one else would be able to detect the obfuscation either, even by sorcerous means. The secrets guarded by the sorcerous script had been veiled once more.

I am sorry, my Guardian. I need to control this information. The right people will have it in time, I promise you.

When she was done he rolled down his sleeves again and tied the front of his shirt closed. He seemed to be moving more easily now, and his color definitely looked a shade better than before. But he was a battered, bloodstained figure all the same, and she wondered what kind of reaction they would get when they suddenly appeared . . . well, wherever.

Drawing in a deep breath, she focused her attention inside herself and began to summon power.

The map on the table was old, as were the brass weights that pinned it down at the corners, solid nuggets with the Kierdwyn family crest inscribed on them. Smaller markers had been placed along the southern border of the Protectorate, near where the High Kingdom began. Seven in all.

The Lord Protector Stevan Kierdwyn stood with his hands behind his back, studying each marker in turn, his expression growing more and more solemn as he absorbed each new bit of information. His advisers were accustomed to such thoughtful silence and waited patiently until he chose to speak.

"These raids," he said at last. "How sure are we of their true source?"

The lord constable's expression was grim. "You've seen the artifacts, Sire." He gestured toward the sideboard, where a variety of items had been laid out for his inspection. A soldier's short sword, such as troops in the High Kingdom carried. A leather supply pack, whose construction betrayed its martial origins. A bloodied pewter button cast with a double-headed hawk, torn loose from some anchoring uniform. "The Seers confirms they are all of military origin. Which means—"

Stevan waved him to silence. "I know what it means," he said sharply.

"Yes, Sire."

They were from the High Kingdom. There was no way around that fact. Seven brutal raids had taken place along Kierdwyn's southern border that appeared to be the work of mountain bandits—but those bandits had been outfitted with military weapons and supplies. And disguises. Good disguises. The people in the villages they had raided had believed themselves to be at the mercy of common outlaws. The women they had raped—

Rage flared inside the Lord Protector; it took all his willpower to keep it from consuming him.

Calm. Calm. Those who protect the civilized world must be calm.

Why would Salvator sanction something like this? What did he stand to gain?

Salvator would never order something like this. His faith would not allow it.

But a prince could set things in motion without ordering them directly. A single comment overheard by the wrong overzealous minister might result in actions he himself would never have approved. Some kings, like Danton, used that to their advantage, manipulating men without ever seeming to do so. Others, less savvy—or perhaps simply less careful—might well find themselves having to pass judgment on men at a later date whose only crime had been the blind passion of their service.

He did not want to think that the son of Danton Aurelius—his own grandchild!—could be so careless. But the only other viable explanation was that Salvator was losing control over his northern border, and that was not a good thing either. Gwynofar's marriage had been meant to secure a lasting peace in that region so that both the Protectorate and the High Kingdom might focus their attentions elsewhere. On new conquests in Danton's case, and ancient duties in Stevan's. Salvator had sworn that he would honor that treaty. So what was happening now?

Kierdwyn would have to move troops down to the trouble spot. There was no way around that. Whether the threat was from roving bandits or soldiers in disguise, his people had to be protected. And all of this was coming at the worst possible time, with their ancient enemy returning to the human lands. He could not attend to that threat properly with his soldiers having to spread out, ready for trouble anywhere along the border—

"Sire!"

Startled, he looked up just in time to see the air in the center of the room begin to ripple oddly. Sorcery! His lord constable moved forward quickly, putting himself between the Lord Protector and whatever unknown spell was about to manifest. Stevan moved back, giving his officer room to defend him if need be. Who would enter his home like this, unannounced?

Magisters generally had better manners, and witches rarely used their power for transportation.

Then two figures stepped through the rippling portal, and with a rushing sound the illusion vanished behind them. For a moment Stevan did not recognize either of them, then—

"Rhys?"

The Guardian was dazed and unsteady, and his shirt was streaked with blood. There was a woman by his side who the Lord Protector did not recognize at all, a fiery redhead dressed in a man's raiment who met his eyes proudly—nay, defiantly— as he took her measure. Both of them were wearing matching uniforms of some kind, and both looked like they had just fought their way through the seven hells and back.

Then the alarm came from his Seers, magical words lancing red-hot into his brain. *There is sorcery in the palace!* Were his Seers watching the castle right now, or had they set up some kind of magical alarm? Either way, he offered his mental reassurance. *All is as it should be.* Whatever was happening here, it was not cause for alarm . . . yet.

"Sire." Whispering the word, Rhys went down on one knee; the gesture seemed as much the product of sheer exhaustion as social courtesy. "Forgive us for the sudden intrusion." The woman at his side said nothing, and offered no gesture of obeisance. Was she the witch that had brought them here? If so, that was a noteworthy sacrifice.

"There is nothing to forgive," the Lord Protector told his son. "You would not have come here without good cause. So speak."

Rhys raised up his head; the expression in his bloodshot eyes was an empty and terrible thing. "The Wrath has been breached," he whispered. "In Alkali. The Guardians are corrupted."

A cold chill ran down Stevan's spine. "Does Favias know?"

Rhys shook his head. "I . . . we . . . came straight here. You are the first. . . ."

And then the faint light in the Guardian's eyes flickered and died. The strength bled out of his limbs as his lids fell shut, and he collapsed into a crumpled heap upon the floor.

Alarmed, the Lord Protector knelt down beside him, pressing fingers against Rhys' wrist to see if there was still a pulse. A servant stepped forward to help him.

"His wounds are healing," the witch told them. "But he has not slept in a very long time."

Rhys' pulse was strong. Racing, in fact, despite his collapse. Stevan felt an odd ridge on the inside of his son's wrist, and pushed up the sleeve to see what it was. Then further.

"What are these?" he demanded. Strange, angular symbols had been crudely etched into Rhys' flesh. They looked oddly familiar, as though he had seen something like this sometime in the past, but he could not place when or where.

"It is a long story," the witch said, "and one I am sure he would rather tell you himself. But give him a place to sleep for now, so that his spirit can restore itself, and I will explain as much as I can."

He nodded shortly and signaled for his servants to pick up the fallen warrior. "Put him in the finest guest chamber. Have food brought and a bath drawn for when he awakens, and see that he is attended at all times." The servants hurried to obey, one of them hoisting Rhys up onto his shoulder, while the other ran ahead to open the chamber doors ahead of him.

Stevan turned to face the witch. She awaited his word politely enough, but he could see the spark of defiance in her eyes, and she offered him no greater obeisance than a stiff, measured bow of her head: the absolute minimum that his rank required.

That was good. Witches should have spirit.

"Send word to Master Favias," he ordered his men, all the while never taking his eyes off her.

Was she from the Protectorates? Did she understand the significance of Rhys' warning? If so, she gave no sign of it.

"My name is Kamala," she said quietly.

He nodded solemnly. "Kierdwyn is in your debt, Kamala. As is its Lord Protector."

Raising a hand to silence her for a moment, he looked to his lord constable. "I want an estimate of the manpower and supplies needed to secure the most vulnerable portions of the southern border. Assume that we may soon have two fronts to deal with." *There could not possibly be a worse time for this sort of trouble,* he thought. *Not if the Wrath is truly failing.* "We will meet again after Rhys gives his report."

He held out a hand toward a small door at the back of the map room, gesturing for the witch to join him. "Come," he said to Kamala. "We will talk."

———

Nightmare creatures with wings of slivered glass fill the sky. Ravenous monsters from out of legend, now manifested. Rhys stands in their shadow, naked and unarmed. Alone. No Guardians are left in all the world but him. No hope will be left in all the world if he cannot stand up to these creatures.

An arctic wind sends a chill down his spine as the great beasts circle overhead, their black-scaled bodies devouring the sunlight. All around him on the ground lie the bodies of long-dead witches, frozen in the postures of their deaths. Did they struggle when they were first brought here? Did they have to be beaten into submission in order to thrust them into their cramped tombs? Did they comfort themselves with knowing that their suffering would serve a greater cause, or were they merely terrified?

Wasted lives. Wasted dreams.

All for nothing.

Turning his face up to the sky, Rhys howls his despair into the wind. It is a terrible sound, empty and hopeless. Who will save the world after he is gone? Who will serve a cause that sanctions such atrocities?

The gods, he knows now, will not help mankind. If they even exist—which he is no longer certain of—it is clear they do not care what happens. Perhaps they will even applaud when the last monuments of the Second Age of Kings crumble to dust, and the men who once worshipped them are reduced to the level of beasts. Perhaps that is what they intended all along.

The power of the creatures circling overhead batters at his soul. He no longer has the conviction needed to stand strong against them. Life drains out of him like blood from an open wound; he falls heavily to his knees as the strength in his legs fail him. The ground beneath him is red with blood—

But he is not alone.

The realization comes to him in a sudden jolt. Who else would be here, in this terrible place? Who is so hated by all the living gods that they must share this horror with him?

He twists about and sees a form some paces distant, wrapped in veils of darkness. Scattered bits of daylight play across the figure as the Souleaters circle overhead, filtering the sun through their wings. The light teases his eye with details: Sleek, pale skin. Green eyes. Hair the color of fire—

Kamala?

And then glittering wings unfurl from her shoulders, and a sound like rushing water fills his ears as the last of his living energy fails him—

———

Rhys woke suddenly to find himself lying between linen sheets, drenched in a cold sweat. His head throbbed painfully. His stomach was a cold, hard knot. For a moment he could not remember where he was.

"Welcome back."

Kamala sat beside him on the great bed, her hand only just now withdrawing from his. Her touch had brought him back from his dream, he realized. He shuddered as he remembered how she had appeared in it.

Was it only a dream? Some *lyr* were said to have the gift of prophecy in their veins. What if this had been a true vision, brought on by the power of his blood? Some kind of warning?

The glittering wings unfurl from her shoulders—

He forced himself to sit up, trying to loosen the grip of the dream upon his soul. "How long has it been?" His throat was so dry that he could barely get the words out. That was good. Less likely she would catch the note of uncertainty in his voice that way.

"Since our arrival?" She got up from the bed and went to pour him a cup of water from the sideboard then returned to hand it to him. She looked ready to help him sit up if need be, but he'd be damned if he would look that helpless in front of her.

Glittering wings of slivered glass—

He shut his eyes for a moment, trying to rid himself of the

memory. It was only a dream, he told himself. Fragmented memories and random emotions, woven into a narrative that was horrific, but not truly meaningful. At least not in the way that the dreams of a Seer were meaningful.

"Rhys? Are you all right?"

He focused his attention on the cup in his hand, and upon the act of drinking. *Just a dream,* he told himself. *Just a dream, just a dream, just a dream. . . .* He could sense her watching him, clearly concerned, but he dared not look at her or that would break the spell.

Slowly, his trembling subsided. Slowly, the images from his dream faded. For now.

"So what happened?" he asked at last.

She shrugged stiffly. "Healers have come and gone, attending to every wound three times over. Seers came to gaze at your soul, and declared it troubled. The Lord and Lady Protector have visited several times, asking the same questions of me on each occasion, as though hearing the same answers over and over again might give them some new insight."

He had to ask it. "What did you tell them?"

"That we traveled to the Spear in Alkali. That we discovered it had been broken open. That there was some kind of writing inside, and you recorded it. They copied the figures from your arms, but said they did not recognize them. I also told them that the Guardians in Alkali probably no longer serve their original cause." She bit her lip. "They wanted more details from me, but I said they should wait until you were awake and let you tell it. What do I know of Guardian politics?"

"Thank you." He handed the cup back to her; his hand was almost steady now. "I am surprised they let me sleep this long, considering all that."

"I told them you had been exhausted to the point where you could no longer remember things clearly, and would not be able to give them the information they wanted until you had gotten some sleep. They didn't believe me, so they brought in some Seers who confirmed my diagnosis." She got up from the bed and walked back to the sideboard. "The Lord Protector wasn't happy about it, but he trusted their opinion and declared that you must be allowed to sleep until you awakened naturally." For a fleeting moment her expression darkened; her eyes were hard and cold, like diamonds. *Your father trusted the Seers,* they seemed to say, *but not me.* "Do you want some more?"

It took him a minute to realize what she was asking. "No. Thank you."

"I should go and tell them you are awake. No doubt they will want to bring in a score of Seers to confirm the fact." She indicated the sideboard. "There's some food here for you, and I'm sure they'll set out a proper feast once they know you are up and about again."

He asked quietly, "Have you been at my side all this time?"

She hesitated, then nodded. "They didn't know what had happened to you, so how could I trust them to watch for trouble? They wouldn't know what to look for."

Trouble. Did she think that he might hurt himself again? That when he woke up he might grab a knife and start lacerating another limb? The others didn't know what he had seen at the Spear, and thus would have no reason to fear such behavior. As far as they were concerned he had simply used his flesh to record a valuable message in the absence of less bloody tools. A finite sacrifice for a finite purpose, gruesome but comprehensible. Only *she* understood that it was more than that. That in the madness of his despair, he might do something foolish.

And she was right, of course. If he had awakened alone, with nothing to focus on but his memories, he might not have done so well.

Once more I am indebted to you, he thought soberly.

They had dressed her in a woman's gown, though the way her hands kept fluttering down to her sides to pick at the fabric made it clear she was not really comfortable with the choice. It was a simple enough outfit, with a saffron-colored gown that fit her body closely and sleeveless surcoat of burgundy wool over it. The surcoat was laced down both sides, loosely enough that the color of the underlayer peeked through, along with a hint of the womanly curves it guarded. The whole of the outfit was a bit too short for her, with the result that the hem fluttered about her ankles as she moved. At first he was surprised that the Lady Protector could not have found something that fit her better, but no, this had probably been by her own choice. He couldn't see her manipulating all the fashionable bits of feminine attire that normally dragged behind a lady, requiring that she *flow* across the floor rather than *walk*. This outfit was suitably practical.

Someone had affixed a veil to her head, a thin piece of white gauze that had been probably been meant to fall softly about her face, disguising her short-cropped hair. Only she had pushed it back out of the way so that it dangled precariously from a single hairpin, utterly failing to accomplish its purpose. It was oddly appealing in its disarray, he realized. As was she.

She must have sensed the nature of his inspection, for she held her skirts out at the sides as if to show them off. The gesture was so unnatural for her it seemed almost like a parody of its type, a caustic comment upon the habits of the feminine sex. "They thought this was more appropriate than a soldier's uniform." A wry half smile flickered across her lips. "Or a grimy man's shirt, no doubt."

A rush of gratitude filled his heart. If not for her he would still be trapped in Anukyat's dungeon. "You will never look more beautiful to me than you did when you appeared in that place," he told her. "Grimy man's shirt and all."

She was clearly shaken by his words. How strange. He'd never seen a woman so startled by a compliment, though many played at it for flirtation's sake. "I'll tell them you're awake," she said quietly, and she slipped out the door. He couldn't tell from her expression whether she was sorry to be leaving him after such an exchange, or grateful to have an excuse to do so. Maybe both.

With a sigh, he pushed his blankets to the side and swung his feet down over the edge of the bed. His arm and leg ached dully where his wounds had been, but that was more memory than real pain. Her witchery had banished any sign of damage, inside and out. Likewise, it appeared to have banished all signs of dirt from his skin. Or maybe someone had bathed him in his sleep.

If not for her, he thought, he would still be in Anukyat's dungeon.

Which meant he would not have seen the Spear.

Which meant he would not have learned the truth.

Thus do the gods torment our souls for their own amusement.

Gathering up the clothes that had been laid out for him, he tried to focus on the task of getting dressed and not think about anything else. But it was hard not to stop and stare at the strange figures etched into his arm, or wonder what in all the hells he was going to say about them to the Lord Protector when he was finally asked.

There was sorcery in the palace.

That was the warning Stevan Kierdwyn's Seer had sent to him.

Not *witchery*. Nor even a vaguely descriptive term like *power*, that might mean any number of things.

Sorcery.

So Rhys' witch must have a Magister as patron who had transported her and Rhys to the palace. Either for reasons of his own, or because he owed her a favor.

Or his Seer could have been wrong.

The last possibility was in some ways the least disturbing, but he knew it wasn't likely. The two uses of soulfire were supposedly so distinct from one another that there was no chance of a Seer confusing them. Witchery was a hot force, molten power spewing forth from the furnace of life. Sorcery was like ice, and chilled the soul if you came too close to it. Or so a Seer had described it to him once when he had asked about it.

So what other sorcerer was active in his Protectorate? And why?

Magisters hated the north. They accepted contracts with the Lord Protectors in order to protect them from the assaults of other Magisters—the same as they did for kings in other places—but for the most part those contracts were in name only. None of them lived this far north. None of them traveled here unless they had to, and if they did, then they stayed only for as long as a given assignment required. Was that because the Wrath was so close by that it disturbed their sorcerous senses? Or were they uncomfortable amid a race of men that claimed that the gods had entrusted them—and not the Magisters—with the saving of the world?

Stevan opened his hand to look once more at the crumpled note within it. It bore the seal of his own Magister Royal and one simple line of script.

I have worked no sorcery upon or within your palace since last we met. Lazaroth.

Was he telling the truth? The Magisters often followed dark and twisted paths and their true motives were always suspect. The Lord Protectors called upon them for aid only when it was absolutely necessary. There were enough witches in the Protectorates who were willing to sacrifice a portion of their life for the common good that Magisters were rarely needed. Like the *lyr*, the Seers had been born for a purpose. Like the Guardians, who honed their weapons and skills in order to prepare to meet the Souleaters in battle, they knew that sacrifice might be required of them, and accepted that. How did the ancient song go?

Our blood was cold and feeble, until Sacrifice lent us strength
Our witchery was earthbound, until Sacrifice gave it wing
Our steel was blunt and brittle, until Sacrifice honed its edge
Our prayers were mute and fearful, until Sacrifice made them
*   sing.*

The Magisters were creatures of self-interest, as unlikely to sacrifice themselves for a worthy cause as any soulless beast. Now it looked as if an unknown Magister was active in Kierdwyn—in Stevan's own palace—and he was not at all pleased by it. In fact he was infuriated by it. How dare a Magister (or anyone!) distract him now, just when it looked like the ancient enemy was returning to the human lands? Just when his people needed him most? The fact that the sorcerers served no higher purpose did not mean they had the right to interfere with his. A Lord Protector answered to the gods themselves. Who was *their* master?

His anger meant little to them, of course. No morati could stand up to a Magister.

But with the Souleaters returning, the *lyr* would have power of their own. Great power. Or so the legends promised.

Be careful, he thought to the nameless offender. *For if you fly too close to this fire, it may just singe your wings.*

CHAPTER 17

YOSEFA'S FAMILY was just sitting down to dinner when the screaming started.

It had been a quiet day until that point. Her husband had worked hard loading and unloading ships in the harbor, and she could see from how he leaned on the table how grateful he was to finally sit down and rest. Her oldest child had been helping her cook and for once hadn't made a mess of things. Her two younger children, both boys, had managed to get through the day without getting into trouble, which was nothing sort of a miracle.

Then the screams had started.

Her daughter was bringing a pot of stew to the table at the time; the sound startled her so badly that she stumbled and fell, spilling the hot contents across the table and into the lap of the youngest boy. He opened his mouth and was about to start screaming himself, but Yosefa reached over and covered his mouth with her hand, forcing him to be silent.

Men were screaming in the distance. Women also. More of them now, voices rising in pitch and volume with each passing second. The sound of raw, unadulterated terror.

It seemed to be coming from the harbor.

Her husband rose up. She could see his eyes going to the heavy cleaver by the fire, and knew what he was planning. "Sorran—" she began, reaching out her hand to stop him. Whatever was going on, she didn't want him in the middle of it.

Then, somewhere in the distance, a child added its voice to the rest. Shrill and terrified, infant lungs stressed beyond tolerance, squeezing out a single note of terror. The terrible sound vibrated across her motherly nerves like fingernails on slate.

She let her hand fall. "Go," she whispered, her voice shaking.

"I'll find out what's happening and come right back. I promise." He grabbed up the cleaver and a heavy staff from beside the door. "Keep the children safe."

And then he was gone.

"Mama, what's happening?" Her daughter was pulling at her skirts. The youngest boy was starting to cry, which meant that the other one would join in soon.

They had to go somewhere safe. Somewhere that no enemies could find them.

"Take a blanket off the bed," she ordered the girl. "Gather food into it. Quickly!"

Shaken, her daughter ran off to obey. She was so frightened she didn't think to ask her question again. How could Yosefa have answered? She did not have a clue what was going on. She only knew with a mother's certain instinct that they needed to get away from the house as soon as possible, before something terrible happened to them all.

Kneeling by the hearth, she lifted up one of the flat stones, uncovering a small secret space beneath it. A handful of coins were in there, along with a few pieces of silver jewelry. Bridal adornments mostly, now tarnished by time; a dowry they had never spent. She fingered the pieces for a moment and then thrust them into her pocket along with all the rest. It wasn't much, but it would have to do.

"Come," she ordered, gathering up the youngest boy, gesturing for her daughter to take the hand of the other. "Shush," she told them both. "Stop crying now. I need you to be quiet. I need you to be brave." To her amazement, it seemed to work. At least they subsided to a quieter form of terror, whimpering softly as she led them all out.

The town bell was tolling in the distance now, a deep, resonant sound. Usually it was used to mark meetings of the elders or to announce the arrival of important visitors. Clearly this time it was being rung as a warning. But of what?

"Come!" she whispered fiercely, as she set off westward, wending her way down the narrow streets. Women and children huddled in doorways and peered through windows as she passed; hungry, worried faces turned to her as she passed, begging her silently for news. *I don't know any more than you do!* she thought wildly. Why weren't they fleeing? If their menfolk had gone off to see what the trouble was, as her husband had done, surely they'd rather have their wives and children safe in the hills than clinging to their homes out of some mistaken belief that mud-patched walls could protect them!

There was less screaming from the harbor now. Was that good or bad? She feared the worst. Finally a few women did join her, dragging terrified children along with them. Too few, too few! What was wrong with all the others? Couldn't they smell the danger in the air?

Then a bloodcurdling scream arose from within the town itself. A woman's voice this time, and not from very far away. Yosefa broke into a run, dragging her terrified children along with her.

An older girl who was joining the exodus caught up her other boy in her arms and began to run by her side so they could all move faster. Yosefa had no breath to spare to thank her.

Out of the narrow streets they ran, into the open field near the trash pits. Yosefa could smell fire behind them now, and the acrid smell of burning meat. Tears ran down her eyes as she finally reached the far end of the field and started up the hillside that was beyond it. In better days she and her family might have come up here to relax, eating a meal in the open air as they watched the ships sail in and out of the harbor. Now, with the thickets of trees that crowned the hill, it seemed the safest place to go. To hide.

A few children stumbled and fell, trying to run up the slope. But no one cried out. Their mothers grabbed them by the arm and dragged them up the hill, but no one complained. White-faced with terror, they all seemed to understand the need for silence. Even Yosefa's two boys were quiet now, though they whimpered softly in their throats like frightened puppies.

Finally she and her family reached the top of the hill and with it the shelter of the thickset trees beyond. Not until the greenery had swallowed them up did Yosefa fall to her knees, trembling as she gasped for breath. Leaves weren't much of a barrier, but at least whatever nightmare was in the town would not be able to see them easily. And with the open field behind them, they'd be able to see anyone or anything that tried to take up their trail.

"Look," one of the women whispered hoarsely. Yosefa saw her standing by the edge of the thicket, gazing back at the town.

She stood up to where she could see in that direction also, and looked.

The town was burning.

Thick black clouds billowed up from the streets they had just abandoned, and from the rest of the town as well. Here and there the smoke would part for a moment, allowing her to see that bodies lay strewn upon the ground. Silent and still— so very still—lying in pools of blood. Some of the bodies were whole, and might have seemed asleep save for the red puddles surrounding them. Some had limbs missing, or even heads. It was all so surreal she could hardly absorb it.

Then one of the women gasped, and pointed to the harbor.

There were three ships there, narrow and long and shallow of draught, with prows that were carved into the shape of great bestial heads. Scales along the hull seemed to transform the whole of each ship into a vast serpentine creature, ending in a high, curling tail at the stern. Yosefa had never seen such a thing before, but had once heard a street minstrel sing of snake-ships that had existed in an earlier time, in a faraway place. How was it that they were here now?

Men were returning to the ships now, and a few armored women as well; bloody weapons were thrust into their belts, bags of booty slung over their shoulders. Yosefa saw two burly men herding a group of terrified young girls onto one of the ships, roped together by their neck. The oldest could not have been more than ten.

Instinctively Yosefa reached out for her own children and gathered them close to her, as if to protect them. She could feel their hearts pounding against her own as she watched the bloody procession

"What is it, Mama?" Her daughter pressed herself close to her side. She, too, was trembling. "What are they doing?"

The town of Soladin had always been a peaceful place. Its harbor served all travelers equally, so all travelers respected it.

Long ago it was said that princes had fought over who owned the surrounding territory, but Danton Aurelius had put a stop to all that. *The peace of the sword,* he had called it. He had made it clear to everyone in the region that disturbing Soladin would cost them dearly, and none had dared test him. The harbor and its surroundings had become a center of regional trade and had prospered accordingly. The yearly tithe that was required of Soladin seemed a small price to pay for the High King's protection.

Salvator Aurelius must be told about this, she thought feverishly. The new High King would surely step into his father's shoes and crush the ones who had done this. He would know what to do.

The monstrous ships were loaded now. Children huddled together in the center of the open decks as long oars were thrust out over the water on both sides, then dipped down into the waves in perfect unison. The ships began to move out of the harbor; slowly at first, then with increasing speed. As they reached the open sea their sails were unfurled, brilliant sheets of white canvas with some kind of crimson serpent painted upon them.

Sorran may still be alive. Yosefa thought. *I need to go find him.* But nothing in the town was moving now except twisting columns of fire and smoke, roiled by a restless wind.

And then the horror of it all was simply too much for her, and she fell to her knees upon the damp, mossy earth and wept.

RECKONING

Cry sorrow, mothers, for brave sons devoured!
Cry sorrow, fallen kings, for glory lost!
And when you tell the tale, a hundred lifetimes hence,
Say that you failed your god, and paid the cost.

Book of Penitence
Lamentations 24:13

CHAPTER 18

*N*YUKU REMEMBERS:
From his vantage point high above the plains, Nyuku could see the place where the world ended.

Shimmering in the air above the snowbound landscape was the hateful spell that divided his universe, a wall of eerie iridescence that was visible to his mind's eye but not to his human vision. To see it he had to close his eyes and let the ikati's senses pour into him, along with all the primitive emotions they inspired. He could taste the wind under his belly then, could feel the thin northern sunlight play along his broad wings, heating his blood (but never enough!). He could feel currents of air shift beneath him as he passed over an expanse of naked granite, then over snow once more, and somewhere in another world his human thighs tightened around the great beast as his powerful wings beat against the cold arctic air, striving to maintain his height. But most of all he could taste the ikati's rage, his bestial fury as he approached the sorcerous barrier that kept him from entering the warm lands to the south. An obscene creation that kept him from chasing the sun southward, as all of his animal instincts cried out for him to do.

The rage filled Nyuku as well, which is why he made no protest as the ikati suddenly canted in midair and headed directly for the barrier. Crouching down low against his consort's back, his legs pressing into natural hollows just behind the rear wings, he was one with the ikati and with his rage. When he howled in fury, Nyuku did so as well, as loudly as he could, until the whole of the sky seemed to shake from the force of their defiance.

But the mystical barrier remained unmoved. It stretched across the land as far as he could see, and extended upward into the sky, a glimmering supernatural curtain without visible end or flaw. Or hope.

Soon the sun would set beyond the world's edge for the last time that season and the Long Night would come once again. The air would grow cold and inhospitable and the ikati would be forced to crawl into narrow caverns, where the heat of the buried Sun Stone would keep them alive until spring. It went against every instinct that the great creatures had to be bound up in a confined space for so long, near enough to others of their kind that they could smell the scent of rivals seeping through cracks in the rock, maddening them with territorial fury. By the time the Sun returned every year the ikati were half mad from their confinement, and the first few flights of the season would often devolve into terrible duels as they vented all their pent-up frustration on one another. Sometimes their riders would channel that aggression into their own affairs and turn on one another on the ground, even as their mounts did the same overhead, until the snow-covered earth was soaked in scarlet and the weakest members of the colony, of both species, had gasped their last breaths.

After that the surviving men would gather up the bodies of the fallen ikati, stripping bone plates and skin to make into weapons and clothing. At first the creatures had reviled the practice, for the foreign smells that clung to the clothing of their human consorts made them feel as if others of their kind were mounting them—an intolerable offense!—but the humans were fragile creatures and needed the kind of protection that only the tough, supple hides could offer. So in time the ikati came to tolerate the practice, even derive a sense of triumph from it as the smells of the skins" original owners faded over time, replaced by their living and powerful musk: the weak giving way to the strong.

As for the orphaned riders, if they had not been driven mad already by the months of close confinement, losing their winged consorts in the spring frenzy completed the job. Some would stagger along the bloodstained slopes howling like wounded animals, a sound more empty and terrible than anything Nyuku would have imagined might come from a human throat. Others turned their gleaming iridescent knives upon themselves, preferring to die than live with only half a soul. A precious few—not wholly mad, but not wholly sane either—wandered off into the wasteland where others could not see them, and somehow managed to survive until the blooding of the next clutch. Then and only then they would return to the colony and try to win the favor of a newly blooded male. If they succeeded, then their spirits might be made whole again. If not, then they ended their life as food, the same as every other rejected creature in the barren landscape. The harsh northern climate allowed for no other options.

Once it had been otherwise.

Once (the eldest members of the colony told him) the ikati

had ruled the skies of the southlands. The air was so warm there that they were able to fly freely even after the Sun set, not needing its rays upon their wings to heat their blood. And the Sun rose every morning, no matter what the season, to heat the earth anew. There was even a place where snow never fell at all (or so he was told), and herd beasts could graze in the fields whenever they liked! Born to a world of ice and snow, his entire existence circumscribed by the narrow margins of a Sun Stone's heat, Nyuku could not even imagine such a place. Indeed, when the eldest first told him it existed, he had thought it no more than a wild dream. How could such a place be real?

But then one day at the height of summer he had flown southward for many days, far enough to see the mysterious barrier that marked the end of the world, and to feel its power. The half of him that was ikati knew with certain animal instinct that his ancestors had indeed come from the far side of that cursed barrier and that he was destined to return there, to a world neither Nyuku nor the ikati had ever seen, but that both now hungered for with every fiber of their joint being.

It was their birthright.

Now. Now. The ikati's need, fiery and terrible, pounded into him with each new wingstroke. They must follow the Sun. They must do it *now.* The drive was so powerful he could not resist it—he did not *want* to resist it—and he screamed out his defiance to the ancient witches who had erected the barrier, daring them to do their worst to him. Bloodless cowards all of them, who had enchanted this stretch of ground so that no living creature could cross it, then gone back to the warm and welcoming lands of the south to live in comfort! He cursed them with all his strength as his ikati picked up speed, energized by his hatred. Soon he would break through to the other side, then those mewling cowards of the south would pay the price for their handiwork!

Others of the colony had attempted the same feat and come back with their tails against their bellies, he knew that. But those others had not been born to this icy land, nor had they been tempered in their youth by its harshness. Now he would show the elders of the colony what a true son of the ice was capable of. Then they would have to eat every word of disdain they had ever directed at him. He would prove himself better than any of them!

Closer and closer the ikati flew to the great barrier, his great wings casting blue and violet shadows along the snow. From this close to the barrier Nyuku could see individual whorls and eddies of power rippling through it, like streamers of the aurora rippling across a midnight sky. It seemed to him he could hear a distant screaming, too, and the sound of it sent shivers down his spine. Other had come this far and turned back, he knew. But he would not stop. Nothing mattered now but the fact that the Sun would soon set on the far side of that barrier, and he—*they*—must follow it. From the moment he had been born, he understood now, that this was his destiny.

The screaming grew louder as they approached. And louder. It filled the frozen air around them, a terrible agonized wailing; the sheer pressure of it sent sparks of pain lancing through Nyuku's head, as if his skull were about to explode. In its wake came a storm of fearsome emotions, raw and unfettered, that assailed not only his ears but his mind, crowding out all rational thought. *Blinding terror. Starvation. Despair*. The sensations curled over him like black, frothing waves, their depths suffocating; he gripped the ikati with all his might while his spirit struggled to surface. *Suffocation. Starvation. Fear*. Beneath him he could feel his consort's back muscles tighten as he, too, reeled before the onslaught. Raw, bestial panic from the ikati poured into his brain, threatening to drown out the last fragments of his human sanity.

Then the creature faltered in his flight, his wingstrokes losing their synchronicity; for one gut wrenching moment it was as if the air beneath them had suddenly ceased to exist and they began to plummet downward. Squeezing his eyes shut, focusing all his concentration inward, Nyuku struggled to lend his ikati strength. It worked for a handful of seconds—the creature regained his composure long enough for a dozen wingstrokes, then two—and then the witchery of the barrier overcame them both. The great wings faltered and they began to fall once more. The snow-covered landscape rushed up to meet them and Nyuku knew with dread certainty that if they fell to earth within range of the dreaded barrier they would never be able to rise again. They would be trapped here forever, while all the power of that ancient witchery poured into their heads.

Trapped here forever!

What madness had driven him to come here, to test himself against a curse so powerful that it had effectively divided the world in two? Even if his consort could have remained airborne long enough to breach the barrier, they would both have been doomed the minute they crossed it. Their bodies might pass through to the other side but their souls would surely be sucked out of their skins and bound to this place, their screams added to the chorus of spirits already trapped here. Other men, sensing their presence, would recoil in horror and turn back before it was too late.

As he should have done.

"Go back!" he gasped. It took every ounce of strength he had to form the human words; the best he could manage was a hoarse whisper. But the ikati heard him. A shudder passed through his long body as he struggled to focus on Nyuku's voice, to drive back the tide of madness. For a moment Nyuku thought they would hit the ground before the creature could regain control of himself, but at the last moment the broad wings fell into an ordered pattern once more and the snow just beneath them was beaten into whirlwinds as the ikati struggled to pull out of his fall. Against all odds, he succeeded. Struggling for each wingbeat, he managed to rise up a few feet and turn himself back north. Putting the barrier behind him seemed to help him focus. Inch by inch he regained altitude, until the ground was a safe distance beneath them. Slowly but surely he carried Nyuku northward, away from the dreaded barrier and certain destruction.

Trapped here! the voices screamed inside him. *Taste the pain! Taste the fear! Be one with our dying!*

But the sensations that had almost overwhelmed him were fading now, and after a few minutes of flight the volume of the voices began to fade. Nyuku's hands, white-knuckled, finally released their death grip on the ikati's spine ridge. But in his heart a black resentment burned and he knew from the tension in the great creature's back that his consort shared it.

That *thing* had defeated them.

Not a man. Not a beast. Not any other respectable sort of enemy. Simply a human creation. Words spoken over a line in the snow, witchery used to mark a location.

Defeated him!

Between his legs he could feel the ikati's seething frustration. All his bestial instincts demanded that he go back and confront his enemy, not turn tail and run. But the trickle of human intelligence he absorbed from Nyuku cautioned that such a move would be suicidal and that they must flee instead. Flee! Did the ikati flee from his rivals when the queen took flight? Did he flee those who challenged him for rank, or territory, or a choice bit of meat? Lifting his long throat into the wind, the ikati bellowed his defiance.

And he was answered.

Startled, Nyuku and his mount looked around for the source. It was in the distance, outlined against the redness of the sunset: another ikati. Hot rage surged through them both at the sight; it did not matter in that moment who the strangers were, or what they wanted; the mere fact that they had seen them in their moment of weakness was offense enough.

Nyuku's ikati screamed out his challenge to the skies, and was answered.

It began to fly toward the intruder.

Dimly, as if in another world, Nyuku realized he should be afraid. When the ikati challenged one another they usually did so as beasts and beasts alone, leaving their fragile human companions safely on the ground. But hatred and rage were pounding in the ikati's veins now, and from there into Nyuku's own, discouraging all rational thought. A strange, distant part of Nyuku knew that he needed to exert some kind of control over his mount or he would surely be crushed to death between feuding ikati. But it was only a distant instinct, a *human* instinct, and right now he was not wholly human.

Nyuku could not see his opponent's face clearly in the dying light, but he recognized the ikati he was riding, and that told him all he needed to know. The man seated between those wings was one of the original members of the colony, a quiet but cunning man who had frustrated Nyuku's ambitions on more than one occasion. His mount was fast and flexible and truly fearsome in combat; more than once Nyuku's own had been forced to give way to him in mating season. The wounds that he had received on such occasions might have healed since then, but the wounds to his pride never had.

Nyuku's ikati bellowed again, this time in pure hatred, and Nyuku screamed with him. All that mattered now was how he would cry his triumph to the winds when his rival was finally torn to pieces. Loudly he would scream it out; loudly enough for his rivals to hear, that they might fear him; loudly enough for the queen of their kind to hear from her hiding place, so that she might desire him. Images of heat and hunger surged through their merged consciousness and Nyuku's groin stiffened in response. Pressed against the ikati's tough hide, he flinched in pleasure and pain at each rhythmic thrust of the powerful wing muscles beneath him. The small wings at the base of the ikati's neck flared briefly—a sexual display—then folded back tightly over him, pinning him in place. The musky odor of the creature filled his nostrils, drowning out the last of his human resistance. A heady drug, powerfully addictive. How could any man ever have enough of it?

Now they were truly one.

Backlit by crimson skies, the ikati faced off against each other. They had come as close as they dared in their approach and now circled each other restlessly, seeking an opening to strike. In mating season they might have spread their display wings wide, enhancing their size and fierceness tenfold, each trying to cow the other into retreat. But with the men on their backs such tactics were not possible. Nor could they afford to waste much time in ritual posturing. The air was cold and the Sun was already low in the heavens, near to setting; the energy required for sustained combat was simply not available. Not unless the ikati devoured their riders for strength—an unspeakable crime that the colony would never accept.

The intruder struck.

His movements were a blur, violet wings beating against the frigid winds as he twisted suddenly, reaching out with his razor-sharp talons. But the movement was merely a feint to drive them where the intruder wanted them, and even as they dodged the blow, his long tail came whipping toward them with a force that cracked in the air, cutting off their retreat. Nyuku's mount dropped down—straight down—barely fast enough to save himself. The tail tip passed between his wing layers, deadly blades just missing their target.

Nyuku's ikati lunged upward. It was all that Nyuku could do to hold onto the spine ridge as they came up under their opponent, daring a vertical assault. It was a maneuver that made Nyuku's heart lurch in his chest, but the risk paid off. His mount's great jaws snapped shut on the lower edge of the intruder's neck, dragging him downward until his own wings failed. Then the ikati were in freefall, riders clinging desperately to their backs, spiraling about each other as each tried to reclaim the skies at the other's expense.

Many times Nyuku had watched while the ikati fought, admiring the grace of their combat. How like a dance it had all seemed then, great serpentine bodies twisting about each other in endlessly changing patterns, each striving to gain an advantageous position for the split second it would take to launch the perfect strike. Their bodies might be well armored but their wings were vulnerable in combat and nature had outfitted them accordingly; a single cut from a tail tip, a single slice from a talon, might end an ikati's flying for a season—or forever.

It was not a dance this time. Not with men right in the middle of it. Not with claws and teeth passing mere inches from their backs and the sharp blades at the end of those long, whiplike tails whistling just past their heads. Nature had equipped the ikati to tear each other to pieces and human survival was not necessarily part of that equation.

Suddenly the intruder slashed at the forward wing of Nyuku's mount, gashing it deeply before the ikati could pull free. Sympathetic pain shot through Nyuku's right arm as his winged brother struggled to steady his flight, blood seeping from the wound. The wing membrane was still holding its shape, but for how long? The moment the skin began to separate from the delicate framework that supported it they would lose their mobility, and with it any hope of winning this deadly contest. Nyuku felt the powerful muscles beneath him tighten in sudden anticipation, and then suddenly they were twisting in a spiral, but headed upward instead of downward. His ikati reared back, driving him up and into the wings of his opponent. The force of the impact stunned Nyuku and for a few terrifying seconds the entire world spun madly about his head. Desperately he gripped the ikati's spine ridge, flattening himself against the creature's back. If he lost hold now, he thought, nothing would be able to save him.

Heart pounding, a cold sweat covering his forehead, it took him several long seconds to realize that the combat had ended.

The intruder was gone.

His ikati struggled to steady his flight, favoring his damaged wing. Nyuku looked out over the sunset-reddened landscape to find the intruder. He was some distance from them now, and badly wounded. Apparently Nyuku's mount had driven himself straight into his opponent's wingspan, sharp spinal spikes tearing his rival's wings to pieces, ripping membrane from bone. Now as the creature struggled, his lopsided wingstroke was bringing him down in a tight spiral—directly toward the cursed barrier.

Nyuku watched in horrified fascination, wondering at what point the terrible voices would start to scream to them, bringing madness in their wake. The ikati seemed to convulse as he fell, muscles spasming down the length of his body as he fought for control, but with two wings torn to pieces there was little hope. With a final desperate thrust of his remaining wings the great beast lunged upward one last time, as if sheer force of will could hold gravity in abeyance. The forward wings lost their strength then, falling suddenly open, and a small, dark shape fell from the creature's back. Was it by chance or intent that the rider had abandoned his mount? Did he deem it a better fate to fall to earth on his own, or had the madness of the barrier's curse weakened his grip so that nothing else was possible? Nyuku watched in horrified fascination as the man plummeted to the earth, unable to save himself. What was it like to see death coming so very clearly and yet be unable to escape it?

That could have been me.

The ikati struck the ground with an impact that shook the earth. His neck was doubled at an unnatural angle and his wings were crushed beneath his torso. If he was not dead yet, he would be soon enough. The rider, on the other hand, had landed in a deep snow bank, and it was possible some spark of life still clung to him. But he was within range of the barrier's witchery now, and the spirits would be moving in to claim him. Soon he might well regret that he had not died cleanly in the fall. It was not the kind of end that Nyuku would have wished upon anyone, but there was no denying the rush of elation he felt to see him dying thus. Soon he would have one less rival to deal with.

His consort clearly wanted to get close enough to the man's body to claim the last sparks of his life-essence. Ikati did not normally feed on the humans who served their kind—such an act would stress their fragile society to the breaking point—but an orphaned rider was fair game. With the sun setting for the last time in months, and the air chilled by the coming winter, the ikati had little energy to spare right now and needed every fresh drop he could gather. But the man's body was too close to the barrier for them to approach safely, and in the end the ikati had to withdraw. At full strength he might have dared the approach and tried to face down the madness that the barrier would pour into his brain, but with his wing torn and bleeding and pain attending every movement, he dared not take such a risk. Already Nyuku could feel a deadly chill creeping into his consort's flesh and he knew they had very little time before the last of his strength was gone and winter's lethargy began to set in. They had to get within range of the Sun Stone's heat before that happened; the wing would never heal properly otherwise.

But this year there would be one less rider wintering in the crowded caverns, he thought with elation. One less elder to frustrate his ambitions come spring. That was surely worth a little pain, yes?

Slowly, carefully, the wounded ikati turned north once more and began the long flight home. While behind his back the shadows of the Long Night crept in from the edges of the sky, eager to devour the icelands and all who were too weak to survive them.

CHAPTER 19

"MAJESTY."

Gwynofar looked up to find that one of the royal pages had entered. A young lad who stood stiff and upright, trying to be worthy of the message he carried. "Yes, Petro?"

"The High King asks that you please attend him."

Brow furrowed, she set aside her book and rose, smoothing her long skirts as she stood. Her maidservant rose as well, prepared to accompany her, but Gwynofar waved her back.

It was odd for Salvator to send for her this way. Normally if he had something to say to her, he just came to wherever she was and did so. The formality of this request was disconcerting.

The page led her to the threshold of an audience chamber overlooking the courtyard. Two guards with grim expressions flanked the double doors; one knocked upon a dark oak panel sharply before opening it, admitting her.

Salvator was inside with one of his witches. That was not a good sign. Her son never relied upon mystical powers when mundane efforts would suffice. A woman was kneeling before him, her clothing torn and stained, and Gwynofar could see that she was trembling from fear and exhaustion.

She wondered for a moment if perhaps Salvator was the cause of the woman's distress, but as her son looked up to acknowledge her entrance, she could see in his expression that this was not the case. The anger in his eyes was focused on someone or something far beyond this room.

While the door was still open, he waved for one of the guards to come in and attend to the woman on the floor. "See that our guest is given food and drink, and anything else she requires. With a guard by her door while she sleeps, if she desires it. She has come far, and done us a great service today."

He waited while the guards helped the woman out—how weak she looked, walking unsteadily between them!—and then he nodded for the witch to follow them as well. "Please, leave us."

The man bowed and obeyed, and shut the heavy door behind him, leaving Salvator and Gwynofar alone.

The High King walked over to one of the room's two sideboards, where an assortment of metal pieces had been laid out on a soiled woolen blanket. For a moment he just stood there, hands joined behind his back, gazing down at them.

Finally he said, "Skandir has attacked one of our northern provinces."

Gwynofar drew in a sharp breath. "You are sure?"

He nodded toward the chamber doors and the woman who had just passed between them. "That was a very tired and terrified messenger, but also an honest one. And fairly accurate, according to my witch. Her words 'resonated with truth.' Or so he said."

"Why on earth would Skandir attack the High Kingdom?"

"Why indeed?" He did not look up as she came up to the table, but kept his eyes fixed on the pieces laid out before him. Knives and buckles, a man's roundel belt, a worn leather bracer studded with iron bits, a set of brass bracelets, and several smaller pieces. "Mind you, they did not exactly announce themselves as being from Skandir. Three ships full of warriors fell upon the harbor town of Soladin without warning. They slaughtered nearly everyone who was there at the time, took what they wanted of the town's possessions, and burned the rest to the ground." His expression was hard. "This woman Yosefa, she says that fewer than two dozen survived by hiding on the outskirts of town. Fortunately they had the mental wherewithal afterward to collect what they could find of the warriors' gear that had survived the fire. Apparently the locals had put up a good enough fight to take down a couple of the invaders, leaving us with the relics that you see here before you."

He gazed at the collection of objects a moment longer. And then, without warning, he swept his arm across the table and sent them flying across the room.

Startled, Gwynofar stepped back quickly so as not to be hit by the falling debris. She knew Salvator well enough by now to guess at the cause behind his silent fury, to understand that it probably had as much to do with his own sense of failure as any external threat.

He sees this as his fault, she thought. *The weight of all those deaths is on his shoulders because he failed to prevent them.* It was the teachings of his barbaric faith, reveling in guilt that prompted such feelings. How she secretly hated it! What good could come from any religion that tormented its worshippers so?

Finally her son seemed to pull himself together enough to be able to speak again, though his voice was a strained and hollow thing. "Tell me why this happened, Mother. You are from the northlands. Tell me what this is about." He shook his head grimly. "An army moving against the High Kingdom I might understand, but this—" He shook his head. "This makes no sense to me."

"I am not from Skandir."

"No, but you are from a Protectorate. Yes? All of them serving one great mission to the exclusion of else. Isn't that what you taught me, Mother? What was that mission supposed to be? *Make ready to fight the Souleaters when they return! Let nothing come before that!*" He gestured angrily towards the mess on the floor. "Well, the Souleaters are back now. And where are Skandir's warriors? At my border, slaughtering my people. I want to know *why*."

"Perhaps they were not from Skandir."

"Oh, no. My witch used his power upon these relics and confirmed their source. Or is that not good enough?" he said angrily. "Should I consult another? Or sell my soul to a Magister, perhaps, to get better answers?"

Gwynofar did not respond. Any discussion of Magisters was likely to spur on other angers, other frustrations, and that was one thing they did not need right now.

Is Skandir doing these things because Danton is gone? she wondered. *Do they doubt Salvator's ability to guide this kingdom and mean to test his hold upon the border? Or is there some darker purpose here?*

"They were sea raiders once, you know." Salvator's voice was steadier now, but she could sense the effort it was taking to manage that. "They were the only army that came to the final campaign by ship instead of over land. After the Wrath appeared and victory was declared, they warred with Alkali for some time over who would control the coastal territories."

"That is ancient history," she told him. "Those borders have been stable for centuries."

"And this was painted upon the sails of the ships that Yosefa saw." He handed her a small piece of paper that had been crumpled in his hand. Cheap paper, with the figure of a strange creature drawn upon it. It had a serpentine body joined to a lizardlike head, the body folded back upon itself in a complex figure-eight pattern. "Do you recognize it, Mother?"

She felt her heart skip a beat. "Mordi?"

"The serpent of the open seas. War god of the early Skandir. Now absorbed into the northern pantheon with all the rest. But, oh, he must be hungry, after so many centuries without human sacrifice."

She looked up at him sharply. "That is quite a leap of logic, Salvator."

"Is it?" He leaned down and picked up one of the items on the floor: a wide brass bracelet inscribed with various patterns. "The woman Yosefa told me that when the raiders left her homeland, they took a number of captives with them. All children."

She shut her eyes and instinctively whispered a prayer to her gods. It was not something she normally did in Salvator's presence, but this news required it.

"The worshippers of Mordi used to sacrifice children to him before their battles," Salvator said. "They believed that if they sated his hunger for blood before they engaged the enemy, he would not seek theirs on the battlefield. Now three ships appear in my kingdom with the mark of the Sea Serpent upon their sails and raid my lands not only for wealth, but for children."

"Those customs existed a thousand years ago," she told him. Which of them was she trying to convince? "A god of the Dark Times, abandoned long ago."

"Maybe not, Mother. The Souleaters are returning, yes? Maybe the ancient gods are returning as well, and they are not such benevolent creatures as your people would like to believe. Nor will they be satisfied with a few drops of blood smeared onto trees. Not when war can loose rivers of blood to sate their hunger."

She could feel her expression harden. "Do not defame your own heritage, Salvator."

"What heritage is that?" he demanded. "The *lyr* gift, which will supposedly save us all? If so, it is well overdue, don't you think? Or maybe you are referring to those self-proclaimed saviors of the material world, the *Guardians of the Wrath*. Freelance warriors who go where they wish and do whatever it strikes their fancy to do, knowing that the gods themselves will surely strike down any prince who dares to question them."

Anger flared hotly inside her. "You go too far, Salvator—"

"Do I?" he demanded. "Or am I only saying what should have been said years ago? Maybe if someone had asked more questions at the beginning of all this, the gods would not have sent their demons back to us now. Maybe if your Guardians spent less time spilling blood to sate their idols, rather than facing the truth behind the legends, the Destroyer would not loose plagues among us now!"

Speechless in her rage, Gwynofar whirled about and started toward the door. If she stayed a moment longer she would surely say things she would regret. But he grabbed her arm and jerked her back, his grip tight enough to cause her pain.

"Behold your precious mission, Mother." He held up the Skandir bracelet in front of her face. "Behold what your traditions have brought us!"

For a moment she could not even focus upon the object, she was so enraged. She tried to jerk away from him, but his grip on her was too strong. Still he held the piece of jewelry before her face, demanding she look at it. Finally she did so, and he turned it in the light so that one by one its decorative images caught the light, ancient Skandir runes meant to inspire and protect the wearer—

And then she saw it.

The color drained from her face. Her legs lost all their strength. If not for Salvator's grip on her arm, she would surely have collapsed.

"No," she whispered. "It can't be."

"It is," he said. His own voice was shaking. Beneath the rage now she could now hear a subtle strain of some other emotion in it. Doubt? Fear? Her head was swimming. "The witch confirmed it."

Slowly, heart pounding, she took the bracelet from him. She turned it in the light so that she could see the terrible figure that was inscribed upon it. A shield with seven upright spears, bound together where they crossed.

The symbol of the Guardians.

"It must have been stolen," she whispered. "Or . . . or . . ." Her voice failed her.

Firmly but gently, he took her by the shoulders and turned her to face him. He waited until she looked up from the bracelet to meet his eyes once more, then said to her, very quietly, "No, Mother. I'm sorry. I thought that at first, too. So I had a witch test it. Twice over, in fact. To be sure." He took the bracelet back from her. "This piece was last worn by a true Guardian who died by the sword in Soladin."

She shut her eyes for a moment. He urged her gently to the side a few steps, then placed her hand upon the back of a chair. She found its seat and lowered herself into it, trembling.

"It makes no sense," she whispered. "Why would Guardians do such a thing? What would it gain them?"

"I cannot tell you that. Nor can I tell you if this is related to the recent trouble on our border with Kierdwyn . . . five raids now within our territory . . . but the timing is suspicious, is it not?"

She looked up sharply. "Kierdwyn would never act against the High Kingdom!"

"The Lord Protector himself, no. But a group of warriors that owes no more than token respect to his rule? That defines its own mission, defines its own wars, and effectively answers to no one?"

"Rhys is one of those warriors," she reminded him. "Do you honestly believe he would serve such a cause? The slaughter of innocents in a foreign kingdom? For what? Booty? Bloodshed? No. Not Rhys. Not possible."

"You have great faith in the motives of men. But blind faith in good intentions is a luxury a High King cannot afford. What evidence is there that I can bank my policy upon? What truth is so certain that lives may be risked in its name?"

"I will go to Kierdwyn and find you evidence," she said. "Whatever it takes. Is that good enough for you?" And she added defiantly, "They are my people. They will answer my questions."

He considered it, then nodded. "I will have an escort ready for you in the morning."

"No."

He raised an eyebrow.

She wiped a bit of moisture from her eye. Her hand was no longer trembling. "Horses take too long. And your witches cannot afford such a sacrifice. I will make my own arrangements."

His expression darkened. "Mother—"

"*Time matters,* Salvator. There is no other way." When he looked as if he were about to protest she added, "Respect my choices, as I have respected yours."

He bit his lip for a moment; she held her breath, waiting.

"There is no Magister here," he said at last.

She exhaled gratefully. "I know how to call one."

"And what will he ask in return?"

"Nothing. He owes me a favor."

"Who?" Salvator demanded.

"Ramirus." When he did not respond she offered, "Your father trusted him."

"My father trusted no Magister. And taught me to do the same."

She said nothing.

Finally, with a sigh, he nodded. "Very well. As long as you will not be indebted to him for it, I will not stand in your way."

It is you who are indebted to him, she thought. *Without him, you would have been killed by enemies of the High Kingdom within hours of your coronation. But I can never tell you that, can I? Your god would not allow you to accept the truth.*

He held out the bracelet to her. Shuddering slightly, she took it from him. The brass was still warm from his touch.

"Bring me word of what my uncle says about this," he told her, "That I may know the name of my enemy."

He looked toward the doors and his eyes narrowed, remembering the woman who had just passed between them. "For I swear to you, Mother, by my father's throne, Soladin will have justice. Even if those of my own blood are implicated."

CHAPTER 20

GWYNOFAR STOOD in the doorway, her golden hair gleaming in the late afternoon sunlight, eyes the blue of a clear summer morning. Kierdwyn blue. She was dressed in a cream-colored gown in the southern style, the long ends of her sleeves all but sweeping the floor. A belt of golden links, each in the form of a double-headed hawk, was clasped about her slender waist. The arms of House Aurelius.

It took Rhys a few seconds to realize that she was there, and then a few seconds more to respond. Thinking had come hard to him ever since his visit to the Spear. "Gwyn?"

She did not answer him, but simply crossed the room to where he stood and embraced him. He resisted for a moment, not wanting to let his guard down even for her, but it could not last; with a shudder of surrender he felt the tension bleed out of his limbs as he finally responded in kind, wrapping his arms tightly about her. The perfume of her hair was a tonic to his senses: familiar, reassuring. Trembling, he closed his eyes and simply drank in the smell of her, trying to lose himself in the memory of better times. For a brief instant the shadows surrounding him seemed to release their stranglehold on his heart. But only for an instant. The newfound darkness in his soul was not to be banished so easily.

When she drew back from him at last her pained expression made it clear just how worried she was about him. Gods alone knew how he looked to her right now, with his bloodshot eyes, week-old stubble, and fading bruises. Probably bad enough to frighten children.

Kamala had wanted to clean him up a bit, but he had forbidden her to try. He would not have a witch wasting her life force for his vanity. Anything a bath and change of clothing could not fix would just have to stay the way it was.

He had not trusted himself enough to wield a razor.

"They called you here?" he said. A question. Her visit warmed his spirit, but it also dismayed him. He had secrets to guard now, and she was the one person that he had never been able to lie to. "They shouldn't have."

But she shook her head. "I didn't even know you were here until I arrived. Mother told me. I came here right away." She reached out and brushed a stray braid back from his face; it was like a mother's touch, gentle and comforting. "I was sent here on Salvator's business and now I am glad for it."

Her concern was almost too intense for him to bear; he was no longer worthy of such affection. "What did they tell you?" he asked, trying not to meet her eyes.

"That you went on some mission into Alkali territory, your companion was killed, and you were imprisoned by the Master Guardian there. That a witch helped you gain your freedom and brought you back home. That the Guardians of Alkali have all gone mad."

The corner of his mouth twitched slightly. In an earlier, more innocent time, it might have become a smile. "Her name is Kamala."

"And that you found a broken Spear."

He felt himself stiffen. "Yes." The word had a terrible power in such context; he dared do no more than whisper it.

"Mother told me that seeing it wounded your soul, somehow. That your spirit still bleeds, even though you are surrounded by family now."

Startled, he looked up at her. "She said that?"

Gwynofar nodded. "She cares about you, Rhys."

He shut his eyes. "She shouldn't," he whispered. "I am a shame to her house."

With a sigh she reached out and touched his face. "You are a joy to your sister and you make your father proud. Maybe those things matter to her."

He said nothing.

"What happened out there, Rhys? I saw you after you fought the Souleater, when it had nearly crushed the life out of you, and you looked more alive even then than you do right now." Her eyes narrowed as she studied him from top to bottom; clearly what she saw disturbed her. "What is it, my brother? Tell me."

He drew in a deep breath, trying to steady his voice. "I saw a Spear broken beyond repair. I saw the Wrath weakening. I learned that the Souleater I had killed was not the only one to enter the human lands. Probably only the first of many." He rubbed his forehead stiffly, as if that could banish the memories. "That is enough to break any man's spirit, I think."

And I learned that the ancient gods do not exist . . . or at least do not care if we live or die. That our sacred mission is rooted in a human atrocity so terrible that the merest echoes of it produced the world's greatest curse. I learned that legends lie.

Perhaps she might have said something to him then that would have broken him down, so that he was forced to tell her the truth. Gods knew that he wanted to share it with someone, to force out all the darkness that was inside him until the pressure in his chest was gone. Until he could breathe again. If anyone would be willing to share his burden with him, it was Gwynofar.

But before his resolve could weaken someone knocked on the door, shattering the moment's intimacy. Rhys drew in a deep breath as Gwynofar stepped forward to open it, revealing one of the Lord Protector's servants.

"It is time," the man announced, with a bow. "Their Lordships bid you attend them in the map room."

"We shall come," Rhys told him; he bowed and withdrew, no doubt to alert another attendee.

Gwynofar raised an eyebrow.

"The master archivist has been working on translating some figures that were inscribed inside the broken Spear," Rhys told her. "We've been waiting for his report."

She nodded and held out one delicate hand toward him. He hesitated, then offered her his arm to lead her to the meeting. He tried not to shiver as her slender fingers pressed the fabric of his sleeve against the scars that lay hidden underneath, conjuring memories of a desolate plain, a pile of shattered brick, and a mummified body screaming out its terror. . . .

He wanted to cut the wounds open again. He wanted to feel the hot blood flowing out of them, purifying his flesh. Did chirurgeons not teach that all bodily ills could be traced to an imbalance of vital fluids? Maybe if he did that the darkness inside his soul would bleed out as well so that he could feel clean again.

Dark thoughts swirling about his head like a colony of rabid bats, he led his royal half sister to the Lord Protector's map chamber.

———

They had invited Kamala to their meeting.

Maybe they would not have, if Rhys hadn't insisted. Maybe their natural distrust of outsiders would have won out over curiosity and the door would have been shut in her face. Certainly the lord constable had been suspicious of her and might have interrogated her for hours had not Rhys intervened. *(Why were you in Alkali? What do you know about the situation there? How is it you appeared at Rhys' side at the exact moment he needed to be rescued?)* She had smoothed over the roughest edges of his nerves with sorcery, but only sparingly; too much mental alteration might have been noticed by those who knew him best.

But when all was said and done, Rhys' argument to the Lord and Lady Protector won out. Kamala had seen the Spear. She had felt its power, tasted its madness, and might remember things about it that he did not. If they meant to discuss what to do about the Wrath failing, then they needed her input.

And so here she was, surrounded by nobles and sorcerers and the commanders of Kierdwyn's armies. And Rhys, of course. How out of place he looked here! When he had left Kierdwyn these people had been like family to him: trusted friends and allies, colleagues at arms, commanders. Now, standing in the midst of that family, he seemed utterly alone. The secret knowledge that he had brought back from Alkali was a prison that he could not breach without revealing the truth. Only Kamala, who knew his secret, could cross that threshold and stand beside him in spirit as well as body. Only she could give his soul comfort.

It was a strange—and uncomfortable—responsibility.

She had asked him, *Shouldn't you tell them the truth? Don't they have the right to know?*

He had answered, *They have a war to fight. Should I destroy the very source of their courage when they need it most?*

But he didn't sound confident and he hadn't been sleeping well and she didn't know how much longer he could go on like this without breaking.

Now his sister was here, and she seemed to bring him some comfort. She was a pale and slender thing, with a delicacy of presence that invited one to forget just how powerful she was. Gwynofar Kierdwyn, Queen Mother to Salvator Aurelius . . . and to Prince Andovan. Poor, doomed Andovan, whom Kamala had killed, sucking him dry of life to fuel her sorcery. How like him his mother looked, despite the disparity in gender! It was like having the ghost of Andovan at the table. Unnerving.

But the woman brought some measure of calm to Rhys' spirit and that was a good thing, wasn't it?

By Gwynofar's side sat the Magister who had brought her to Kierdwyn, an older man with snow-white hair and a long beard. That would be Ramirus. Kamala bound a whisper of power to remember what Ethanus had once said about him.

He is ancient and powerful and dangerously insightful, and fond of pursuing odd experiments with morati princes as his pawns. Some of his games take centuries to play out and no one but him really understands their purpose. He is prouder than most of our kind and enjoys the trappings of morati power; that is his greatest weakness. But he is also a renowned scholar in arcane matters and his word carries great weight among our brotherhood. And then he had added a sober warning: *Be doubly careful if you lie to this one; he does not require sorcery to sniff out an untruth.*

With a start Kamala realized that he was the Magister who had watched her fight the Souleater outside Danton's palace. Her heart began to pound fiercely and she had to remind herself that he had never seen her face and so could not possibly recognize her now. Of all the Magisters, only Colivar knew what she looked like.

There was one other Magister present, a brooding sorcerer whom the Lord Protector introduced as Lazaroth, Magister Royal to Kierdwyn's court. He was a pale man with short-cropped black hair who did not seem at all pleased to be present. His almond-shaped eyes and full lips were strangely compelling, almost sensual in aspect, but also disturbing in a way that Kamala could not put a name to; a shiver ran down her spine whenever he looked at her. Ethanus had not mentioned this one's name at all but that did not mean that he was not a sorcerer to be reckoned with; some Magisters changed names as casually as they changed the flesh they wore.

Also present were the Master Guardian Favias and his chief archivist, both of whom had been summoned to the palace as soon as Rhys and Kamala had arrived. Beside them sat Kierdwyn's lord constable, and then, at the head of the table, Lord and Lady Kierdwyn themselves. The two monarchs appeared more like brother and sister to Kamala's eyes than man and wife. That was the result of a thousand years of inbreeding among the *lyr* bloodlines, Rhys had explained. Supposedly the northern gods had dictated such practices after the Great War and provided special magics to protect the children of *lyr* unions from the normal consequences of incestuous couplings. Thus could the magical bloodlines be preserved and strengthened to weather the ages.

It all seemed unwholesome to Kamala.

The Lord Protector waited until all eyes were upon him

before speaking. "I thank you all for coming here on such short notice. Most of you have heard the gist of current events, including the reports of a Souleater appearing in Corialanus and another in Danton's capital city. I regret to say that I have now confirmed both reports. And of course we have witnesses to the second event sitting among us tonight." He nodded toward Ramirus and then toward where Kamala was sitting; startled, it took her a moment to realize that he was referring to Rhys. "Let no one mistake what these signs mean. Our ancient enemy has returned.

"Guardian Rhys was able to dispatch one of creatures. But our agents have been unable to locate the other one, and now there are rumors of nests being found in several remote locations. So it seems that the war we have feared for so long is finally upon us. It will not be fought along the northern border, as we anticipated, but in the very heart of human territory."

He drew in a deep breath; his expression was grim. "Thanks to the courage of Rhys and his companion Kamala, we now know that a Spear in Alkali has been damaged, weakening the Wrath enough to allow the Souleaters to cross. The ancient curse is still active, but it is not as strong or as finely focused as it used to be. The entire area now suffers from its baleful influence and arcane powers are severely compromised. Meanwhile it appears that the Master Guardian of Alkali serves some new agenda that has turned him against his own kind. None of his people have been seen in the other Protectorates for some months now. Is that correct, Master Favias?"

Favias nodded grimly. "Aye, sire."

"Master Anukyat's ultimate intentions are unknown—as are his motives—but it is clear that he and his followers do not want anyone to know about the damaged Spear. He is likely to stand in the way of any attempt to approach it and study it, much less repair it." His eyes narrowed. "In this he has made himself the enemy of Kierdwyn . . . and of the gods that guide us all."

Rhys' jaw twitched at the mention of gods and he looked away.

"What most of you here do not know is that Guardian Rhys was able to inspect the interior of the broken Spear. I will leave it to him to describe it to you."

For a moment it seemed as if Rhys had not heard him. Only Kamala was close enough to see his hands clench into fists beneath the table's edge as he struggled to tame his emotions. Then—in a voice so low that the men on the far side of the table had to lean forward to hear him—he said, "Its core was a hollow cylinder of brick with a domed top. The inside had been smoothed over with mortar, and the outside thickly reinforced with the same. It was our repairs being layered over it, year after year, century after century, that gave it another shape." A muscle tensed along the line of his jaw. "There was no tool of the gods at the center of it. Nothing. Just bricks, of the same type used in ordinary structures. Common mortar. And of course rubble, where the thing had been broken open."

He paused, then, and Kamala wondered if he was going to tell them the rest of the story. But the moment passed in silence and he only shook his head, a haunting sadness in his eyes. "Nothing sacred," he muttered. "Nothing that we might use as a weapon."

"Tell us of the symbols you saw there."

Rhys rubbed at the place on his arm where the cuts were hidden by his sleeve. "They were inscribed in continuous bands around the inside of the cylinder, with no visible beginning or end, or anything I recognized as punctuation. Perhaps there was something in the broken section to explain that. Kamala said—" He looked at her, as if seeking permission to continue. She nodded. "She thought it might be a spell of some kind." He hesitated, and Kamala could see the torment of indecision in his eyes. What would these men do if he went on with his story, he wondered; what if he told them the whole truth? Would their faith be shattered, as his had been? Could they do what needed to be done to save the human kingdoms from ruin without the illusion of divine favor to bolster their courage?

Finally he lowered his head and said simply, "I copied them."

The Lord Protector nodded. "Archivist Rommel. You have made some progress interpreting these figures, I understand?"

The archivist cleared his throat noisily as he reached for the pile of vellum sheets; he spread them out across the table so that all might see the strange shapes scribed upon them. "The figures appear to be in Karsi, a pictographic system that was created for merchants to use back in the First Age of Kings. Every domain had its own language in those days, you see, so communication could be slow and unwieldy. A caravan that traveled great distances might require a whole staff of translators to facilitate its business. So the merchants of the time created this script. Rather ingenious, really. You see, these letters are not sounds—not even really letters as such—but rather pictures, highly stylized. Each one represents an item or a concept. If you know what the pictures stand for you can make out what the writing says, regardless of what language you speak. A truly universal system. Quite amazing. We have read about it for years, and collected examples of individuals signs, but no sample this extensive has been seen for centuries." He ran his hand over the lines of writing as reverently as a sempstress might caress a bolt of the finest velvet. "Many of the ancient signs have been forgotten. Others—preserved as part of a family crest, perhaps, or used by witches as a sign of power—have been corrupted over time and their original meanings lost. Thus I regret that we cannot interpret this text as precisely as I would like."

"Tell us what you have managed," the Lord Protector said.

Rommel drew in a deep breath; clearly he was not used to such command performances. "The text appears to be divided into three sections. The first is clearly an invocation of some sort." Rommel pointed to individual figures as he described them. "This one refers to *seers,* and this one to *diviners,* and this one to *healers.*" Kamala found herself leaning forward as he spoke. "There are several more in that vein, all referring to witches of some type." He moved his finger down to the second line of figures. "These appear to describe the forces of nature: *wind, air, earth, fire . . . stars* are referenced here, and *sun,* and a symbol that means one or both *moons . . .* and then here is another set of figures I could not identify. Presumably another natural force."

All the power that is in the world, Kamala thought suddenly, remembering her dream. Suddenly the two Magisters had turned to look at her, and her heart skipped a beat. What had she done to draw their attention? Were they somehow listening to her thoughts? Or were their sorcerous senses simply attuned to any insight? Trembling inwardly, she bolstered the arcane defenses that she had prepared for this meeting so that even their most piercing inquiries could not break through. Carefully. Carefully. If they tasted sorcery in her aura they might assume that some past patron had gifted her with a protective spell, but if they caught her actually working a spell herself, right in front of them, there would be no mistaking its nature. Or hers.

Lazaroth turned away after a moment, focusing upon Rommel's scribblings, but Ramirus' eyes remained fixed upon her. She thought she could feel the ice-cold touch of a sorcerous query slithering across her skin. Gritting her teeth, she forced herself not to flinch or let him see in any other way that she was aware of its presence. After a few seconds it seemed to withdraw from her, unsatisfied. Her defenses were holding strong.

". . . We believe that the purpose of this list was to invoke all the forms of power known to the witches of that time to aid in some sort of grand spell," Rommel was saying. "For obvious reasons, sorcerers were not included."

"Are there any gods mentioned?" Rhys asked abruptly.

"Not among the figures we were able to interpret." Rommel's brow furrowed. "That does seem rather odd, doesn't it? Perhaps that was in the portion of text that was damaged. You say that part of the Spear had crumbled, yes? Or perhaps the writer only meant to invoke those powers that mankind could comprehend. Gods are a different sort of creature altogether. Yes?"

Rhys' expression darkened, but he said nothing.

"This next portion speaks of sacrifice. I believe that it chronicles the passage of the witches into the northlands and the fate they expected to suffer there while hunting down the last of the Souleaters. A very gloomy picture, to be sure. These figures here indicate *hunger, death,* and *fear* . . . there are many more along that line. A detailed list of human misery. As for the third and final section. . . ." Rommel scowled at the final pages of his work. "I regret that we could not make much sense of it. This string of symbols here refers to *three ladies,* this one to *truth,* then down here a *twilight chair*, and later a *throne of tears*, possibly references to the same thing, then there are a few references to *blood*, each with a different qualifier, and the number seven appears several times." He sighed. "We are still researching this section, but its form suggests that it may be some sort of warning, or even a prophecy. If so, it is unlikely its meaning can be unraveled without a precise translation of all the figures. Something we do not yet have the resources to provide."

The Lord Protector turned to his Magister Royal. "Lazaroth?"

"I will check once more to see if there are additional resources to be found," the Magister Royal responded coolly. "However, in my experience the archivists are quite thorough. It is doubtful any reference exists that they do not already know about."

"The Spear itself is beyond your reach?" he asked.

"Regretfully so, my liege. The Wrath will befoul any sorcery that touches it, regardless of where the source of that sorcery lies. We might manage to establish a connection if we tried hard enough, but there is no saying whether the information thus gathered would be accurate or not. A wasted effort at best and a misleading one at worst."

"Then we shall do our best with more mundane efforts," The Lord Protector said. He looked back to the archivist. "Anything more, Master Rommel?"

"That is all for now, sire." Rommel gathered the papers together again, handling them as reverently as if they were made of beaten gold. "We continue to work on it."

Stevan nodded and turned to Master Guardian. "Master Favias'. Your thoughts, please."

Favias' eyes narrowed thoughtfully. "Tradition says that the gods thrust their weapons into the ground and then caused the earth to rise up and cover them, in order to preserve them for the day we might need them again. Now we discover that the only thing inside one such monument is a handful of symbols." He paused, stroking his short beard as he considered the puzzle before him. "Perhaps the words themselves are the weapon we seek. A grand spell that the gods provided for our use, in case their curse should ever falter."

The Lady Protector spoke for the first time. "Do not forget the cost of the first spell. It is said that all the witches that were in the world offered up their lives in sacrifice, that the gods might hear their prayers. Do you imagine we might repair it with any less effort? The witches of our own age are unlikely to make such a sacrifice." Her clear eyes glittered in the lamp-light. "They do not yet understand what we face," she said softly. "They do not yet fear the enemy enough."

Rhys' fists were clenched so tightly now that that his finger-nails drew blood from the palms. Kamala could only imagine what he was thinking. Would they judge such an enterprise more practical if they knew it did not require a willing sacrifice but could be managed by mass murder instead? Would they be willing to pay that cost? All he needed to do was speak the truth to them, and they would know the price of power for what it was.

And lose their faith.

"It is clear we require a more precise translation of the inscription before we can decide upon a course of action," the Lord Protector said. "I remain open to any suggestions of how that might be accomplished. In the meantime, there are other matters I wish to discuss."

His cool blue eyes fixed upon his daughter. "Since you are here, Gwynofar, I would like to address a matter that speaks to the High Kingdom. Perhaps related to all this. Family should be direct with family, for that is the way of the *lyr*. Don't you agree?"

"Of course," Gwynofar said, nodding gracefully in assent.

"Do you find the current company acceptable? Or would you prefer a more private setting? I have no wish to make you uncomfortable."

The High Queen looked around the table. Everyone present was either a member of Kierdwyn's ruling family or a trusted adviser who would expect to be part of any such discussion. All except for Kamala, that is. Gwynofar's eyes paused for a second as they fell upon her—taking her measure, no doubt—but Rhys reached out and took the witch's hand, holding it tightly where all could see it. The message was clear.

She nodded. "It is acceptable."

The Lord Protector drummed his fingers sharply on the oak table as he ordered his thoughts. "Your late husband Danton wanted peace along his northern border. Your marriage was arranged to seal that peace. As *lyra*, you understand the importance of such a contract. Our bloodlines have a duty to look beyond ephemeral politics to a greater mission. We do not wish to waste time and manpower in petty skirmishes over border disputes. Danton, meanwhile, wanted to focus his imperialistic instincts elsewhere, without having to worry that we might stir up trouble on his rear flank while he was doing so to test his strength."

"The alliance served us well," she agreed.

"And Salvator honors it?"

The question seemed to surprise her. "Of course."

The Lord Protector's eyes narrowed. "You should know that there have been raids against our people along our common border. Supposedly the work of bandits, but they left relics of his soldiery behind. If Salvator's men are not performing the raids themselves, then they may be supplying those who are."

Gwynofar's eyes flared. "Salvator has no reason to do such a thing."

"His antipathy toward the Protectorates is well known. His creator god disapproves of our mission, does he not?" Again the fingers drummed restlessly on the table. "Perhaps he feels that distracting the *lyr* from their vigilance would be a service to his god."

His wife put her own hand gently over his, quieting his fingers.

"I do not deny the distasteful nature of his religion," Gwynofar countered. "But he is Danton's son, and understands that his first duty is to maintain the stability of his domain. That would hardly be accomplished by sending out bandits to harass an ally."

The Lord Protector nodded, but his expression did not soften. "And the source of the relics?" he challenged her.

Gwynofar hesitated a moment, then reached into her pouch and drew out a wide brass cuff. "Perhaps the same as the source of this."

She turned it in the light so that the designs etched into it were visible to all. Kamala heard a sharp intake of breath from the Master Guardian.

"Where did you get this?" Favias demanded, rising from his seat as he reached for it.

"From the body of a dead Skandir raider. Three ships full of them attacked the harbor town of Soladin some days ago and left nothing alive in their wake." She handed the item to him and watched him as he turned it over in his hand, studying the engravings. "It is a Guardian's bracelet, is it not?"

Favias looked sharply at Rhys, then offered him the item to inspect.

"Namanti," Rhys whispered, as he took it. All the color had drained from his face, "She was wearing this when we left Kierdwyn."

Favias turned to Gwynofar; his voice was steady, but the effort required to make it so was apparent. "Let me understand this, Majesty. You are claiming that Guardians from Skandir raided your shores?"

Gwynofar drew herself up proudly. "I have shown you what one of the raiders wore while she helped put my subjects to the sword. You tell me what that means, if not that she was one of yours."

"Jewelry can be stolen," he challenged her. "Traded. Lost."

Gwynofar looked to Ramirus.

"The bracelet was taken from the body of its true owner in Soladin," the Magister said quietly. "That much I have confirmed myself. I am sorry."

Favias drew in a sharp breath. "With all due respect, how can you know—"

"NO!" Rhys slammed his fist down on the table; the noise was like an explosion. He stood up suddenly, sending the heavy oak chair clattering to the floor behind him. "Namanti was with *me*. She died in Alkali. I saw her crushed beneath her horse. . . ."

And then words failed him utterly, as the truth sank in.

With a hoarse cry of rage—or was it grief?—he turned his back on the others and started toward the door.

"Rhys!" Gwynofar reached out as if to stop him, but he showed no sign of even knowing she was there. He struck the oak doors at a near run, scattering the servants outside as he rushed from the chamber.

Kamala bound a whisper of sorcery to read his intentions, then quickly rose from her own seat as the answer came. Ignoring all the proper protocol for one of her rank—which would no doubt dictate some complex dance of curtseys and apologies before leaving such exalted company—she headed straight for the door, following in Rhys' wake. Let them take her to task for it later, if they liked. She would not put him at risk for such foolishness.

Why do you care what happens to him? she asked herself.

There was no time to answer.

Through the castle she hurried, following the trail of Rhys' grief as it wended its way through room after room. The force of his misery was as clear to her Sight as a trail of animal droppings would have been to a tracker. Once her long skirt caught underfoot and she cursed in language that would make a sailor blush, but she didn't want to spare so much as a single second of concentration to shorten it, so she just grabbed the fabric and raised it up in front of her to scandalous height—calf-high—and kept moving.

Servants scattered as she approached, perhaps fearing that if they did not get out of the way fast enough she would run right over them. Rightly so.

She passed through an iron-barred door and was suddenly outside. High, high up, on a walkway edged by a waist-high parapet, somewhere near the summit of Kierdwyn's castle. Two half moons shone overhead and she could see Rhys clearly by their light, standing unsteadily by the parapet, facing outward into the night. The ornaments in his hair glittered like captive stars as his braids stirred in the breeze; Kamala thought she could see a thin line of blood trickling down from his injured palm where he gripped the cold stone.

She knew without asking why he was so very still as he gazed out over the battlements. She knew that he was considering how far he would have to fall to have his life snuffed cleanly out rather than leaving his body broken but alive. Such a fall would have no meaning if all it accomplished was to test a healer's art.

For what seemed like an eternity Kamala stood there in silence, afraid to speak aloud or move toward him lest that be the final impetus that forced him over the edge.

"She was *alive*," he said at last, his voice hoarse with misery. Was he speaking to her, or to himself? "I watched her fall and I saw her crushed and I thought she was dead . . . I *believed* them when they told me she was dead . . . would she be alive now if I had not been such a fool? Could I have saved her?"

"The servants there genuinely believed she was dead." Kamala's tone was as gentle as she could make it. "Probably the jailer also." If she moved closer, if she reached out to touch him, would he accept that? Or would he vault himself over the parapet and be lost forever? "Questioning them more would have accomplished nothing."

"Don't you understand?" He turned back to face her. His face was streaked with sweat—or perhaps with tears?—and his gray eyes were bloodshot and haunted. "I should have refused to leave Alkali until we found her! I should have torn that Citadel apart, brick by brick if necessary, until I either knew that she was safe, or held her body in my own hands! Do you understand now? *Can* you understand? I failed her!" He shut his eyes and whispered fiercely, "I failed my duty."

Kamala did not know what to say. She was not a creature of instinctive compassion and had no experience with bringing men comfort. She just stood there in silence, hoping that her presence would be enough to bind him to the living world. Enough to matter.

Why do you care if he lives or dies? the inner voice persisted.

"Did they kill her back then, do you think?" Rhys' voice dropped to a hoarse whisper. "Did they preserve her body with sorcery so that it would not rot, then leave it to be found in Soladin, as if it had been freshly killed? Or maybe they used spells to wipe out her mind, turned her into a mindless puppet that could do nothing but obey them, even when they ordered her to betray her mission. Her *sacred* mission!" He struck his fist against the parapet behind him, hard enough that Kamala heard the crack of bone. Pain flared briefly in his eyes, followed by a dark and terrible satisfaction. She had seen that expression once before, when he had gouged the symbols from the Spear into his flesh. It was no less unnerving this time.

"The Guardians will avenge her," Kamala said quietly. The words seemed insufficient even to her when weighed against his grief, but they were the best she had to offer. "Don't you want to be there for that? Don't you want to help make it happen?"

"And what makes you think I will not fail in that as well?" he rasped. "They are all better off without me."

He looked out over the parapet—toward the deep, dark shadows that lay below—and shuddered. For a moment Kamala thought that he would indeed jump, and she summoned enough power to stop him—but then a soft voice rang out across the evening air, all the more startling for its gentle tone. "Rhys."

Shaken, he turned back to see who it was.

Gwynofar Aurelius walked slowly toward him, past where Kamala stood, holding out a hand to him. Moonlight cast a halo about her head, turning her hair nearly as pale as his own;

in such light she looked like some delicate fairy creature, come from another world to save him.

"Don't leave us, Rhys. Not now." She paused, and when he did not respond, added quietly, "Don't leave *me*."

For a moment the entire world seemed frozen; even the breeze seemed to grow still waiting for his answer. Kamala found that she was holding her breath. Still no response from Rhys.

Gwynofar took one step forward, then another. Her half brother shivered and glanced back over the parapet once more, but he did not move away from her.

And then her slender white hand touched his arm, oh, so gently, and all the strength seemed to drain out of his body in a single breath. She caught him as he slumped, holding him tightly in her arms. After a moment he returned the embrace, his face buried in her hair. Weeping, perhaps. The dam had broken at last.

"There is so much to do now," Gwynofar whispered to him. "So much that you are needed for. Have strength, my brother."

For a moment longer Kamala watched them, a vague and nameless hunger stirring in her heart. Jealousy? Flushing at the thought, she finally forced herself to turn away, granting them their privacy. Not jealousy, she told herself, as she eased open the door that led back into the castle. What was there to be jealous of? She slipped inside and then shut the door softly behind her, so very softly, not wanting the sound of it to disturb them.

With her back against the door she took several deep breaths, trying to sort out what was in her heart. So many strange feelings to process. So many unfamiliar questions. If she had some of this mysterious *lyr* blood in her veins, would it all make more sense?

There is no Magister among the lyr, she remembered. Why was that? Logically it made no sense at all; any population with an innate propensity for arcane power should produce more Magisters, not fewer. Yet here the opposite had happened.

There had to be a reason, she thought.

"Lady Kamala."

Startled, she looked up to find that Ramirus had entered the room. What had he seen in her when she had thought herself alone, her expression unguarded? Silently she cursed her own carelessness. In a place like this she should never let her guard down; one never knew who was watching.

When she did not respond he pressed, "That is the name you prefer. Is it not?"

She pushed herself stiffly away from the door, aware that now every movement of hers was going to be watched, analyzed, memorized. The thought was daunting, but also strangely invigorating; *suspicion* was an arena much more comfortable to her than that of sympathy and sentiment. "It is."

"The meeting has been adjourned till the morrow, for obvious reasons. His Lordship has sent out servants to inform all concerned, but I offered to carry the message to you myself." Clear eyes set deeply into folds of parchment-textured skin took her measure, offered nothing in return. "I thought perhaps we might speak."

"Of course." She nodded in what she hoped was a suitably gracious manner, though her pulse was racing. In any other company she might have used sorcery to calm her heart, but in front of a Magister that was far too dangerous. Better to respond like a morati and take her chances. "You honor me with such attention."

The aged lips curled into a thin smile. "Rhys speaks highly of you."

She bowed her head in what she hoped was a suitably humble manner. "He honors me as well."

"How fortunate it was that he came across you when he did. Otherwise he might still be imprisoned in Alkali . . . or perhaps even worse."

"Indeed." It did not matter what words she gave him, she knew; his true purpose was to read her hidden responses, if not with sorcery than with simple human insight. Such a man could learn more from how she listened to a question than the words she used to answer it. "Clearly the gods favored his mission."

Ramirus chuckled softly; she would have sold her soul at that moment to know the exact cause of his amusement. Stroking his long beard with a wrinkled hand, he said, "I was surprised you did not say much at the meeting."

She shrugged. "I was not asked to speak."

"And if you had been?"

Now it was her turn to smile enigmatically. "That would depend on what the question was."

"Regardless, I am sure you would have had much to offer. You were with Rhys when he found the broken Spear. You saw the same Karsi figures that he did, and must have wondered at their meaning."

"Of course."

"No doubt you would have made your own observations, as well."

"Perhaps." She felt like a fly dancing around the edges of a spider's web. Where was he heading with all this?

"And being a witch, no doubt you also viewed the situation as witches do, who are sensitive to the requirements of arcane power."

The hairs on the back of her neck rose instinctively. "I am not sure I understand your meaning."

"I think that perhaps you do." The challenge in his voice was all the more sharply honed for being quietly voiced. "Once you left the Spear's vicinity, you knew you would be unable to access its secrets any longer. Unless you brought back something to serve as an anchor, to use in a place where the Wrath had no power."

She felt the flicker of surprise come into in her eyes before she could stop it. *Well done,* she thought to him, even as she struggled to keep any more emotion from showing on her face. *I should have anticipated that you would guess that. I should have been prepared for it.* "Is that a question?"

A strange, cold smile spread across his face. "No. Not at all. The question is . . . what information did you gather that Rhys did not, and why do you not offer it up to those who need it?"

"There are a lot of assumptions in that question."

"But not necessarily false ones." The cold eyes glittered.

She shrugged. "I was not asked for information today. If I am tomorrow, we shall see then how I answer." She paused, wondering how best to regain control of the conversation. "Unless there is some reason you think I should keep my silence."

"Quite the contrary. I am looking forward to what you have to say. In fact, I was hoping we might share a few words on the matter tonight. Let us say, a *professional* discussion."

A cold hatred welled suddenly up inside her. She knew exactly how Magisters felt about witches, and it wasn't a collegial relationship by a long shot. There was a reason they called them morati—death-bound, ignorant—a word usually reserved for the helpless mortals of the world who couldn't summon enough power to tie a shoelace. Witches were failures: men and women who were ambitious enough to grasp at power, but not strong enough to hold onto it. The ones that were worthy of respect became Magisters. The rest of them died young and were forgotten.

Normally if there was a piece of information a Magister wanted, he would just use sorcery to steal it. But Kamala's defenses were strong enough to repel such efforts. Ramirus could not use sorcery to loosen her tongue without running up against that armor. So he was forced to rely upon this mundane seduction that assumed her own ignorance of Magister bigotry.

But she was not ignorant. She knew exactly what he wanted—and why he wanted it.

He is prouder than most of our kind.

Lazaroth was Magister Royal here. Any sorcerous investigation that took place in Kierdwyn would be subject to his authority. For another Magister to become involved, as Ramirus had done today, bordered on insult; no doubt that was why Lazaroth had been in such a foul mood. If Ramirus now provided some vital piece of information that his rival had failed to uncover . . . ah, that would be a move to savor in the fierce competition which passed for social concourse among their kind! Rarely did a Magister come across such a perfect opportunity to embarrass a rival while appearing to aid him.

"Such information is valuable," she said quietly.

"That depends on what it is."

"I know its value to me. The favor of a Lord Protector, at the very least." She paused. "That is a high price to bid against, Magister Ramirus."

The bluntness of her challenge seemed to startle him. Good. If there was one thing she had learned in her whoring days it was the power of keeping a man off balance.

Another cold tendril of power slithered over her skin, seeking some chink in her armor; it was easily banished. Finally he said, "You have a price in mind."

She cocked her head to one side, pretending to consider. Could he hear how hard her heart was beating? "Frankly, there is not much that I need."

His eyes narrowed ominously; the warning in them was clear. *I could crush you without pausing for breath, witch, and then summon your secrets forth from your ashes. Do not toy with me.*

"But we could call it a favor owed," she concluded, seemingly oblivious to his displeasure. "I am sure in the future something appropriate will come to mind."

He raised an eyebrow. "That is quite an audacious request."

She shrugged. "If you find it unacceptable, I am quite content to discuss my findings when our meeting resumes tomorrow. I am sure their lordships will appreciate my contribution."

She began to move past him to the exit. Would he try to stop her? If so, he was in for one hell of a surprise. She could already feel her power gathering inside her, molten and eager. *I have already killed one Magister,* she thought to him. *Don't tempt me to make it two.*

But he did nothing to stop her from leaving, and she was halfway out the door when he finally said, "A favor without limits is an invitation to misunderstanding."

Since he could not see her face, she allowed herself to smile. "Well now, we do not want misunderstanding by any means." Slowly she turned back, her mind racing. She was under no illusion about the subtext of this conversation; he was putting on a show for her benefit to convince her that her request had real meaning. As a Magister herself, Kamala knew better. No promise made to a morati was considered binding. Who was going to enforce payment? He could promise whatever he wanted to her, without limits or logic, and neither law nor ethics would require that he honor it.

The game was on now, and she hoped he would not realize where it was headed. "Very well, let us say . . . something reasonable. Counsel, perhaps; the benefit of your knowledge. Guidance, when morati wisdom falls short. Perhaps protection in some simple matter. Nothing so vast it would stress your resources, nothing that would put your morati allies at risk or any contract with them. A single, finite act. Is that reasonable?"

His brow furrowed as he pretended to think it over. All a farce, of course. It hardly mattered what conditions he agreed to; he would keep his promise if it suited him to do so and ignore it otherwise. But the drama of the moment had to be played out for as long as he thought it had meaning to her. "Agreed," he said at last, with suitable solemnity.

"Excellent." She let her eyes fill with gratitude, and gave him a moment to drink it in. *See how grateful the poor little witch is for your magnanimous favor.* "Now seal your promise with an oath upon your Law, and we will call the bargain sealed."

Now it was his turn to be startled. "The Law is for Magisters. An oath to a witch would be . . . meaningless."

"Ah." She appeared to reconsider. "Then perhaps when the time comes to call in my favor, I will have a Magister do it for me. Does that sound reasonable?"

An oath sworn upon the Law was sacrosanct, Kamala knew. It was one of the handful of customs that kept Magister society from tearing itself to pieces, and all would respect it.

Ramirus' eyes narrowed as he reassessed her. Bereft of sorcery, he had only his human senses to rely upon. She, however, had spent half her lifetime lying to men, getting them to believe that she possessed the one thing they wanted most in the world, then convincing them they wanted to pay for it.

"What you ask is unprecedented," he said at last, clearly displeased with where his negotiations had led him. "Show me that what you have is worth such a price."

Looking down quickly so that he would not see the triumph in her eyes, she untied a small leather purse from her belt and loosened the cord that kept it closed. Upending it, she spilled forth a handful of rubble into her upturned palm.

Brick.

Mortar.

"The substance of the Spear itself," she told him. "Enough of an anchor to allow sorcery to divine the history of that artifact, its message, its makers' intent." She looked up at him. "I trust that has value to you?"

His face revealed nothing. Of course. He was a master of manipulation, and would let nothing of his true desire show.

Then: "Very well." He said it gruffly, as if the promise he was about to give her was of no real consequence anyway. "By the Law that governs Magisters, you shall have what you ask for."

Reining in her jubilation so that he would not see it, Kamala handed the precious rubble over to him. She hoped he would never discover that she had prepared the fragments for just such a bargain. They might reveal many secrets to Ramirus, including the meaning of the Spear's Karsi text—they would certainly enable him to upstage and embarrass his rival—but they would not betray the one secret that mattered most. All the traces of human sacrifice had been cleansed from the fragments; the screams of the dying had been silenced, and no man's sorcery could restore them without her agreement.

My gift to you, Rhys. She thought it gently, softly, and wished it could give the Guardian comfort. *Do with that secret as your spirit guides you.*

CHAPTER 21

DREAMBOUND, SIDEREA flew.

Or perhaps not dreambound. Nor waking, exactly. Rather some state that was in between, that quieted the flesh but stirred the soul. A sense of *otherness* that allowed her to extend her senses beyond the limits of her human body and embrace the other half of herself. To share in the Souleater's flight, her energy . . . her joy.

Broad, shimmering wings beat the air into whirlwinds beneath her. She could feel them lift her up and over the rocky peaks, while below her all sorts of animals fled in terror. That was all right. She was not hungry right now, so she let them run. But if she had wanted one . . . ah, the pleasure of the hunt! To feel the power surging outward from her until it stopped her prey in its tracks, until her target fell to its knees before her, inviting her to sup upon the essence of its life until it expired. An ecstasy of dying. The Souleater queen had not truly savored such things before; to her the world was simply divided into *those who eat* and *those who are eaten,* and devouring her prey was a simple animal indulgence. But now she had access to Siderea's subtler instincts, and the Witch-Queen recognized the seduction of the kill for what it truly was. And it pleased her—it pleased them both—to have such power over other living creatures.

Amalik matched us well, Siderea thought, and she could feel the sentiment echo in the distance, couched in terms a Souleater might understand. Along with a mental growl of warning, should the man approach either of them again without the proper courtesies.

She had not seen him since the day at the ravine. Which was as it should be. He was a companion of Souleaters and understood the male's proper status.

Sometimes Siderea dreamed of tearing him limb from limb, along with his Souleater consort. They were terrifying dreams, but also pleasurable ones. Sometimes she would lie in bed for hours afterward, savoring the smell of Souleater blood and the screams of his dying, sharing that pleasure with the one who now shared her soul.

As it should be.

"Majesty?"

She returned from her distant flight drowsily, regretfully. *Do not fly too high,* she warned her consort as they parted. Not that there was need for such warnings any longer. The Souleater had absorbed enough of Siderea's own knowledge of the world to understand why such secrecy was needed and how to maintain it.

But how she longed to fly high and free, daring all the other Souleaters to pursue her! No longer a secret invader who must hide her presence from men, but a true queen, master over all the earth!

Soon, the thought came. *It will be soon.*

"Yes? What is it?"

The servant bowed as Siderea shifted herself upon the silken cushions of the couch.

"Petrana Bellisi has arrived." Despite the fact that Siderea was fully dressed and alone, the servant averted his eyes as he spoke; clearly he felt as if he had somehow interrupted an intimate moment.

Perhaps he had.

She rose up from the couch and clapped her hands sharply, so that her maidservant might come running. She had plans for Petrana Bellisi, and they required her looking her best. "Have her greeted as her rank deserves," she told her servant. "Bring out the best of our wine and see that she is encouraged to relax. I shall be there shortly. Quickly now!" she prompted, when he did not leave immediately. A maidservant squeezed by him as he backed out of the doorway; Siderea indicated her sleep-tousled hair and the girl took up a brush and began to work on it. Shutting her eyes, the queen gave herself over to the sensations of the coiffure: warm fingers tickling her scalp, the sharp bite of pins as each curl and ringlet was fixed in place, the gentle tug of the brush as it smoothed out the snarls in the long hanging tresses, the soft weight of ornaments as they were positioned amid the strands.

?

The question was wordless, but she understood its meaning. Her consort did not comprehend why she would preen herself for another woman. As always, Siderea was never quite sure if the Souleater was actually observing her affairs or responding instinctively to thoughts and emotions that seeped from one mind to the other without context.

Desire is power, she explained.

It was getting hard to focus upon human company these days.

Hard to shut out that other soul—so powerful, so primal!—and limit herself to human words and human thoughts. Her other self was a creature of pure self-indulgence whose every instinct became action as soon as it was conceived. A human queen, on the other hand, was a creature of plots and contrivances for whom every word must be chosen with care, voiced in just the perfect tone, then studied as it took effect. How much easier it seemed to just live in the moment, to simply *be*. Sometimes Siderea envied her Souleater counterpart.

She took a moment to glance in the mirror and was pleased by what she saw. The Souleater's vitality had brought new color to her cheeks, and the deep ruddy tone of her lips no longer needed enhancement. Only a bit of kohl was required to blacken her lashes, drawing attention to her wide, dark eyes. Her body was draped in layers of ruddy silk, bound with a twisted girdle that accentuated the curves of her form. Pearl-headed pins peeked out from rich black curls about her face while the rest of her hair cascaded down over her shoulders in long, coiled tendrils. No man could resist her thus. Perhaps no woman either.

She chose a pair of long earrings that tinkled softly as she moved, misted herself with one of her more delicate perfumes—the tastes of men and women were so different in matters of smell!—and finally was ready. A strange, fluttering excitement filled her stomach; was that the Souleater? Was she watching her dress? Siderea took an extra moment at the mirror, just in case. *What do you think?* she whispered to her consort. There was no answer. But she thought to her as she left the room, silken skirts swirling around her ankles, *Now you will learn how to fly without wings.*

Petrana Bellisi was waiting in the atrium. She stood up quickly when Siderea entered and offered a quick curtsy. Clearly she was not quite sure what manner of greeting was expected now that they were in the Witch-Queen's home territory. Beside her was a glass of wine, still full. *We shall have to fix that,* Siderea thought.

"My dear Petrana." She held out her arms in welcome, then, when the visitor hesitated, moved forward to embrace her. A tender kiss on each cheek lingered just long enough to bring a warm flush to Petrana's face; the woman was unaccustomed to such casual intimacy.

She was dressed in silk the color of twilight, an odd choice for a summer afternoon. The neckline was somewhat lower than her accustomed style, which was perhaps why she had chosen it; she was clearly trying to follow Siderea's advice in looking less somber. But she had draped a veil across her bosom and tucked it into the dress in such a manner that whatever womanly gifts she might have possessed were effectively hidden from sight. Were the veil of thinner silk, or more artfully draped, it might have offered a seductive enhancement, enticing one to search for hidden treasures beneath. As it was, it seemed intended to serve as armor.

For the body or the soul? Siderea wondered.

"Your Majesty is kind to receive me."

The Witch-Queen shook her head and touched a perfumed finger to her visitor's lips. "Shush. No titles, my dear. I will not have it." Taking Petrana's hand in her own, she urged her to sit down once more by the abandoned glass of wine. "You are in my home now, not some foreign court. Siderea will do." She signaled for a nearby servant to bring her a glass of wine as well.

—and a low growl sounded within her brain, as the scent of the visitor filled her nostrils—

"A lovely gown," she murmured, startled by the mental intrusion. She ran her fingers down one of Petrana's sleeves, along the edges where the fine white chemise peeked through. "Sendalese silk, is it? They make the finest blues." A glass of wine was handed to her; she brought it to her lips and paused a moment, drinking in its scent before sipping. "Ah, exquisite. You must try some." She lifted Petrana's glass and handed it to her. "Our southern vineyards have no equal, when the rainfall is right." She waited while her guest sipped from her glass, then smiled and drank more fully. It was a vintage Siderea usually saved for seduction: smooth, sweet, and laced delicately with herbs that were said to enhance the senses.

Her own were certainly more acute than usual. She could smell the residue of soap in her visitor's hair, the faint minty fragrance from where she had brushed against one of Siderea's plants, the thin sheen of nervous sweat upon her brow. Never had she experienced a person's scent so acutely before. Was this another symptom of her partnership with the Souleater? If so, it was delightful.

Again the low growl sounded in the back of her brain.

Shhh, she thought to her consort. *All is well*.

She encouraged her guest to speak of her recent travels, all the while plying her with wine. Servants brought them plates of food as well: delicate savories made from the rarest of cheeses, Sendalese olives sculpted into flowers, slivers of smoked fish arranged in delicate patterns upon salted wafers. All of which increased Petrana's thirst, of course. Her wine glass was refilled several times while they chatted. Of course. What Siderea meant to teach Petrana today required preparation.

Finally Siderea judged the time was right. She waited for an appropriate opening in the conversation, then laughed softly.

Her long earrings tinkled with the movement. "But you must forgive me. Here I have plied you with questions, and not given you a moment to address the reason you came! What a poor hostess I am!" She set her glass of wine aside and then took Petrana's from her, and set it aside as well. Then she took her guest's hands in her own and gazed into her eyes, noting as she did so that the young woman's pupils were more than a little dilated. "Pleased though I am to have such delightful company, it would be poor hospitality not to address the reason you came. Or do I mistake what that might be?"

A bright flush rose to Petrana's cheeks. "You said at Salvator's coronation that you would be able to . . . advise me. About, ah . . . men." She tried to wring her hands together, but Siderea held them tightly.

"And so I did. And look what you have brought me to work with!" She smiled her most encouraging smile. "You are quite lovely, my dear. You know that? With a bit of powder and a few social tricks you could have any man you desired—even a High King. And that would be good for all of us, yes?"

She stood, drawing Petrana up with her. "Come, first I will show you how to make the most of what Nature has given you. Later, other lessons."

Holding her firmly by the hand, she led her through the public portion of the palace back to her own private rooms. A whispered command sent her servants scurrying out, and caused the richly carved doors to be shut behind them. Petrana seemed to be breathless. Was that from the wine, or something more?

Wrong. Wrong. The intrusive thought had no words, but her own mind supplied them, translating animal instinct into human language. *This place is ours!*

Shhh, she thought back. *It's all right. Watch.*

She brought Petrana over to her vanity and had her sit before the mirror. It was a Magister's gift from long ago and offered a more perfect reflection than polished metal ever could. Clearly Petrana was not accustomed to such luxuries and she gasped as her reflection came into focus, raising up a hand to her cheek as if to test whether the image was her own.

"You see? You have so much potential, my dear." Siderea stood behind her, close enough to feel the woman's warmth against her flesh. Her fingers toyed gently with the tightly-bound hair, teasing bits of it loose. "May I take this down?"

Clearly out of her element, Petrana nodded.

Slowly, aware that every motion was being watched in the mirror, Siderea unpinned her guest's hair. It was dark and thick, and fell luxuriously down about her shoulders, lock by lock. She stroked it gently, as if testing its weight. "Is it the custom in your home, to wear it all up like that?"

"My father thinks it best. He says a lady of quality should not make a spectacle of herself."

Siderea laughed softly. "Ah, my dear, there is a world of difference between making the most of one's charms, and 'making a spectacle of oneself.'" Siderea took up a lock of hair and twisted it around her finger. "Not that fathers always have insight into such things."

She took up a soft brush and began to work over the dark tresses. Petrana sighed, relaxing into the rhythm of the caress. "You think I have promise?" she breathed. "Truly?"

"Absolutely." She ran her hand down the long locks on either side, positioning them delicately on either side of Petrana's face, smoothing the long ends down along the sides of her breasts. "You see, this style will draw a man's eye to where one wishes it to go—such a subtle game—if they only knew how easily we manipulated them." She touched the veil that was tucked into her neckline. "May I?"

Petrana seemed startled. "I'm not sure—"

"Simply to see what we have to work with." She smiled. "It is hard to advise you on dress without knowing what it is that must be clothed. Yes?"

The young woman hesitated, then nodded. She watched in the mirror as Sidera leaned over her from behind, slowly working the layered veil loose. Once the lacquered nails slipped down into the neckline of her dress, bushing unexpectedly against the tip of her breast, and Petrana drew in a sharp breath.

"There, you see?" She put the veil aside. Petrana instinctively reached up to put her hand over her bosom, but Siderea caught it in her own and kept her from covering herself. "Look what you have been hiding, my dear."

In truth the young woman had a fine figure, with full, high breasts that rose and fell with every breath. Any man in his right mind would be aroused by them. Judging from the flush in Petrana's cheeks, this was the first time she had considered that. She let her look into the mirror for a few minutes, imagining what it would be like to have a man assessing her charms. Desiring her. A delicate flush rose to her cheeks.

"Come, now. Stand."

This time Petrana obeyed wordlessly. Siderea positioned her before the mirror and then stood behind her, close enough that the heat of the young woman's body warmed her own flesh. "We shall have to have something fashioned that suits your figure better than this gown." She ran her hands down along the sides of Petrana's body, pulling the dress taught across her flesh. "Ah, see, there is the figure that will entrance a High King! This dress does it no justice at all. Come, let us see what is under it."

Eyes wide, Petrana turned toward her. "I can't . . . I mean . . ." She floundered for words.

Siderea put a finger softly to her guest's lips, quieting her protest. "Surely such a lovely young woman is not ashamed of her body! There are no men here to see you disrobe. No one to compromise your honor." But I can hardly teach you how to dress if I do not see what there is to work with. That gown gives no hint of it." She paused. "Would it make you feel more comfortable if I disrobed as well? I shall be happy to do so, if it sets you at ease."

Without waiting for an answer she stepped back from Petrana and began to unwrap her long belt. Her expression was playful, almost teasing: *How silly you are, to be afraid!* In the back of her mind that odd growling started up again, but she ignored it. If the Souleater was going to share Siderea's life, she would have to learn how to play these games.

The belt dropped to the floor, and she opened the clasp securing her gown. The soft silk parted easily, caught for a moment on the fullness of her breasts, and then whispered to the ground. Beneath it she wore only a thin white chemise that did little to hide her charms. She smiled in pleasure as Petrana stared at her, fascinated despite herself, clearly unable to look away. "There, you see how easy it is?" Now Siderea loosened the neck of her chemise and let that, too, fall to the ground. Her skin was a rich copper, rare in these regions, and it glistened with a fine sheen of summer sweat: exotic, enticing. A few choice bits of jewelry glittered in various places, drawing the eye to where Siderea wanted it to go. She turned about slowly, inviting Petrana to look at every inch of her. "Nothing to be ashamed of." She smiled as she turned back to face her guest, pleased to see the bright flush that had risen in Petrana's cheeks. "Now it is your turn."

Petrana made no protest this time, turning as Siderea prompted her to face the mirror once more. Siderea leaned her naked body against her back as she reached around on both sides to undo the front of her gown. The young woman's heart was pounding so hard it was possible to feel its beat through her fingertips. There was so much hunger in this one, Siderea mused. And so much fear. This was what men did to women when they locked them away from pleasure all their lives and swaddled them in yards of heavy fabric, as if somehow that might protect them from their own natural instincts. All under the guise of protecting them. It wound them up so tightly that a single touch rendered them utterly vulnerable, where otherwise they might have been able to muster a defense.

I promised you I would teach you how to manipulate men, she thought to her guest, as she eased the blue dress slowly open. In the mirror before them she could see Petrana watching, lips parted, as she was disrobed. The sight seemed to mesmerize her. Beneath the thin fabric of her chemise the tips of her breasts were surprisingly dark, and she gasped as Siderea's hands rubbed against them. *And so I shall,* she promised, pushing the gown down over her hips, until its own weight finally carried it to the floor.

There was nothing between them now but Petrana's own chemise, more of an enticement than a barrier. Drawing the young woman against her, letting her feel the heat of her body against her back, Siderea pulled at the cord that held the gathered neckline shut, drawing it slowly out. Petrana leaned back against her with a soft sigh as the cord finally came loose, and the final fabric barrier fluttered to the ground around her feet.

Wrong wrong wrong wrong wrong, keened a voice in her head. How beautiful she was, Siderea thought, as she ran one hand down the inside of Petrana's thigh, the chemise cord tangled in her fingers. How very beautiful. Breasts so high and taut, as only youth would have them. She traced circles about the tip of one with her fingernail and heard her guest gasp softly as she surrendered to the touch. So lovely. So helpless. Men would like that. Men would flock to this one, fight over her, expend their best energies in courting her. A cold shudder ran through Siderea's body. *She* had been that young, once. Men had fought over her once. Now . . . now this one would take her place. Her beautiful puppet.

A low growl rose in the back of her throat.

Suddenly the scent of Petrana's desire was no longer sweet to her, as it should have been, but foul. Enraging. It made the hackles at the back of Siderea's neck rise up, and her left hand gripped the cord it held, tightly. She should not have invited this woman here. She should not have allowed another female into her territory. She should not have awakened this one's mating instincts, so that she would now be a competitor.

She slid one arm tightly about Petrana's chest, pinning her back against her. Her forearm rubbed hard against her breast, causing the young woman to gasp at the sudden mixture of pleasure and pain. Yes, she would please men well, this one. An untouched virgin, banking on the one commodity with which Siderea could never compete.

She could not allow it.

She *would* not allow it.

With a low growl, Siderea brought up her hands to the sides of Petrana's neck. For a moment she paused there, as her rival mistook the motion for some new caress and leaned back into her grip. What a pleasure it would be just to sink her teeth into the girl's soft throat and rip it open, to feel the gush of her life blood spilling out as she beat her wings in agony . . . but a human body was ill-equipped for such things. Instead, Siderea took one end of the chemise cord in each hand and pulled it up and back, forcing it to bite deeply into her visitor's neck. Petrana's eyes shot open in surprise and she reached for the cord, trying to pull it loose, but Siderea's grip was too strong. She yanked her visitor off her feet, so that her own weight would help choke her. Both of Petrana's hands were now scratching desperately at the cord, but it had sunk deeply into her flesh and could not be dislodged. Her eyes bulged in horror and she opened her mouth as if to scream, but only a gurgle came forth. Her feet scrabbled desperately for purchase on the floor beneath her to provide some leverage for her struggles, but she slipped on one of the garments strewn about her feet and went down, hard. Siderea thought she heard something in her neck crack but she kept tight hold of the cord, pulling upward against the female's weight.

The hands stopped their fluttering. The legs went limp. Siderea felt a hot gush of urine run down her legs as Petrana's bladder suddenly voided itself. A wordless voice inside her head screamed in triumph.

Then the thrashing subsided. Petrana's pale hands stopped their scratching and fell limply down by her sides. What had once been a warm, living body became a dead weight in Siderea's arms, and she let it fall with a dull thud to the floor.

This is good, an inner voice crooned.

Siderea blinked as if she were coming out of a trance. For a moment she just stared at the huddled body by her feet, struggling to comprehend what had happened. Confused, she looked at the mirror. And back to the body.

What happened?

The room seemed to swim in her vision. The smells surrounding her were suddenly overwhelming—urine and sex and fear—and she doubled over, fighting the urge to vomit.

What have I done?

She stared in horror at the body at her feet, as if seeing it for the first time. Petrana's eyes stared emptily at the ceiling now; the whites were spotted with crimson. Siderea's own flesh felt suddenly cold and she fumbled to pick up her gown, to cover herself again. *What have I done?*

Within her, the Souleater queen keened her triumph. Formless bestial instincts took on the shape of words inside her head: *You protected what is rightfully ours.*

"This is not right!" she whispered hoarsely. "The woman was an ally!" Raw visceral horror was giving way now to political horror, which was equally compelling. How was she going to handle this so that it did not bring her down? What was she supposed to tell Petrana's family? It wasn't a question of whether the girl was dead—assassinations were a common enough affair in the Free States—but how openly, how brazenly it had been done. Not to mentioned that the Free States' best chance to wield influence in the High King's court was now lying dead on the floor, in a pool of her own urine. What monarch in his right mind would be so reckless as to do that?

She would have to clean up the body. She'd use sorcery to remove the marks of murder from Petrana's flesh and substitute other signs that would serve as witness to a more natural illness. Petrana had come to visit, had complained of dizziness, and shortly afterward had suffered a seizure that took her life so quickly that even Siderea's witchery could not save her. Even a Magister could not raise the dead.

Her family would want to believe that, she told herself.

Not because they would believe the Witch-Queen incapable of killing, but because they knew she would never be so utterly reckless with her own reputation as to do it like this. If Siderea Aminestas wanted to kill someone it would be done through poison in the night, or the kiss of a nameless stiletto in some foreign place, or else perhaps by witchery, unseen and unsuspected. Not like this. Never like this.

Her hands still shaking, she began to gather up the dead girl's clothing and to summon the power needed to set her plan in motion. To mask the fact that she had murdered an ally.

There are no allies among queens, the Souleater told her.

CHAPTER 22

THE BOOK was bound in brown leather, well-worn, and its parchment pages were yellow and crisp with age. The inked figures that filled its pages had no doubt been a deep black in their youth, but now were a faded brown or in some cases little more than ghostly echoes of the original.

Rommel turned the pages with the kind of reverence usually reserved for sacred texts, his wrinkled fingers so gentle upon the paper that the dust that clung to their edges was not disturbed. As he smoothed each page into place, it was possible to see that the figures scribed upon it were a remarkable match to some of the ones that Rhys had cut into his arm. Still others were vaguely similar, but differed in the curve of a tail, the angle of an ascender. A small number were reflected nowhere in the figures Rhys had copied.

As for the original lists that Rommel had drawn up, they now had notes scrawled all over them: translations, Karsi-style drawings, and his own commentary.

". . . A remarkable work," he was saying. "It has enabled me to go much further in interpreting these symbols than I had thought would be possible." The archivist looked up at Ramirus. "We are all indebted to you."

Kamala coughed gently into her hand, masking any hint of a smile. Whatever she had imagined the bearded Magister might do with the information from her brick fragments, counterfeiting ancient texts had not been on the list. But it was a brilliant move. Lazaroth had already announced that his own sorcery had not been able to locate any new Karsi resources; now Ramirus was presenting an item which appeared to be exactly that. It would be hard to imagine a Magister being more effectively embarrassed than Lazaroth was right now. And in front of his royal patron, no less! Ramirus must have been very pleased with himself.

But it did not show on his face, of course. That was all part of the game. Kamala guessed that he had woven enough sorcery into his "ancient" book to prevent any other Magister from being able to uncover its true origin, no doubt under guise of a protective spell to reinforce its fragile pages. Lazaroth might suspect that a trick had been played on him, but he could never be sure of it.

Rommel pushed the book aside and spread out his original drawings once more. "The first portion of text is now confirmed as an evocation to earthly and arcane powers to attend upon some great project. Outside of adding a few new elements to the list I recited yesterday, Ramirus' source offers no new insight. I do note that some of the pictoglyphs Rhys brought back from the Spear differ slightly from the versions in this book; I have had to take some liberties in correcting them.

"The second portion likewise becomes more detailed with this new information, but does not change in its general purpose. It provides a lengthy list of human sufferings, no doubt meant to describe the effect of the Wrath upon living minds. However, this does raise one question. This inscription was supposedly created *before* the Wrath came into existence, yes? But our records tell us that our ancestors did not know what the gods were about to do for them; when the Wrath fell upon the land its power was a surprise to man and Souleater alike. So how can its effect be described in such detail here, before it even existed?" He shook his head. "We will need more than a simple translation to make sense of all this, I fear."

"And the third section?" the Lord Protector asked. "You said it might be a prophecy of some sort."

"That or a list of instructions. I will let you judge for yourselves." He cleared his throat as he pulled a new set of notes toward him. "Mind you, there is no way to know the proper rhythm of the thing without knowing what language the original writer spoke though the passage clearly falls into three quatrains. Here is the meaning of it, in our current tongue:

> *Seven times seven the flame is passed*
> *Seven times seven forgotten*
> *Fire banked low in seven souls*
> *Vigilance blood-slumbering*

> *What is lost, three ladies guard*
> *What is sought, the eldest provides.*
> *What is unknown, the twilight throne reveals*
> *What is forgotten, blood remembers.*

> *Birthright in balance, Seven together,*
> *Offered as one in the eagle's nest*
> *Upon a chair of bones and wings*
> *Conjures light from dark, and life from death.*

When he was done he leaned back in his chair, breathless, as if he had just completed some great physical exertion. "That is all," he said.

He shut the leather-bound book that Ramirus had provided, wrapped it lovingly in a piece of oilcloth, and tied the package safely shut. Lazaroth glared at it.

"Prophecy or otherwise," the Lord Protector said, "the intent of all this seems clear enough. These words were meant to be seen if the Spear was ever broken open."

"And they were meant for us to read and understand," Favias offered. "Else they would not have been scribed in this universal script."

Rommel nodded. "Every scholar of the First Age would have known how to read this. They would have no reason to anticipate that such a useful tool would be forgotten."

Ramirus looked to him. "Have you been able to make sense of any of these passages?"

The archivist licked his lips. "Some of it. The first line seems clear enough. The Seven were the generals that survived the final battle, the first Protectors. Legend says they each took seven wives, the better to spread out the gods' gift to the population. Well, except for the one woman among them, who presumably took seven husbands . . . or something like that."

"Are the legends true?" The Lady Protector asked. "Do the actual records support this?" There was an edge to Evaine's voice that Kamala had not heard there before, but it came and went too quickly for her to read meaning into it.

"Yes and no." Rommel took a new sheaf of papers from a leather portfolio by his side and spread them out upon the table. Genealogical charts. "Every one of them took care to spread his seed about, and in many cases that did indeed result in exactly seven children, but as you can see, this Protector had a few more and several had fewer."

"Nevertheless," Ramirus said, "the reference seems clear."

"Yes. Yes. Of course . . ." He cleared his throat. "One is tempted to read the second line as referring to the number of children in the generation after that, but there is no support for that interpretation. Even allowing for unrecorded bastards—" He looked at Rhys as though he was about to apologize for the reference, then thought better of it "—there is nothing near that number of offspring in the *lyr* lines. Especially during the Dark Times. Families were small for a long time after that."

"Perhaps these numbers refer to the generations themselves," Kamala said.

Rommel looked at her. "Pardon me?"

"How long has it been since this prophecy was written? About a thousand years, correct? Forty-nine generations is almost that."

As the archivist's brow furrowed in concentration, Kamala sensed Ramirus' eyes fixed on her. *Well, did you think I would not conjure knowledge for myself before giving you my relics?* Despite the danger of baiting him, she found she was enjoying the game immensely. Did that mean she was truly a Magister at heart?

"Yes, yes, that could be the meaning," Rommel agreed. "Perhaps not intended literally, as an exact number, but simply to indicate a considerable period of time. Long enough for the *lyr* to forget some things about their own heritage."

"The image of a flame might refer to the gift of the gods," the Lady Protector offered. "In which case, the meaning of the entire prophecy becomes clear: After enough time, men will forget the nature of that gift, or how to use it."

Rommel nodded excitedly. "Yes, and what is most interesting about all this is the next section is clearly meant to show us

how to retrieve that knowledge. If we can decipher it properly."
His eyes narrowed in concentration as he studied his notes.
"Three ladies . . . the eldest . . . some kind of lineage reference?"

Kamala paused just long enough for her to look as if she had
to think about her answer. "There are some monuments in
Alkali," she mused. She turned to Rhys. "What did you say
they were called?"

"Three Sisters. Wind-carved towers, at the north end of
Alkali's central plain. They're called the Three Sisters." There
was an odd look in Rhys' eyes as he said that; it took her a
moment to realize why.

Rhys had talked to Namanti about the Three Sisters, not to
Kamala. That was well before Kamala had joined him. So how
did she know what he had said to his companion said back
then?

"So." Rommel dipped his quill in ink and began scribbling
new notes next to the old ones. "The Three Sisters in Alkali.
That means the eldest would be—"

"The tallest one," Lazaroth said. Thus far he had been silent,
his dark eyes brooding as Kamala and Ramirus had offered up
their tidbits of stolen knowledge. He was sharp enough to know
that something was up, and he was not pleased.

Rhys nodded stiffly. "That is the one which Anukyat's Citadel
guards. The base of the monument is part of its structure."

"And this reference to a twilight throne?"

Kamala smiled with satisfaction; this answer did not require
sorcery. "The servants of the Citadel spoke of such a thing when
I was there. Some great antique chair made of bones, covered
by blue-black leather. The color of twilight, they said. The
servants believed that it was at the top of the tower. They called
it the Throne of Tears." She paused, remembering. "Every now

and then some foolish boy would climb up, looking for it. They never came back."

Gwynofar nodded. "It is said that in the ancient days there was a throne fashioned from the bones and wings of Souleaters. Some now believe it was never real, only legend."

"Apparently Anukyat believes in it," Favias muttered. "Why else have a fortified outpost in the middle of nowhere?"

"So, some sort of blood offering must be made in front of this chair," Rhys said. "Is that the idea? And that will awaken ancient magics, reveal forgotten truths, call down the favor of the gods to protect us from the Souleaters?" It was the first time that he had allowed his voice to express the full measure of his newfound cynicism and Kamala felt herself holding her breath as she wondered if the others would take note of it. But they seemed too wrapped up in unraveling this mystery to notice the bitter edge in his voice—or else they just chose to ignore it.

"There is nothing of gods in this prophecy," Rommel pointed out. It was a simple factual statement, but ironically, it was just the response that Rhys needed to hear; Kamala could see her traveling companion relax slightly, as he realized he was not going to have to pretend to honor the gods that had abandoned him.

"It speaks of the seven ruling bloodlines acting as one." Ramirus said. "Perhaps embodied in a single individual." He stroked his long beard thoughtfully, pretending to muse over the problem. In reality, Kamala's handful of brick fragments had already provided him with most of the information he needed. The rest was all showmanship, for Lazaroth's sake. "With the same number of ancestors from each bloodline, perhaps?"

Deep furrows appeared in Rommel's brow as he considered the question. "Well, it would not be so simple as all that, since each ancestor after the first would carry multiple strains himself, in varying proportions, but theoretically it could be worked out. See here . . ." He spread out his genealogical charts on the table. "If we can figure in the dilution of each succeeding generation properly, we can produce a formula which allows us to evaluate the blood of each existing *lyr* for its precise relationship to each of the original seven founders. Lord Kierdwyn, for instance, traces his heritage back to the bloodlines of Kierdwyn, Abeja, Brusus, Han, and Tonado most strongly, with lesser strains of Skandir and Alkali. All the *lyr* can be mapped thus, turning the whole problem into a simple mathematical exercise."

"Hardly simple," the Lord Protector mused.

Rommel flushed. "Forgive me, your Lordship, I—"

Stevan waved his protest short. "I meant it as a compliment, Rommel. Ten centuries of genealogical records are no small thing to wade through, much less reduce to mathematical measure, simple or otherwise. So do you think you will be able to find us one of these . . . well, I suppose we shall have to come up with a new word for it . . . a *lyr* whose birthright is in balance? In whom all seven bloodlines are equally represented?

"Oh, I am sure, Your Lordship. If Magister Lazaroth will help me send word to all the other archivists, we can start work on it right away. We may not be able to find a lineage that is as perfectly proportioned as the prophecy would like, but we can certainly locate the best candidate for you." He hesitated. "That said, it will take time of course. . . ."

"All the more reason to begin immediately." The Lord Protector looked to Lazaroth. "Please give Archivist Rommel all the help he needs."

"Of course."

Kierdwyn turned to look at his lord constable. "Ullar, you are quiet today. Have you nothing to add?"

The officer snorted. "I am a man of war, my liege, not a jongleur. The fine points of poetry I leave to others, prophetic or otherwise."

"But if we wished to send in a force to claim this relic, that would be a different story, yes?"

The constable bit his lip as he considered. With his coarse stubble and his hard, cold eyes, the expression gave him a particularly fierce look. Then, without a word, he got up and went to the sideboard, where several maps had been laid out. Sensing his intention, Rommel quickly gathered up his drawings and Favias moved the pen and inkwell safely out of the way. Just in time. A large map was unrolled across the table and those sitting nearest the corners instinctively reached out to hold it flat.

Alkali.

Every mountain and valley of the rogue Protectorate was mapped out in meticulous detail, including the pass that Rhys and Namanti had originally intended to access; there had not yet been time to update it. With a shudder, Kamala saw a plateau marked the northern edge of the map, and a hard black line cutting across it. The Wrath. It seemed almost obscene that a curse of such baleful power could be reduced to a simple pen stroke.

Anukyat's Citadel was marked on the map as well, along with details of the outer and inner defensive walls. According to the map, it commanded the highest inhabitable ground for miles in every direction. All but bare of trees, the area immediately surrounding it offered little cover to protect invaders. The map showed that clearly, too.

"Its defenses aren't what they used to be," the constable told them. "But the place was designed to withstand a siege at least long enough for reinforcements to arrive from the south. Rough terrain to the west means bringing in supplies won't be easy, at least from Kierdwyn." He looked up at Kamala. "You could not work spells there?"

Surprised to be consulted, it took her a moment to find her voice. "No. Not reliably."

Master Favias said, "The Wrath has expanded its geographical area of influence. Presumably since the Spear was damaged."

"Which means it may continue to do so," Ullar noted, "so relying on sorcery for anything would be a mistake. That is not a pretty picture, especially once winter comes." He looked up at his rulers. "You tell me you want to conquer a fortress in the middle of Alkali, I can come up with a plan for that. We'd have to bring in our supply lines from the southwest, so that Lazaroth could protect them—I'd wager his skills against that pissant Alkali Magister any day—and that means we'd have to control a few key transit points, here, here, and here. And then hold this pass to protect our flank." He indicated various places on the map as he spoke, too quickly for Kamala to do anything more than acknowledge they were there. "But that kind of campaign takes time. Possibly a lot of time. And I'm hearing we don't have that."

"No," the Lord Protector agreed. "Not if the Souleaters are already here."

Ullar clucked his tongue as he studied the map. "Well, there is an alternative," he said at last. "But it would be a chancy thing without sorcery to back it."

"What is that?"

"First, your Lordship, please clarify something for me. What is the real goal here? Getting hold of some piece of mystical furniture and bringing it back here so we can bring in our best-bred *lyr* and have them try it out? Or just getting someone with the right birthright to sit down in the thing, possibly right where it is?"

Kamala could feel a wave of tension come over the table as they all realized what he was proposing.

"Well," the Lord Protector said slowly, "It might require more than merely 'sitting down' . . . but yes, sending someone to it would be an option."

"A dangerous option," his wife offered.

Ullar snorted. "War is dangerous. One does not win it without taking risks. And we know what the battlefield will look like in the end if we lose."

He stroked his stubbled chin as he studied the map; Kamala could almost hear his brain churning. Finally he turned to Rhys. "Am I correct in understanding that the Citadel flanks this tower, it does not surround it?"

Startled, Rhys looked to Kamala for confirmation; evidently he thought her memory would be better than his. When she nodded he said, "Yes. That's right."

"Well that is good then. But hells!" He cursed softly under his breath. "I would give my right eye to be able to send someone in for a good reconnaissance right now."

"Why can't you?" the Lady Protector asked him

"Because the damned thing is surrounded by enough open ground that getting close to it unobserved will be all but impossible without some kind of arcane support. And according to the witch here, we can't rely upon that."

"Ah," Kamala coughed gently into her hand. "I didn't say that, exactly."

Heads around the table turned toward her.

"You asked me about spellcasting," she said. "*That* was nearly impossible. But witchery performed elsewhere was unaffected, at least as far as my experience went."

"Explain this to me," Ullar said. "Assume that I do not know your art at all, and make it simple."

She didn't really want to elaborate, but there was no way to back out of it now. "I had shape changed before entering the area in question," she said, a hint of defiance in her voice. Would the Magisters wonder why a mere witch was performing such a costly move? Would it make them question what she really was? "I had no trouble maintaining that form as I approached the Wrath." She shivered inwardly, remembering how that experiment had ended. "Changing back within the affected region almost cost me my life. Spells I tried later were all unstable. Perhaps it is the art of binding and shaping power that is affected there. Perhaps a human spirit subjected to the Wrath cannot manage the concentration required. But spells that were crafted elsewhere seemed to hold true, even when we were standing before the Spear itself." *And remained true afterward*, she thought with satisfaction. *Your own Magisters still cannot break through them.*

For a moment Ullar stared at her, digesting that information. Then he turned to Lazaroth.

The Magister nodded, anticipating his thoughts. "Send me your scouts. I will give them wings." He glanced at Kamala, his dark eyes narrowing. "May the gods prove you right, *witch*." He spoke the last word as though it tasted vile on his tongue. "Otherwise we may lose some good men."

"Enough," the Lord Protector said. He offered a nod of appreciation to Kamala. "Your testimony is appreciated." Then he turned his attention to Ullar again. "Even with sorcery to guard our 'chosen one,' this is a risky venture. We have no way of knowing what safeguards already exist in that place to detect such invasion. Perhaps even sorceries established long ago, before the Wrath began to falter."

"Aye," Ullar agreed. "We will have to distract the enemy."

With a calloused hand the constable indicated the border between Kierdwyn and Alkali. "Let us bring war to Alkali. Armed men prepared to fight, gathered along the border, who honestly believe they are about to attack in force. That way any sorcery focused upon them will get the proper message. Here, and here also—" He indicated several points along the border. "—we will gather our forces and focus such reconnaissance spells upon the enemy as a real war would require. That should keep their Magister busy enough. Meanwhile, if we can get the High Kingdom to join forces with us, threatening a two-pronged attack, that will double the deception. . . ." He raised an eyebrow as he looked at Gwynofar. "Your Majesty?"

To her surprise, Gwynofar found herself falling easily into the mindset of war; a lifetime of marriage to Danton Aurelius had prepared her for such things. "Salvator might agree to such a feint if he were convinced of the need, but I am not sure he could get an army here in the time frame required. The distance is great, and he will not allow the use of sorcery to shorten it."

"Not an unreasonable stand, for once," Ramirus said. "Sorcerous transportation is risky at best, and must be managed one man at a time, or something very close to that. Some will be lost along the way; that is inevitable." He looked at Ullar. "An acceptable cost in war, but perhaps less so when one is merely dealing with the illusion of war."

The constable grunted. "I see I did not make myself clear.

This will be a 'real' war to everyone but us. Not even my generals will know the truth." He looked at Stevan. "Anything less would make us vulnerable to the enemy's divination."

The Lord Protector nodded. "Quite correct."

Evaine turned to Gwynofar. "Will you speak to your son? Convince him of the need for this?"

She sighed. "I will do my best. But he is Aurelius, and therefore stubborn. Do not make plans that depend upon his compromising his beliefs." She paused. "We do have several garrisons in our northern provinces. It might be possible to position them as you require within a reasonable time frame. Not as many troops as an all-out war would require, but perhaps as an auxiliary to your own efforts it would be convincing enough."

Ullar nodded. "Good. The goal is to threaten enough of the border that Alkali's attention is focused there and its defensive forces spread thin. With luck, if Anukyat believes that he is safely out of the line of fire, he may even send down some of his own Guardians to help out."

"While we do what, exactly?" the Lady Protector asked. "I wish to be clear on this."

Ullar scowled. "Hard to answer that precisely, until my scouts report. But if this tower can be scaled from the outside, I'm thinking it might be a lesser battle to try to sneak our 'chosen one' into place than to bring this relic to us." He looked to the two rulers. "With your approval of course, Your Lordships."

For a moment the room was so silent Kamala could hear herself breathing. Then, with a soft rustle of silk, the Lady Protector turned to face her husband. Her face was pale, her hand trembling where it lay on the table; clearly the conversation had unsettled her. For a long moment they just looked at one another, communing as couples do who have lived together for so long that they no longer need words to communicate.

Finally Stevan turned back to Ullar. "We will hear what your scouts have to say," he declared, "and then we will decide. In the meantime, let it be known among your men that Kierdwyn is going to war. One way or another, that is the truth of it."

"Yes, Your Lordship. Immediately."

"I assume you will provide a well-layered plan so that anyone using arcane powers to investigate this matter will find enough secrets and diversions to keep him busy."

"Plots within plots," Ullar promised him.

"Excellent." the Lord Protector turned to Rommel once more. "You and your colleagues must find us someone who can play the role of this 'chosen one,' with all dispatch. Someone whom the prophecy—and the gods—will favor. Nothing can be decided until we know who that is, and what he is capable of."

Rommel bowed his head. "Understood, my liege."

"Your Lordship." It was Lazaroth. "Transportation is a difficult and time-consuming task for any sorcerer, especially when large numbers of men are involved. I am sure my colleague Ramirus will be happy to assist in this matter, for what else could his presence at this meeting be meant to communicate?" The dark eyes sparkled maliciously. "Even so, I would respectfully suggest that we bring in at least one more Magister to assist us. Given how quickly we may need to move your troops."

"Indeed. Have you someone in mind who can be trusted with our secrets? And who would be willing to serve?"

Lazaroth's smile was a cold thing. "Magister Colivar is said to know more about the Souleaters than any other man alive. I am sure he would be willing to trade his sorcery for a chance to be front and center in such a historic campaign."

It said much for Ramirus' self-control that his expression remained impassive. Kamala could sense a black fury raging inside him; whatever dark and malevolent chess game he and Lazaroth were playing, Ramirus had just lost control of the board. But the terms of that game were nothing he could admit to any morati, and so he simply nodded stiffly, acknowledging the move.

"Very well," the Lord Protector said. "I leave it to you to contact him, Lazaroth." He looked around the table. "Is there anything else that requires discussion?" When no one answered in the affirmative he took his wife's hand in his, and the two of them rose. Chairs scraped back as their guests stood respectfully, several bowing their heads in obeisance. Rhys stood also, with Kamala by his side, but he held his head high. Perhaps it was meant as an act of defiance. Or perhaps it was a comment upon what he thought of the plan that had been presented thus far. Or perhaps . . . perhaps he was simply too exhausted by all that he had seen and done in the past few weeks to care anymore.

Kamala was hard pressed to decide which possibility bothered her more.

———

The memorial path was long and twisting and flanked by a forest of blue pines so dense that only the most enterprising beams of sunlight could ever hope to make it to the ground. Nearly every trunk had been carved into one shape or another; some of the trees were so ancient that they had long ago given up trying to sprout branches to cover over the mutilations, while a few younger ones still had fresh scars from their spring pruning. The summer air was heavy with the pungent perfume of the trees, underscored by the moist scent of lichens and the fertile decay of fallen needles: the scent of memories.

Moving from tree to tree, Gwynofar ran her hands along the bark-shrouded features, trying to assign names to all the faces. In her childhood she had known them all and had prided herself on being able to recite them. How clear the faces had seemed to her back then! Now, after many years" absence, she was struck by how muted the carvings had become. The trees kept struggling to swallow up the sculptures as their trunks grew thicker. Her parents kept a sculptor on hand for the trees that needed attention, but in a memorial forest this large it was hard to keep up.

Even so, it was like walking through a forest of ghosts. As if she could hear her ancestors whispering all around her as she followed the winding path to its end.

Finally there was only a single tree that stood alone, positioned atop a hill which had been stripped of all other brush. It was an ancient thing, with long, needle-heavy boughs that spread out from the summit like a vast blue parasol. Tradition said that this tree had been old even before the Great War began and supposedly the spirits of all the men who had been killed by the Souleaters in that war took shelter beneath its branches. Its trunk had been carved in the shape of a man but not merely with a disembodied face as was the usual custom. This ancestor appeared to be emerging from the wood even as one watched, sword drawn, gazing outward fiercely as if to search out the enemy wherever it might be hiding. Gwynofar found the great tree both eerie and fascinating and when she was younger she had come here often just to stare at it, as if daring it to move while she was watching. Thus far it had not done so.

Thus was Liam, the first Protector of Kierdwyn, memorialized. Beside the tree stood Evaine Kierdwyn. She waited as her daughter came up the hill, watching her pass from shadow to sunlight and then into shadow once more as she approached the great pine. The Lady Protector held a scroll case of simple leather in her hands, neither labeled nor adorned, and her fingers played restlessly about the edge of the cap as she waited. She looked nervous, which struck Gwynofar as odd. Evaine Kierdwyn was adept at masking her feelings and rarely looked anything but calm.

Walking up to her, Gwynofar embraced her warmly. That seemed odd as well. It was as if there were some secret, unnamed tension in her mother's body. Something not yet acknowledged, but very wrong.

"I am so glad you could come," Evaine said.

Gwynofar smiled in what she hoped would be a reassuring manner. "It's not as if I have much else to do, Mother. Since you and Father both insist on treating me as a guest and not as family."

A faint smile played across the Lady Protector's face. "Would you rather be kneading bread in the kitchen?"

"No." She laughed softly. "But if you offered me a chance to go rummaging among dusty scrolls in the library, in search of forgotten lore, I might not turn you down."

"Ah." A strange, haunting sadness entered Evaine's eyes. "Ancient scrolls sometimes teach us things we don't want to know." Her fingers tightened around the leather case. "Would you read each last one that you found, knowing that to be the case? Or shy away from those that might be troubling?"

Gwynofar hesitated. She sensed that her mother wanted to discuss something very private—why else would she have asked to meet with her out here, so far from any witnesses?—but didn't know how to start. And without some clue as to what it was all about, Gwynofar was unable to help her. "I would read them, if I could. And expect to be troubled. What was it my tutor used to say? 'Knowledge is a double-edged sword, and the hand that grasps it too eagerly may pay for his eagerness in blood.'"

Her mother turned away from her. Gwynofar watched her for a moment, noting the subtle trembling of her shoulders. Gently, she put a hand on her arm. Despite the warmth of the air surrounding them, the Lady Protector's flesh felt chill beneath her sleeve.

"What is it, Mother?" She whispered the words. "Please tell me."

With a sigh, Evaine looked down at the tube in her hands. For a long moment she did not respond, merely ran one fingernail around the edge of its cap. Finally she said, very quietly, "If you knew that your duty as a *lyra* called you to act, but that doing so might cost you everything you held dear, what would you do, Gwynofar? Would you want to know the details? Or would you prefer the safety of ignorance? Knowledge is power in many respects, but it brings with it responsibility."

A cold chill ran down her spine. "Mother, I—"

"Don't answer too quickly, Gwynofar. Some secrets, once they are released from their cage, cannot be put back again. Be very sure you want to share in this one."

She shut her eyes for a moment and concentrated upon quieting the wild beating of her heart. Finally she drew in a long, deep breath and looked at her mother once more. "I am *lyra*." She said it quietly but firmly. "I've known all my life that someday the gods might call upon me to serve them. That they have not seen fit to do so up until now does not excuse me from my duty."

A strange look came over Evaine. Part pride; part pain. "You would not compromise that duty, my daughter? Even to save one of your own family from harm? Or perhaps from shame?"

"Mother . . ." She looked deep into the older woman's eyes, seeking whatever clues might be found there. But there was nothing she knew how to read. "Tell me what is wrong. Please."

With a sigh her mother looked down at the leather tube in her hands. After a moment she removed the cap and upended the tube to remove the contents. All done without a word. The only sound on the hillside was the soft rustling of pine branches in the afternoon breeze and an occasional whirring of insects.

When a tightly rolled document finally slid out Evaine held it in her hand for a moment, hesitating. Then she gave it to Gwynofar. "Here, my daughter. See for yourself."

Gwynofar unrolled the vellum sheet so that she might read it. It was a genealogical chart, drawn up according to the customs of the *lyr*. Each name had beside it a collections of tiny symbols, indicating which bloodlines were the most prevalent in that person's heritage. The *lyr* used such charts to choose mates for their children, identifying unions that would bring new blood into their line. Or perhaps to avoid new blood, if what they wanted most was to enhance the characteristics of their own lineage. Different families had different customs, and the archivists recorded them all, passing judgment on none. Not with the precision that Rommel's current project required, of course, but well enough for planning marital contracts.

Gwynofar scrolled through the document until she began to see familiar names: her immediate ancestors. Stevan Kierdwyn was on the final branch, with two sons by his first wife, then came Evaine and their two children Gwynofar and Arian. But the final entry by Gwynofar's name did not look right, somehow. It too her a minute to figure out why.

There was a Skandir sigil by her name. "This is wrong," she murmured. She knew for a fact that she had very little Skandir blood in her veins. Her twin brother Arian had been married to a Skandir princess for just that reason, though in the end he had died in a hunting accident before siring any children.

"Follow it back," her mother said quietly. "Find the source of the aberration."

She did as directed, her eyes traveling back along the various branches of her family tree, searching for anything else that did not seem right. Her father's family looked correct, back as far as she could remember the details. But her mother's branch—

She stopped.

And read the entry.

And read it again.

"I don't understand," she whispered. "How can this be?"

Her mother said nothing.

The mistake was two generations back, in the name provided for Gwynofar's maternal grandfather. Instead of Casigo III, a prince of the Umrah line, the chart listed someone else entirely. Haralt? Some lordling of Skandir descent with a noteworthy strain of Alkali blood in him as well. Gwynofar had never heard the name before.

She looked up at Evaine, confused.

"He was your grandfather," the Lady Protector said.

"But Lady Desira . . . your mother . . . she was only married once. And her husband's name is not even on this chart."

"No," Evaine agreed. "It is not."

And then the truth of it sank in. The only possible answer. *Oh, my gods . . .*

"Where did you get this?" Gwynofar whispered. She reached

out for the trunk of the tree for support, as the world swirled dizzily around her.

"I drew it up myself, when you were born. As my mother had done for me, upon my birth. Who else could be trusted with such knowledge? I made a copy for your brother, too, but he . . . he never learned the truth." She paused, remembering. "I buried his copy with him."

How sad her eyes were. How lost. Gwynofar could not begin to imagine what keeping such a secret had cost her.

"Does Father know this?"

Evaine shook her head slowly from side to side. "No one knows. Not since the day my mother died, taking her secret with her. Only myself . . . and now you."

Gwynofar stared at the scroll, struggling to absorb its message. "How did it happen?"

"She had an affair. It was short-lived—or so my mother claimed—but apparently productive. My father thought I was his child, and my mother never corrected him. All the official histories—and genealogies—reflect that lie."

"But how could she have been sure who the father was? Casigo would not have believed the child was his unless they'd had relations in the proper time frame, which means. . . ." She was finding it all hard to process. "How could she be so sure?"

"Aside from the gift of a *lyra* to know her own child?" She smiled sadly. "Rather mundane, actually. A simple birthmark, not significant in any other sense. But clearly inherited. Perhaps the gods marked us thus because they wished us to know the truth, or perhaps they did it to mock her infidelity. At any rate, this is your true lineage Gwynofar."

Speechless, Gwynofar stared at the matriarchal branch of her family. Beyond Haralt's, they were all unfamiliar.

"Have you figured out why this matters, Gwynofar? Why I am showing this to you now, instead of taking the secret with me to my grave?"

She shook her head.

The older woman pointed to the symbols scribed by Gwynofar's name. Tiny sigils identifying each of the sacred bloodlines that had contributed to her heritage. "Count them," she said quietly.

There were seven.

A cold shiver coursed through Gwynofar's flesh. Her hands holding the chart suddenly felt numb, the vellum insubstantial.

"You are the child of all seven bloodlines, Gwynofar. And while I don't have Rommel's formulae to determine the exact proportions of your heritage, I'm willing to bet that they are— what did the prophecy say? *Birthright in balance.*"

"You can't know that," she whispered. "No one can."

"No? Even your sons, with only half your strength, could smell when the enemy was near. Didn't you tell me that? That was when I realized that the gift of the gods was unusually strong in you. But I did not know why." She gestured toward the scroll. "Now I do."

"But Rommel doesn't know any of this." She had to struggle to get the words out. "No one knows."

"That is true." Gently Evaine took hold of the vellum, working it loose from Gwynofar's hands. She rolled it up tightly and slid it back into its protective shell, capping the tube once more. "And no one will know . . . unless you choose to reveal it."

She looked up at her mother.

"You are a queen, Gwynofar. Even if you tell them the truth, no one will ask you to risk your life in this affair. No one will *want* you to risk your life. You will have to fight for the right to do so, defying all those who want to protect you, who feel that your political station should put you above such risk. It will be hard enough to convince people here, where we all share the same sense of duty, but I can't even imagine how you could get Salvator to understand."

Gwynofar shuddered. "I could never tell Salvator."

Evaine took her daughter's hand in her own. "Listen to me, my child. We can tuck this chart away in some secret place, and no one will ever know it exists. If that is what you want. Or I can deliver it to Rommel, along with . . . explanations." A shadow passed over her face. "Not a conversation I am looking forward to, if I must be honest."

Shutting her eyes, Gwynofar tried to bring some kind of order to her thoughts. She wanted to feel brave, but she didn't. She wanted her faith to give her strength, so that she didn't feel so small and frightened and completely overwhelmed by all this. She wanted some kind of sign from the gods that this was the right thing to do. Anything.

But there was nothing.

They have given us powers and prophecies, she thought, *and now they sit back and watch us, waiting to see what we will make of it all. Whether in the end we will prove worthy of their gifts, or else cower and weep and beg someone else to provide us with salvation.*

Her mother was watching her. Waiting for her answer.

I am lyra, she thought. *Born and bred to protect mankind when the Great War begins anew. Now that time has come, and the gods have dictated how the war shall be waged. Who am I to deny their will? What will all my accomplishments in life be worth, if I shirk this final duty?*

"I will tell Rommel," she whispered. The words hung heavy in the air.

Her mother nodded. "And I will tell your father." She sighed heavily. "Though to be honest, that is the part I am dreading the most."

"He will understand. He has his own infidelities." *Like Rhys,* she thought. Did this explain the strange chemistry between her mother and her brother? Was Evaine more tolerant of Stevan's indiscretions because she knew her own heritage was rooted in similar weakness? Suddenly a lot of things made more sense.

"Gwynofar. My precious daughter." Evaine reached up to stroke her cheek. "Infidelity by itself means little. The annals of every royal history are full of it. Even lying about infidelity, in order to avoid a public scandal, is common enough. Such a crime might be forgiven in time." She sighed. "But for a *lyra* to falsify genealogical charts, to insert a lie which will gain in scope and power with each new generation, that will not be forgiven so easily."

Her hand fell from her daughter's face. Her eyes were sad, but determined.

"In time of war we must all make sacrifice," she said. "This is mine."

CHAPTER 23

"IS IT really from her?" Salvator demanded. "Are you sure?"

The witch drew in a deep breath and tried to focus her power. It was hard, with the High King standing over her like a vulture, but she was getting used to that. Slowly she turned the letter over in her hand, rubbing the fine vellum between her fingertips as she tested its substance with her power. Once she finally managed to focus her mind, it was a simple enough item to read. Only one layer of meaning adhered to it, without supernatural obfuscation or enhancement, and there were only a few handlers to detect. Someone had cried over the ink at some point, and somewhere in the process of producing the vellum a child had been beaten, but those were all minor notes that had little real significance. The central story was clear.

"This was written by the Queen Mother," she affirmed, "in her own hand, by her own will. Nowhere about it is there any trace of coercion. Or deception." Actually there was a faint echo of lies being told over the ink while it was being bottled— something about a young girl's virginity—but she guessed that the High King did not want to hear about such trivial details.

"Likewise I can confirm that it was indeed delivered to your chamber by Magister Ramirus, by a common transportation spell, that expired when the letter arrived. There is no sign of any residual sorcery that should be of concern to you." *Not that I could detect a Magister's tricks if he meant to keep them a secret,* she thought dryly. But there was no need to volunteer that information. "Nor is there sign of any man or woman handling it besides those who produced the vellum and those two persons I have named. And of course now yourself, Sire."

Salvator stared at the witch in silence for a few seconds, then nodded and held out his hand. Glad to be done with the matter, she gave him back the letter. Royal assignments paid well, but the new High King made her nervous. Especially today. His manner was calm enough, but she sensed that rage simmered just beneath the surface, and she wanted to be far away from him when it boiled over.

Salvator watched as the witch backed her way out of the chamber, offering repeated obeisance as she went. Not until she was gone, and the door was shut solidly behind her, did the High King open the letter and read it again.

My dearest Salvator,

I apologize to you for writing to you with this news, rather than delivering it in person. I had intended to return home by now, as you know, but some matters here in Kierdwyn require my personal attention, and so I will be staying a while longer.

I do assure you, upon the honor of my crown, that Kierdwyn intends no challenge to your authority, and has no connection to the raiders who have plagued the High

Kingdom of late. I have also seen compelling evidence that the raiders who attacked Soladin were not from Skandir at all, but actors in a military subterfuge meant to turn you against that ally. In fact our true enemy appears to be in Alkali, a man named Anukyat, and though we do not yet know his true motivation or the extent of his power, it seems clear that he is planting the seeds of war where he feels they are most likely to bear fruit, encouraging allies to turn on one another. Including some of the Guardians.

You must deny him victory.

The Souleaters that have been sighted in the human kingdoms may have come south through Alkali. We do not yet know how or why. It is the search for answers that will keep me in the north longer than I had originally intended; please forgive me for my absence.

Even as I write this letter, my father is gathering his warriors to address these matters. He asks for your assistance. He requests that you direct your own military forces to the Alkali border as if you were preparing to invade. An actual invasion will not be necessary, but their presence on the border will help distract the enemy and thus facilitate the true invasion from my father's lands.

There is one special condition required to make this work, and that is that no man other than yourself may know that this mobilization is merely a subterfuge. Each man you send to the border must believe, with all his heart and soul, that he is to be sent into battle. Please allow no exceptions.

I am sure you understand why such things matter.

Time is of the essence here. Before the eyes of the gods gaze down upon us again, action will be taken to address this matter. The more you can do to make a show of threatening the border by that time, the more lives may be saved on other fronts.

As your Queen Mother, and as royal emissary to Kierdwyn, I pass along this request to you, from your allies, the Lord and Lady Protector of the Kierdwyn Protectorate. As your Queen Mother, and as your counselor, I assure you that this is the best course for the High Kingdom at this time. You and may I disagree at times over interpreting fine points of our history, but surely the need for decisive action at this time is clear, and I hope you will agree with me on this.

There is no subterfuge here, Salvator. Not where you are concerned. The blood of the lyr runs in your veins, which makes your alliance with my parents a matter of sacred trust for them, not merely political expediency. I know that does not mean much by the measure of your faith, but trust me, it is a bedrock upon which you can rely.

My son, I know you must have many questions, and I deeply regret that I cannot return home to answer them. The shadow of war falls swiftly upon us, and I fear this is only the first campaign of many. Pray to your creator god for strength and clear judgment, if you believe that he can provide such things, for surely this will be a test for us all.

Your witches can use this letter to send me a response, if you wish. Meanwhile trust in Ramirus if he contacts you, for I know what his interest is in this matter, and his loyalty is certain.

Writ by my hand this day, in love and honor, for House Aurelius,

Gwynofar

Salvator shut his eyes and counted slowly to ten, drawing in a deep breath as he did so, reciting such meditations in his mind as would help to settle his spirit. Anger was a bestial emotion the priests of the Creator taught, frustration a bestial response. A man who understood that could master his emotions, if he wanted to. A man who served the two-faced god had a responsibility to do so.

When he felt that his spirit was finally calm enough for him to think clearly he offered up a prayer to his god, but not as Creator. It was his god's Destroyer aspect that would oversee this affair, deciding whether a given battle would be won or lost and how many men would die. The Souleaters were one tool of the Destroyer, but not his only one. Suspicion, doubt, greed, and fear were all part of his arsenal as well. Even the so-called "northern gods" could serve his purpose, in tempting men away from their proper path. What were those idols after all but illusions of power, seductive legends of greed and violence that encouraged men to accept their baser instincts rather than struggle against them?

When he had finished with his prayer he opened his eyes and looked to his mother's letter again. In his momentary lapse of spirit he had crushed it in his hand, and now he smoothed it open again and read it slowly, carefully, testing each word in his mind for all the hidden meanings that it might contain. The Magisters were conspicuous for not being mentioned in her strategy. Did Gwynofar think that he would believe they played no part in this? What other purpose could possibly be served by making sure that every last soldier believed a lie "with all his heart and soul," if not to trick those who could peer into the hearts of men?

It was said that in the ancient days, before the coming of

the Magisters, wars had been fought with blood and steel and courage. Nothing more. Strength pitted against strength, strategy against strategy, with the kind of brutal directness that had marked the First Age of Kings. Life had been simpler then. Easier for a king to manage. All was changed now.

I am my father's son as well as my mother's, he thought darkly.

What did they expect of him now? That he would perform the role his mother had scripted for him, crafting his strategy to suit the games of Magisters? That for fear of sorcery, he would keep his generals ignorant of their true purpose, and let his men be herded like sheep to a battle they did not comprehend, against an enemy whose name they did not even know?

What was it that his god would expect him to do?

Since the day he had sworn an oath to serve the Creator, he had prayed that the final war would never come. He had served in the monastery to help make that possible, humbling himself to his Creator on behalf of all mankind, offering up his personal sacrifices to weigh against the sins of others. Yet clearly it had not been enough. All the prayers of all the priests, all the sacrifices of monks and acolytes, even the offerings of common worshippers—who might cast away a bit of bread in sacrifice, refrain from wine, or quiet a moment's song—had not been enough.

Judgment had been rendered. Redemption denied. The Destroyer's face was turned toward them at last. And he was a king now, not a monk any longer, and must accept a king's duties.

His heart heavy, Salvator took up a fresh quill, uncapped a bottle of ink, and began to write out his orders.

Chapter 24

T HE STONE tower was narrow and tall, with parallel furrows running vertically down its surface. Some were shallow and clean and looked as if a monstrous clawed hand had gouged them out with a single swipe; others were carved more deeply into the stone, perhaps giving access to whatever interior space existed; still others had been eroded by wind and ice into twisted, pitted channels whose depths were lost in shadow. The side of the monument that faced the Citadel was uneven and broken, with stairlike formations in several places, albeit sized for a giant's stride. The outer face was much more forbidding, with no possibility of interior access on its lower half, and little hope after that.

"You have everything you need?" Lazaroth asked.

The archivist scratched a few more hurried lines onto his drawing, added a few notes, and then nodded.

The image of the tower faded from their sight, leaving the table in the map room empty but for Rommel's notes. Twenty men and women now filled it to capacity and a subtle current of shifting flesh coursed through the room periodically, as the casual movement of one required that all the others reposition themselves to keep an acceptable space between them.

"These have been prepared for the climb," Lazaroth said. He put two heavy burlap bags on the table, then conjured a small boulder into place beside them. Removing an iron spike from the bag, he thrust it into the rock. Sparks flew and chips of stone went flying across the room as the spike sank deeply into the stone surface. After a moment it appeared to be held fast, and when Lazaroth lifted up the spike to demonstrate his art, the rock came with it. When he knew that everyone had seen it he nodded, and it vanished once more.

"The sorcery is intrinsic to the spikes and will be triggered when you strike the point against your target. Whether that will work or not once you get close to the Wrath I cannot begin to guess, but hopefully it will come under the heading of 'spells cast elsewhere' and function properly. As the witch Kamala suggests it may." His lips curled in subtle distaste as he spoke her name. Was it because he disdained all witches, Kamala wondered, or just her in particular? "Do not bank your lives on these until that theory has been tested."

He handed one of the sacks to Favias and one to Ullar. The lord constable hefted his briefly, as if testing its weight, then handed it off gruffly to one of the men crowding behind him. As commander of Kierdwyn's armies he would have to remain behind to orchestrate the military phase of the campaign and that clearly did not please him. Was it because he wanted to see to Gwynofar's safety personally, as he claimed, or was there something more subtle going on, some sort of rivalry between Kierdwyn's common soldiers and the Guardians? Trying to catch all the subtle signs of it made Kamala's head hurt.

Four Guardians would be accompanying Gwynofar, and four

soldiers, with two more to watch over the horses once they were left behind. It was the best they had been able to agree on, with each faction fighting for control of the expedition. Both sides would have been happier sending a hundred men to guard Gwynofar, but the larger the expedition was, the harder it would be to hide it from the enemy's surveillance. In the end the Magisters had advised no more than a dozen participants, and the Lord Protector had backed their call.

That night's discussion had ended in a fierce argument between Favias and the lord constable over exactly who was going, who would not be going, why some particular combination of soldiers and Guardians would be better than another until at last Kamala had abandoned the field of battle to get some sleep. When she was given an update in the morning, she was told they had reached a compromise, but it seemed clear that both were less than happy with it.

Four Guardians would ride with Gwynofar, to mastermind the assault on the monument, and hopefully to get her safely to the top. Four soldiers would guard her rear from assault during their climb and later prepare the way back down. More than that would only be counterproductive, Ullar had argued, given the physical parameters of the situation. For once, Favias had agreed. It was clear they were both unhappy about that situation and wished that Gwynofar would pass the torch on to someone . . . well, to someone more expendable.

And then there were the Souleaters to worry about.

We don't know how many of the creatures exist on this side of the Wrath, the Lord Protector said, *or where they are located right now. The best we can do is try to draw their attention to another battlefront while you make your approach and hope they respond.*

No one talked about what would happen to Kierdwyn's armies

if that plan worked. They all understood the sacrifice that might be necessary.

Colivar was coming from the south to help, along with Sulah, a student of his; that much had been confirmed by Lazaroth, with an ill-guarded smirk of triumph as he watched his rival's reaction. But Ramirus was not taken by surprise this time and simply nodded his acknowledgment of the arrangement. His eternally impassive expression offered little insight into his true feelings, but Kamala sensed that he was far from pleased by that part of the plan. It seemed odd to her, given that she'd seen Ramirus and Colivar standing side by side when Rhys fought the Souleater, and she stored the observation away in the back of her mind for when she might make use of it. The Magisters would move Kierdwyn's troops into position along a vulnerable flank of the Alkali Protectorate, hopefully with enough speed that true invasion appeared imminent. Ullar had seen to it that rumors of a coming campaign had been leaked to the right spies and Lazaroth had backed up the rumors with enough sorcerous obfuscation that any Magister who tried to confirm Kierdwyn's plans would learn only what the Lord Protector wanted him to. So dense and powerful were the deceptive spells being cast in the castle that at times it was hard for Kamala herself to remember what the master plan really was. Magister Lazaroth's skills were formidable.

Another piece of information to remember.

Then of course there was the biggest question of all, at least from Kamala's standpoint. What part would she play in all this? Logic—and self-preservation—dictated that she should be as far from the affected region as possible. The first time she had approached the Wrath she had not properly understood its power and had been deep within its area of effect before she knew what the danger was. This time she understood that all her sorcery would not be worth a rat's ass in that place. If anything went wrong—and it was a sure bet that something would—she would not be able help the expedition and she would not be able to protect herself.

But.

She had already experienced the power that arcane knowledge could wield when she'd bound Ramirus to a Magister's oath for a single serving of it. More information would mean more power over more Magisters, leveraged against the day when she would need to call in those favors. For the first time since she had killed the Magister in Gansang, she really felt as if she had some direction. Now this insane expedition (and she did regard it as insane) offered a new opportunity. The very power that made it dangerous for her to approach the Wrath meant that no other Magister would dare go there.

Because they are intelligent, she told herself dryly. *Because they understand what a fragile thing immortality can be, and how they should not take chances with it.*

But the kind of knowledge that Magisters valued might not be the sort that morati would think to collect for her. Not to mention the Guardians had other priorities. So as the only Magister who would be present at the assault, she would have an unparalleled opportunity to gather the kind of knowledge the other Magisters would value. And be willing to pay for. And maybe even fight over, if she handled it well enough.

That was the real reason she was going. That was the only reason. No human sentiment was involved. No desire for the sense of elation that accompanied taking risks and surmounting them. No pleasure in outwitting the kind of men who had abused her so casually in her youth, no joy in robbing them of what they wanted most and leaving them with empty hands, to wonder what in all the hells had happened. Until that day when one of them (probably Colivar) called for her death and all the others were forced to defend her. And certainly no fondness for Rhys, or respect for the courage and honor of his family. No Magister would be so foolish as to let such emotions sway him. Especially not when his survival might be at issue.

It was just about knowledge, she told herself sternly. Nothing else.

———

"You are sure you want to do this, Majesty?" Ramirus' sober expression made his own feelings about the matter quite clear. "You understand the risk?"

"I am *lyra*," Gwynofar said quietly. "This is my duty."

He raised an eyebrow. "So the gift of the *lyr* is named at last: stubbornness."

Despite her dark mood Gwynofar smiled. "What other gift could make us cling to a cause a thousand years after most men had forgotten its name? Danton asked me that once." She sighed, twisting a bit of her mourning dress between her fingers, remembering him. "In his eyes all the *lyr* were foolish dreamers . . . but he admired our passion."

"Dreams aside, you are a queen, not a mountain climber. Passion can accomplish much, but it does not negate the force of gravity."

For a moment Gwynofar didn't answer. Then she went to the window and looked outward, over the lands that surrounded her parents' castle. It was a rugged terrain, spotted with pine trees and naked stone ridges. There were mountains to the west that soared high above the alpine line, their peaks clad in snow even during the reign of summer. "When I was a girl I used to run about freely; the servants were exhausted trying to keep up with me. I would climb trees and rocks, and wriggle into caves, and in general do everything I could that tasted of adventure. My parents encouraged such a spirit in me. They believed it would make me strong." She looked at him defiantly. "And it did."

Ramirus sighed. "With all due respect, Majesty, that was twenty years ago. And six children. How long has it been since the last time you climbed a tree? Or even rode astride on a horse?"

"The spirit remembers such things—"

"Aye, but the body forgets. Age is a thief that robs a man of his vital energies in secret. One morning he wakes up and realizes he is not the same creature he was ten, twenty, thirty years ago. If he is fortunate, that does not occur in a place where his life depends upon the strength of youth. I do not want you discovering too late that while Gwynofar the girl might have handled this task with ease, Gwynofar the woman should have considered another approach."

"You were at the same meeting I was, Ramirus. There is no other way. And no better qualified candidate than I."

"That we have yet found. There may be others."

"Time matters. You said so yourself."

He shook his head. "You know I cannot go with you. Not to this place. Sorcery will not function that close to the Wrath. Nor can I protect you from a distance, once you are within range of its power. There is no telling what my sorcery might become by the time it reached you. We cannot take that chance."

She said it quietly. "I understand."

With a heavy sigh he reached out and took her hand in his

own; it was such an uncharacteristic gesture that she turned back to face him, surprised. "I can make you stronger," he told her. "Strength is a function of form, and your form can be altered. I can enhance your perceptive senses in the same manner, and even add to your endurance, because those are also qualities of the flesh. But you must understand, every change that I make to your body will entail some new risk. Your limbs may not respond as you are used to. The world may look different, sound different. Distracting. Under normal circumstances it would not matter so much. You would get used to it in time. But clinging to a cliff face hundreds of feet above the ground, with enemies on all sides of you . . . it is a risk."

"But less so than physical weakness, I think." She nodded soberly. "You are quite correct in your assessment, painful though it is to hear. It has been a very long time since I have tested my physical capacity in anything other than childbirth." Suddenly it seemed that something fluttered inside her. She put a hand to her stomach, surprised. Was it possible that her child was stirring? Surely it was too early for such things. "My son—"

"He will not be harmed," the Magister promised. But something in his tone hinted at unvoiced reservations. Clearly her pregnancy concerned him more than he was going to admit. Was he simply concerned about how much it might tax her body and perhaps distract her at a crucial time? Or was he wondering about the prophecy he had once uttered, when divining the child's future?

He will not be a hero himself, though he will help bring a hero into existence. His strength will never be measured, but he will test the strength of others. He will attend upon death without seeing it, change the fate of the world without knowing it, and inspire sacrifice without understanding it.

It was all too much for Gwynofar to process right now; she would go crazy if she tried.

Squeezing the Magister's hand in what she hoped was a confident manner, she forced a smile to her face. "Then give me a man's strength if you can, Ramirus. And a man's endurance to match. Those are the things that will matter most, I think. The rest . . . the rest is not worth the added risk."

He did as she asked. Wielding sorcery that turned key muscles to fire, remolding them as a master sculptor might remold clay. Pouring liquid sorcery into her heart until her body took it up, beat after beat, driving it into her veins, her flesh until she shook from the force of it and tears came to her eyes.

But it would not hurt her child. He promised her that, before they began.

All the rest could be endured.

———

"You don't have to go," Rhys said quietly.

He stood with his back to the bedroom window, moonlight casting a halo about his shoulders. With his pale hair glimmering like liquid fire, he looked like one of the angels Kamala's mother had told her about, who lived in a place where everything was perfect and beautiful. Children who obeyed their parents might go there someday, her mother had said, to play among the clouds and eat candies made of sunshine.

Empty fantasies. She hadn't believed in them even back then.

She forced a smile to her face. "You really think I'm going to let you go to the Citadel without me? Look what happened the last time."

The angel stepped forward suddenly and took her face in his hands; she could feel the tremor in them. "Last time you didn't know what the place would do to you. You told me that. This time you know. All your witchery will be gone."

Her gaze hardened slightly. "And without it I will be helpless? Was I such a helpless woman when I rescued you?"

Now it was his expression that grew stern. "That isn't what I meant."

He was trying to protect her. How strange it felt. How . . . intimate.

"I will only watch," she promised him. "From a height, to scan the countryside for danger, but out of range of any battle. Is that acceptable? You will need such surveillance. I can warn you if any danger approaches."

"And if a Souleater comes?"

She could not help the shiver that ran through her body at the thought. And she knew from the narrowing of his eyes that he was aware of it.

"Then may the gods help us all," she whispered. Wasn't that what they said in this place, whenever the demons were mentioned? Leave fate to the gods so men do not have to feel responsible for it.

He kissed her suddenly. Tentatively at first, and then, when he sensed that his advance was not unwelcome, more hungrily. Fiercely. Was there any kind of love in that kiss, or only desperation? The fire of life was burning inside him, demanding an outlet, she understood that. She felt it herself.

The door to the chamber was open. She didn't care. Let them watch. Let them all watch.

He lifted her up and carried to her over to the curtained bed and world outside simply ceased to matter.

The portal spell shimmered in the air before them, rippling slowly, like waves of heat over a sun-baked desert. Kamala could feel its power prickling her skin from several yards away; even by Magister standards it was an impressive piece of work. Ramirus had bound enough soulfire into the spell that it would be able to transport all of them halfway across Alkali without his needing to summon more athra. That was the safest option when other Magisters were watching, because it did not require that he cast a new spell for every individual he was transporting, but it was a costly one. She had no doubt that last night some distant consort had parted with the last meager fragments of his life as Ramirus cast that one aside in favor of fresh blood. Even a brand new consort would have to give up many years of life to power this kind of spell; it would not be unreasonable for Ramirus to cast that one aside as well, as soon as this enterprise was over. Paranoia was a powerful master.

The Lord Protector stood to one side of the portal, watching the preparations with grim approval. His wife was not with him. She had not been seen by the company since the prophecy had been translated. *She is unwell,* her husband said. His tone was sympathetic, but his eyes were cold. *She has asked me to beg your forgiveness for her absence and to offer you her prayers.*

One by one he went to them now, clasping a hand to each man's shoulder, gazing into each man's eyes. One by one the soldiers and Guardians saluted him, each as his rank required. They were dressed in the uniforms of Anukyat's men, with more concealing clothes in their saddlebags. Lazaroth had cast a spell to allow them to move unnoticed through enemy territory, but there was no telling until they got there whether or not it would work. All manners of subterfuge had been prepared, just in case.

Finally the Lord Protector came to where Kamala stood,

dressed once more in her Alkali uniform. Kierdwyn's semp-stresses had fitted it to her lean form, and provided suitable undergarments to hide her sex, so this time the disguise was not quite so haphazard. The Lord Protector nodded as he studied her, then bowed his head ever so slightly in formal appreciation. "House Kierdwyn is grateful for the service you have rendered us thus far, and the risks you accept this day in order to serve us still. Know that for as long as you walk this earth you will be welcomed as a friend in our halls."

Startled, she nodded, and muttered something about being honored. Her life thus far had not prepared her for such moments.

Finally the Lord Protector came to where his daughter stood. Gwynofar was dressed in male costume as well, but it was not nearly as effective a disguise on her as it was on Kamala. Her slight frame and delicate features made a lie of any masculine identity and she did not bear herself with the kind of casual arrogance that befit armed and uniformed men. But she stood up straight and proud as her father looked her over, and once more Kamala had a sense of hidden strength inside her.

The Lord Protector embraced his daughter and held her tightly for a long, solemn moment. "Be careful," he whispered. "Come home safe when you are done."

"I will," she promised him.

Stepping back at last, Lord Kierdwyn signaled to his men. The soldiers began to move forward in single file, each man leading his horse through the sorcerous portal. The animals were clearly not happy about the situation and snorted nerv-ously as the shimmering air engulfed them, but they had been well trained, and ultimately all allowed themselves to be walked through the portal. Watching the sorcery take hold of them was like watching them enter a pool of water: one moment the surface was rippling as it engulfed them, the next they were gone from sight.

Finally it was Rhys' turn. Kamala stepped forward and took his hand. Looking up defiantly at Ramirus, she thought she saw a spark of amusement in his eyes. Perhaps even appreciation. Not that he would necessarily have made the portal fail as she passed through it, but she had felt it best not to tempt him.

Bracing herself for the cold shock of another man's sorcery, she shut her eyes, squeezed Rhys' hand, and stepped through.

Alkali awaited.

CHAPTER 25

ANUKYAT REMEMBERS:
The Seers were leaving.

Anukyat could not stop them. Gods know he had tried. He had shaken duty in their faces like a pennant of war, seeking to stir the fire of their conscience. It made them humble. It made them silent. It had even made a few of them weep as they abandoned their posts, for they knew that in doing so they were abandoning the task that the gods once gave them.

But.

He could feel it in his sleep now. A pounding in his brain, so fierce that it threatened to crack his skull in two. A sense of foreboding so black and terrible that it twisted all his dreams into nightmares. An awareness of human screaming, just below the threshold of his hearing, that made him dread the moment it would finally break through and be heard.

He could shut such torments out by sheer force of will if he had to; he'd been doing so for some time now. But the Seers were more vulnerable to mental disturbances, and keeping protective spells in place constantly would simply cost them too much power. Not even the gods would ask them to throw away their lives like that. Or so they had argued when they finally told him they were leaving. All the orders in the world meant nothing, they told him, if they died before they could fulfill them.

They had counseled him to leave as well. The Wrath was expanding its influence, they said, and no man seemed able to stop it. Today its dire power it was lapping at the feet of the smallest Sister; tomorrow it might well swallow the Citadel whole. Did Anukyat expect to stay here when that happened? What would he do when the sanity of his Guardians began to slip away and there were no witches left to help them recover?

I must stay here, he told them stubbornly. *Duty demands it.*

Soon the last of them would be gone.

The sky to the north was no longer red. Was that a good or a bad thing? Several seasons ago the sunsets had been a deep, bruised purple and crimson clouds, the color of fresh blood, had gathered about the northern horizon. The Seers had suffered from dreams of fire and ash for much of that winter and some had awakened screaming. *Bodies burning!* they had gasped, their bedclothes drenched in sweat. *Skies smoking!* Night after night the visions had grown worse, but no one could make any sense of them. Whatever event or artifact the Seers needed to draw upon for knowledge was locked away on the far side of the Wrath, where no witch could access it. All they had on this side were dreams and confusion.

Anukyat had sent Guardians to the north to make an offering to the Spears. They never returned.

He had sent out yet more Guardians, to find out what had happened to the first group.

They never returned either.

Maybe he should have called for help at that point. Someday soon he would probably have to, informing the other Masters that something in Alkali had gone terribly wrong and that he could not handle it alone. But not yet. Not until he could put give a name to what they would be fighting. That was his pride speaking, but it was the same pride that had given him the courage to stand his ground as long as he had, the same pride that he lent to his men to keep them strong. He would not abandon it lightly. The Master of Alkali's Guardians would discover the source of this phenomenon and learn what had happened to his missing men, and if he had to call upon outsiders for help after that he would do so as a Master Guardian should, commander to commander. No foreigner would look down upon the Guardians of Alkali—or their Master—for being too weak to do their job properly.

Was it pride that motivated him now to put on his own armor and set out after his missing men? He handpicked men to accompany him, eight of his fiercest Guardians, as proud and as determined as he was. Men of Alkali blood who had proven themselves by the harsh measure of the north for many seasons now, braving blizzards in the depth of winter to perform the rituals needed to repair the Spears, braving bloody battles when war was called for, to protect them. Anukyat had Guardians of mixed heritage as well, but he was leaving them behind. Nothing was fiercer or more determined than a true Alkali warrior.

The ride north turned out to be a nightmare, even by the measure of men whose normal duty was to guard the source of all nightmares. In the end the horses would go no farther and the men were forced to dismount and continue on foot. Would the animals be strong enough to hold onto their sanity until the men returned? There was no way to know.

The ground was frozen and slick with ice and snow still guarded the mountain heights; the going was slow, the men's breath frosting in the still air. No one said a word now; moving forward against the force of the Wrath required every available ounce of energy. This close to the barrier there was no denying that something was seriously wrong; the curse that had always been tightly bound to its markers was now leaking out across the landscape, poisoning the very air they were breathing. Every step required a monumental effort and there were many steps left to go. Even the most determined spirit wavered as they drew inexorably closer to their goal.

I should have come here earlier, Anukyat thought grimly. But how could he have known that his Guardians—carefully chosen, mercilessly tested—would have proven inadequate to the task?

Soon they would reach the Spear. Then they would know the truth.

The valley floor they had been following for hours began to slope upward, and Anukyat knew that they would have to climb over a sharp ridge to reach the plateau where the nearest Spear was located. He hoped that one would give them some clue as to what was going on. If not, well, there were other Spears in Alkali, and if he had to visit them one after another to unravel this puzzle, he was ready to do so. He owed his missing men that much—and it was his duty to the gods.

Suddenly, without warning, a man stepped out from the shadows of the valley ahead of him directly into his path.

He heard the whisper of steel blades being drawn behind him even as he pulled his own sword free of its scabbard. The presence of his archers was like a cold prickling on the back of his neck, and he heard the frozen ground crunch as they positioned themselves for combat. The spirit of every Guardian was

on fire, despite the cold; whatever had struck down the previous
expeditions, these men were determined not to fall prey to it.

The newcomer was clearly of Alkali blood, with little or no
foreign inheritance. He wore his hair in long braids, tangled
and filthy; ornaments of wood or bone had been thrust into
them so long ago that time and dirt had fixed them permanently
into place. His garments were strange, some sort of close-fitting
armor that had the texture of waxed leather, but not its color.
At first glance it appeared a deep black—almost the Magisters'
black—but then as he moved, as shadows and sunlight moved
across its surface, Anukyat could make out glimmering blue
highlights, utterly unlike any fabric or hide he had ever seen.
Each garment was pieced together out of irregular scraps, like
some strange, mad quiltwork, then molded to the human form;
the result fit its owner like a second skin. A strange smell arose
from the stranger, sweet and musky and sour all at once, strong
enough to taint the chill air between them. It was like an odd
cross between the rankness of human sweat and the pungence
of a stag in rut.

"Who are you?" Anukyat demanded, hefting his sword
suggestively. If this man had anything to do with the disappearance of his Guardians, he would have much to answer for.

A strange, twisted smile crossed the stranger's face. "I am the
conscience of Alkali." He spoke the regional tongue well enough,
but with an accent that Anukyat never heard before; it was
clipped and coarse and gave the impression that its owner did
not spend much time practicing the fine art of conversation.
"You may call me the 'voice of the lost.'"

Anukyat snorted. "Well, I am Master Guardian of Alkali and
I do not care for riddles. You are in my lands and will identify
yourself now. Or must I seek that information by other means?"

A brief, black hatred stirred in the depths of the stranger's eyes. For a moment Anukyat thought the man was about to strike at him and his hand tightened reflexively on the grip of his sword. He was dimly aware that some dark and terrible power was coiled inside this man and knew that if they came to blows, he might wind up fighting something that was more dangerous than a mere human being. But that was fine with him. As a Guardian he was trained to fight supernatural creatures, and if this creature was the one responsible for the disappearance of his men, he would take personal pleasure in hacking him to bits, human or otherwise.

Suddenly there was a noise above him, on both sides of the valley. He heard one of his Guardians gasp, and against his better judgment he took his eyes off the stranger for half a second to glance upward.

The missing Guardians.

They were gathered high up on both sides of the valley, gazing down upon the confrontation. Ashen in color, hollow-eyed, they looked more like ghosts than like men, and when they met Anukyat's eyes there was barely a flicker of recognition. One of them even turned away rather than return Anukyat's gaze. Had the malignant power of this place sapped their strength, battered their spirits? Or was there something more subtle going on?

Fury hot in his heart, he turned on the stranger. "What have you done to them?" he demanded.

"I gave them the truth." The stranger's thin mouth twitched into a smile. "And I told them to wait here, so that you would come to me. Nothing more."

Anukyat's patience was at an end. "I warned you against riddles." He raised his left hand to signal the archers to ready themselves and heard the subtle friction of bowstrings being drawn as they took aim at the stranger. "Name yourself now, and explain what you mean by *truth*, or so help me gods, I will drag your corpse back to my witches and let them conjure explanations for me."

"No riddles," the stranger said sharply. His smile vanished. "Look at me, Guardian!" He spread his arms wide. "What do you see? Kannoket, yes? Like yourself. Like your men. All Kannoket. Now you call yourselves Alkali, but *we* are not Alkali, *we* were not saved by one of your seven heroes, *we* do not take his name. We are Kannoket . . . like you."

Kannoket. It was an ancient name, from another era. The Kannoket had once ruled the north, braving its harsh winters and fierce storms and serving its bloodthirsty gods. Then outsiders had arrived, self-righteous invaders who drove the winged demons called Souleaters before them. *Help us to drive them farther north*, they had told the Kannoket. *When they are far from the sun that they love, and have no more men to prey upon, surely they will perish.* And so the final great battle had taken place on Kannoket land, and the blood of Kannoket warriors had been spilled upon the earth in offering, until the gods saw fit to send down their Wrath to end all the killing.

The victors had divided the land into Protectorates after that, one for each of the war's great heroes to rule over. Only one hero was of Kannoket blood, the one called Alkali. The rest were simply foreign invaders who, having seen the true beauty of the north, decided to claim pieces of it for themselves. Or so the priests taught.

"What did the invaders say?" the stranger demanded. "That the lands of ice were empty of men. Empty of life. But they lied! There were Kannoket living there, and the outsiders knew it.

They said to each other, 'we will sacrifice them, we will give them to the demons for food, and then we can take their land.'"

"This is a mad tale," Anukyat said sharply. But he could not help but glance up at his men on the hillside. *They believe him,* he thought. "What proof have you of any of this?"

"Proof?" The stranger spread his arms wide. "I am proof, Master Guardian. I come from the lands of ice myself to tell you the truth. Is that not proof enough?"

"You mean you came from north of the Wrath?" A shiver ran down his spine. "You have crossed through it?"

"Yes. And more will come soon. More Kannoket. We seek our brothers. Our blood brothers. We will reclaim what is ours. You . . . Alkali . . . will help."

No man can cross the Wrath, Anukyat thought. *Not under normal circumstances. But what if it is changing now? Maybe the same thing that is causing the nightmares to spread has weakened the Wrath so that men might actually cross it.*

In the wake of that thought came one more chilling than all the rest put together: *If men can do that now, so can the Souleaters.*

"You want me to believe that the first Protectors betrayed us," he challenged the stranger. "That they knowingly condemned our people to death, to steal their land. Is that it?"

"And killed their witches, too, so that none would help them. A great sacrifice." The stranger's eyes glittered coldly. "Do you want to see?"

"Do I want to . . . see?"

The stranger gestured up the slope. Toward the ridgeback, the plateau beyond it . . . and the Spear.

He showed something to my men, Anukyat thought. *This is what makes them believe him.*

If the stranger's story were true, it would mean that all the history he'd been taught was a lie. Instead of a brave alliance of seven armies coming to defend the northlands, six armies had come to conquer. His own Kannoket people had been divided and the northernmost tribes condemned to a horrific fate. And the witches who might have done something to stop such a travesty—the Kannoket witches who would not have let their people die—had all been slaughtered. Sacrificed. Or so this stranger claimed.

If so, he thought grimly, that would change everything.

"Show me," he said quietly. Sheathing his sword. Signaling for his archers to stand down.

The stranger nodded and turned away, ready to lead him up the slope. But Anukyat stopped him. "Wait."

He turned back, to see what was needed.

"You have not given me your name."

For a long moment the stranger just stared at him. There was something oddly inhuman about his gaze but whether it was something better or worse than human, Anukyat could not begin to guess.

"Nyuku," he said. "My name is Nyuku."

And they began to climb.

CHAPTER 26

T HE FIRST morning of their journey, Gwynofar threw up. She staggered a few yards away from the camp before she did so, but they all could hear her clearly enough. Rhys started to go after her, but Kamala caught him by the arm and said quietly, "woman's business." In her experience that phrase was enough to make any man back down immediately, and indeed it worked this time.

It seemed obligatory that someone should help Gwynofar, and as she was the only other female in the camp, Kamala grabbed up a nearby rag—actually it was a spare shirt, but it would have to serve as a rag for now—and followed her.

She found the Queen Mother on her knees, shaking in the aftermath of a bout of sickness. It took Gwynofar a minute to notice Kamala standing there beside her; when she finally did, Kamala handed her the rag.

"Thank you." She wiped off her face with it, and then reached down to the ground to brush some dirt and moss over the mess she had made until it was all neatly covered up. Like a cat, Kamala thought. All neat and tidy.

Perhaps she shouldn't have said anything but the words just came out. "You are with child?"

Gwynofar sighed. Then nodded.

"Do the others know?"

"Rhys does. Ramirus. I am not sure who else was told."

"So . . . let me be sure I understand this. You are going into enemy territory to risk your life, in a campaign requiring strength and endurance . . . pregnant?"

A dry smile flickered across the blonde woman's lips. "That is the gist of the plan, yes."

Kamala shook her head in amazement. "You are either very brave or very foolish."

"I am *lyra*." She rose unsteadily to her feet. "One of the gifts the gods gave us was the ability to bear our children without pain or illness." She put a hand on her stomach. "My son will not slow me down."

"So do the *lyra* usually vomit in the morning?" Kamala could not keep the edge from her voice. "Just like common peasants do?

A shadow passed over Gwynofar's face. She said nothing.

"You've had other children," Kamala persisted. "Did the other ones make you ill when they were in the womb?"

"No," she said quietly. "No, they did not."

"So maybe the Wrath distorts this *lyr* magic as well as the other types." It was a cruel thing to say and she knew it, but something about the woman's quiet arrogance just brought out the worst in her.

Gwynofar drew in a sharp breath. For a moment she was very still. Kamala was aware of the noise of the men working behind them to get the horses ready for a hard day's ride, as everyone pointedly left the two women alone.

"Why do you dislike me so much?" Gwynofar asked. "I don't remember having treated you badly."

Because you are soft and you are fragile and men fawn upon you as though the sun rose and set at your command. From the day of your birth you have had everything handed to you on a silver platter and I doubt you asked the cost of any of it. Even when it comes to the pain of childbearing—the one arena in which all women are brought down to the same level—you have miraculously been spared. In short, you have everything a woman might desire, and you do not know the true value of any of it, for you have never been tested. So if you vomit like a peasant, my Lady Queen, maybe it is because there is still a tad of justice in this world.

"I don't dislike you," Kamala said.

Gwynofar looked at her sharply, then reached down to brush the leaves and dirt from her leggings. "The task at hand requires that we rely upon one another, Lady Kamala. Possibly for our lives. I don't know how you normally go about preparing for such a thing, but I believe that lies are a poor way to start."

For a long moment Kamala just stared at her. What was behind that delicate facade that gave her such strength of spirit? Dressed in an Alkali uniform for the journey she looked even smaller than usual, and she wouldn't pass for a grown man in anything but the dimmest of light. Yet she bore the weight of her armor without complaint, and had kept her seat astride her horse through a long day of riding when even the more experienced men were sore. Little wonder she had thrown up, all things considered. It might not even have anything to do with the pregnancy.

She's got courage at least. No man can fault her for that.

Finally she said, "Kamala. My name. Just Kamala."

The queen drew in a deep breath. "And mine is Gwynofar.

Just Gwynofar." A faint smile flickered across her face. "For this trip, at least. Fair enough?"

She handed her back the shirt. Without even thinking, Kamala bound a whisper of power to clean it.

Gwynofar seemed startled. "Are you sure you should do that?"

"It'll be another day before we're close enough to the Wrath for it to be a problem," Kamala said. *Gods forbid the Magisters should have risked their precious necks by landing us somewhere closer.* But she understood why the sorcerers had decided to play it safe. It wasn't like there was a line drawn in the dirt that was labeled "sorcery works here" on one side and "sorcery doesn't work here" on the other. Better to play it safe, especially when royalty was involved, and ride into the affected region by purely mundane means.

"But the cost you must pay for such an inconsequential spell. No one here would ask that of you."

Ah, hells. She had missed the woman's meaning entirely.

A real witch would not have wasted her power on such a mundane task. What woman in her right mind would give up even one minute of her life to wash the vomit out of a shirt? *You make a lousy witch,* she told herself.

"I forgot myself," she muttered. That much was certainly true.

Gwynofar touched her lightly on the arm. "You are very generous, Kamala."

No, I'm not, she thought. *I'm a cold-hearted cannibalistic monster, the same as those Souleaters you are all so afraid of. You just haven't figured it out yet.* "The men are waiting for us." She nodded toward the camp without meeting Gwynofar's eyes.

Why did the woman's praise make her feel so damned guilty?

By the time they got back to the camp the horses were saddled and ready. Kamala gave the shirt back to the soldier whose pack she had borrowed it from, who looked at it suspiciously and then stuffed it in one of his bags. None of them really trusted her. During their last night in the castle she'd used sorcery to listen in on several heated arguments over why she was being allowed to come along at all. "Do you know who she really is?" Ullar had demanded. "Or where she's really from? For all we know she could be Anukyat's own agent, sent here to spy upon us. That would certainly explain how she appeared at just the right moment to rescue Rhys when only Anukyat knew where he was."

But Rhys trusted her, and Gwynofar trusted Rhys . . . and so the others were eventually overruled. A *lyr* thing, apparently. In matters such as these, the instincts of their ancient bloodline were considered sacrosanct.

What was it like to be raised your whole life to serve a cause like that? To be expected to put aside your entire life to chase after legends? The depth of their faith was something Kamala could not comprehend; her world was a much simpler place.

The camp was silent when they returned to it, all eyes fixed upon a point in space where the air had just begun to ripple ominously. Kamala heard steel being drawn as both soldiers and Guardians braced themselves to meet . . . what? If a Magister came through that portal, were they going to confront him with simple steel? That battle would not last very long.

And then the spell was completed and a sorcerer stepped through. When she saw his face, Kamala's heart almost stopped beating.

Colivar.

His dark eyes glittered with cold amusement as he saw how his arrival had disconcerted the company. His black shirt and doublet were of a simple black—morati black—but everyone present seemed to know what he was. A few of the men sheathed their weapons as they recognized him, but a few did not. Clearly those men were willing to go down fighting a sorcerer if that was what their duty required.

Fine olive skin. Long black hair, sweeping down to his shoulders. Jet black eyes above finely chiseled features. The hint of a cold, condescending smirk, as if the entire world existed for his amusement. Kamala remembered him well. She also remembered his last words to her when they had arrived outside Danton's palace, hinting that he knew her darkest secret: not only what she truly was, but what she had done.

Test me if you like, she thought defiantly. Bracing herself to channel the fire in her soul. *I am ready for you.*

But Colivar's eyes passed over her with maddening disinterest and fixed upon Gwynofar instead. "I bring you news from the eastern front, Majesty. Your son has mobilized his armies and is moving them toward the Skandir border. It would appear that he has his own ideas about who the real enemy is."

The color bled from Gywnofar's face, but her expression did not falter. "You are sure of this?"

"I am. And Ramirus has confirmed it."

"Then why did he not come here himself to tell us that? Or send Lazaroth?"

He chuckled coldly. "Hard as it may be to accept that Ramirus and I are allied in this matter, I assure you that is the case. As for Lazaroth, he was concerned that you might be too close to the Wrath by now for sorcerous transportation to be safe. So I volunteered." A faint, sardonic smile curled his lips. "Perhaps I am less afraid of 'the curse of the gods' than most of my kind."

"The line between courage and recklessness is sometimes thin," Kamala murmured.

"Indeed." The black eyes fixed on her. For one brief moment he allowed her to see the power that was behind them, and to catch the echoes of all dark and terrible things that lurked in their depths. "You are the one they call Kamala, yes? I would not wish to mistake you for someone else."

"It is my name," she said, refusing to be baited.

"I thought you would have taken on wings by now. Wasn't that the plan?" He shook his head. "Perhaps you are afraid of using your power this close to the Wrath? Concerned that as a *witch* you are not up to the challenge?" Shadows of mockery hung about the term, along with an unvoiced subtext: *we both know that is not what you are.* "If so, I would be glad to assist you. I assure you my sorcery is . . . trustworthy."

"Thank you," she said sweetly, "but I thought I would wait until we got closer to our target. You might not want to be casting spells there yourself. I hear it's quite dangerous."

There was no telling what his response might have been had not Gwynofar stepped between them at that moment. "Thank you for the report, Magister Colivar. I am so sorry we cannot offer you better hospitality right now, but as you can see, we are getting ready to ride out." She held out her hand to him, smiling with the kind of polished radiance that noblewomen spent years working to perfect. "Please do give Magisters Ramirus and Lazaroth my best, and assure them we will return to them soon."

For a moment Colivar's expression was unreadable. Then, with a courtly nod he accepted her hand, raising it to his lips to kiss it gently. "Of course, Your Majesty. And I am sure they will be grateful for the reassurance."

The air behind him began to ripple once more as he released her hand; his eyes met Kamala's for a moment—she nodded

graciously, trying to make her own smile suitably enigmatic—
and then a step backward brought him within range of the
portal spell. Swiftly he vanished from their sight. A moment
later the breezes settled back into their normal pattern and there
was no sign of his ever having been present save for a few horses
that nickered uneasily, clearly less than happy about people that
appeared and disappeared in front of them.

Kamala didn't realize how fast her heart had been beating
until he was gone. Shutting her eyes, she tried to quiet her spirit
once more.

"You are either very brave or very foolish," Gwynofar told
her, once the others had turned back to their business.

Both, Kamala thought.

But Colivar had been right. The time for riding on horseback along with the rest of this company had passed. Last night
she had felt the first stirring of fear in her brain, presaging the
nightmares to come. Soon, now, her sorcery would become
unstable. Soon any attempt to shapechange might well backfire on her and cause her irreparable damage. The time for delay
had ended.

Clasping Rhys' hand for a moment (and how much
communion was in that touch, without the need for words to
be spoken!) she stepped away from the others, into an open
space, and summoned the power to her. Bidding it envelop her
body, uncreate her human flesh, and craft something else in its
place. Her new feathered wings were broad and soft; they would
be silent in approaching the Citadel. Her new eyes were sharp
and focused. Her talons were long and sharp, powerful enough
to tear flesh to pieces, sensitive enough to carry an egg without
breaking it. It was not her usual choice of bird form but it was
the one best suited to the final phase of this journey, and that

was what mattered most. And if her skin was tougher than the skin of this seed-eating species should have been, her muscles stronger, her talons sharper . . . well, that was just good design work. The fact that shape changing required some sort of natural template to follow did not mean that nature's rules could not be prodded a bit.

With a short cry she flapped her wings, took to the air, and rose up swiftly into the bright morning sky.

———

The Magister stood alone in the early morning light, his long black robes stirred by an occasional restless breeze. Even without sorcery he could make out the distant sound of a horse's approach and while he might have been tempted in any other place to enhance his senses and gather more information about it, he was too close to the Citadel right now to chance it. Mere human hearing would have to do.

He waited.

The sound was coming close enough now for him to make out individual hoofbeats and he could see the shape of a single rider approaching. Only one. That was a curious choice, he thought. Not what he had expected. But then, the Master Guardian of Alkali was an eccentric sort.

The Magister called his birds to him; the air shimmered with sorcery briefly to one side of him and a few seconds later a wooden crate appeared. The birds inside were silent, their incessant cooing muted by the shock of sorcerous transportation. A pleasant change from their normal chatter.

Then the rider pulled up his horse right in front of the box, setting them to beating their wings in panic. It got them nowhere, of course.

"Magister Thelas?"

It seemed to him a foolish question under the circumstances, but he nodded.

Anukyat dismounted smoothly, his booted feet raising dust as they hit the ground. "Your messenger arrived but two hours ago. Cutting it close, yes?"

"Events move quickly," Thelas said. "Especially in wartime."

"That does not sound good."

"It is not." The birds were starting to scratch at their crate. Hardly a surprise. Animals hated this place. "Salvator is moving his armies east, to the Skandir border. It would appear that he means to go after those who ravaged Soladin."

"Well, that is good news, yes? Just what the Lord Protector wanted."

"It would be good news," he agreed, "if it were true."

Anukyat breathed in sharply. "What do you mean?"

"Apparently the leader of the campaign carries sealed orders from King Salvator, that no man has yet read. Sealed by witchery in addition to more common methods, so that it cannot even be read from a distance, nor its purpose divined."

"But you managed to do so, yes? Else we would not be standing here."

Alkali's Magister Royal nodded. "When Salvator's troops reach the place where Skandir's border abuts our own, they will learn that their true target is Alkali. By then they be within easy march of several key cities, with access to the whole of the eastern plateau—"

"And those cities have already sent their garrisons west to face off against Kierdwyn's men."

"Exactly."

"So Aurelius and Kierdwyn are working together."

The Magister's expression was grim. "You promised Alkali's Lord Protector that was not going to happen."

He bit back a sharp retort. "That promise came from another. I told His Lordship that."

"It matters little, once the promise is broken."

"And assigning blame wins us no battles." He waved his hand, dismissing the subject. "So what is it you want from me, Thelas? I am sure you did not come all the way out here just for a friendly chat. What does His Lordship require of the Guardians?"

"The eastern threat must be removed. Or at the very least delayed long enough for him to deal with the threat from Kierdwyn."

Anukyat's eyes narrowed suspiciously. "And how do I fit into this?"

"You have men here. More than you need."

He hissed softly. "My men are not common soldiers."

"No," the Magister agreed. "They are elite soldiers, specially skilled at operating in small groups, and at range. Such men could be especially useful in this matter."

"The road to the Spear must be protected. Our ally demands that much."

"So keep enough men with you to handle that task. The rest go south." He smiled dryly. "Never fear, we will keep your units separate, and not mix them with . . . *common* soldiers." The condescension in his voice was unmasked.

"This is not wise," Anukyat said quietly.

"That is not your call to make," the Magister responded. "Nor mine. Once we cede to princes the right to rule us, we owe them obedience until another that is more qualified takes their place. So if you wish to take the throne for yourself," he said dryly, "now is the time. If not, then I will expect your men to meet me here tomorrow at daybreak, when I will see to their transportation."

"With sorcery?" He scowled. "That is risky, is it not?"

"In large numbers, aye. You will most likely lose a few men along the way. But there is no time for slower measures, so make your peace with it." The Magister reached down and picked up the crate of birds. "You can use these to send any urgent messages you may have."

"Homing pigeons?" He took the crate and hefted it to eye level, glaring at the birds. "You really think they will keep their bearing in this region? Even men can barely stand this place, and they get paid to be here."

"They are but simple birds, bearing the marks of my sorcery. When you release one from the Citadel it will make for the south with all due haste, terrified by what lies in the other direction. As soon as it comes within range I will call it to me. Far more efficient than any human messenger could be, under the circumstances." He paused. "Not to mention, a bird can deliver its message alive or dead."

"So when do I get my men back?"

"When Salvator decides this is not a war he wishes to fight, so that the Lord Protector can focus his attention on the western front."

Anukyat smiled darkly. "Salvator is a son of the monastery; he has no stomach for war. And he has no Magister to help him fight it. It should be easy enough to frighten him away."

"Let us hope so. For your sake." The Magister's eyes narrowed. "This war began with your revelation and was nurtured by your counsel. It would not be a good thing for you if the Lord Protector decided he had been ill advised."

Anukyat stiffened. "Is it *ill advised* to answer an ancient wrongdoing? To aid our abandoned brothers in their vengeance?"

Thelas raised a hand to silence him. "Save your arguments for the Lord Protector. I am only his messenger in this matter." Then he waved his hand at the empty space beside him and the air began to shift and shimmer once more. The horse neighed sharply and tried to move away from the sorcerous display, but Anukyat was holding the reins and so he could not go far.

"I will expect your men in the morning," Thelas said. And then he stepped into the portal and was gone.

Anukyat waited until the spell faded completely before he finally vented his fury, cursing the Magister, the Lord Protector, and most of all the pitiful monk Salvator who thought he was a real king. The curse was complex and colorful and it ran through half a dozen languages, among them an ancient dialect of Kannoket that had not been spoken this far south of the Wrath for nearly a thousand years.

Nyuku would not be pleased by all this, he thought darkly. Nyuku would not be pleased at all.

———

I didn't really lie to them, Kamala thought, flying toward Anukyat's Citadel. *I will do reconnaissance for them. I will just do other things as well.*

Morati scouts had already taken the measure of the tower, thanks to Lazaroth's sorcery. Wearing borrowed wings, they had brought back enough information to allow Favias and Ullar to map out the company's best route of approach. But their observations were of limited scope, and therefore limited value. Magisters were used to shape changing—it was a cornerstone of their art—and they could refine the flesh they wore into a fine-tuned creation that suited their needs exactly. Morati were not nearly so comfortable in animal form and sometimes did not adjust well to seeing the world through an animal's senses.

Kamala had other things to do here, private things, and so she had offered to back up their efforts with her own observations, once they got within range of the tower.

High overhead she soared now, until the trees were mere pinpoints beneath her. The land here was not like the forests surrounding Ethanus' mountain retreat, where she had first practiced shapechanging. That was a lush, green place where only the steepest cliffs and tallest peaks revealed any expanse of dirt or stone. This region was far less inviting. Trees were few and far between, and the kind of thick brush that her companions would have liked to use for cover was next to nonexistent near the Citadel itself.

Ramirus had cast a spell upon the company that would theoretically aid them in approaching the enemy's haven unseen . . . assuming it worked at all. And assuming it did not backfire. It was a subtle sorcery, which would not render them invisible per se, but would rather encourage any men who saw them to over look their presence. Guards along the road would believe them to be fellow guards, unremarkable and uninteresting. And if someone spotted them while they were climbing the tower, in theory they would be mistaken for someone or something that would normally be hanging from the side of a tower. Kamala had her doubts about how well all that would work, but she understood the need for subtlety. If such a spell were scrambled by the Wrath, it was unlikely the result would threaten their mission. A spell of true invisibility that backfired, however, could become a beacon that drew the attention of every living being within miles. Better by far to play it safe and tread lightly in matters metaphysical than to risk some more dramatic failure.

Which meant that they all had to look like guards and act like guards in order to support Ramirus' sorcery. The less work there was for the spell to do, he had explained to them, the more likely it was to work. What he did not say—and what no one dared suggest—was that if the Wrath cancelled out his sorcery, or changed its effect entirely, their lives might well depend upon the quality of their subterfuge. A spell that kept them from being noticed, if warped by the Wrath, might draw attention to them instead.

With so few places in the area where they could take shelter, that was not a happy prospect.

Flying high over the desolate countryside, Kamala practiced speaking. It was harder than she had expected it to be. Normally when one took on an animal form one had an innate sense of how to control the body, but apparently that did not extend to such fine motor control as bird speech required. She had taken the precaution of transforming herself into a type of bird that was capable of imitating human speech—Ethanus had conjured one for her to study early in her apprenticeship—but without lips, teeth, or anything like a human tongue, it took her a while to figure out how to make it work. When she finally succeeded, the resulting speech was odd and screechy, with a quality not unlike fingernails on slate. Comprehensible, but far from pleasing.

She doubted her companions would care about aesthetics.

When she finally arrived at the Citadel she slowly circled above it a few times to see if anyone noticed her. No one did. It was hardly definitive proof that Ramirus' sorcery was operative, but given how rare large birds were in this region, it was a promising sign. Then, coming in behind the monument, where the Citadel's guards would be unable to see her, she flew in closer to the great rock to get a better look at it.

The morati scouts had focused upon the outer structure of the third Sister, collecting the kind of details that climbers would need to ascend to the top, making note of a few large openings that appeared to give access to an interior space. Uncomfortable in their borrowed avian flesh, however, they had deemed it too dangerous to risk going inside. But Kamala was more practiced in transformation, and was ready to do so. She had designed her feathers to be a perfect match to the weathered stone, so even if Ramirus' spell was not working, though such a disguise would not guarantee her safety, it brought the level of risk down to an acceptable level.

Which is what? she wondered. Was she really risking her life for someone else's cause?

I am risking my life for knowledge, she told herself sternly, *and the things that knowledge can buy. Nothing more.*

Landing on a narrow ledge beside one of larger openings near the top, she waited a few minutes to see if anyone noticed her there—no one did—and then eased her way inside the structure. The window was naturally formed, a deep crack in the monument's surface that time and wind had widened, but the interior of the tower had clearly been carved out by a human hand. Probably by a sorcerer's hand, given the polished perfection of the work. That was only to be expected. Until recently the Wrath's effect had not reached this far south, so all things had been possible, including hollowing out a natural monument and outfitting it for human purposes.

The chamber she entered was round—perfectly round—and beams of sunlight poured in through the irregular openings about its circumference. Most of those natural windows were too narrow to admit a grown man, but she took note of several that might allow it. She also noted that the room as a whole offered a complete view of the land on the far side of the monument. That was not good news. Anukyat had not built an observational tower on this side of the Citadel because he'd had no need for one; the monument itself was his guard tower.

Not used very often, she thought, making note of the thick layer of dust on the floor. A line of scuff marks led from the staircase to the nearest window and from there around the outside of the chamber, but they were old enough that fresh dust and dried leaves had begun to cover them up again. Clearly this place was not part of the Citadel's normal sentry rounds.

A stone spiral staircase came up through the floor in the center of the chamber. It was so narrow that only one man at a time would be able to ascend it while those defending the chamber could easily spread out and surround him. Kamala could see spears affixed to braces on the wall, awaiting the need for such action. Under normal circumstances that would not be good news for Kierdwyn's company, but in this case it could be turned to their advantage; if they could get control of this chamber themselves, it would be next to impossible for Anukyat's men to dislodge them.

Overhead there was a trap door leading upward with a ladder set beside it. Realizing that she would not be able to push the door open from below in her current body, Kamala slipped out the window again and sought access to the next level of the monument. There were natural windows up there as well, but these were much narrower; she didn't see any that were large enough to admit a grown man. So much for direct access.

Easing herself into one of the windows, alert for any sign or sound of human presence, she peered into the topmost chamber.

It was there.

Not until that moment would she have admitted to herself that she had doubted whether the legendary throne would actually be here, since they'd had no more than a thousand-year-old prophecy to point the way. But there it was, covered by a length of black oilskin, which in turn was blanketed by a layer of dust that looked centuries old, though the shape of the thing was clear enough. Taller than a man, with a back as broad as the outstretched reach of a warrior, it revealed just enough of its form through the covering that she could see it was a indeed a chair, and a massive one. She hungered to pull the covering off it so that she could see its details, but she knew there was no way to do that without disturbing the dust that coated it. Doing that now would risk the locals finding out that she had been here and perhaps drawing the obvious conclusion.

The floor of the room was likewise covered in dust, with old leaves and dried bird droppings all over the place. Clearly the upkeep of this chamber was not high on Anukyat's priority list. The bolt of the trapdoor was unlocked, but there were no tracks in the dust, nor any other sign that living men had visited the place in recent memory. It appeared that Anukyat's primary interest in the monument was as a guard tower, and had taken no special precautions to protect the artifact it harbored. Why should he? Anyone who meant to storm the tower must take the Citadel first. Right?

She spent a few more minutes considering whether there was any way to get a look under the oilskin without leaving a telltale mark on the dusty film that covered everything, but finally decided against it. Exiting through a narrow window, she flew low about the monument, peeking into cracks and crevices as she went. The spiral staircase that dominated the Sister's interior was wide enough for comfort in most places, and maybe even for combat; it was only at the very top of its course that it narrowed, as it channeled men through the floor of the observation tower. She located a few natural windows that were big enough for her companions to pass through and took note of what they looked like from the outside. Then, with one last glance at the Citadel beneath her, she took to the open sky again, heading west instead of east, just in case anyone was watching. She could circle about to get back to her traveling companions later.

Now for her own private business.

It took her several hours to find a suitable subject for her experiment. Animals in this region were mostly tiny and nervous, and the species of bird she had used for her model was designed for gathering seeds, not hunting game. But finally, just as the sun began to drop below the western mountains, she spotted a nervous hare, and she settled down onto a nearby tree branch to watch him forage.

Shapechanging, Ethanus had taught her, was one of the most complex and dangerous spells to attempt. A body must not only be capable of sustaining life in its original form and its final form, but of sustaining life through every transitional form in between. The slightest miscalculation could result in death. All of which meant that such a spell was particularly lethal in this region. It didn't even matter exactly what effect the Wrath had upon such sorcery, or even if it was the same effect every time; any interference at all, of any kind, could make shape changing a lethal enterprise.

Carefully she gathered her consort's athra to her, enough to fuel such a costly spell. Then, with the hare in her sights, she released it. In any other place, that spell would have transformed the small animal into another sort of creature. But here?

The animal's body contorted suddenly and a terrible sound came out of its throat, a sound no natural hare could have made. She watched as the small body became distended, distorted, its limbs twisting in on themselves, blood pouring from its eyes, ears, and mouth. The soft fur gave way to something pink and raw, with glistening gray coils protruding from gashes in its belly. Intestines? Fascinated, she had to remind herself just how much this experiment was costing her, and she regretfully she let the sorcery fade.

The hare—or what was left of the hare—was dead.

So. She was not without power here, after all.

Granted, it was a costly trick, which meant she could not perform it often. The last thing she wanted was to be forced into transition in this blighted region. Once her lifeline to her current consort was severed, her sorcery might not work well enough to find her a new one. No Magister had tested the power of the Wrath in that manner, and she did not mean to be the first.

But she was not helpless. Not any longer.

Savoring that thought, she took flight once more, anxious to rejoin her morati companions before the last of the day's light was gone.

———

The Seer's chamber was small and dark, with a heavy oak door that was bolted shut from the outside. For her own protection, of course. There was a small window set in the door through which one could see a room with few furnishings; its most noteworthy feature was a large canopied bed directly in its center. There was a woman in the bed at the moment, tossing and turning and mumbling in her sleep as if in the grip of a nightmare.

Anukyat waved for the door to be opened and stood to one side while a servant obeyed. The maidservant who had brought him to the room waited behind him, her hands twisting nervously in her apron.

The air in the room was close and humid, its smell a mixture of sweat and fear. There was no point in trying to air it out, Anukyat knew. As long as he kept a talented Seer within range of the Wrath, the supply of sweat and fear was endless.

He stood by one side of the bed, watching while the maidservant sat down on the other side, blotting at her mistress' forehead with a linen handkerchief. "She was muttering something about sorcery," she told Anukyat. "It didn't make any sense to me, but I came to get you right away. I thought that maybe—"

With a wave of his hand he silenced her so that he could listen for himself. The Seer was not saying anything now, but that did not surprise him. Sanity came in fits and starts to such a talent, coherence likewise. An unfortunate necessity of bringing such a rare and vulnerable talent within range of the Wrath.

As he watched, the Seer began to toss and turn, clearly in the early stages of some new nightmare. With the Wrath pouring its malignant essence directly into her brain, unfettered by the kind of mental defenses that most humans took for granted, it was nothing short of a wonder that she ever woke up at all.

Then her eyes shot open. For a moment she just stared at the ceiling without focus or comprehension. Then, turning her head in Anukyat's direction, she stared intently at him. Or through him.

"Dead flesh," she whispered hoarsely. "Dead flesh, unshaped. Should have left with the others! Should have run! Look, even the maggots are afraid. . . ."

"Sorcery," he prompted. She was not sane enough to comprehend direct orders, much less respond to them, but sometimes she could be prodded in the right direction. "What about the sorcery?"

She shut her eyes and shivered violently. "Cold, so cold. The power is death. Stolen from far away. Someone else's death. Can you see it? Blacker than ink. Colder than ice. So near to the Citadel. Will anyone notice it? No one looks for sorcery here."

Her body shuddered suddenly and then became still; her breathing was rapid and shallow, like a dog panting. Anukyat waited for a short while to see if she would resume her description and when she did not, touched a hand to her cheek. Her body lurched as her spirit rose to consciousness once more, clearly a painful process.

"Where?" Anukyat demanded. "Where is the sorcery?"

For a moment it seemed like she did not hear him. Then, just as he was about to ask the question again, she whispered, "The setting sun, the setting sun! Shadow of the smallest Sister. Look at the blood on the ground! The flies will not feast, they are afraid. Go back, go back! Now we can kill. Now we are strong."

A chill coursed through Anukyat's veins as he heard those words. But no matter how he prodded her after that, physically or verbally, he could not coax forth more details, only the same cryptic phrases over and over again.

Finally, with a scowl, he rose from the bed. "Record everything she says," he told the maidservant. "Call me immediately if there is anything new."

He left her in the chamber to tend to the Seer. It was an unhappy job, but she was paid well for it.

There was sorcery being worked within his domain.

Thelas had assured him that was impossible. Neither witch nor sorcerer could raise any kind of power within range of the Wrath, the Magister Royal had said. Even before the barrier had become unstable, the Guardians had needed a phalanx of spell casters, guarded by ancient rituals, to tame it. Now even that was no longer possible. For Anukyat to be without magical defenses, therefore, meant nothing, because magic could not be wielded against him. Nothing for him to worry about.

Anukyat had never really trusted that assessment. So he had ordered the Seers to assign one of their number to him, despite the obvious risks, and unhappily they had obeyed. This Seer had come to him nearly a year ago, a young woman with stars in her eyes, ready to take on the nightmarish power of the Wrath in order to serve the Guardians' cause.

She did not yet know that her cause was a false one, and that while she slept it had been abandoned. She did not know that in order to bring justice to the Kannoket it would first be necessary to teach their so-called allies the cost of past betrayals, and make sure they could never offend again. She did not know that the nightmares she endured, and the visions she channeled, were all in service to that task.

So what was the source of this mysterious sorcery? And what was its purpose? He could not believe a Magister would enter this region of his own free will; even Thelas, who was accustomed to dealing with the Wrath, had made it clear he never would do so. Yet this Seer had picked up on something. And his Seers were rarely wrong.

The setting sun, the Seer had said. *Shadow of the smallest Sister.*

To the west, then. Somewhere close by the smallest of the three monuments. Would his Guardians be able to find the source of this sorcery if they went there? Even more to the point: would the Citadel be safe in their absence? He cursed Thelas under his breath for taking so many of his men away from him. It was almost as if the gods were mocking him now, with this new bit of trouble. *Choose between security and reconnaissance,* they teased him. Knowing that he no longer had enough men for both duties.

This region is mine, he thought fiercely. Feeling a black and terrible anger toward whatever sorcerer had dared to leave his mark on his land, so close to his Citadel. He would no more tolerate it than he would let a stray dog piss on his battlements.

Come dawn he would send out a few men to investigate this matter—there was no way to avoid that—but he would also send out one of the birds that Thelas had given him to carry news of this sorcerous outrage directly to Alkali's Magister Royal. If the sorcerer did not respond promptly—immediately!— well, then, next time he would find that his word had little weight in this region.

And with the Kannoket and their winged allies returning from long exile, that would not be a good thing for him. Not good at all.

———

Quiet. The darkness of midnight. Fire crackling low in a circle of stones. Fitful snoring from one of the sleeping Guardians.

Gwynofar lay awake, absorbing it all. A final taste of peace. Tomorrow they would pass into the blighted region (as Kamala called it) and who could say when there would be peace again? If ever?

Slowly she shut her eyes, turning her attention within herself. Sensing the flow of blood within her veins, the slow throb of her heart within her chest . . . and lower down, cradled between her hips, the fluttering of something that was almost a heart, the stirring of something that was almost a child, the fire of something that was almost a soul.

Allowing her *lyr* gift to guide her, she embraced the tiny spark of life inside herself and felt the world about her shift in response. Gone now was the darkness of the forest night, gone were the huffs and snorts of her companions, gone was everything that spoke of stress or uncertainty or fear.

Surrounded by sunlight, she cradled a baby in her arms. He was a beautiful child, with wisps of blond hair that curled about his temples and pale blue eyes that reminded her of Andovan. The sight of him made her heart ache, even if it was only an illusion. How young she had been when her third child had been born! It seemed an eternity ago. Another lifetime.

You were conceived in an act of violence, she thought to the pink-cheeked infant in her arms, *but that was not your fault. You are the son of a great king and brother to princes, and your mother will love you as dearly as she loved those who came before you. Even more, for you comfort her in her mourning.*

Carefully she inspected the infant, looking for any signs of ill health. If there were any problems with her pregnancy they would manifest thus, and she could channel the power needed to fix things by attending to the child appropriately. The baby in her arms might be an illusion, but by tending it to it she could channel healing power to her real child as he needed it. It was part of the gift that the gods had granted to every *lyra*, allowing her to tend to her son's needs even while he was still in the womb. But despite the long hours on horseback and all other stresses of the journey, the child in her arms was healthy, which meant that all was well with her pregnancy.

She held the illusionary baby close to her breast for a long time, taking comfort from the warmth of his flesh against her own, from the sweet scent of his skin and then, regretfully, she let the illusion fade. Gods alone knew if she would be capable of such visions once they entered the area where the Wrath held sway. It was a form of witchery, after all. But for now, at least, her child was healthy and safe. And that was what mattered most.

Closing her eyes, she willed herself to forget about everything else in the world and surrendered to what might be her last peaceful sleep for some time.

Chapter 27

THE SKY was a sullen, swollen purple with dark and angry clouds that seemed about to split open, spilling their festering contents upon the earth below. The air was thick with poisonous smells, a strange and sickening mixture of putrid elements that made Salvator's stomach lurch. If he closed his eyes and judged by smell alone he could easily believe the whole earth was rotting, a bloated corpse beneath his feet, too vast for man to comprehend. He shuddered at the image and for a moment it was all he could do to fight off the urge to add to its putrescence with his own vomit.

For a moment he wondered if he had died and been sent to some kind of transitional underworld where he would be judged by his god before being committed permanently to eternal reward or suffering. Could a man die and not even know that it had happened? Then, a moment later, the answer came to him, and with it a modicum of sanity: *This is a dream.*

It was easier to deal with his surroundings in that context. He could even open his eyes and take a look around without being overwhelmed by it all. He found that he was standing atop a mountain, bare of vegetation, that dropped down precipitously into a deep gorge. At the bottom, where a river had probably flowed in wetter seasons, a column of men was now marching. Soldiers, grim-faced, who ignored the occasional bones at their feet, not stopping to take note of the fact that some of them appeared to be human remains. Salvator saw one man step upon a long femur and snap it in two. His stride never faltered, and the soldier behind him ground the fragments deep into the ground as he stepped on them in turn.

What was this place?

"King's Pass," came a voice. Its soft, feminine substance parted the foul winds like a knife. "The troops of Corialanus, heading north."

He turned to find the source of the words. Behind him stood Queen Siderea. She was dressed in a gown of amethyst silk that clung to her body like a second skin with streamers of chiffon that fluttered from her shoulders like dragonfly wings. Her arms were bare, her breasts nearly so; and her copper skin gleamed against the dismal landscape like the final fires of a setting sun.

"You sent this dream," he said. Both offended and intrigued by the concept.

The full lips smiled; a secret amusement glittered in the depths of her eyes. "A vision, King Salvator. Not a dream."

"What is the difference?"

She waved one long, sleek arm out across the gorge; golden bracelets along its length shimmered with the motion. "What you see before you is really taking place, hundreds of miles from where you sleep. I have merely enhanced your power of vision with my own, that you might witness it from a distance."

He could not keep the edge from his voice. "Without my permission."

A slender eyebrow, plucked to perfection, arched upward. "The offering of an ally, my King. Would you not wish to have such a service?"

He looked back down at the scene below him. The river-carved gorge twisted and turned in its course, and not far from where he stood it curved out of his line of sight, both to the right and left of him. Thus he could not see the front of the line of soldiers, nor guess at where the end was. But the part that was passing before him was long enough to hint at a major campaign. Hundreds of men, at least. Perhaps thousands?

Behind him he could feel the Witch-Queen approach. Close, very close. The warmth of her body tickled against his back, though her flesh did not touch him. Something male inside him stirred in response.

"They head toward the High Kingdom." Her whisper was hot against his ear. "Knowing you are distracted right now and that your focus is elsewhere."

"Then they make dangerous assumptions." How much did Corialanus really know and how much was the Witch-Queen milking him for state secrets? Gwynofar's letter to him had passed through no other hands, his own witch had assured him of that. And as much as Salvator despised the Magisters, he knew that Ramirus would not have allowed Gwynofar's words to be leaked by any other means. The man he remembered from his childhood had always been meticulous about such matters. It was unlikely that anyone, Corialanus included, knew the truth of his intentions.

A finger stroked the length of his back, leaving a trail of fire in its wake. "They say you are a weak king who does not understand how much it will cost him to have turned the Magisters away. By the time Corialanus is ready to strike at your border it will be too late for you to send your armies there without a sorcerer's help. Will you compromise your ethics, then, and meet them in battle as Danton would have done, with your armies transported to battle by some Magister? So that all men know the weakness of your faith? Or will you cede them this victory, in the name of your god, and show the High Kingdom that you cannot defend its borders? Either way, your enemies will celebrate, for they will have won more than land or gold."

Silently he clenched his teeth. It took all his self-control to keep the dismay in his heart from showing on his face, but if there was one thing that a monk of the Creator learned early on, it was self-control.

It may not even be true, he reminded himself. *Thus far the only evidence of this is a dream sent by a witch.*

"What is your interest in this?" he demanded.

A long nail, razor-sharp, brushed against his cheek, delicately urging him to face her. "Right now Corialanus is part of the High Kingdom; as such it cannot act against your allies. As a free state, however, who knows how far her ambitions might extend? I value the current arrangement. It leaves me free to focus upon other things . . . more important things." Her lips were so close to his cheek that he could feel her breath on his skin. His groin tightened reflexively. "Our interests are allied in this, High King. Else why would I come here and warn you?"

Why, indeed? It was getting hard to think of the options. His body wanted another kind of conversation entirely.

Soft hands slid from the sides of his face down to his chest, creasing the fabric of his robe. Copper fingers banded with golden rings, copper skin as fine and as lustrous as Sengalese silk. Heat rushed to his loins as his body responded to her touch. *Never mind politics,* a voice seemed to whisper in his head. *Never mind treaties. Some alliances are sealed by sweeter stuff.*

She moved closer, sliding her arms up around his neck, drawing him down to her. Her body pressed close against his, the warm, full weight of her breasts a maddening enticement. Desire surged through his veins with a force that he could neither deny nor contain, and his hands moved of their own accord over her shoulders, along her back, and down over her hips and buttocks. Fingers hungry for her soft curves, her fierce heat. With a sigh of pleasure she began to move against him, slowly at first, then with greater strength, teasing the swollen flesh that was trapped between them. He reached down suddenly to grasp the soft silk of her skirt, sliding his hand beneath it, stroking the sleek copper skin of her inner thigh, seeking the moist heat that lay beyond. Never before had he desired a woman so desperately, so blindly. Never before had he felt so utterly out of control, as if his rational human self had somehow been consumed by a beast that knew only hunger and lust and cared nothing for human concerns.

She drew a leg up about his hips and he pushed aside his own clothes, thrusting inside her with a force that drove the air from her lungs in a gasp. Copper hands reached for his hair, drawing him down to her lips as he thrust harder and harder into her engulfing heat. Soft moans of pleasure were offered for him to devour and he kissed her fiercely, claiming them. Not afraid of hurting her because he knew somehow, in that primitive part of him that had been unleashed, that she was as strong as he was. Worthy allies, equal in passion. How they deserved one another! Not like the weak creatures marching below them who pretended to be men. Vermin from Corialanus, all of them, who played at being wolves while they crept up upon his territory like rats, thinking he did not notice. But he would show them. He would show them! The molten heat of masculine pride filled his veins to the breaking point and he clutched the Witch-Queen to him as images filled his brain, accompanying each wave of pleasure. His armies waiting at the north end of King's Pass. Surprising the enemy. Mountains drenched in blood. Sovereignty defended. His land! His empire! No man could take what was rightfully his! No enemy would dare to challenge him again once he had taught Corialanus the price of defiance!

(a strange bitterness on her lips, not right)

Strength proclaimed!

(foul odor mixed with sweet perfume)

Sovereignty assured!

(slick and cold, beneath the heat)

He knew something was wrong but he could not stop himself, nor rein in the beast that had been given control of his flesh. She cried out as he came at last inside her, not in pleasure but in triumph, and even as the waves of unbearable pleasure surged through his flesh he could feel her witchery taking hold of him. It was a cold and clammy thing that offered pleasure to the bestial parts of his brain if they would serve her will, and strangled those parts which might question what was happening. As the wild pounding of his heart began to subside at last he pushed her away from him, not knowing exactly what was wrong but knowing with certain instinct—*human* instinct—that he must fight it with all his strength.

How cold her eyes were now, with all the illusion stripped from them! Black jeweled eyes, without iris or white. Her silken dress had taken on an unwholesome sheen, like that of a wet eel, and the chiffon strips of her sleeves spread out like wings behind her, snapping in the wind. And the smell! No longer an offense limited to the earth and sky, it now seemed to emanate directly from her, like some foul perfume. And now it was on him as well. Soaked into his velvet gown, lathered along his loins. His whole body reeked of it.

"You have no power over me." He tried to pour all his strength into the words, but they came out no louder than a whisper. "I will not allow you to have power over me!"

"Salvator. Sweet Salvator." She reached out to touch his cheek but he pulled away from her. She seemed surprised by his defiance. Did she not realize that he had seen through her mask? That he had somehow broken free of her spell and was seeing her as she truly was? Not human any longer, but something alien and evil that made every fiber of his soul scream out in revulsion? "You have no choice in this. Don't you understand? The ancient drives are too strong to deny. Can't you feel them now, simmering inside you? Too long denied. My poor monk." Her voice dropped to a low whisper; she probably intended to sound seductive, but with his senses now alert to her corruption he could hear the echoes of baleful power behind it. "Forget the northern border," she breathed into his skin. "The real danger is here, in King's Pass. There is still time to redeploy. . . ." He could feel the words seeping in through his pores, wrapping themselves about his soul. So hard to think clearly. So hard to remember why Alkali mattered. . . .

No!

He jerked back from her. It took every ounce of strength that he had, and at first his legs would not even respond to him. He could feel her spells shattering like rotten silk as he struggled against them, the tapestry of their shared dream unraveling about them. Clouds shivered into nothingness overhead; the soldiers marching below lost their bodily cohesion and bled out into the surrounding scenery. Something wailed in the distance that didn't belong in any world, and then—still nameless—was silenced.

"You have no power over me," he repeated. His voice was stronger now; control of his body seemed to be returning, and with it confidence. Did she think he had wasted his four years in the monastery? Did she think a four-year vow of celibacy was lightly sworn or easily maintained, a casual flirtation with self-denial that would not affect the kind of man he became? He had faced down the beast within his own soul and vanquished it before; he could do so again if need be. Even in the midst of this cursed dream and with the sweat of her passion still clinging to his skin.

The smell in the air had changed now. No longer was it sweet, even in its undertones. Acrid fumes filled his nostrils and stung his eyes, making them water. He remembered what his mother had told him about the foul odor that had been in the palace when Kostas had lived there. Not a real smell, she had said, with a physical source that other men might notice, but something that only their family could detect.

Then the fabric of his dream came crashing down about him. Dark images flooded his brain, choked off his breath. He struggled to break free of them and surface. Somewhere beyond all this was the real world, the Creator's world, and he knew if he could just connect to it again this vile magic would lose its hold on him. Feverishly he prayed, using the familiar phrases to focus his mind and fortify his soul: *Holy Father, who created the world that man might live in it, and placed within us all the things that he requires. . . .* Slowly, oh, so slowly, the nightmare images began to fade. Black jeweled eyes. Amethyst wings. Soldiers marching north to claim his territory—

And a sudden pounding on the door.

He opened his eyes and blinked until they focused. The light of dawn had just begun to creep in through the windows, illuminating a chamber that looked jarringly normal. His bed was soaked with cold sweat, but it smelled refreshingly human. Whatever witchery had taken hold of his soul for a brief time, no trace of it remained.

He whispered his thanks to his god.

"Majesty! Are you all right?"

Before he could find his voice the door swung open, and two of his guards entered the room. One had already drawn a sword, and he seemed quite startled to discover there was no one in the room but the three of them. He peered suspiciously into all the corners of the room as his companion bowed nervously. "Forgive us for disturbing you, but Your Majesty cried out—"

Salvator waved him to silence. "I am fine. As you see. But I thank you for your concern."

They began to bow out of the room, but he signaled for them to wait. "I am done with sleeping for tonight," he told them, swinging his feet over the edge of the bed so that he might rise. "Order a cold breakfast laid out for me. And a bath. Cold as well. And for after that . . ." His eyes narrowed thoughtfully. "Order my council to attend me. We have much to discuss."

He wondered briefly what his mother would have made of his dream, but only briefly. In the end it was his faith in the Creator that had saved him, and his training among the holy brothers, not some mysterious gift that no man knew the name of.

Such strength could be yours as well, he thought to Gwynofar, *if you only would let go of empty legends.*

CHAPTER 28

THE THIRD Sister arose from a sea of morning mist like a whale breaking through the surface of the ocean. Fog filled the low points of the landscape, rendering everything all but invisible and wisps of it swirled like silken veils over all the rest. The sun was beginning to rise, the blackness of night just starting to drain out of the sky along the eastern horizon, and the first hint of morning light lent a ghostly glow to the edges of the fog drifts.

Gwynofar's company stood still for a long time, taking it all in. No doubt those who led the expedition were making precise calculations about how best to approach the Citadel in order to maximize their cover while not losing sight of necessary landmarks, but to Gwynofar's eye the view was simply magical, as if they were in some fairy realm and the object of their attention was rooted not in solid earth but in clouds and dreams.

"A while longer," the captain of the expedition ordered. "We need more light."

They were sheltered in the last sizeable patch of forest east of the citadel. They had reached it by moonlight alone, not daring to use any artificial light this close to their target. Fire could be seen from miles away in the night the captain had explained to Gwynofar. Even a single candle flame would be dangerous.

Now they were waiting for the moment when dawn would provide enough light that they could be sure of their footing, but no more. The air itself would seem heavy and gray, then, and from a distance land and sky would appear to merge into a single entity. The company had dressed with such surroundings in mind, setting aside their brightly colored uniforms for garments of gray, layered pieces daubed with paint to match the colors of the monument. Hopefully it would be enough for Ramirus' spell to be effective.

They already knew that his sorcery was working from the contact they'd had with a company of guards the day before. The locals had saluted them in passing, apparently not noting the various details that might have put a lie to their disguise, not least among them the fact that several of Kierdwyn's men had their hands on their swords, ready to draw them the instant there was any sign that they were not well received. But the meeting had passed without incident, Ramirus' sorcery muting the locals' suspicious instincts, making it seem that all was as it should be. Kamala's analysis of the Wrath's effect—and how the sorcerers might weave their spells around it—had apparently been accurate. They had all breathed a little easier after that.

But this part of the journey would test Ramirus' sorcery anew. It was one thing to pass for a guard when one looked like a guard, in a place where guards were doing what guards presumably were supposed to be doing. But no one should be traveling in this stretch of open land. No one should be climbing the tower. No mere disguise would convince Anukyat's men that the invaders belonged here if they were sighted in this phase of their operation. Thus the captain had called for making the approach in the tenuous light of early dawn, so that they would have some cover from the darkness while moving in, then full sunlight soon afterward to facilitate their climb.

When he thought conditions were right, the captain led them along a serpentine path, from one patch of mist to another. While they were inside the fog banks it was hard for Gwynofar to see any farther than the two men directly in front of her, and she had to trust to the column to keep its bearing and just follow blindly along. But that meant that from the outside they were all but invisible. Perhaps the gods were favoring this enterprise after all, she thought.

Quickly but carefully the company moved, leather boot soles slick against the wet grass, bits and pieces of climbing gear slapping softly against the backs and thighs of the men who carried them. Overhead—nearly invisible against the predawn sky—Kamala flew in erratic patterns while she watched for danger, wary of adopting any configuration that might reveal her interest in a particular stretch of ground beneath her. But there was no sign of trouble . . . yet.

As for the tower ahead of them, Gwynofar did not have time to look up at it yet. That was probably best. Fear would come in time, no doubt, but that did not mean she had to issue it a formal invitation. The magnitude of this undertaking was just starting to sink in. Even if fate favored them and they managed to get into the Citadel safely, climb it, and locate the so-called Throne of Tears—and channel its power properly—what were the odds they could withdraw safely after that and get home without incident? No one had ever asked the question aloud—at least in her presence—but she knew that they were all thinking it. Kamala in her bird form could carry word home of anything they discovered, but she could not carry people.

One thing at a time, she told herself. *Focus on what is before you.*

Finally they reached the base of the tower. The earth gave way to a rubbled slope and then to solid rock, cold and damp to the touch. The captain led the way up a short incline to a place where a jutting ledge overhead would block the view of any sentries above them. It was a larger protrusion than Gwynofar had expected it to be based on the images they'd studied in their preparations. In fact, all the sculptural features of the tower looked much larger up close than she had expected.

Which led her to finally peek out around the ledge and look up to see the true size of the thing.

Against the early morning sky it soared: majestic and arrogant, immeasurable. The first direct rays of dawn struck its summit even as Gwynofar watched, capping the tower in fire. The view was dizzying; it seemed to her that she could feel the weight of the massive monument looming over her, daring her to take its solidity for granted. Daring her to feel safe.

Rhys put a hand on her shoulder, directing her attention back to the business at hand. The men were already stripping off their outer boots, and she began to do the same. Lazaroth had provided them with special shoes for climbing, designed to the Guardians' specifications, as well as soft boots to wear over them while approaching the target. The leather of the tight climbing shoes was so thin that Gwynofar could feel the texture of the rock underfoot, and Lazaroth had added something to the soles that he said would give them a better grip. She tried to slide a foot forward along the dew-dampened rock, and it was surprisingly difficult. That discovery should have reassured her—it meant that one more bit of sorcery was working as it should— but in fact it did just the opposite. For the first time since their departure from Kierdwyn, the magnitude of their task suddenly struck home. She looked up at the monument again—its whole summit was glowing with golden light now, a blazing beacon against an ever-lightening sky—and thought, with a sudden wave of nausea, *that's where we are going*.

The first part of the climb would be along a series of angled formations, not much more challenging than some of the rock formations she had climbed as a young girl. But after that the monument became abruptly vertical with few handholds that she could see, and nothing to break a fall except the sharp rocks at the bottom. Ullar had decided that the best course of action was for his scouts to climb that part first, segment by segment, then pull her up behind them. Now that she saw the monument up close she was relieved to have such a plan. She remembered Ramirus' words of warning about her enhanced strength, and how it might affect her coordination, and she knew that the last thing she wanted to do was maneuver on that steep rock face alone.

Now Rhys came over and wrapped a thick piece of rope around her waist, knotting it so that there was a secure loop in front. Another man took all their discarded gear and tucked it into a shadowy crevice, covering it with a piece of gray cloth that matched their clothing. From a distance it should be all but invisible. Through all this they were silent. So silent. Each person knew what was required of him and did it, wary of offering up so much as a whisper of sound for the enemy to hear. There was no way they could predict when Ramirus' sorcery would or would not protect them; they would proceed as though there were nothing to protect them from discovery but their own stealth.

The need for silence had cost them one of their most valuable tools. Lazaroth's spikes had been tested on a rock outcropping the day before, and while they had worked well enough, they were far from silent. That hadn't seemed like an issue in Kierdwyn's castle, but here it could mean the difference between life and death. Too much risk, the captain had assessed. They could not afford to stress Ramirus' protective spell that much. Gwynofar hadn't been all that sure she agreed, but now that she was here, in the midst of this vast silence, she realized that he'd been right.

Which meant that the men would have to make their climb with nothing more than stubbornness and a few mundane tools to support them.

I believe in you, Rhys mouthed to Gwynofar as he tightened the last knot on her harness, and he kissed her on the forehead; she hugged him tightly, allowing herself the luxury of trembling in his arms for one last time. He would be nearby to protect her if anything went wrong.

Watching as the first climbers began their ascent, Gwynofar could not help but hold her breath. They moved with eerie agility, one limb at a time, clinging to such subtle cracks and protrusions that sometimes it was easier to believe they possessed a spider's power of adhesion than a human's clumsy grasp. At one point they abandoned handholds entirely, bracing their backs against one side of a vertical gap and their feet against the other, their bodies bridging the open space as they inched their way up the walls with nothing but friction and raw muscular strength keeping them in place. It was slow and painful work, and Gwynofar's body ached just watching them.

But they had left a trail of new handholds behind them, twists of rope that they had anchored into various crevices along the way for those who must follow. As the other men began to climb, the first two took shelter on a ledge high overhead. Once they had found a solid anchor for their ropes, they lowered one end to Gwynofar, and Rhys helped her hook it onto her belt. There was a pulley system to help distribute her weight as they pulled her up to the ledge, but that did not lessen the sensation of vertigo as the ground suddenly dropped from beneath her, or her instinctive panic when the motion of the rope swung her against a jagged outcropping. She did her best to keep in contact with the monument as she moved, bracing herself against it in order to stabilize her motion. It took enough concentration that she had no time to look down, which was probably a good thing.

When she reached the ledge two of the men lifted her up, positioning her with her back to the monument while they unhooked the pulley system from her belt and replaced it with a safety line. The lead climbers had already begun the next part of the ascent. Three more to go, she remembered. She was already high enough that looking down made her heart lurch in her chest. But that was good, right? Each new pitch meant that they were that much closer to their objective. And thus far no one had seen them.

We've gotten this far, she thought. *We're going to make it.*

She could not see Kamala anymore. But with the monument blocking her view in several directions, it was not something she was going to worry about.

Shutting her eyes, she waited for her turn at the next ascent.

Kamala was directly over the Citadel when she saw a man emerge on top of one of the towers, carrying a plain wooden box. He was not dressed like a guard, but wore a pricey gown of blue brocade that glittered with golden highlights when the first rays of the rising sun struck it. Probably one of the people in charge of this place. For one wild moment she was tempted to strike him down where he stood, but she knew the risk was too great. Such an action would raise alarms all over the Citadel. Brave as her companions were, she had no illusion about them being able to hold their own against the full might of Anukyat's forces in battle. Stealth was of paramount importance.

Her senses on high alert, she watched intently as he looked out across the landscape, studying the land in all directions. The sight of it made her blood run cold. Rhys' people had reached the base of the tower already and so were safely out of his line of sight. But if what this man wanted was a vantage point from which he might look out over the entire area, he might well decide to visit the upper chamber of the third Sister himself, or send others to do the job. And that would be very bad right now. Less than an hour ago Kamala had scouted the upper tower and confirmed to Rhys and his company that it was empty. Under normal circumstances it would probably stay that way. But this new variable could change everything.

Kamala watched as he leaned down to unlatch the box, reached inside, and came up holding a gray bird in his hands. He held it still for a moment, then raised up his hands and let go. The pigeon took to the air with a frenetic flurry of wings, clearly anxious to escape this place as quickly as possible. As it flew off southward, Kamala could see that there was some small object strapped to its leg.

A messenger pigeon.

She would have taken off after it immediately, but the man was still on the roof, watching it fly into the distance. If he saw a larger bird suddenly appear out of nowhere to snatch up his messenger, that would surely put him—and perhaps the whole Citadel—on high alert. But if the bird got too far for Kamala to catch up with it . . . well, that would depend upon what sort of message he was sending out. She felt her avian heart beating wildly as she waited, precious seconds passing with agonizing slowness. *Surely you have something better to do,* she urged him silently. *Go do it.*

By the time he finally went back inside the Citadel, the pigeon was so far away that chasing it down would not be a quick or easy task. Kamala did not want to leave her watch station for any length of time while Rhys' company was making its climb, but if Anukyat were trying to contact his allies, that was even more urgent. Some of those allies had very large wingspans and would have no trouble picking Rhys' men off the side of the great monument.

Which left her no real choice.

She took off like an arrow, following the small bird. Though her current form was not that of a predator built for speed, she was still a good deal larger than the pigeon, and the muscular beat of her wings slowly but surely began to close the gap between them. As she did so she made one attempt to strike it down with sorcery, as she had struck down the hare, but evidently she was too far away for that to work. Or perhaps she just could not manage the concentration needed while flying herself.

Or maybe it was a warning that she no longer had enough athra left in her consort to manage such a spell safely.

As she finally managed to get close to the bird it became

erratic in its flight, evading her best attempts to grab hold of it. Prey instinct. If she had been wearing the body of a hawk, perhaps she would have known how to compensate for it. Precious seconds passed while she struggled to compensate for its instinctive tactics. It seemed like hours. At last she dug her talons squarely into the pigeon's body, holding on with all her strength as it began to flap wildly, trying to break free. It took all her skill to keep from being dragged out of the sky as she tried to kill the thing, as the body she had made for herself was not designed for killing. Finally, in frustration, she let loose a bit more transformative sorcery, and this time it did what it was supposed to. As the mangled body went limp beneath her she grabbed hold of the message tube with her beak and tore it loose, letting the rest of the bird fall. Finally!

Turning sharply, she began to fly with all her strength back to the Citadel, hoping that her absence would not cost the company too dearly.

Kamala should have reported in by now, Rhys thought.

He held Gwynofar steady while the first four warriors slipped into the tower. Or perhaps more accurately, they *scraped* into the tower. The jagged crevice that gave them access to the interior was big enough for a grown man to squeeze through, but barely. Garments and gear scraped against the raw edges of the opening as the warriors forced their way through, and one man had to divest himself of some of his climbing gear in order to fit. When Gwynofar's turn finally came she went through much more easily, but her legs were trembling so badly by the time she dropped inside that Rhys had to help support her. All the fear of the past few hours was finally hitting home, he guessed.

But that was fine. She'd managed the ascent well enough, which was the part that mattered most. Any trouble that turned up now the warriors would deal with.

Quickly the men rearranged their gear, making sure all their weapons were ready at hand. They worked as quickly and quietly as possible, but in the close confines of the tower every sound seemed to echo back at them and it was hard to imagine anyone else who might be inside could fail to hear them.

The inside of the tower was much as Kamala had described it, with a vast spiral staircase carved into the native stone, wide enough for two men abreast if all they did was walk, but uncomfortably close quarters for combat. The situation clearly didn't please Ullar's men, but they'd chosen their weapons accordingly and were ready to fight for every step if necessary. Hopefully there was no one above them to get in the way. As for coming down again later . . . that was something none of them really wanted to think about. Could they find this relic and uncover its secrets without any of the locals knowing that they were here? Much less hope for a clean retreat afterward?

Stay with Gwynofar once we reach the throne, Rhys had told Kamala. *See what she sees, learn what she learns, commit to memory all that happens to her. You may well be the one who has to carry that information back to Kierdwyn so that others can act upon it.*

So where was Kamala now? She should have reported in before this, if for no other reason then to confirm that the upper levels were still unoccupied. She had given them the go-ahead on that count before they started climbing, but he would have liked to have it confirmed. So much depended upon that one condition.

He looked over the men, bristling with weapons and determination, and thought, *there is no going back now.* Any confrontation on the staircase was bound to be brutal, but Ullar's men looked ready for it. Even eager. Hanging off the side of a monolith for several hours while waiting to see if Souleaters would show up to pick them off wasn't the kind of operation they'd been trained for. But for the Guardians . . . well, that was precisely what they had been trained for, and Rhys knew that if a Souleater had shown up they would have given it a damned good fight, even if they had to do it hanging from ropes.

As they separated into two groups, preparing for the next phase of the operation, he saw one of the Guardians moving his lips silently. Probably praying. A cold knot formed in Rhys' gut and he had to fight the impulse to tell the man that his faith was misplaced. No god cared about this battle one way or the other. And if the enemy fell upon them now, no god would lift a metaphysical finger to help them.

Faith is the core of their strength, he told himself harshly. *Shatter the illusion and you strip them of that strength.*

How he envied them the comfort of their ignorance!

Moving quickly up the staircase, sandwiched between four warriors ahead of them and four behind, Rhys stayed close by Gwynofar's side, ready to help her if she needed it. She struggled gamely to keep up with the men and gave no sign of being either tired or worried. Indeed, when one of the soldiers glanced back at her to see how she was doing, she beamed back at him with such confidence that Rhys knew the man's own courage was bolstered. That was always her gift, he thought—giving strength to others—and never had it been needed more than now.

Then, just as they had completed a their second turn of the staircase and were passing by another one of the jagged windows, the sudden flutter of wings drew them up short.

Kamala.

For a moment she didn't say anything. And that said it all. Rhys felt his stomach knot, and it took all his self-control to keep his voice steady as he asked, "How many are there?"

"Six that I could see," the bird rasped. Barely a whisper, but the words were significant enough that no one missed them.

"Chamber or stairs?"

"Chamber."

Six men could easily hold the upper chamber against an assault from below, given its configuration. The knot in Rhys' stomach tightened.

The captain asked quietly, "Do they know we are here yet?"

"I don't think so," the bird responded. "They are looking for something outside the tower."

Signs of our passage, Rhys thought grimly. Ramirus' sorcery had prevented the enemy from inspecting them too closely, but the trail they left behind would be fair game. And if the Alkali started looking too closely at the tower itself they would realize what must have happened. There were signs of it, if one looked in the right places.

Time was running out.

"Were they guarding the entrance?" the captain asked.

Kamala thought for a moment, then shook her head.

The captain's expression was grim. "We still have Ramirus' protection." He kept his voice to a half whisper so that his voice would not carry beyond the small company. "Though we don't know how effective it will be in this place. That might enable us to breach the upper chamber, though we shouldn't count on it protecting us once they are alerted to our presence." His eyes narrowed as he took in their painted gray garments, so obviously out of place in this setting. Maybe Ramirus' spell would be up to the task of masking such a thing, maybe not. The Citadel might even have defensive sorcery of its own, cast in a happier time, that negated such spells entirely. They would not know until they put their lives on the line to test it.

It is all or nothing now, Rhys thought grimly. And with that knowledge came a cold and compelling certainty: *I am ready to die.*

"I will go first," he said.

The captain shook his head. "You stay with the queen. This is our task."

Gwynofar nodded. If she understood how desperate their situation had just become, she gave no outward sign of it. "Where do you want us?"

"At the rear. If we can take the upper chamber, you will follow us. If not . . ." His expression was grim.

"I will see to her safety," Rhys promised. Brave-sounding words; did Gwynofar sense how little substance there was behind them? If these men failed in their assault, her only hope would be a rapid retreat. To where? For what purpose? The task they had come to do could not be left undone. Too much depended upon it. Where was there to go, once the enemy knew they were here?

The captain nodded grimly, then looked at the bird. "Let us know if anything changes."

Kamala bobbed her head once and headed back out the window.

"All right then." The captain shut his eyes for a moment, his lips moving silently in prayer. "The will of the gods be done," he whispered at last. And he nodded for his men to begin their ascent.

The six Alkali guards didn't know exactly what Master Anukyat had sent them to the top of the tower to find, but they could guess the cost of coming back without it. "Search land and sky for anything unnatural," he had ordered them. "Anything that might indicate an attempt to use sorcery."

Several of the guards muttered imprecations under their breath as they stared out the narrow windows in the observation chamber, trying to figure out just what that was supposed to mean in a land where the Wrath made just about everything seem unnatural. What did sorcery look like anyway? Last they'd all heard it couldn't be used in this region at all, so what did that make of their master's request?

As one of the guards turned his attention from one empty vista to another, he thought he saw motion out of the corner of his eye in the center of the room. Someone else was coming up from below to assist them. That was just wonderful, he thought. More help doing nothing. He opened his mouth to make a sardonic comment as he turned to greet the newcomer, but the words never got out of his mouth.

The man was dressed in shades of mottled gray, unlike any clothing the guard had ever seen, and he carried a short sword in one hand and a small round shield in another. His posture was likewise inappropriate, betraying the kind of innate muscular tension that would normally presage combat. But what was there to fight up here? And why was he wearing those outlandish garments? It seemed to him that he should be able to figure that out, but his mind seemed loath to focus on the problem.

Then the newcomer stepped forward to make way for another to follow him, and something inside the guard snapped into focus.

"To arms—" he called out, and he might have said more had

the stranger not swung his sword at that moment. The blade whipped across his throat in a blinding arc, and when it passed through there was no more sound possible. Choking on blood as he sagged to his knees, the guard saw his companions turning to face the invasion just in time. A second man was inside the room now, and he was just as oddly dressed and well-armed as the first. And there was a third warrior making the ascent behind him. *Someone is attacking the tower,* the wounded man thought, as everything faded into darkness. And in his last conscious moment: *Why?*

The spilling of blood seemed to awaken them all to the danger they were in and their martial training kicked in. Three of the guards grabbed spears from their brackets on the wall and brought them to bear upon the staircase, determined to drive back the third invader and then keep anyone else from entering the chamber. Gods alone knew how many there were on the staircase below preparing to join the assault! But the man refused by be intimidated by their bristling weaponry, and deftly turned one thrust aside with the shield on his left arm, while his sword parried another. His movements were clean and minimal, and he turned about as he fought, making it harder for one of them to get behind him. Step by step he cleared his way up into the room and the best of their efforts did not seem able to stop him.

All the Alkali were drawing their weapons now, released from whatever spell had previously dulled their senses. But the loss of initiative had already cost them dearly. Treading in puddles of blood from their fallen comrades, the remaining pair attacked the other invaders fiercely, unwilling to cede a moment's advantage. Blood flowed from an arm on one side, a leg on the other, as gleaming steel blades played back and forth, snaking past shield and parry on both sides. One of the Alkali nearly lost his footing on a blood slick and an attacker was quick to take advantage of it, his own soft shoes gripping the floor with supernatural tenacity as he thrust his blade through the man's forward shoulder, severing vital muscles. But the Alkali just took up his sword in his other hand and kept fighting, a look of grim determination on his face. *Blood will not stop me,* it warned, *nor pain.*

Then one of the lancers managed to get through the guard of the third invader, driving his spear in under his raised arm and deep into his torso. He could feel the blade grating on bone as he forced it home, and was rewarded with a gush of fresh blood for his efforts. Pinned, the man could no longer maneuver away from his Alkali opponents, and another thrust forward and opened a gash in his neck as well. As the body slumped, twitching, the third man grabbed hold of it and dragged it into the room, so that no one below could use it to shield himself as he attempted to follow. For a fraction of a second the gauntlet of spears was compromised and a fourth attacker began to rush up the staircase. But the first guard jerked his weapon free and turned to guard the entranceway, and in concert with his companions they forced the invader back down into the depths of the tower.

And then one of the Alkali did something that should have been done earlier. Stepping back from the battle, he reached for a horn that hung between two windows. One of the invaders realized what he was doing and lunged to stop him, but he was too late. Another Alkali rammed into the invader from the side, forcing him out of the way. Out of reach.

The guard put the horn to his lips and blew.

The sound was piercing, a shrill note that reverberated from the stone walls and rang out across the courtyard far below.

Men began to pour out of the Citadel, grabbing up arms as they headed for the base of the tower. Whoever or whatever was behind this assault, they would soon find themselves outflanked. With their entrance into the chamber cut off and the tower about to be stormed from below, the invaders would not last long. All the Alkali had to do now was delay these two long enough for reinforcements to arrive, and all the rest would follow.

Dropping the horn, the Alkali let out a roar of rage, raised his sword high, and rejoined the battle.

The sound of the alarm call reverberated through the monument. Rhys cursed under his breath and descended half a turn to where a narrow crevice offered him a limited view of the citadel's courtyard. Looking outside, he cursed again.

Their access to the upper chamber had effectively been cut off. Three men now had tried to force their way up through the narrow entrance; one was presumed dead and the other two, severely wounded, had been forced to withdraw. In time the men who had succeeded in invading the chamber might find a way provide their brothers with an opening but for now, they had run out of time.

How slowly the world seemed to move, in that one moment. Slowly enough that when Rhys looked up at his companions, the silent communication between them encompassed all their options, played out to every possible conclusion. In the time it took to draw a single breath every course was weighed, every outcome evaluated.

Short of a miracle, they were going to die here.

Beneath them now they could hear other noises within the

tower. Voices. Footsteps. The sound of steel being drawn. All resonating in the staircase like echoes in a tomb.

It cannot end here, Rhys thought.

Gwynofar's face was white. She, too, required no words to understand what had happened. Or what sort of fate it must inexorably lead to.

She might even be spared, he thought. Taken captive, a vulnerable vessel from which all the group's secrets could presumably be squeezed, by Magisters if not by common torture. Later a hostage in the great war to come, used against her own people to undermine their strength and their purpose.

He saw her hand move to the knife at her belt. Saw the resolve in her eyes.

My beloved sister, there is as much courage in you as in any of these warriors.

Then he saw the window behind her. It was one of the larger ones, a deep crevice nearly as tall as a man, but far too narrow for any man to pass through. A slender woman, though, might just squeeze through. Barely.

She followed his gaze. The last color drained from her face. "Rhys—"

The sounds from below were closer now. Too close. The men began to take up a defensive posture. As if it would do anything but delay the inevitable.

"There is no other way," he told her.

"But you—"

"My fate lies here," he told her. "Yours has yet to be resolved."

Do not let us die in vain.

As if she had heard his thoughts, she nodded. He could see her trembling, but she did not hesitate as he cupped his hands to give her a lift up to the crevice. For a moment it looked like she would say something more to him, but there was simply no time for it. The noises from below were too close now.

With a brief kiss to his forehead, she stepped up to the opening.

He did not watch as she began to squeeze her way out through the narrow crack. There was no time for such luxuries. If she was to get safely away, Rhys would have to provide a distraction. He could not risk the enemy coming upon them here, where she was still visible.

Grimly, he gestured for the other Guardians to join him. No words were necessary. They all understood.

There was a time when he might have prayed first. A time when he had believed that someone or something listened to such prayers and cared about what happened to him. Now he had no prayers left in his heart, but in their place was something equally powerful. A willingness to die. Perhaps even a hunger for it.

Letting loose a battle cry that shook the very walls of the tower, he led his fellow Guardians in a charge down the staircase to earn Gwynofar as much time as he could with his death.

———

Squeezing out through the narrow crevice, Gwynofar saw the whole of Alkali spread out before her. It took every ounce of self-control she had not to hesitate. But survival—and the gods—had offered her no alternative.

They gave their lives to bring me this far. I cannot fail them now.

Turning to one side, she grabbed hold of a pillarlike formation that flanked the window and, with a whispered prayer, pulled herself around it. Her toes wedged themselves into a crack too small to think about, while her hands struggled to grab hold of a small horizontal ridge overhead for balance. Behind her she could hear a terrible war cry—was that Rhys?— and then the sound of warriors passing by the window she had just exited. She pressed herself close to the rock, praying for their safety. And hoping that when the enemy got this far they would not think to look outside and find her here. But why should they? What kind of insane creature would come out here without the proper equipment, planning, or experience? Such a move would be downright suicidal, wouldn't it?

For a moment she just stayed where she was, gripping the stone with all her might, trying to gather her courage. Her heart was pounding so hard she could feel it pulse in her fingertips. *Don't look down*, she told herself, fighting the sudden wave of vertigo that threatened to overcome her at the very thought. *Just don't look down.*

Finally, when she felt she could move her head without being sick, she looked around for anything nearby that she might grab hold of to help her move farther away from the window. For a moment the sheer magnitude of the task was so overwhelming that all the strength seemed to leak out of her limbs; a sudden gust of wind broadsided her and she nearly lost her balance. How was she supposed to climb up from here? What route would get her to the top? Trembling, she tried to remember the detailed drawings she had seen of the monument back in the planning stages of this trip, but she didn't even know what window she had come out of, from that perspective. How was she to get her bearings?

A sudden flapping sound overhead startled her and for a moment she feared it was a Souleater approaching. But no, the sound was closer than that, and smaller. Her heart pounding, she turned her head carefully to look for the source.

Kamala.

The gray-and-black bird was perched on a narrow ledge some distance overhead, beating the rock with her wings to get the queen's attention. When she saw that Gwynofar was finally looking up at her, Kamala inched sideways along the ledge to a point midway between two narrow windows. And then she stopped there, and cocked her head to one side. For a moment Gwynofar just stared at her, unable to make sense of the strange dance. Then she nodded her understanding. Kamala could see the whole of the monument from her avian perspective and had picked the best route for her. She would have to trust in it.

Drawing in a deep breath, wiping her hands one after the other on the fabric of her shirt so as to keep them as dry as possible, Gwynofar began to climb. Inch by inch she struggled to find some purchase for her grip, slender fingers working their way into cracks and around protrusions wherever she could find them, trying to remember how the other climbers had moved and to get her own body to do the same. Her altered muscles ached from the unaccustomed effort, but they did not fail her. Thank Ramirus for that.

How she envied the climbers their ropes! How much she wished she had even one safeguard in place, even one hint of a safety net right now, that might grant her the illusion of safety!

The wind was beginning to intensify now, and gusted past her with increasing force; somewhere not too far away a storm must be gathering. She tried not to think about what would happen if it started raining while she was still out here. *One thing at a time*, she told herself fiercely. *Focus on the task at hand.* At least Anukyat's men were not following her yet. Gods willing, Rhys and his men would be able to deal with them. Rhys . . . she had to blink tears out of her eyes before she could move again. *Please keep him safe,* she prayed to her gods, more afraid for him than she had ever been for himself. She could not bear to lose him now. Not like this.

You can't afford to think about him now. You can't afford to think about anything but climbing.

It seemed to take forever to climb up to the ledge that Kamala had indicated; by the time she got there she was thoroughly winded and had to stop to catch her breath. Mercifully, the top of the monument was more weathered than the lower reaches had been, offering more handholds for her to work with. But even that would not have saved her if Ramirus had not enhanced her capacity so that she was physically up to the task.

By the time she finally reached the place where Kamala waited, the muscles of her arms felt as if they were on fire and she knew that it was only his sorcery that was keeping her body from doubling over with cramps.

She paused for a minute to catch her breath, then edged out onto the narrow ledge that Kamala had indicated. Slowly she inched along on the inside edges of her feet, her body pressed close to the stone, hands grasping for anything they could find to hold onto. At one point the rock beneath her right foot broke away and her heart almost stopped, but she managed to hang on solidly enough to shift her weight back to her other foot and kept her balance. After a few shaky breaths she inched her right foot out again, trembling, and found solid purchase beyond the break. She tested it a few times with her toes before trusting her weight to it, painfully aware of her lack of experience. Would she even know what a rotten ledge felt like if she tested one? But when she finally committed her full weight to the move, the rock held beneath her and she slowly released the breath she'd been holding as she began to make progress once more.

Finally the ledge widened out a bit, almost enough for her to fit her whole foot onto it. A welcome luxury. She worked her way slowly around a narrow column, body scraping against the rough rock; she saw that she was leaving a thin smear of blood behind her, but she didn't have the luxury of stopping to see where it was coming from. At last she reached a shelter of sorts, a deep vertical groove that ran between two of the columns, large enough for her body to fit inside. The ledge she'd been following widened out into a platform there, big enough for her to stand up comfortably. She tucked herself into the shadows gratefully, wedging herself in tightly enough that nothing short of an earthquake should be able to dislodge her . . . and then the tears came. She let them flow. Gods alone knew if the others were still alive, but even if they were the whole of the mission rested on her shoulders now.

Finally she wiped the wetness from her face with a torn and grimy sleeve and gathered herself to face the task at hand. *Need to be strong. Need to keep going.* Once her vision cleared she could see why Kamala had directed her to this place. Her shelter was the lower end of a narrow chimney, scored by a series of diagonal faults that would provide a wealth of handholds going up. Climbing it, she would be surrounded by solid stone on three sides, as opposed to open air. A comforting illusion of safety, at least.

I can do this, she thought. And then: *I have to do this.*

There was a sudden squawk from Kamala, a clear alarm. Startled, Gwynofar pressed herself back into the shadows of the chimney as fast as she could. As she did so she could see shadows moving in the area she had just left. Was someone going to follow her out the window? She didn't dare lean far enough forward to be sure. Heart pounding wildly, she tried to make herself as small as possible and drew up her arms in front of her face, so that the coarse gray wool of her shirt would help hide the gleaming pallor of her skin. One second passed. Two. An eternity of waiting, while the cold wind whistled across the front of her rocky shelter. Finally the bird cheeped again, softly this time, and then fluttered down to a perch next to her and whispered, "Stay here."

She nodded.

Kamala began to move around the monument, peering intently around each obstacle before going past it, as if searching for something in particular. Her plumage was so perfectly matched to the color and texture of the tower that once she got more than ten yards away it was all but impossible to see her. Eventually she ducked into the shadow of a deep vertical crack and Gwynofar lost sight of her completely.

Wait, she told herself. *Just wait. She knows what she's doing.*

There were other sounds she could hear now that she was still, carried to her by the wind. Banging sounds. Clashing sounds. Shouting. She could not help but think of the men that she had left behind, fighting for their lives within the monument. Offering up their life's blood to give her the time she needed to reach the uppermost chamber.

Their sacrifice must not be in vain.

Finally the soft scratching of talons above her head alerted her to Kamala's return.

"There have been guards at some of the windows," she whispered to Gwynofar. "Checking for trouble on this side of the monument. I don't think they saw you. You should be able to go straight up this chimney, almost to the top, and you'll be invisible from most vantage points."

"The fighting. Is it . . . ?" She couldn't finish the question.

"I don't know," the bird said shortly and then she flapped her wings and moved to a distant perch. Too far away for any more questions.

Drawing in a deep breath, Gwynofar began to climb again. It was easier now, with the solid wall of the chimney to brace herself against, but her arms ached from the day's exertions, and her hand had been scraped badly enough that it was starting to ooze blood along the palm. She rubbed it against her clothing whenever she could to dry it off, but sometimes that just wasn't possible.

At last, trembling from exhaustion, she reached the top of the narrow channel, where a jutting formation overhead cut off any hope of further progress. Wedging herself into the tight space beneath it, she took a moment to catch her breath as the bird flew off into the distance once more. Every muscle in her body was shaking from exhaustion now; she prayed that Ramirus' sorcerous enhancements would last long enough to get her to her objective.

Then the bird was back. "This way," it whispered, and then added, "there are no guards."

The transverse course was a more generous ledge, nearly as wide as her feet. Slowly she worked her way along it until she felt the stone wall beneath her outstretched hand give way to empty space. A window. Her legs were shaking as she worked her way over to it, and at last she was able to grasp the edge of the opening solidly enough to pull herself into it. It was a tight fit, more so than she had anticipated, and there was no question that the men in their company could not have made it through with armor on. She was forced to wriggle out of her own harness first, prying at the knots with trembling fingers until they finally gave way. Even then the window was so narrow that the rough stone scraped her flesh painfully as she forced her way through and she could feel the warm trickle of blood along her back.

But she was inside at last.

She fell to the floor and for a moment could do no more than lie there, panting for breath. But only for a moment. Gods alone knew how little time she had before the locals came up here and found her; she had to do what she had come for before that happened.

Raising herself up from the floor on trembling hands, she looked around at the chamber. It was round, with tall, narrow windows at irregular intervals; if they were man-made, there had been no effort to make them uniform in shape. She could see now that Kamala had led her to the widest of all the windows; it was doubtful she could have fit through any of the others. She was dimly aware of a heavy trap door to one side of her, no doubt leading down to the observation chamber the men had tried to storm earlier. But she did not stop to look at that. She did not stop to look at anything more, save the item that was in the middle of the room.

Draped in black oilcloth and a thick layer of dust, it was at least as tall as she was, and wider than her outstretched hands. She felt a thrill rush through her veins as she reached out to grab hold of the cloth cover; it looked like no one had touched the thing for years. Getting a good grip on it with both hands, she pulled as hard as she could. Clouds of dust filled the room and set her to coughing; for a moment it was not possible to see anything at all.

Then the dust cleared and the Throne of Tears was before her in all its darksome glory.

It was regal and elegant and indisputably grotesque; the very sight of it sent a cold chill down her spine. At first glance it seemed to be carved from polished ebony, but where sunlight played over its surface it raised cobalt highlights that pooled upon its surface like puddles of oil. The seat and back of the throne were covered in polished leather of the same color, with a glistening texture. The arms and legs terminated in a ball-and-claw motif, but in the place of carved wood, long, curving teeth had been set into them, their ivory enamel in stark contrast with the fist-sized globes of black crystal that they grasped.

And then there were the wings. They fanned outward from the back of the chair like silk veils frozen in midmotion: impossibly delicate, chillingly beautiful. The beams of sunlight that passed through them were filtered as if through stained glass, sending shards of color streaming across the walls and floor and ceiling of the chamber.

For a moment Gwynofar was mesmerized by the sight of the terrible sculpture. Was this truly the last hope of her people? She trembled to consider what manner of power might be vested in such a thing, or what the price might be of awakening it. But there was no other choice. Men had died to give her this opportunity; she could not let them down.

Breathing deeply, she stepped up onto the stone dais that supported the ghastly seat and muttered a final prayer under her breath, bracing herself for whatever the gods might require of her. And then she sat down in it, running her hands down the arms of the great chair until her fingers slid between the polished teeth, grasping the jeweled globes with her own pale fingers.

Nothing happened.

All the dangers of the past few days did not strike such terror into her heart as that single moment of failure. All the planning that had been required to bring her here, all the lives that had been risked—and possibly lost—to make this possible . . . was that all to be wasted? *No*, she thought fiercely. Defiantly. *Not possible!* She grasped the arms of the throne in her hands and squeezed them, willing the grotesque throne to respond to her. Still nothing happened.

What was wrong? Was she not the right candidate after all? Had the ancient magics faded over time? Or had they interpreted the prophecy incorrectly?

There were muffled sounds coming from beneath the trap door now. Kamala had managed to shut the iron bolt on the trap door, but that would only work for so long. Armed men with enough determination could surely break through.

What had the prophecy said, exactly? Gwynofar struggled to remember the exact words.

> *Birthright in balance, Seven together,*
> *Offered as one in the eagle's nest*
> *Upon a chair of bones and wings. . . .*

"Blood," the bird said abruptly.

Kamala was right, Gwynofar thought. The *lyr* birthright was measured in blood; it would be an appropriate offering.

She took her bruised hand and dragged it against point of one of the chair's talons; her flesh tore open and blood began to flow freely. She let drops of it fall upon the claws of the chair and the black globes they grasped. Upon the center of the seat. Upon the back. She located every carved motif on the thing that might provide an appropriate site for blood sacrifice and offered up prayers as she smeared her *lyr* blood on each one. But still nothing happened, no matter what she did. Not even when she sat in the bloody chair afterward, willing all her innate magic into it. Still nothing.

The voices were less muffled now. Alkali voices, approaching from below.

Tears of frustration ran down her face . . . and tears of fear as well. Could it be that the sacrifice of her life was required in order to unlock the throne's secrets? Was that what the prophecy was hinting at? It was the only other thing that she could think of.

"All right!" she whispered fiercely. "Take it! Take me! My blood, my life . . . whatever you require! Only give the *lyr* what they need. Show them how to fight these creatures!"

She closed her eyes, trembling. And waited for the dire magic of the throne to devour her soul.

Nothing happened.

Despair came crashing down around her. In her worst fears she had never imagined that her quest would end like this: sitting on the legendary throne, prepared to make whatever sacrifice was required to awaken its power, and not having a clue how to do so.

What if the Wrath itself were responsible, she thought suddenly. What if the same baleful power that had befouled all other magic in this region had affected this priceless artifact as well? Then all their efforts would have been wasted and there was truly no hope.

I won't believe that. There must be a way. . . .

Someone banged on the underside of the trap door, startling her. The bolt held it closed for now, but how long would that last?

Gods of the Wrath, she prayed, *have mercy upon your servant. Tell me what I must do.*

But there was no answer.

The trap door thudded heavily as someone below tried to break it open; the sudden force shook the iron bolt, loosening its mooring. A rush of hot fear surged through Gwynofar. How many men had died to get her this far? How many more would die in the coming war, if the *lyr* could not access their god-given powers? She could not fail them all.

Gods of the Wrath, she prayed desperately, *whatever price is required for this knowledge, I willingly pay it. My life, my soul, all that I possess . . . all of it is yours. Freely offered in sacrifice, on behalf of my people. Take from me whatever is required, that the* lyr *may learn the name of their gift. . . .*

A cold wind seemed to stir in the room. She drew in a sharp breath and closed her eyes, trying to shut out the voices from below. The arms of the throne were growing warm beneath her touch, its heat filling her lungs as she drew in a long, trembling breath—

And then, suddenly, she understood.

The child.

Her body stiffened reflexively, she put a hand over her stomach, as if to protect the child within.

No!

It was Danton's child who defied the prophecy. Not because he was tainted by sorcery—Ramirus had assured her that was not the case—but simply because he was what he was: his father's child. Half his heritage was *lyr*, but the other half was not; that alien inheritance was now wedded to her flesh. Gwynofar could not sacrifice her own life without offering up his life as well. And he did not satisfy the conditions of the prophecy.

"No," she whispered. Remembering her other lost children,

lying dead at her feet in a pool of blood. A part of her soul had died that day. "Don't ask this of me. . . ."

But it was too late.

The trap door jerked upward, forcing the bolt partway out of its mooring. "Who is in there?" a voice demanded from below. "Open this door!"

And then the voices were gone, and all the noises of the world outside, and there was only a terrible silence within her . . .

. . . and memory.

His strength will never be measured, Ramirus had told her, *but he will test the strength of others. He will attend upon death without seeing it, change the fate of the world without knowing it, and inspire sacrifice without understanding it.*

Kostas had understood the power of such a pregnancy. That was why he had baited Danton into raping her, and had used his own sorcery to guarantee conception. As long as the High King's son was wedded to her flesh she could not manifest her full potential as *lyra*. Oh, the vile creature couldn't possibly have known how important Gwynofar's unique heritage would turn out to be, but on the eve of the Souleater's return, any *lyr* who might be neutralized was one less enemy to worry about later. The fact that her poor innocent child now held the fate of the world hostage was something none of them could have foreseen.

Don't ask this of me, she begged silently. But the offer had already been made, and could not be recalled.

Pain lanced through her abdomen as the trap door slammed open. With a cry she doubled over in pain, as her body struggled to protect the child it had nurtured for so long. But the power of the throne—or the gods—was stronger. A rough hand grabbed her arm as her womb convulsed—

And then something bright and terrible exploded inside her. Power, raw and unfettered, surged through her with such unexpected force that it drove the air from her lungs. The hand that had grabbed hold of her arm fell away, and from somewhere in the distance she heard a man's cry of pain. But she could not focus on anything outside her own flesh now. A firestorm had taken root in her soul and molten power poured through her veins, agony and ecstasy combined into one terrible conflagration.

Just when she thought that her body could not contain it any longer, the power burst out of her, flooding the world beyond with its fire. It surged through the souls of the men surrounding her, then into the guards who waited below, and into all the inhabitants of the Citadel . . . she could feel it as it swallowed each new soul, spitting out those very few who had no northern blood in their veins, claiming all the others. Into the Alkali Protectorate it surged, where thousands cried out in fear and pain as the power suddenly claimed them at their tables, at their work, in their beds. Into the other Protectorates it rushed, and beyond them. Into the High Kingdom and past it, to all the continents beyond, claiming every man, woman, and child whose heritage bound them to the *lyr*. Gwynofar could sense the moment when the power first touched Salvator, and she could taste his terror. She could feel it envelop her other children in rapid succession, and then each of her grandchildren in his turn, down to the tiniest newborn babe in his cradle. Each one taken by surprise as the mystical fire poured into them, engulfed too swiftly to protest or resist it.

And then the power paused, and for a moment it seemed to Gwynofar that she sat at the heart of a vast burning web that covered the whole of the earth, whose fiery strands bound each new *lyr* into a vast and complex pattern. She could sense the anchor cords that connected her soul to each of the seven founding bloodlines, perfectly balanced in strength and tenor. Had it been unbalanced, she realized, the forces involved would have torn the whole construct to pieces, and her along with it.

But how perfect a construct it was! Each new bit of soulfire that the throne's power absorbed fed its strength into the greater whole, be it borrowed from the spirit of a true *lyr*, born and bred for power, or from some long-forgotten descendant with only the faintest echo of northern blood in his veins. All of them were bound together now in a vast metaphysical conflagration, as if their souls had joined hands together for strength and support.

And then the images came. Rushing into Gwynofar's head with a force that threw her back against the throne, traveling down the lines of inheritance to every other soul in the burning web, drowning them all in a flood of memory so powerful that every other thought was extinguished, leaving only—

—*Wingshadows passing low over the farmlands, fertile fields made barren by abandonment. A young boy sleeps by his plow, perhaps forever; his body twitches as the demon's shadow passes over him. In the distance his family gathers—what is left of his family—for a meal of dried tubers and rotten berries, the best they could gather from fields long since gone wild. Rats in the corner have eaten their way through the burlap bag that guards their stores, but no one notices. No one has the energy to notice. The war with the rats cannot be won because they are stronger than men now; the winged demons have reordered nature to suit their hunger—*

—*Winter's cordwood running out and all there is left to burn for heat is furniture, artwork, books. Why mourn their loss? There is no need for such things anymore. An ax lies unused by the door, for none have the strength—or perhaps strength of will—to wield it. The child in the cradle shivers in his sleep, but will not awaken. The strength has been sucked out of its soul, and all that is left now in an empty shell, too weak to dream of its mother's lost milk—*

—Golden cities stripped of their burnish by time and neglect, overgrown with weeds. Proud stone temples robbed of their marble for building supplies, for projects abandoned in their turn. Ebony idols broken apart for fuel. Priceless tapestries torn to pieces when all other clothing is gone, or else perhaps laid out whole upon the earth to serve as bedding, until time and damp rot them away—

—Staggering across the dying landscape, a handful of survivors struggle to find others of their kind before it is too late. A lone demon circles high overhead, picking at their souls like a carrion bird tearing at rotting meat, but it cannot devour these spirits as quickly or as easily as it does the souls of other men. A gift of the gods? Or merely a quirk of nature? One of the survivors falls and does not get up, but the others are stronger. More determined. They expend enough energy to build him a cairn—itself an act of defiance—and then persist in their journey. Somewhere there must be others like them, resistant to the power of the demons, perhaps even a few who are wholly immune—

—Weaker ones left behind in the towns they pass through, stronger ones invited to join them. North they travel, seeking the comfort of cold skies and snowbound fields, in the sunless lands that the demons despise. Men and women of different colors, different shapes, different languages. Sometimes a handful from one town, sometimes only a single traveler, desolate among strangers. Children

among them as well, running to keep up. Gaunt faces, haunted eyes. Some of the young ones have left their parents far behind, while others drag them along behind them like oversized dolls, not understanding that the spirit within them has long since expired—

—Witches screaming out their power to the skies, sculpting vast illusions with their final breath. Monstrous images with cobalt scales and stained-glass wings, ten times larger than the invaders, driving them fearfully northward. Clouds of witchery blotting out the sun in all directions but one, herding the demons northward. Always northward. No spell can last long when crafted on such a scale, but as each witch falls another rises to take his place, for all know the cost of failure—

—Marking the anchor points for what will be man's final defense, a curse so fearsome that no living creature can cross it. But who will protect the natives of the ice fields that live beyond this point once that final spell is cast? Alkali answers: they cannot be saved. Let us mourn their sacrifice—

—Blood on the ice, broken wings in the snow, the scent of demons: these things mark the way for the hunters who will follow. For the enemy is wounded now, and the cold skies offer them neither comfort nor healing—

—Witches mutter prayers as they craft the cylindrical walls of their own tombs, laying brick upon brick themselves, scribing from the inside of their mausoleums the song of their final sacrifice. Thus do we die, so that the world will not have to. Remember our courage. Remember our sacrifice. Treasure the gift of freedom which we

bequeath to all the generations that follow us, and do not let it
flounder, lest our suffering be in vain—

As quickly as they had come, the images vanished. For a brief
moment it seemed that Gwynofar could sense all the other *lyr*
souls she was connected to, and she knew that the strongest ones
had shared her visions in their entirety, while all the others had
felt only a brief and terrifying rush of power that left in its wake
fragmentary images, as if from some half-remembered nightmare.
For a moment Gwynofar could sense them all—their confusion,
their fear—and the image of a burning web that was burned into
her brain. And then all that vanished. The firestorm was over.

Silence.

Shivering in pain, she forced herself to open her eyes and
look about the chamber. Near her feet lay a body that might
once have been human, but its head was a mound of shapeless
flesh, as if it had exploded from the inside. Beyond that stood
two of Anukyat's Guardians, clearly rendered speechless by what
they had just experienced. Drawing in a deep breath, she gathered her strength and rose to her feet, calling upon all her years
of professional majesty to look stronger than she felt. In fact
her legs were shaking so badly they could hardly support her;
she wished she had a woman's gown on to hide their trembling.

She should be talking to these men. Establishing the proper
context for their visions. Telling them that it did not matter
whether a gift of the gods was in their blood or simply a quirk
of nature. The end result was the same. The northern bloodlines were resistant to the Souleaters' power. They must work
together to combat the coming invasion.

But her child was dead within her and she could not find
her voice.

On shaking legs, she stumbled to the trap door. Neither man moved to stop her. One even backed up a bit, getting out of her way. Their eyes were wide. *They think that I did this*, she realized. *That it was my power that reached out to them and showed them the truth.*

The hand of one guard opened, and his sword clattered noisily to the floor. He hesitated for a moment, then lowered himself to one knee before her. The other followed suit, laying his own sword before her in offering.

She knew that some kind of acknowledgment was called for, but she was too numb with sorrow to offer it. She could focus on only one thing right now. *Rhys.* Shaking, she backed down the ladder to the observation chamber. *Must find Rhys.* Bodies littered the floor, puddles of blood slick beneath her feet as she made her way to the head of the great staircase. An Alkali guard was still standing, and he stepped quickly out of her way. What a ghoulish sight she must be right now! Her body covered with dust and her face streaked with tears, her clothing soaked with blood from her various offerings . . . little wonder he moved out of her way so rapidly.

Three turns down the staircase. Four. She passed the place where she had parted with her half brother to sneak out through a narrow window, half a lifetime ago. Five turns. Six. Stepping over bodies as she searched for her brother among the living and the dead. The warriors who were standing were so dazed that they hardly noticed her, still stunned by the power of the nightmare visions she had channeled. Dare she hope that Rhys might be alive as well? With increasing urgency she stumbled over fallen bodies and forgotten weapons, seeking the one person who mattered most.

And she found him. Lying diagonally across the stairs, his

head resting against the base of the inner wall. His eyes were shut almost peacefully, as though he had only just fallen asleep. She knelt down beside him with a sharp sob and stroked his cheek, calling his name. "Rhys! Rhys!" But his chest was not moving and his eyes did not open. As his head lolled to one side in response to his touch she could see the deep gash in the side of his neck and the pool of blood beneath it. Still warm. By the gods, he was still warm . . . !

The final dam let loose then, and she wept. Lowering her head to his unbreathing chest, allowing all the sorrow and fear that had been building up inside her to pour out at last, unfettered. There was no reason left to hold it back. Rhys was gone. Her child was gone. Nothing was left that mattered.

And when the local guards finally came to bind up the living and gather up the dead she would not let them take Rhys away, but she curled up against his side, shivering uncontrollably. Until finally, mercifully, exhaustion claimed her and all the world slipped away into darkness.

CHAPTER 29

A STORM WAS coming.

Standing atop the third Sister, Anukyat could see it gathering along the southern horizon. Thick black clouds with sheets of rain that swept down across the landscape, slowly moving closer and closer to where he stood. Lightning flashed across the sky from north to south, and the thunder reached him a few seconds later, setting the rock vibrating beneath his feet.

He knew he should go inside before the rain reached the Citadel. The rock surface would grow slick very quickly and be hard to manage. The last thing he wanted now was to loose his footing in the very same place where he had so recently lost his honor.

Or perhaps that would be an appropriate end.

He had come up here to pray, but once he arrived he found that he could not. He could not even curse, or rail at the heavens, or in any other way give vent to what was inside him. The emotions that were tearing his soul to pieces were too vast for words, too volatile to be contained by anything as concrete and finite as *language*.

He had failed.

The scope of that failure defied rational limits. The roots of it lay a thousand years in the past, and the future . . . the future had yet to make itself known. All he could be sure of right now was that his ancestors had offered up their lives for a cause, and he had betrayed it. And his descendants would now pay the price.

It was more than a human heart could absorb.

Lightning fractured the storm clouds for a moment, bright enough to blind him. He shut his eyes against the glare, counting down the seconds before a whiplike crack of thunder split the air. Five. Only five. The storm would be upon him soon.

And there was another sound, a slow rhythmic beat, like pennants whipping in the wind. He shuddered to hear it but did not turn around, not even when he heard the scraping of talons on the rock behind him. Or the sound of human feet hitting the stone surface.

"They will repair the Wrath." Anukyat spoke without turning. "There are those who will make the sacrifice, now that they know the truth." *I would,* he thought, *if I believed the gods would accept a traitor's sacrifice.*

"It is too late," Nyuku said.

Slowly, the Master Guardian turned to face his visitor. Or rather *both* his visitors. The first, a man, was garbed in gleaming blue-black armor that had been polished to a fine sheen; his hair had been pulled back tightly into a queue, baring his Kannoket features. The second, behind him, was a beast from out of legend whose broad veined wings beat the air slowly as it crouched at the edge of the monument, its long serpentine tail coiling rest-lessly about its master's feet as it waited. Its hide was the same color as the man's armor, making the pair of them seem more like extensions of a single creature than two separate individuals. Which was in fact accurate enough.

"You lied to me," Anukyat accused. The lightning cracked again. A few drops of rain splattered upon the granite spire, vanguard of the coming storm.

"About what? Your ancestry? The fate of the Kannoket? None of that was a lie." Nyuku smiled coldly. "None of it needed to be a lie."

How smooth he was in his manner now, in his speech! The bestial mannerisms that had once betrayed his origin were long gone; he had become polished enough to walk among morati princes as if he were one of them. Anukyat had helped teach him that. Doubtless the others of his kind would learn the trick as well. Their early mistakes would not be repeated.

"Why do you bring these creatures back to our world?" Anukyat demanded. "You must know what they will do."

A flash of lightning behind Anukyat turned Nyuku's eyes silver for a instant, reflective like a cat's. "They are no longer merely beasts," he said.

The anger that until this moment had been self-directed suddenly had an outward focus. "Do they no longer feed upon human souls?" Anukyat demanded. "Do they no longer rob men of the very spark that makes them human? Are you claming to have 'tamed' them, so that they can live among us peaceably?" He stared at the ikati with raw, unfettered hatred. It was a strangely cleansing sensation, as though all the despicable things he had done recently were oozing out of his pores, like some noxious poison. "Somehow I doubt that is possible."

"Many men will die," Nyuku agreed. "That is the price they pay for driving us into exile. A thousand years of being cut off from the world, away from the very heartbeat of humanity! And now we are free at last."

The words came unbidden to his lips. "Not all of you."

Anger flashed like lightning in Nyuku's eyes. "The rest will follow us. Those of us who were strong enough to make the crossing will pave the way for them. Once mankind has submitted to our rule we will come back here and tear the Wrath down in its entirety."

Lightning flashed across the sky; the crack of thunder that followed was loud enough to make his ears ring. *He would not tell me all this if he meant for me to live,* Anukyat realized. Strangely, the insight did not really disturb him. Perhaps he had grown numb to fear . . . or perhaps he was more afraid of remaining alive and witnessing the consequences of his treachery.

"The *lyr* will find you," he said quietly. "They know what you are now. They know how to find you."

"And by the time they mobilize we will be far from this region. They will not even know where to look." The tail of the ikati twitched against Nyuku's thigh; he reached out a hand to stroke its glistening surface. "It is a long flight from here, Anukyat." He said it softly. "I am sure you understand."

He did.

The beast's black eyes captured his and held them fast, so that he could not look away. The power of the ikati licked at his soul, loosening his life force from its moorings, ripping it loose like raw meat. While lightning struck behind Anukyat, its brief flash reflected a thousand time over in the black facets of the ikati's eyes.

"Bugger yourself," he said.

And he jumped.

For a brief moment longer he could feel the ikati's hunger

burning inside him, then the sensations of the fall drowned all that out. Air rushing by his head. Raindrops racing him to the ground. The sweet embrace of gravity, serene and incorruptible. And at the end of the fall, rushing up toward him: freedom.

Nyuku stood silently at the top of the monument, gazing down in frustration at the broken body far below him. Behind him his consort fidgeted restlessly. He was hungry. All the other human food had left this place. He would have to begin his flight with nothing more than a few local snakes and frogs for sustenance. And in the rain, no less. Clearly the great beast was not happy.

Nyuku looked northward. The malignant power of the Wrath was visible from here: a wounded curse, slowly bleeding out its life force. The *lyr* would focus their efforts upon it now and would attempt to kill any of his people who tried to cross it. Perhaps in time they would even succeed in repairing the barrier, after a fashion. But even that could do no more than delay the inevitable. Enough of his brothers had made it through already to set his plans in motion. And there was a queen in the southlands now, which meant that they were no longer bound to the land of darkness and ice. The whole world was theirs for the taking.

"I will come back for you, my brothers." He whispered his words into the growing wind. "I promise."

Then the rain began to fall in earnest and the ikati screeched in protest. Quickly Nyuku climbed up on his back once more and let the stained-glass wings fold about him protectively. And then the ground dropped away from them both and the long journey began.

South.

CHAPTER 30

B Y THE time Rhys' body was brought out and set upon the bier, both moons had risen high in the sky. A cool, ghostly light picked out highlights on his armor, his sword, the ornaments in his hair. His pale skin was perfect, seemingly untouched by death, and his hands across his chest were so artfully folded that it looked as if he might stir at any moment, making a fool of Death. Such was the gift of witchery that the Seers had insisted on providing for their fallen brother, refusing Lazaroth's offer of sorcery to do the same at lesser cost. Their sacrifice was a statement of their mourning.

They had dressed him in his armor, weapons by his side. His pale blond braids were spread out like a halo about his head, tiny ornaments glittering in the moonlight. Several wooden boxes and small fabric bundles had been placed on the wooden platform beside him. They contained his most precious personal possessions, Gwynofar had explained to Kamala. A man should be surrounded by the things he valued most when he left this world.

Finally the Lord Protector stepped forward and the crowd

of mourners grew hushed. Holding out his hand, he beckoned a woman to join him. She was dressed in dark garments, her hair loose and undressed about her shoulders, and the tears that trickled down her cheeks as she stepped forward cut paths through the streaks of dried salt already there. Rhys' mother. Gwynofar came forward as well, and helped them unroll a length of sheer white linen that they then placed gently over the corpse. It was thin enough that one could see Rhys' face through it, his expression as peaceful as though he were merely sleeping.

"This is my son," the Lord Protector announced to the crowd of mourners, "lent to us by the gods and now returned to them. He lived in honor and died with courage, offering up his life that others might live. He will be memorialized among the trees of Kierdwyn's ancestors, as a prince of our line, for he has earned his place among them."

He held out a hand to one side, and a servant stepped forward and placed a gleaming kris knife into his hand. Thrusting it through the cloth of his sleeve, the Lord Protector tore loose a ragged piece of cloth that he set down on top of the white linen. He then handed the knife hilt first to Rhys' mother, who performed the same odd ritual. When it came to Gwynofar's turn she did not rend her garment, but cut off a lock of her hair, lying it reverently beside her half brother, leaning over him to kiss his forehead lovingly through the layer of gauze.

A solemn procession followed. Salvator, the Lady Protector, and all the sons and cousins of Kierdwyn went first, passing the knife from one to another, each one tearing loose some bit of fabric or hair to honor Rhys' memory. Several had brought small items as well that they left on top of the white cloth. Gifts of remembrance. Magisters Lazaroth, Ramirus, and Colivar were present, and they offered their respects in turn.

But they refused the knife that was offered, and Kamala was sure that the gifts they laid beside the fallen Guardian were strictly impersonal. Only a fool among Magisters would leave behind items that could be used against him by others of his kind, especially with rivals present.

And then it was her turn.

How quiet the night seemed in that moment! Darkness swallowed the other mourners as she approached the body, granting her an eerie privacy. Someone handed her the ritual knife and then faded back into the shadows. She and Rhys were alone.

Looking down at the body of her traveling companion, she felt a tightness in her chest. Some cold, uncomfortable emotion stirred in the deepest recesses of her soul, making it hard to breathe.

I killed you.

There was no denying that truth. If she had remained at her watch-post while the Guardians were climbing the monument, she would have seen the soldiers entering the upper chamber. She could have warned Rhys' men in time to keep them from being trapped there.

I saw an alarm being sent out from the Citadel, she thought. *I had to intercept it.*

But what if it wasn't the alarm she thought it was? The tiny leather message capsule was in her pocket, still unopened. Every time she took it out, her hands shook so badly that she could not get the clasp undone. A call for Souleaters to come protect the Citadel would have been well worth the risk she had taken; a single one of the great winged creatures could have picked the warriors off their precarious perch, Gwynofar included. The men would all have died then, and their mission would have failed as well. This way at least the mission had succeeded. Any of the Guardians would have made the same choice, surely.

But what if the message wasn't that?

Gazing down at her companion's still form, Kamala found it hard to sort out her emotions. Certainly Rhys himself had not feared death. Even before the revelation of Alkali's Spear had worked its spiritual corruption on him, making him hunger for the peace that death might bring, he had dedicated his life to a mission that was firmly rooted in the concept of self-sacrifice. He once told her that he would march into hell with his head held high if he thought it would gain his brothers some advantage over their winged adversaries. And she did not doubt that it was true. Life had been sweet to him, but duty meant more.

Gently she reached out and touched the side of his face; his skin was cool beneath the linen veil. What was it like to value some outside agency or goal more than life itself? The concept was so alien to her that she could barely frame the question. From her earliest days she had fixed her own sight on a single goal, willing to sacrifice anything and everything to achieve it. Even her humanity. Yet in the end, what had she gained? Eternal life in which to do . . . what? Standing before Rhys' body, she was acutely aware that she had no answer to such a question. Was that why the Magisters invested so much time and energy into their incessant rivalries? she wondered. Not to ward off the boredom of the centuries, as they claimed, but to give themselves the illusion of purpose?

With a shiver she leaned down over Rhys' body and kissed him gently on the forehead. And in that moment, she knew the name of the emotion that was so disquieting.

Envy.

Taking up the ritual knife with its serpentine blade, she reached up and cut off a lock of her hair, then laid it gently beside him. Binding it to the linen shroud securely enough with her power that not even a single hair could be removed without a sorcerous wrestling match first. She could sense Colivar's eyes on her back as he watched her make the morati-style offering, but she did not look up. For the sacrifice that Rhys had made, he deserved to be honored thus.

Then she passed the knife on to another, and stepped back into the shadows herself. Watching for over an hour as mourners filed past—Guardians and lovers, soldiers and friends—until his body was surrounded by a circle of tokens. Then another layer of linen was carefully lowered over the platform and tied down at the corners, to keep the wind from disturbing the offerings. Guardians then took up the poles at both ends of the mourning platform and lifted it from its stand, carrying it over to where the makings of a funeral pyre were waiting. Soon Rhys lay at the top of a pyramid, its stacked-wood base fragrant with the natural perfumes of the forest. A priest circled the construct three times with a torch, chanting prayers, then touched his flame to the dry tinder. The smell of burning pine needles filled the air as flames soared skyward, flickering veils of light surrounding Rhys for one glorious moment before the platform itself went up in flames. In the end, Kamala knew, his ashes and bones would be gathered up and buried at the base of some great pine that would later be carved into his image so that future generations might seek communion with his spirit.

She stood by the fire for a long time after that, well after the royal family had withdrawn from public view and the last of the mourners had begun to scatter. Then she reached into her pocket and drew out the message tube that she had taken from Anukyat's pigeon. Turning it over slowly in her hand, she drew in a deep breath, then worked loose the leather thong that held it shut. Teasing out the tightly rolled piece of paper that was inside it, she held it in her hand for a few moments before finally unrolling and reading it.

> *Sorcery detected where none should be. Inform our allies and send help immediately.*

Slowly, silently, she rolled the paper up tightly once more and slid it back into its tube. Then she cast it at the funeral pyre. Up it sailed, high over the blazing wood, until it landed in the center of the conflagration, on what was left of the funeral platform.

Not until the fire had burned down to embers, and all the offerings to ash, did she leave finally leave the site.

––––––––––

In the shadows at the far end of the field, the Lord Protector and his family watched the fire burn. Colivar stood beside them, enjoying the vague discomfort his presence was causing Ramirus. Unless he missed his guess, the white-haired Magister had struck some kind of deal with the Aurelius household, or at least with Gwynofar. If so, then the two of them were serving rival monarchs once more. Just like old times.

Not that it was likely to stay that way for long. Colivar had been so busy tracking down hints of the Souleaters' presence in recent days that he'd hardly had time for his royal duties. King Farah had been understanding about it—the Souleaters were a global threat, after all—but in the end, an absent Magister Royal wasn't all that much better than not having one at all.

Soon Colivar would have to give up his position if he meant to go on with his investigation.

Why were the creatures so important to him? Was it because their return threatened the world he lived in, the civilization he had come to take for granted, or was the reasons more intimate, more personal? Certainly the mere thought of them flying free in the skies again awakened memories that he was not entirely ready to handle and hinted at personal weaknesses that until now he had not realized he'd possessed. Better to search those things out now, he thought, than be surprised by them later.

Looking out over the crowd, he saw that Salvator was approaching. Now that was interesting. Apparently he'd had a witch transport him here, preferring—as always—to sap the living strength of morati rather than trust to the seemingly endless power of the Magisters. Not that there was much difference between the two in the end, of course. Someone, somewhere, had to provide the life-essence for such a spell. It was only a question of whose athra it was, and whether the donor was willing.

The new High King came to where the Lord Protector was standing, nodding his head respectfully to Kierdwyn and Gwynofar. Not to the Magisters, though. They might as well be stone monuments for all Salvator seemed to care. It seemed a foolish move, but at least one had to admire the man's consistency. Colivar could see the displeasure in Ramirus' eyes, and Lazaroth's expression was as warm as a glacier.

Colivar chuckled to himself. *Careful, Magisters. Your pride is showing.*

"Your son was greatly loved," Salvator said to his grandfather. "This funeral does him honor."

In the distance Guardians were stepping forward now to stir

the embers of the funeral pyre, making sure that every bit of flammable material was properly burned. By the time the sun rose, there would be nothing left but bones and ash.

"My people honor Rhys' mission as well as his person," Kierdwyn responded solemnly. "It is the way of the *lyr*."

Salvator nodded respectfully. "Such a mission is worthy of honor."

The Lord Protector raised an eyebrow. "That is a different sentiment than one normally hears from you."

"We have all learned much of our natures these past few weeks. Some of those lessons were . . . surprising."

"Indeed." A shadow passed over the Lord Protector's face. "I would think a Penitent would be pleased by all this. Legends of the ancient gods proven to be no more than a seductive fantasy, the mysterious 'gift of the *lyr*' no more than a natural resistance to the Souleaters' power. Granted it was useful, but hardly supernatural."

Salvator spoke quietly. "On the contrary, the hand of the Creator is now evident in this matter. Was it not he that created mankind to begin with, along with all the talents and proclivities that make us human? If so, then it is he who seeded that immunity among us in the first place, anticipating our need. By proving the *lyr* gift to be a natural power, part and parcel of mankind's creation, you have in fact confirmed it as a divine endowment." He paused. "But what of your people? How are they dealing with this?"

Kierdwyn shrugged stiffly. "Most received only fragments of Gwynofar's visions and are relying upon the priests to sort things out. I am not sure where it will lead. Certainly our duty is not altered, and with the Souleaters returning I suspect there will be little time to worry about anything else. For myself . . ." He bit his lip for a moment. "I wonder, if we had known the truth from the beginning, if we would have been quite so meticulous in preserving the *lyr* bloodlines. It is the legends that kept us committed to that cause through all the centuries. Repairing the Spears, preserving ancient lore, concentrating the gift that is in the blood of the seven great families . . . a man will do things in service to his gods that he would not do for himself. So perhaps the legends we believed in for so long were part of the gods' plan all along, to keep us properly focused. Perhaps."

Colivar could not resist the opening. "And the Magisters? What is our part in all of this supposed to be?"

Salvator's expression was chill. "In light of what has just been revealed, I find it noteworthy that there has never been a Magister of *lyr* blood. Perhaps when we understand why that is so, we may be able to answer your question as it deserves."

Hardly a mystery, Colivar thought dryly. *The* lyr *exist for a purpose. A Magister's only purpose is to ensure his own survival. The two philosophies are incompatible.*

"So you accept your heritage now?" the Lord Protector asked his grandson.

"I do. In fact . . ." He looked over at the three Magisters, perhaps considering whether he really wanted to hold this discussion in front of them. Finally, with a grim nod of acceptance, he turned back to Kierdwyn. "I had a dream, while our armies were gathering. It seemed rather straightforward at the time. Now, in light of the visions that Gwynofar provided, I must wonder."

"The one with the Witch-Queen?"

Salvator nodded tightly.

"You said that she tried to convince you to withdraw your troops from the north."

"Indeed. The political implications seemed clear at the time, so I did not question it further. But she tried to use witchery to drive her message home. And could not. I would like to take credit for her failure and claim that my soul is so well guarded against spiritual assaults that she could make no headway. But in light of what the Throne has revealed, I must now question that assumption. Especially as . . ." He hesitated. "In the dream's final moments, I saw her change. Her eyes became black, and faceted. For a moment I thought I saw wings. Nightmares often have such imagery. But now I wonder if these were perhaps more significant."

Colivar could feel the color drain from his face; words came out before he could stop them. "The scent of a queen."

Kierdwyn turned to him. "Magister Colivar?"

"The Souleater's scent. It was in her palace, the last time I saw her. On her skin. I had forgotten . . ." He shook his head sharply, banishing the tide of memory. *Not now, Colivar. Not in front of all these people.* "She was channeling their power." He looked at Salvator. "That is why she could not take control of you. Your *lyr* heritage protected you."

The High King's expression was grim. "So she was not only allied to Alkali, but to the monsters themselves?"

"So it would appear," Colivar agreed.

"How is that possible?" Salvator demanded.

Colivar did not answer him. Dared not answer him. "I don't know," he said at last, turning away. He could sense the eyes of the other Magisters on him with questions of their own, but none of those could be answered in the presence of morati. If at all.

A few awkward seconds passed, and then, when it was clear he had nothing more to offer, the tide of conversation moved on without him. He waited until the morati were safely focused on other things, then quietly took his leave of their company. There were memories stirring inside him now that he did not know how to handle, and he did not wish them to witness his disquiet. Feelings he thought he had conquered long ago.

Not until they were out of hearing of the small group, and nearly out of their sight, did Ramirus say quietly from behind him, "It is not enough, you know."

Colivar stopped walking, but did not turn back.

"You have the knowledge of how to stop these creatures," Ramirus said, "but you cannot do it alone. Sooner or later, you must have allies."

"Are you suggesting I trust other Magisters?"

"Would you rather rely upon the morati?"

"You also assume I wish to do battle with these creatures."

"Not at all." Ramirus' tone was a silken thing. "But I do believe we will come to the point when we must do that, or else surrender our sovereignty to them. And I suspect the Souleaters will not take kindly to having rivals about."

"No." A cold shiver ran down Colivar's spine. "They will not."

"Just something to think on, for the moment. No need to act on it just yet." There was a pause. "Perhaps something to discuss on the way to Sankara?"

Colivar drew in a deep breath, then exhaled it slowly, willing his soul to be calm. *If you knew the real reason that Magisters do not trust one another, you would never suggest an alliance.* "I don't know how to stop the creatures," he warned Ramirus. "No man does."

"Understood." A cold smile crept across the Magister's face. "In the meantime, I believe we have some business to take care of."

Gwynofar stood by her mother in the early dawn light, staring at the hole they had just dug in the moist earth. The air was heavy with smells from the surrounding forest: pine needles, damp moss, the faint musk of deer preparing for their morning forage.

Peaceful, she thought. So peaceful. This was a good place.

"Are you ready?" her mother asked gently.

Gwynofar drew in a deep breath, exhaled it slowly, and then nodded. She took a small wooden box out of her pocket and knelt down before the hole, holding it out before her.

"This is my son," she said, "lent to us by the gods, and now returned to them. He never knew what life was, nor understood why it was taken from him—"

She had to stop for a moment, biting her lip as she fought against a wave of sorrow. *I am sorry, my son. I would have died myself to save you, if the gods had allowed it.* "He died that others might live," she whispered. "May the gods honor his sacrifice."

She opened the box and overturned it; a small bit of ash fell to the bottom of the hole, barely visible in the dim light.

Reaching over to one side, her mother picked up the small tree they had brought with them. It was barely two feet high, its spiny blue branches just beginning to spread. The two women lowered it into the grave together, on top of the ashes. Evaine then held the root ball in place while Gwynofar packed fresh dirt in around it. By the time she was done her fingernails were black, and fresh tears streaked her cheeks.

Finally she sat back on her heels, gazing in sorrow at the tiny grave. "He has no face," she whispered. "There will be nothing to carve on his tree."

Her mother put an arm around her shoulder and squeezed gently. "Have you given him a name?"

Gwynofar nodded. "Anrhys. After his uncle." She wiped a hand across her face, leaving a streak of dirt behind. "He was one of the bravest men I ever knew."

"It is a good name," her mother said softly. "And it will be a strong tree."

They waited together in silence until the first rays of the morning sun fell upon the grave, then whispered the closing prayers.

Rest in peace, my son.

———

The Witch-Queen's palace gleamed emptily in the early morning light, bereft of any sign of life. The sense of stillness about it was palpable, broken only by the shimmering of the portal spell that allowed four Magisters to pass through, and that only briefly. Once the sorcery vanished, its job completed, the atmosphere was like that of a tomb.

Sulah drew in a sharp breath. Even he, the most recent addition to Siderea's stable of sorcerous lovers, could sense the shadow of *wrongness* hanging about the place. "I don't like this."

Lazaroth and Ramirus looked equally disturbed, though Colivar doubted that either had been here before. He said nothing himself, but headed straight for the gleaming white arches that marked the entrance to the palace.

No servants came to greet them, or even to acknowledge their existence. Colivar led them to the atrium, and from there to the other public chambers. Nothing. Only when they headed toward the Witch-Queen's private chambers was there a hint of movement, and that turned out to be a bird at the window.

We are too late, Colivar thought.

Outside her bedchamber he paused. That strange, sweet scent was noticeable here, and now that he recognized what it was, it brought memories in its wake. Fierce memories, primitive in tenor, that were wholly out of keeping with his current mode of existence. For a moment he had to put a hand against the wall to steady himself, as he fought to free himself from the mnemonic riptide.

A queen's power has touched this place, he mused when the worst of the storm had passed. Wonder and horror attended the thought.

Inside the chamber there was no Witch-Queen, but they found their first sign of life. A maidservant lay on the floor by the great bed, curled up on her side like a child, asleep. Lazaroth knelt down and prodded her, but she did not stir. He prodded her more harshly. Still no response. Finally he slapped her face, hard enough to leave the imprint of his hand across her pale flesh, but still she slumbered on.

"The Black Sleep." Ramirus's tone was grim. "Will she recover?"

"She may," Colivar said. "If the cause of it does not return."

Just then there was a sound from outside the bedchamber. The Magisters turned quickly, just in time to see a young boy enter. His eyes were wide and tear-filled, his clothing dirty and disheveled. "Have you come to help?" he asked. His voice was trembling. "Do you know what happened here?"

Sulah said, "We were hoping you would tell us."

The boy shut his eyes for a moment. "There was a great beast, with wings like sapphires. It hovered over the palace for an hour or more. At first men went up onto the roof to see it better, and some said they should kill the thing. They never came down again. And then people began to get dizzy.

And weak. And then they fell down wherever they were, and just . . . went to sleep. I couldn't wake them up." Tears poured down his face. "I kept trying and trying, but it was like they were dead. They couldn't hear me."

"Where is your queen?" Colivar demanded.

"She went up onto the roof after all the others. She never came down. The flying thing left soon after that, heading out over the sea. I thought that everyone might wake up then, but they didn't. So I . . . I went to hide. In case it came back. I didn't want it to get me, too."

"How long ago was that?" Ramirus asked.

"I don't know," the boy said miserably. "I'm sorry. I've been in the cellar. It seemed like the safest place."

"You're safe now," Colivar told him. *Even if the rest of the world isn't.*

On the roof they found some of the missing people. Most were comatose. A few were dead. One looked as if large chunks of flesh had been gouged from his body. Flies were thick about the meat, but no maggots had appeared yet. So all this had happened fairly recently, Colivar thought. He gathered his sorcery about him to narrow down the time frame, but he could not bring himself to release it. Not when the whole place smelled of *her*.

"She was readying herself for a long flight," he said. Trying to keep his voice steady. "Possibly to a place where food would be scarce. I doubt she will come back."

"She?" Lazaroth asked sharply.

"A female Souleater," he said. "The most dangerous of her kind."

But not for any reason you would understand.

Had Colivar thought he could escape them forever? That

the Wrath would protect him from ever needing to confront his memories? From having to define his loyalties? If so, that illusion was shattered now.

He had never expected a queen to appear in the south.

You will take up the sword again soon, he told himself. *But on which side will you fight?*

extras

about the author

Celia Friedman has been a voracious reader from her earliest days and began writing at the age of thirteen. At university, she studied maths, then theatre, before following her love of costume design to study and pursue a career in that field. She taught Costume Design at a northern Virginian university and has designed period dress patterns for a historical supply company. She now writes full-time and teaches a creative writing course at a local high school.

To find out more about Celia Friedman and other Orbit authors you can register for the free monthly newsletter at www.orbitbooks.net

if you enjoyed
WINGS OF WRATH
look out for
THE HUNDRED THOUSAND KINGDOMS

by

N. K. Jemison

I

Grandfather

I AM NOT AS I ONCE WAS. They have done this to me, broken me open and torn out my heart. I do not know who I am anymore.

I must try to remember.

My people tell stories of the night I was born. They say my mother crossed her legs in the middle of labor and fought with all her strength not to release me into the world. I was born anyhow, of course; nature cannot be denied. Yet it does not surprise me that she tried.

My mother was an heiress of the Arameri. There was a ball for the lesser nobility—the sort of thing that happens once a decade as a backhanded sop to their self-esteem. My father dared ask my mother to dance; she deigned to consent. I have often wondered what he said and did that night to make her fall in love with him so powerfully, for she eventually abdicated her position to be with him. It is the stuff of great tales, yes? Very romantic. In the tales, such a couple lives happily ever after. The tales do not say what happens when the most powerful family in the world is offended in the process.

*   *   *

But I forget myself. Who was I, again? Ah, yes.

My name is Yeine. In my people's way I am Yeine dau she Kinneth tai wer Somem kanna Darre, which means that I am the daughter of Kinneth, and that my tribe within the Darre people is called Somem. Tribes mean little to us these days, though before the Gods' War they were more important.

I am nineteen years old. I also am, or was, the chieftain of my people, called *ennu*. In the Arameri way, which is the way of the Amn race from whom they originated, I am the Baroness Yeine Darr.

One month after my mother died, I received a message from my grandfather Dekarta Arameri, inviting me to visit the family seat. Because one does not refuse an invitation from the Arameri, I set forth. It took the better part of three months to travel from the High North continent to Senm, across the Repentance Sea. Despite Darr's relative poverty, I traveled in style the whole way, first by palanquin and ocean vessel, and finally by chauffeured horse-coach. This was not my choice. The Darre Warriors' Council, which rather desperately hoped that I might restore us to the Arameri's good graces, thought that this extravagance would help. It is well known that Amn respect displays of wealth.

Thus arrayed, I arrived at my destination on the cusp of the winter solstice. And as the driver stopped the coach on a hill outside the city, ostensibly to water the horses but more likely because he was a local and liked to watch foreigners gawk, I got my first glimpse of the Hundred Thousand Kingdoms' heart.

There is a rose that is famous in High North. (This is not a digression.) It is called the altarskirt rose. Not only do its petals unfold in a radiance of pearled white, but frequently it grows an incomplete secondary flower about the base of its stem. In its most prized from, the altarskirt grows a layer of overlarge petals that drape the ground. The two bloom in tandem, seedbearing head and skirt, glory above and below.

This was the city called Sky. On the ground, sprawling over a small mountain or an oversize hill: a circle of high walls, mounting tiers of buildings, all resplendent in white, per Arameri decree. Above the city, smaller but brighter, the pearl of its tiers occasionally obscured by scuds of cloud, was the palace—also called Sky, and perhaps more deserving of the name. I knew the column was there, the impossibly thin column that supported such a massive structure, but from that distance I couldn't see it. Palace floated above city, linked in spirit, both so unearthly in their beauty that I held my breath at the sight.

The altarskirt rose is priceless because of the difficulty of producing it. The most famous lines are heavily inbred; it originated as a deformity that some savvy breeder deemed useful. The primary flower's scent, sweet to us, is apparently repugnant to insects; these roses must be pollinated by hand. The secondary flower saps nutrients crucial for the plant's fertility. Seeds are rare, and for every one that grows into a perfect altarskirt, ten others become plants that must be destroyed for their hideousness.

*   *   *

At the gates of Sky (the palace) I was turned away, though not for the reasons I'd expected. My grandfather was not present, it seemed. He had left instructions in the event of my arrival.

Sky is the Arameri's home; business is never done there. This is because, officially, they do not rule the world. The Nobles' Consortium does, with the benevolent assistance of the Order of Itempas. The Consortium meets in the Salon, a huge, stately building—white-walled, of course—that sits among a cluster of official buildings at the foot of the palace. It is very impressive, and would be more so if it did not sit squarely in Sky's elegant shadow.

I went inside and announced myself to the Consortium staff, whereupon they all looked very surprised, though politely so. One of them—a very junior aide, I gathered—was dispatched to escort me to the central chamber, where the day's session was well under way.

As a lesser noble, I had always been welcome to attend a Consortium gathering, but there had never seemed any point. Besides the expense and months of travel time required to attend, Darr was simply too small, poor, and ill-favored to have any clout, even without my mother's abdication adding to our collective stain. Most of High North is regarded as a backwater, and only the largest nations there have enough prestige or money to make their voices heard among our noble peers. So I was not surprised to find that the seat reserved for me on the Consortium floor—in a shadowed area, behind a pillar—was currently occupied by an excess delegate from one of the Senmcontinent nations. It would be terribly rude, the aide stammered anxiously, to dislodge this man, who was elderly and had bad knees. Perhaps I would not mind standing? Since I had just spent many long hours cramped in a carriage, I was happy to agree.

So the aide positioned me at the side of the Consortium floor, where I actually had a good view of the goings-on. The Consortium chamber was magnificently apportioned, with white marble and rich, dark wood that had probably come from Darr's forests in better days. The nobles—three hundred or so in total—sat in comfortable chairs on the chamber's floor or along elevated tiers above. Aides, pages, and scribes occupied the periphery with me, ready to fetch documents or run errands as needed. At the head of the chamber, the Consortium Overseer stood atop an elaborate podium, pointing to members as they indicated a desire to speak. Apparently there was a dispute over water rights in a desert somewhere; five countries were involved. None of the conversation's participants spoke out of turn; no tempers were lost; there were no snide comments or veiled insults. It was all very orderly and polite, despite the size of the gathering and the fact that most of those present were accustomed to speaking however they pleased among their own people.

One reason for this extraordinary good behavior stood on a plinth behind the Overseer's podium: a life-size statue of the Skyfather in one of His most famous poses, the Appeal to Mortal Reason. Hard to speak out of turn under that stern gaze. But more repressive, I suspected, was the stern gaze of the man who sat behind the Overseer in an elevated box. I could not see him well from where I stood, but he was elderly, richly dressed, and flanked by a younger blond man and a dark-haired woman, as well as a handful of retainers.

It did not take much to guess this man's identity, though he wore no crown, had no visible guards, and neither he nor anyone in his entourage spoke throughout the meeting.

"Hello, Grandfather," I murmured to myself, and smiled at him across the chamber, though I knew he could not see me. The pages and scribes gave me the oddest looks for the rest of the afternoon.

* * *

I knelt before my grandfather with my head bowed, hearing titters of laughter.

No, wait.

* * *

There were three gods once.

Only three, I mean. Now there are dozens, perhaps hundreds. They breed like rabbits. But once there were only three, most powerful and glorious of all: the god of day, the god of night, and the goodess of twilight and dawn. Or light and darkness and the shades between. Or order, chaos, and balance. None of that is important because one of them died, the other might as well have, and the last is the only one who matters anymore.

The Arameri get their power from this remaining god. He is called the Skyfather, Bright Itempas, and the ancestors of the Arameri were His most devoted priests. He rewarded them by giving them a weapon so mighty that no army could stand against it. They used this weapon—weapons, really—to make themselves rulers of the world.

That's better. Now.

*   *   *

I knelt before my grandfather with my head bowed and my knife laid on the floor.

We were in Sky, having transferred there following the Consortium session, via the magic of the Vertical Gate. Immediately upon arrival I had been summoned to my grandfather's audience chamber, which felt much like a throne room. The chamber was roughly circular because circles are sacred to Itempas. The vaulted ceiling made the members of the court look taller—unnecessarily, since Amn are a tall people compared to my own. Tall and pale and endlessly poised, like statues of human beings rather than real flesh and blood.

"Most high Lord Arameri," I said. "I am honored to be in your presence."

I had heard titters of laughter when I entered the room. Now they sounded again, muffled by hands and kerchiefs and fans. I was reminded of bird flocks roosting in a forest canopy.

Before me sat Dekarta Arameri, uncrowned king of the world. He was old; perhaps the oldest man I have ever seen, though Amn usually live longer than my people, so this was not surprising. His thin hair had gone completely white, and he was so gaunt and stooped that the elevated stone chair on which he sat—it was never called a throne—seemed to swallow him whole.

"Granddaughter," he said, and the titters stopped. The silence was heavy enough to hold in my hand. He was head of the Arameri family, and his word was law. No one had expected him to acknowledge me as kin, least of all myself.

"Stand," he said. "Let me have a look at you."

I did, reclaiming my knife since no one had taken it. There was more silence. I am not very interesting to look at. It might have been different if I had gotten the traits of my two peoples in a better combination—Amn height with Darre curves, perhaps, or thick straight Darre hair colored Amn-pale. I have Amn eyes: faded green in color, more unnerving than pretty. Otherwise, I am short and flat and brown as forestwood, and my hair is a curled mess. Because I find it unmanageable otherwise, I wear it short. I am sometimes mistaken for a boy.

As the silence wore on, I saw Dekarta frown. There was an odd sort of marking on his forehead, I noticed: a perfect circle of black, as if someone had dipped a coin in ink and pressed it to his flesh. On either side of this was a thick chevron, bracketing the circle.

"You look nothing like her," he said at last. "But I suppose that is just as well. Viraine?"

This last was directed at a man who stood among the courtiers closest to the throne. For an instant I thought he was another elder, then I realized my error: though his hair was stark white, he was only somewhere in his fourth decade. He, too, bore a forehead mark, though his was less elaborate than Dekarta's: just the black circle.

"She's not hopeless," he said, folding his arms. "Nothing to be done about her looks; I doubt even makeup will help. But put her in civilized attire and she can convey . . . nobility, at least." His eyes narrowed, taking me apart by degrees. My best Darren clothing, a long vest of white civvetfur and calf-length leggings, earned me a sigh. (I had gotten the odd look for this outfit at the

Salon, but I hadn't realized it was *that* bad.) He examined my face so long that I wondered if I should show my teeth.

Instead he smiled, showing his. "Her mother has trained her. Look how she shows no fear or resentment, even now."

"She will do, then," said Dekarta.

"Do for what, Grandfather?" I asked. The weight in the room grew heavier, expectant, though he had already named me granddaughter. There was a certain risk involved in my daring to address him the same familiar way, of course—powerful men are touchy over odd things. But my mother had indeed trained me well, and I knew it was worth the risk to establish myself in the court's eyes.

Dekarta Arameri's face did not change; I could not read it. "For my heir, Granddaughter. I intend to name you to that position today."

The silence turned to stone as hard as my grandfather's chair.

I thought he might be joking, but no one laughed. That was what made me believes him at last: the utter shock and horror on the faces of the courtiers as they stared at their lord. Except the one called Viraine. He watched me.

It came to me that some response was expected.

"You already have heirs," I said.

"Not as diplomatic as she could be," Viraine said in a dry tone.

Dekarta ignored this. "It is true, there are two other candidates," he said to me. "My niece and nephew, Scimina and Relad. Your cousins, once removed."

I had heard of them, of course; everyone had. Rumor constantly made one or the other heir, though no one knew for certain which. *Both* was something that had not occurred to me.

"If I may suggest, Grandfather," I said carefully, though it was impossible to be careful in this conversation, "I would make two heirs too many."

It was the eyes that made Dekarta seem so old, I would realize much later. I had no idea what color they had originally been; age had bleached and filmed them to near-white. There were lifetimes in those eyes, none of them happy.

"Indeed," he said. "But just enough for an interesting competition, I think."

"I don't understand, Grandfather."

He lifted his hand in a gesture that would have been graceful, once. Now his hand shook badly. "It is very simple. I have named three heirs. One of you will actually manage to succeed me. The other two will doubtless kill each other or be killed by the victor. As for which lives, and which die—" He shrugged. "That is for you to decide."

My mother had taught me never to show fear, but emotions will not be stilled so easily. I began to sweat. I have been the target of an assassination attempt only once in my life—the benefit of being heir to such a tiny, impoverished nation. No one wanted my job. But now there would be two others who did. Lord Relad and Lady Scimina were wealthy and powerful beyond my wildest dreams. They had spent their whole lives striving against each other toward the goal of ruling the world. And here came I, unknown, with no resources and few friends, into the fray.

"There will be no decision," I said. To my credit, my voice did not shake. "And no contest. They will kill me at once and turn their attention back to each other."

"That is possible," said my grandfather.

I could think of nothing to say that would save me.